BRICK WALLS

L.A. WITT

Brick Walls

First edition

Copyright © 2023 L.A. Witt

Edited by Mackenzie Walton

Cover Art by Lori Witt

Ebook ISBN: 978-1-64230-147-2

Paperback ISBN: 978-1-64230-163-2

Hardcover ISBN: 979-8-37792-993-2

 Created with Vellum

ABOUT BRICK WALLS

Cary "Sol" Solomon isn't just in a slump—he's a mess. His stats have plummeted. Fans hate him. After he caps off two awful seasons with a catastrophic playoff flop, his team is done with him. Worse, thanks to his downward spiral, the addiction that's nearly cost him his career before is rearing its ugly head.

As luck would have it, though, the Seattle Sasquatches are desperate for goalies. When they snatch up Sol off waivers, maybe he has a chance to turn things around... *if* he can stay sober and get back on his game.

Except Sol isn't the Sasquatches' only new netminder.

Once destined for the hall of fame, Josh O'Brien is a trainwreck thanks to an injury and a messy divorce. His illustrious career is a disaster, and now he's an unrestricted free agent who *nobody* wants to sign. He's on the brink of losing the only thing he has left: hockey.

Then Seattle comes knocking with an offer he can't refuse: a huge pay cut, but a shot at redemption. One that means being teammates with the ex whose name still raises Josh's hackles all these years later.

Now Josh and Sol are stuck on the same team, proximity dredging up emotions they've both kept buried for years. Which wouldn't be so bad if the only things coming to the surface were anger and resentment. As they remember all the sparks and feelings that once drew them together, neither can decide which is worse—being together or apart.

And that's before Sol's old demons start showing up.

But they're not just coming for him this time.

CW: On-page struggle with cocaine addiction. If you would like clarification or other additional information about this content warning, please feel free to email the author at gallagherwitt at gmail dot com.

AUTHOR'S NOTE

This book is centered largely around cocaine addiction, which may be a difficult, sensitive subject for some readers. Representation includes on-page struggles with cravings, characters exhibiting signs of active cocaine use, conversations and internal thoughts about what drives a person to use, and the like.

If you would like clarification or have any other questions about how this subject matter appears in this book, please do not hesitate to reach out to the author at gallagherwitt@gmail.com

If you or someone you know is struggling with addiction, please contact the Substance Abuse and Mental Health Services Administration at 1-800-662-HELP or by visiting their website, https://www.samhsa.gov/find-help/national-helpline, or reach out to available rehab and information services in your country.

CHAPTER 1

SOL

Startling Hail Mary for Seattle Defense: Desperate Sasquatches Acquire Netminders Solomon, O'Brien

SEATTLE – In a surprising development to an already chaotic tale, the Seattle Sasquatches have signed two goalies no other team in the league would touch.

The end of this year's hockey season brought with it a cascade of bad luck for the team's goaltending. Backup goalie Liam Farson suffered a career-ending hip injury in the runup to the playoffs. Less than two weeks after Seattle's elimination from contention, emergency backup goalie Cole Archer announced his retirement due to persistent concussion symptoms. Then came the killing blow for Seattle: star netminder David Barnaby decided to test the market as an unrestricted free agent, in which he quickly landed a lucrative five-year contract with the newly crowned Cup champions, the Montreal Royales.

With Seattle's net suddenly and ominously empty, and

with no prospects ready to make the leap, Sasquatches' general manager Lon Caldwell reportedly searched for goalies on the free agent market. According to rumors, he tried a number of trades as well, possibly even offering up valuable players from the top offensive lines and defensive pairs.

Today, Seattle's front office announced that, in addition to bringing up rookie Payton Sweetman from the minors, the Sasquatches have made two shocking acquisitions: Cary Solomon and Josh O'Brien.

A Phoenix Firebird for all nine of years of his professional career, Solomon, 32, was recently put on waivers after back-to-back disappointing seasons followed by a series of catastrophic errors in the playoffs that led to Phoenix's first-round elimination. Many have feared that the struggling Solomon is on track to fall back into old habits —namely, the cocaine addiction that saw him suspended for twenty games during his second season.

Sources have speculated that these fears may have prompted the unusual move of putting a player on unconditional waivers during the off season: that the Firebirds, seeing Solomon as a serious liability, intended to buy out his contract in order to jettison him as quickly as possible. It's unclear whether they anticipated another team claiming him, and Phoenix's front office did not respond to requests for comment.

O'Brien's career has been on a similarly downward trajectory following a series of injuries. Many have also speculated that distraction caused by his tumultuous divorce contributed to the errors plaguing his most recent two seasons. An unrestricted free agent, O'Brien, 30, received no offer to re-sign with the Calgary Chinooks, and no other teams in the league expressed interest in acquiring this netminder who was once destined for the Hall of Fame.

When asked how he believes his team will fare with Solomon and O'Brien, given their recent history, Seattle head coach Heath Maines stated that every player has ups and downs. His added comment that "the alternatives are either an empty net or a prospect who isn't ready for the big leagues" has led to speculation that he's understandably pessimistic about the acquisitions.

Representatives for Solomon and O'Brien did not return calls or emails for comment.

Both goalies are expected to attend training camp with the Sasquatches next week at the team's training center in Northgate.

There was more to the article—something about the goalie coach, I thought—but my brain was going in too many directions to focus. It didn't help that this was one of those sites with a wildly animated ad after every other paragraph, making it a nightmare for me to read. I closed the news app, put my phone facedown on the tray table, and pressed my head back against the first-class seat.

The instant I'd gotten the *Dude, have you seen this shit?* text from my buddy, I should've logged off the plane's Wi-Fi and put the damn phone away. I'd known it was bad. *Known* it. But I'd had to look, because who wouldn't have? I'd have fixated on it whether I'd read it or not, so I'd looked.

And...ugh.

Seriously? Fucking *seriously?*

It wasn't the part where they brought up my addiction like literally *every* reporter did no matter what the article was about. It wasn't the part where the coach was just barely holding back that he hated the decision and probably wanted to go ahead and call up those prospects. As much as I didn't want to admit it, the guy was right to be skeptical. I was lucky he was this desperate and that his farm team goalies weren't ready to play.

No, the part of the article that had me reeling was the *other* newly acquired goalie.

No one had told me that Josh fucking O'Brien was signing with Seattle, too.

I couldn't say that would've changed my mind. With my history and having been put on waivers, I was a beggar who had no business being a chooser. I either played for Seattle or I didn't play hockey. Period. I doubted even the minors or one of the European leagues wanted anything to do with me at this point. It was a legitimate miracle that Seattle was willing to give me the time of day, never mind a contract.

But goddamn, it sure would've been nice to get a heads up that they were also signing my dickhead of an ex-boyfriend.

Maybe they hadn't known. In fact, I doubted they did—few people knew about our history. And anyway, no one would've given a shit about that. Everyone my agent and I had spoken to in Seattle had seemed too hard up to consider anything other than, *"You're an experienced goalie with a pulse and 206 currently unbroken bones? Cool. Sign here."* In fact, she and I both suspected there'd been some kind of behind-closed-doors gentlemen's agreement between Phoenix and Seattle where I'd be put on unconditional waivers so Seattle could snatch me up. Not something that typically happened during the off season, but it would allow Phoenix to wash their hands of me completely without having to buy me out, and it would allow Seattle to sign a much-needed warm body to put in their net.

It was nice to feel so wanted.

Seattle must've been in a serious panic, too, if they were signing me. It was like they were legitimately worried they were going to start off the season with no goalies who'd played above the college level. They had some prospects, but they all needed time in the minors before they were thrust onto this stage. At the very least, the team needed a couple of veterans to hold down the fort while the younger guys cut their teeth.

Enter me.

And, apparently, my ex.

Fuck my life.

Fidgeting in my seat, I wiped a hand over my face, then stared out the window at the mountains poking up through the clouds. There was nothing I could do about any of this. I was going to Seattle, and so was Josh, and if I wanted to hold on to my career, I had to make this work.

I supposed it could've been worse. If we'd been forwards or something, we might've ended up on the same line. Had to work together, night in and night out, even while we wanted to high stick each other for breathing. Or, well, *I'd* want to high stick *him*. God knew how he felt about me anymore. If he felt anything at all. It had been seven years since everything had fallen apart between us. He'd married and divorced since then, so he must have moved on to some extent.

I'd done the same, if I was being honest. I'd had boyfriends since Josh. Even got a little serious with a guy before I found out the reason he loved that one restaurant in Phoenix was because he liked how the sous chef's dick tasted. Thinking about that jerk could still make me gnash my teeth.

Josh, though? He was ancient history.

Right?

I closed my eyes and exhaled, rubbing my heel against the underside of my seat just to expend some nervous energy. No, I didn't lie awake at night thinking about him anymore. No, I hadn't cried myself to sleep over him in a long, long time. No, I didn't choke up when I stumbled across something that reminded me of him. I really had moved on.

Which absolutely explained why, whenever our teams had faced off, seeing him across the ice made my blood boil. And why it was just as well our roles kept us on opposite sides of the sheet whenever we played. If we'd been forwards or D-men, we probably would've gotten into a fist-fight or twelve by now. Every time I saw a video of a rare goalie fight, I imagined him and me meeting at the red line and dropping gloves. Would be a hell of a fight, that was for sure.

Assuming he even knew or cared that I was alive anymore. He had to be somewhat aware of me—came with the territory in the small world that was professional hockey —but he'd moved on with his life. I didn't matter to him anymore.

Did I ever matter to him?

I winced at that thought and swallowed the sudden lump in my throat. This wasn't like me at all. In fact, it probably had nothing to do with Josh. My entire world had just been turned on its ass. First, I'd been put on waivers. I'd assumed I was on my way to the minors at best, but then I'd been snatched up by Seattle. By a team who clearly didn't want me but absolutely needed me because they were out of options. Everything had happened so fast, and I hadn't even had time to sleep or catch my breath. Hell, I'd had to have a friend in Phoenix wrangle movers, Realtors, and all that crap for me, because I'd had to get my ass to Seattle on a moment's notice.

So no, this wasn't because of Josh. Josh signing with the same team was just another layer of *are you fucking serious?* on the shit sundae that my life had become, and I was so worn down that I was ready to crack at the slightest provocation. Even the frenetic pace of the hockey season could wear some of my coping methods thin. All this? Oh God. I'd barely been able to handle my flight being delayed earlier, and I was as used to things like that as anyone could be.

I took and released a few deep breaths, willing myself to calm down. I was just stressed out, that was all. It was change. A lot of it. A lot of big changes happening all at once. It would calm down soon. For now, I just needed to get to Seattle. Get some sleep. Start working with the new team. Concentrate on redeeming myself for the nightmare my career had become in the last couple of years. Stay sober.

That last one was always a challenge, but I'd do it. I wasn't falling apart now. Not again. And sure as shit not because of Josh. Or with him there as a witness.

The thought of seeing his judgmental sneer while I was relapsing made me shudder, and the awful coffee I'd drunk to calm myself down almost made a reappearance. I swallowed it back, though, and debated asking the flight attendant for another. Anything to pull me back down to earth—figuratively, anyway, since we weren't landing for a bit—so I could get through all this.

With any luck, I'd feel better once I'd made it to my hotel room and slept for a few hours. After spending some time on the ice with my new team, even better.

I could do this. I'd been through worse. It was all probably a whole lot bigger in my head than it was in reality. Most things were.

And, I reminded myself again, Josh was probably long since over me. He didn't fixate on things like I did. It had been years—the man did *not* give a shit about me.

I'd be fine.

Josh O'Brien walked into the Seattle Sasquatches' locker room, and I immediately knew three things.

First, that time had been *criminally* kind to him. Christ, he was even hotter than he'd been all those years ago, and that said something. As fit as ever in that snug T-shirt and shorts, lightly tanned like he'd spent the off season someplace warm, with his sun-kissed dark hair perfectly styled to give him that men's fashion model aesthetic. The baby face was long gone. His cheekbones stood out more prominently, and his dark eyes and long lashes were...whoa. I'd forgotten how beautiful they were.

The second thing I knew was that when I'd assumed Josh didn't give a shit about me after all this time, I had been very, *very* wrong.

Because the third thing? Oh, so *that* was what people meant when they said, *"if looks could kill."* Holy shit.

He was in the middle of a conversation with someone who I assumed was a member of the team's staff. Josh had been smiling. Pleasant. As charming as he ever was. Then his gaze had locked on mine, and it had been like the Arizona sun being instantly blotted out by Seattle storm clouds.

And...fuck. Maybe I wasn't over him, either, because all

it took was a split second of eye contact to kick off a barrage of emotions.

You jerk. You son of a bitch.

Did you treat your husband like you did me?

I hope he took your overpaid ass to the cleaners.

There was a sliver of pain in there, too. A sharp, cold sliver that hit all those sensitive places in my chest, filling my brain with flashes of long-forgotten good times before things had gone to shit. How bleak and desolate my world had felt before he'd walked away, and how much worse it had become after he left.

You abandoned me when I needed you the most.

I quickly broke eye contact to resume getting into my gear. At least there was that—goalies wore a ton of crap, and it took time to put it all on. The perfect distraction from that beautiful motherfucker. Something to do besides waiting to see who wound up crying, because it would either be my emotions getting the best of me, or my fist relieving him of a few teeth.

Okay, I wasn't a violent guy. Aside from my one and only fight on the ice and some pushing and shoving now and then— not to mention that ever-present and amusing fantasy of a goalie fight with him—violence wasn't my style. But sometimes thinking about it made me feel better, and right now, I'd take whatever I could get if it meant not losing my shit in front of my old boyfriend *or* my new team. Not that there was anyone else here at the moment besides us and a handful of staff.

I couldn't fuck this up. Seattle was my last chance to hold on to my hockey career. I sure as shit wasn't losing everything I'd worked for—everything I'd already nearly lost more than once before—because of *him*.

What I was going to do, I vowed right then and there,

was play my absolute ass off. Training camp, practice, preseason, regular season—didn't matter. I was going to protect that goal like it was overtime and we were in the damn playoffs.

Because when I'd met Coach Maines the other day, he'd told me he and the goalie coach would decide during training camp if Josh or I would be the starter.

And no way in hell was I playing backup to *that* asshole.

CHAPTER 2

JOSH

I wasn't sure when or how, but I'd pissed off some deity or another. That was the only explanation for why the last three years of my life had been an absolute shitshow that wasn't showing any sign of improving.

Case in point: I was suddenly in the same locker room as Cary Solomon. On the same *team* as him. Heading out onto the same ice to try to prove I was worthy of a place on this team's roster...just like he was.

Seriously, what the hell had I done? Had I assassinated a pope in a past life? Had I been the asshole who started putting pineapple on pizza? Because it must've been something awful to sign me up for all this bullshit as retribution.

And I couldn't do a damn thing about it, because it was either play for the Seattle Sasquatches or kiss my hockey career goodbye. When you're eight years and a Cup deep into your career and you can't even get minor league teams to return your agent's calls, things are...bleak.

I'd just gotten extraordinarily lucky that the Sasquatches—oh my God, what a stupid name—had found themselves in an even more desperate situation than mine.

They hadn't had the cap space to sign any of the halfway decent goalies on the market, and I hadn't been in a position to demand more than they offered me, which was a pretty significant pay cut.

At least it was a paycheck. One from a hockey team.

With my awful luck the last couple of years, I should've known the salary drop and the *"wow, the Sasquatches are scraping the bottom of the barrel"* headlines wouldn't be the end of it. And I'd found out around the time I'd signed my contract this week that it wasn't. It just hadn't really sunk in that Sol would be here until I walked in today and saw him.

Fuck my life.

I wasn't going to let him ruin anything else in my world, though, including this last chance at a hockey career. So, I gritted my teeth and started getting into my gear.

This is the end *of my slump,* I promised myself as I laced up my skates. *No way am I playing backup to* that *piece of shit.*

Hell, maybe coming to this team was a blessing in disguise. I'd been fighting like mad to get back to the level I'd always been, but I didn't imagine there was much that could motivate me to play harder than refusing to let Cary goddamned Solomon snag the starter spot over me.

Once I had on my gear, I grabbed my stick and mask and headed out to the ice. There weren't a lot of people here today; there was prospect camp for the new guys—the actual rookies—later this morning, but the head coach and goalie coach wanted to see the two of us skate a little on our own. We'd join the team for training camp tomorrow.

Sol was skating around the rink without his mask, trapper, or paddle, same as he always did to loosen up before a practice. Like me, he was wearing a blank practice jersey. His was white, mine was blue, with no numbers or names.

Presumably we'd have those by the time we started working with our teammates.

At center ice was Coach Maines, who I'd met briefly this morning, in skates and gloves with a stick in hand and some pucks scattered at his feet. Beside him was, I assumed, Kayla Rooney, the goalie coach. She'd been a phenomenal goalie for Team Canada at three Olympic games, and she'd made headlines a couple of years ago for being one of the only women in coaching roles in the league. Her presence was definitely a silver lining to this whole fiasco—I could stomach a lot if it meant getting to learn from someone of her caliber.

I left my mask and stick on the bench and skated around to loosen up, staying aware of Sol so we didn't end up on the same end of the ice. I could sense his presence as much as I could sense the scrutiny of my new coaches, and I just tried to focus on skating so I didn't wipe out and look like an ass.

I did steal a few looks at him. He was still unreasonably attractive, which didn't seem fair. His blond hair was a little darker now, reminding me of how it looked when it was damp with sweat. When the edges darkened and the ends curled, and his fair skin would be flushed with exertion and gleaming with sweat. How his crystal-blue eyes tracked a puck or a shooter, or how they locked right on me as he drove me closer to—

Nope. Didn't need to think about *that* anymore. Ever. I hated how much I'd enjoyed watching Sol play when we'd been on the same team, but at least that was a more pleasant train of thought than remembering the other situations in which I'd seen him sweat. In which I'd *made* him sweat.

Fortunately, my thoughts were disrupted completely by a whistle. Time to get to work.

I grabbed my equipment off the bench, then skated

toward center ice. At the edge of my peripheral vision, so did Sol.

"Good morning, gentlemen." Peering at us from beneath a weathered blue Sasquatches ballcap, Coach Maines gave us both a curt nod, which we returned. He introduced us to Coach Rooney, who insisted on being called Kayla. "Kayla's going to put the two of you through your paces so we can get a feel for you." He sounded *thrilled*. "Then tomorrow, you'll practice with the team. Between training camp and the preseason, we'll determine which of you will start and who will be backup."

I thought I felt Sol glancing at me, but I kept my gaze fixed on the coaches. I didn't want to look at him. I never did, but especially not now when he was both my teammate and my competition. I was keeping my eye on the prize: that starter position.

"We're counting on both of you," Maines went on. "We've brought up Sweetman as a third, but he is *not* ready to start. He's also still rehabbing from a hip injury. He can handle a few games if we need him, but not the workload of the starter *or* backup."

I nodded as he spoke. Yeah, no pressure. Jesus. The hockey gods had not been kind to this team's netminding department if all the front office could scrounge up were two disasters and a limping kid who wasn't ready for the majors.

I glanced at Sol, and some of my resolve returned. Sweetman's recovery and skill level were going to be moot because I was going to stay healthy myself and get that starter spot if it fucking killed me. I'd let Sol and Sweetman duke it out for the backup and emergency third positions, and if only for the sake of Sweetman, I hoped Sol had his shit together enough to play. The fact that he was still an active player in the league didn't mean much; for all the league insisted they were cracking down on illicit substances, there just wasn't much testing for cocaine use. Otherwise at least two guys on my last team would be in rehab or out of a job by now. And maybe McEnroe would've gotten help before his addiction had spiraled so far out of control.

I didn't let the thoughts linger. I needed to focus on impressing Maines and Kayla, not on how much it stung that I hadn't been able to get re-signed after an injury while my team's top defensive pair had snorted their way to contract extensions. Or how much it had hurt watching someone else I cared about get snowed under by his addiction.

Unaware of my momentary mental short circuit, Maines tapped his stick on the ice. "All right, boys. I'll turn it over to Kayla, and then let's see what the two of you can do."

Kayla probably went easy on us, but it sure didn't feel like it. Not when I was this jetlagged and exhausted. I might've done okay if I'd eased up on myself a little bit. Maybe put in eighty-five percent or so. Coach and Kayla both told us more than once that they didn't expect us to be up to snuff quite yet—this was just to get a look at how we moved, even if it wasn't at full speed or full strength, and how we dealt with the puck.

Sol had always been stronger with his stick than his trapper. My shuffle was a little faster to my left than to my right thanks to an old injury. All things being equal, I was more likely to freeze a puck than play it. Sol preferred to keep it in play. We didn't have to be moving at a hundred percent for some of those patterns to come out, and seeing us in action gave Kayla a baseline so she knew what she had to work with.

But I wasn't about to ease off while Sol was here. I was determined to have that starter spot, and the fight for it started now. Anything to give me an edge. Anything to keep him from outshining me.

From the way Sol was moving and twitching, he had the same idea. When he was listening to one of the coaches, he fidgeted and moved constantly. His thick glove didn't hide the way his fingers danced on the handle of his stick. When I was in the net, he was anything but still—skating small circles, practicing some shuffling and butterflying—which distracted me more than it should have. Part of playing this position meant being able to focus while there was movement and activity all around, and I was damn good at shutting it all out and zeroing in on the puck. I was just annoyed by the ever-present reminder that *he* was *here*.

At least his perpetual motion and twitchiness meant he probably hadn't gone back to his old ways. Or if nothing else, he wasn't using right this minute. If he suddenly settled down and stilled during a game, then I'd get concerned.

"Looking good," Kayla told me as I stopped another puck. "Solomon, let's see how you do."

I put my mask up and skated away from the net so Sol could take over. I made a few circles to loosen up my tired muscles—I'd been training all summer, but my recent stress and lack of sleep had taken a toll.

When I stopped to stretch, I watched Sol. His form was still good. That wasn't surprising. And when he was waiting for Maines or Kayla to fire another puck at him, he was still visibly twitchy. Like he absolutely could *not* stay still. Whenever a puck flew past him into the net, the frustration was visible even through his mask. It was like his intensity dialed up a notch until it was a miracle he wasn't vibrating all over.

No drugs, then, at least not right now, which was a relief.

Thing was, for most people, cocaine was a major stimulant. It made them agitated and even aggressive. Made them talk fast. Either scattered their thoughts or zeroed them in on something to the point that couldn't think about anything else. They were so wired they damn near vibrated, fidgeting nervously and working their jaws in that conspicuous side-to-side way that made my teeth ache just from watching it.

That wasn't the case for Sol. He stilled. His speech slowed down to something closer to normal. He focused more intently than he did sober, but he could shift that focus if he needed to, like if someone changed the subject or another person entered the room. That was why it had taken so long to get anyone to take me seriously when I'd tried to get him help—no one heard that someone was chill and focused and believed they were using cocaine.

The way Sol was right now? Constantly moving, gnawing his lip, shifting from skate to skate—*that* would flag most people that he was on some kind of upper. But no, this was default Sol. A line of blow that would send most people into the rafters made him seem like he'd just done some really good weed.

So he wasn't high right this minute. Good. But that didn't necessarily mean he wasn't using at all. I wouldn't be able to tell for sure if he was still a cokehead until the season kicked off and every goal counted. For our team's sake, I hoped he was still clean. As far as I knew, he had been—or at least he hadn't been caught —since he'd come back from that stint in rehab seven years ago. He'd only been caught in the first place because...

Well. Because of me. Because I'd wanted to get him help. I'd wondered for a long time if he still hated me for that. Judging by the way he'd looked at me when I'd walked into the locker room this morning, I was pretty sure I had my answer.

"O'Brien, you're up," Kayla barked, jarring me back into the present. She pointed at the net with her stick. Sol got out of the way and I took his place again.

It felt good, being in the crease and tracking pucks. Every time I stopped one or batted it away, I got a little bit of a rush. Probably because I'd been convinced there for a while that I wasn't going to be doing this anymore. Not at this level, anyway. Certainly not with a coach of Kayla's caliber. My agent had even told me to start making peace with the idea of, at best, going down to the minors.

"At this point," she'd grimly told me, "even having a Cup under your belt isn't going to keep you from getting bumped down."

Ouch, Tami.

Miraculously, though, I had another chance, and every puck I stopped this morning made this more real. I had a shot. I could redeem myself.

And my God, as if I wasn't motivated enough already, there was that always-moving visage out of the corner of my eye. I couldn't even pretend he was someone else because I could pick Sol out of a crowd just by the way he skated. The way he held his stick. How he'd sometimes make lazy circles on one blade with the other just slightly upraised. Not to mention his height—I was six-three, about average for a goalie, and Sol had a full two inches on me. He was lean and narrow, same as me and also typical of a goalie, but with his gear on? He was *huge*. Impossible to miss in a crowd. Impossible to fucking ignore.

I channeled my irritation into stopping every puck Kayla sent my way as if I were keeping Sol himself out of this net. Out of *my* net.

I didn't stop all of them. Didn't expect to. But I held my own, and both she and Maines seemed pleased. They seemed pleased with Sol, too. Fine. I could shine brighter in training camp and the preseason games. I *would* get the starter position, damn it.

By the time I went into the locker room, my head was, unsurprisingly, throbbing. That was probably from fatigue, but also the noise and lights in the practice rink. At least this facility had LED lights over the sheet, which weren't quite as brutal as fluorescents or mercury vapors. Ever since that last concussion, those lights had given me the worst headaches. The LEDs were better—still bright enough to bother me, but a type of light that was bearable. It would be better when I was wearing my contacts. I couldn't use a visor like the skaters did, so I couldn't wear a tinted one. Instead, I had a waiver that allowed me to wear special lenses to filter out the light that triggered headaches and migraines. My eyes had just been too dry and irritated this morning from flying, so I'd gone without. Tomorrow, I'd have the lenses in, and my head would feel better. I'd get some more sleep, too.

I could do this. I could still be a goalie. I could be a damn better one than my fucking ex. And hey, at least we wouldn't have to play together. Practice and train, yes, but only one of us would be on the ice at a time. I'd seen forwards and defensemen who hated each other, and that could make things...difficult. Any game I played, Sol would spend in a chair by the bench, waiting to tag in if I had to come out. We'd both skate during warm-ups, but we wouldn't have to interact.

For two ex-boyfriends who couldn't stand each other and ended up on the same team, this was the absolute best-case scenario.

Well, no. The absolute best-case scenario was the one where I started and he sat his ass in a chair more games than not. I was still working on that part.

The equipment manager, Jason, came in as we were taking off our gear. He double-checked some information about our skates and pads, and apparently he had a question about Sol's stick. I didn't really listen. Then Jason gestured at his tablet and said to both of us, "I need to know what you two want to do about numbers."

I peered up at him. "Numbers?" But a split second later, I put the pieces together—Sol and I both wore thirty-five. He had since I'd known him. I had since I'd signed with my first team after we split.

"I can only have one thirty-five on the team," Jason said with a shrug. "So, you boys tell me."

Sol and I locked gazes across the room. I kind of wanted to say, "Eh, whatever, you've had it longer," because it really didn't matter that much to me. The way he glared at me, though? Fuck it. I could be a stubborn son of a bitch, too. In unison, we said, "I'll keep it."

I met my ex's challenging look. Had there been less bad blood between us, I'd have suggested a one-on-one scrimmage or something. A coin toss. Paper-rock-scissors. Whatever. Some good-natured way of duking it out. And I usually wasn't this petty or stubborn, but when it came to Sol, what could I say? I was still more hurt and angry over him than I'd realized before today, and I wasn't letting a damn thing go.

Jason pursed his lips, glancing back and forth between us, looking for all the world like a kindergarten teacher waiting for a couple of kids to figure out who got to use the crayons first.

I opened my mouth to speak, but Sol beat me to it.

Voice full of resignation, he said, "He can keep it." As he leaned down to continue unlacing his skates, he added, "I'll take twenty-nine."

That...

Oh, you fucker. Going to take the high road so I look like an asshole?

Okay, I kind of deserved it. Because I *was* being an asshole. As heat rushed into my face and Jason jotted something on his tablet, I was pissed at Sol but furious with myself. We were exes. It was over. It was in the past. Why was I letting him get under my skin like this? Especially since he didn't even seem to *want* under my skin?

"Give me thirty-two," I said.

Both Jason and Sol eyed me.

I shrugged, hoping my face was still flushed from skating so they couldn't see me blush. "Thirty-two was my number before I was a pro." I forced a laugh. "Maybe going back to that will bring me some good luck for a change."

Sol didn't look convinced at all.

Jason clearly didn't care. He tapped something into his tablet, then left us to continue undressing.

There was no one but us in here now. Other staff members were milling around elsewhere in the facility, but no one was in the locker room. There probably wasn't anyone even within earshot.

Neither of us said a word. The sounds of gear creaking and shifting emphasized the silence between us. It reminded me a little of that hush after someone got seriously hurt during a game. When even the crowd went completely quiet. When everyone was just...waiting. Holding their breath. Hearts pounding. Waiting for someone to say how bad he was hurt. Waiting for him to get up or give *some* sign of life so we could all exhale at once. Then he'd finally start to stand, or he'd raise a hand to wave at the crowd, and the whole place would erupt in relieved applause and stick-tapping.

There was no crowd in here. There'd be no sticks tapping. I just couldn't predict how the standoff would finally end.

It was anticlimactic when it finally happened: Sol got up and walked out, heading for the showers.

Alone at last, I released that breath, the room spinning around my thumping head. I leaned forward, resting my elbows on my knees and pressing my fingers into my throbbing temples. At this rate, with the fatigue and the stress and the way I was working myself up, I was going to trigger a damn migraine, which I did not need. I mean, I *never* needed them—they'd always sucked, and they'd only gotten worse since that last concussion—and I was already miserable right now. Didn't need to add that fuckery to the heap.

Sighing, I sat up and rocked my head from side to side to loosen the building tension in my neck. I was being stupid. Sol and I had to coexist. We didn't have to like each other. We didn't have to be friends. We just had to function as teammates working toward a common goal. It wouldn't be so bad, having my name next to his on the Cup, because at least that would mean I'd *won* the damn Cup again. It had been far too long.

And I doubted Sol was even the problem right now. He was just a whole bundle of straws dropping onto the back of this overladen camel, and I wanted to lash out at him because he was there. Because he was an easy target. Because, yes, admittedly I did still have feelings from that shitshow between us almost a decade ago.

But I was exhausted. I was humiliated by what my career had become. After almost two years, I was still struggling to get back to the person and player I'd been before that concussion. And that was to say nothing of what my divorce had done to my ability to function; I was nowhere near over the man who'd left me in the middle of trying to get my health and career back on track.

I did well under pressure—kind of came with the territory in this sport—but I wasn't used to *this* kind of pressure. The kind where so much was riding on my ability to play through pain, heartache, the never-ending aftermath of a head injury, and the proximity of the only ex who'd ever hurt me more than the one who'd divorced me.

Seattle was my last chance. I had to make it here, or I was done.

I was going to make it.

I was going to be the best goalie I'd ever been.

Because fuck the skeptics. Fuck the haters. Fuck everyone who thought I was a washed-up has-been.

And maybe it made me petty and vindictive...

But *fuck* Cary Solomon.

CHAPTER 3

SOL

It was weird, seeing my name in white across a green jersey. Even weirder, seeing it above the number twenty-nine again after all these years. I'd worn it all through my youth hockey and minor league days, only switching after I'd been called up to a team that already had a twenty-nine.

Apart from half a season in the minors, I'd been a Firebird for all nine years of my professional career. Number thirty-five, that whole time. Maybe I should've grabbed thirty-five back after Josh had taken thirty-two. It would be one less change to make my mind jump the tracks like it did at the slightest provocation. On the other hand, if I did go back to thirty-five, then would Josh be a dick about it? I mean, probably—he was a dick about everything—but...

Ugh. Fuck. It's just a number. Why can't I let it go?

Probably because I'd long since hit "change" critical mass during this whole transition. To the point that doing something like changing a skate lace or opening a new pack of stick tape would make my brain completely shut down.

Get a grip, Sol. Come on.

I could do this. I was on a new team and my old number was in a new color, and it was weird, but I could do it.

I glanced across the semi-crowded locker room, immediately zeroing in on the man wearing number thirty-two.

On a new team with my old number and my old boyfriend. Yeah, this was fucking weird.

Hopefully it didn't mean my past was going to repeat itself. I'd put a lot of distance between me and who I was back then. Addiction didn't magically go away, and it was still a daily struggle to stay clean, but I was determined to keep winning that struggle just like I had for the past seven years. Okay, *most* of the past seven years. No matter how much the old me tried to gain ground, I refused to be him again, especially while I was in full view of the asshole who'd deserted me at the worst possible time. No way in hell was I going to let him see me like that again, because no way in hell could I handle seeing that disgust and resentment all over his fucking face again. As if everything I'd done had been a slight on *him* instead of me trying valiantly to self-destruct.

Now that I thought about it, maybe having him on the same team was a good thing. I had a lot of reasons to stay sober even now when I felt like my life was off the rails, and I'd have been lying if I said *don't give Josh O'Brien the satisfaction of watching me fail* wasn't way up on that list.

I'm not going to relapse, because fuck that asshole.

Hey, when your sobriety's hanging by a thread, there's no such thing as a bad reason to stay on the wagon.

And part of staying on that wagon meant strengthening my tenuous grasp on my career. Step one, knock my performance out of the park during training camp so I could snag that coveted starter spot. With that in mind, I grabbed my paddle, trapper, and mask, and headed out to the ice to warm up.

Josh came out not long after, and of course, we made eye contact, which made the cold air around us even colder. We hadn't said a word to each other since I'd first walked into the locker room yesterday, and we didn't say a word to each other now, but the tension was unmistakable. Every time Josh looked at me, my hackles went up. So did his. He probably thought he was being slick about it, but he never was. I doubted I was either.

Whatever. He was here. I was here. Couldn't do anything about that. Instead, I did my best to ignore him and focus on my job. At least today would be less fraught than yesterday because the rest of the team would be here, not to mention a couple dozen prospects from the farm teams.

First things first, some goalie training with Kayla. Usually we'd start training camp at the same time as the rest of the team, but she'd told Coach she wanted to spend an hour with us ahead of each session until we'd found our groove. She hadn't come out and said it was because we'd both been disasters last season and she wanted to make sure we had our bearings—at least, she hadn't said it within earshot of me—but the implication was there. I couldn't even be offended by it. We did need the extra practice. We needed to get used to her and we needed to spend some time in the net without having to focus on what the rest of the team was doing.

Once we were done with some drills, the rest of the team started to skate out onto the ice for their warm-ups. They were split into three units for training—wearing white, green, or blue jerseys—and right now, green and white jerseys were on the ice.

Josh and I had met everyone earlier, though it would take a while to learn names. Now we were out here with them, and I was...overwhelmed. It wasn't unusual for players to be thrown in with a new team shortly after introductions were made. Happened all the time, especially with mid-season trades. Hell, we'd had a forward come to Phoenix last season right at the trade deadline, and he'd flown in on a red-eye, slept a few hours, joined us for the morning skate, and played that night. I had no idea how he did it without losing his mind, because I was kind of losing mine right now.

This was all happening so fast. Maybe it was because I'd been on the same team for so long, I hadn't had to deal with being yeeted onto another roster on a moment's notice the way other players did, so I didn't know how to handle it. Or maybe I just wasn't wired for it. No idea. What I did know was that meeting the whole new team and the parade of prospects at the same time I was starting to practice with them turned out to be a lot more chaotic and nerve-racking than I anticipated. So many people. So many new faces. Thank God everyone had their names on their jerseys for training camp, or I'd have been completely lost.

I knew a few faces. Darby had played with Phoenix for...three seasons? Four? Meyer had been in the minors with me for a little while. And of course I'd met various players over time. Become familiar with them. Hockey was a fairly small sport, and most of us knew each other to some extent. We'd at least played against each other.

I just didn't...*know* them. Not like I had some of my teammates back in Arizona. I didn't have the rapport to shoot the shit during stoppages or chirp in between drills. I couldn't see myself striking up a conversation with any of them in the locker room or on the plane. Despite being familiar names and faces, and even former teammates, they were still strangers.

It was while we were setting up for the scrimmage that the most unnerving truth slowly dawned on me. I'd been so caught up in the panic of potentially losing my career that I'd overlooked the fact that the Firebirds had been my support network. Several players knew about my ongoing struggle to remain sober. When I'd had the occasional crisis and desperately wanted to find a dealer, there'd been guys I could go to who would, without question or judgment, help talk me down. They didn't even have to do that much—my old therapist had taught me a number of ways to ride out a craving, and sometimes all I needed was someone to be there with me. They didn't have to do or say anything—just be there so I wasn't alone. That helped a lot more than any of them probably realized, and aside from two brief relapses, I'd stayed clean for most of my career since the first time I'd left rehab.

Here in Seattle...

On the ice with the Sasquatches and all the prospects...

I was alone.

Completely untethered. Completely without that safety net I'd carefully created over the years.

And that was, even more than the possibility of losing my career altogether, terrifying.

Suddenly, as I took my place in the net and the scrimmage kicked off, everything was too much. Too bright. Too loud. Pucks banging like gunfire off the glass and dashers. Colors and signs I didn't recognize. Banners that weren't what I was used to and were all in the wrong places. The lights were different. The building was different. Everything was different, and it gnawed at me and needled at me and made it exponentially harder to concentrate on the thing I absolutely *had* to get right: tending the goal well enough to secure my place on this team.

I blinked a few times and took a few breaths, then focused hard on the players in green who were currently making a drive for the other net. I could do this. I would do this. I had to do this. Failure truly wasn't an option; I didn't let myself think about what life would look like if I lost my career because it was too terrifying and depressing to imagine. I needed everything that was tied to this contract and this new, unfamiliar jersey that suddenly seemed too tight and too itchy despite being nowhere near my skin. It was all in my head and I knew it—the gear between the jersey and my body was familiar and perfectly fitted, and I'd long ago learned that when it all suddenly became uncomfortable, it was just my brain going haywire. When the pressure was too much, my neck guard felt like it was getting tighter and tighter, cutting off blood and air alike until I couldn't concentrate on anything except—

A shout jerked my attention back to the ice, and thank God my mind snapped into focus. There was a two-on-one rush coming my way, and that beast of a forward was leaving both our guy and his own teammate in the dust as he barreled toward my net. Heart pounding, I watched both him and the puck, glove and paddle ready as I tried to anticipate his next move.

He faked left. Then right. Then he passed without looking back to his teammate, who was ready and waiting to fire a one-timer at me.

It was sheer dumb luck that I was just far enough off-center for the puck to hit my chest instead of going in, and when it landed on the ice, I slammed my trapper down on top of it. A few sticks and bodies crashed into me—carried mostly by momentum but probably also the need to be absolutely sure the puck wasn't loose—before the ref blew the play dead. Everyone cleared out of the crease, and I indulged in a relieved sigh as my heart pounded behind the place the puck had smacked into my pads. Those lucky shots happened during games sometimes, but they could also be lucky for the skater and go right past my shoulder or under my arm.

I had to focus. Had to. This was just a scrimmage, but I was under heavy scrutiny, and I could not afford to blow it.

Volkov, one of the forwards I recognized, came by and tapped my pads with his stick. "Nice save."

I nodded to acknowledge him. I appreciated skaters who appreciated what we did; he just didn't need to know it was physics and the shooter's aim that had stopped that shot from being a point.

Get it together, Sol. Come on.

As the skaters set up for a faceoff, I glanced across the ice. I couldn't see Josh's face from here, but I knew it was him.

Christ. Don't you dare let him see you fall apart.

That sent a surge of determination through me, followed by a jittery rush of panic. I didn't want to fall apart. It just sometimes happened despite my best efforts. I wondered sometimes if it happened *because* of my best efforts. I was a mess. Always had been.

I rolled my shoulders under my pads and slowly pushed out a breath through my nose.

It was in moments like this that sobriety felt less important. One line. Even just a small bump. Then everything in my head would quiet enough for me to make sense of it all. The world would slow down enough for me to keep up. I'd be able to concentrate on the important things—the puck, the way other players were moving—instead of being mentally yanked in too many directions.

That was the toughest part about staying off coke during hockey season—knowing how well it actually improved my game. The hardest moments were when I was in the net, overwhelmed by light and sound and noise and motion, and I *knew* there was something that could bring it all down to a dull, manageable roar. It didn't give me superhuman strength or extra energy like it did other people. It just slowed the world and my brain enough to let me do my job.

I took advantage of another stoppage to close my eyes and take a few slow breaths, trying like hell to quiet the maelstrom in my head so I could focus.

I'd made it through this before. The first practice after rehab had been brutal—all that pressure, all that noise, and my best (or, well, most familiar and effective) coping mechanism had been gone. I hadn't been used to processing all of that—never mind tracking the puck and making saves— without the chemically-induced calm.

But I *had* made it through. I'd had a damn good comeback season after that.

I could do it again. I just needed to get my shit together and keep pucks out of the net, and I wouldn't be wading through the uncharted waters of new sobriety this time.

I could do this. I *would* do this.

I'd get through the scattered focus. I'd get through the cravings. All of it.

And more cravings *would* come. They were inevitable. They were less frequent as time went on, but they happened. And my last relapse was only two years ago, so... that whole "as time went on" thing was still an ongoing process.

I'd have given anything to be able to take one of the

meds on the market for ADHD, but neither my therapists nor the league would go for it. The league had banned meds like Adderall across the board with no exceptions, and even if those drugs were allowed, the effects were too similar to cocaine. My sobriety was difficult enough to maintain without giving myself little tastes of the relief I craved. All I could do was knuckle through. Same as I always did.

Same as I *usually* did.

As activity resumed on the ice, I opened my eyes, and before I could stop it, my gaze locked on Josh. He was in the other goal, his face invisible across that much space and behind his mask, but somehow I could feel him watching me. Could feel him judging the shit out of me because no one knew better than he did what a fuck-up I'd been all those years ago.

Maybe I didn't have meds or cocaine to help me focus, but I did have spite, and a former teammate had once told me that spite could be a hell of a drug.

"If you can't win for yourself," he'd told me over beers one night, *"win because it'll piss off the haters."*

Those immortal words didn't quiet the noise in my head, but they did focus a lot of it on a single goal: shine like I'd never shined before, if only so Josh O'Brien had to be my backup goalie.

I am going to do this.

Because fuck you, that's why.

I made it through day one of training camp by the skin of my teeth. Kayla and Coach were pleased, so apparently I'd been convincingly competent. If they hadn't noticed me on the brink of coming unraveled, then...great. I was still keeping it under the surface.

After I'd showered, I ate in the lounge with some teammates. Some of the guys from the green team invited me to their table, and I was grateful for the company. Not that my aching, overstimulated brain could follow much of the conversation, and I didn't contribute more than a few words here and there. Still, it was more comfortable than sitting alone while everyone else carried on in groups. Safety in numbers. Or at least less anxiety in numbers.

Once other guys started to peel away and head for the parking garage, I left, too. Lucky for me, I just had to walk across the street to the hotel. As much as I hated staying in hotels for any length of time, my head was too much of a mess right now to drive. Instead, all I had to do was walk about a block and a half, get up to my room, and faceplant in that bed.

I couldn't sleep when the sun was up. Never had been able to. Napping didn't work for me—not when my mind was always going too fast and in too many directions—but just lying there and not doing anything helped. The hamsters inside my skull could do their thing, and I could just close my eyes instead of pretending I could follow a puck or a conversation. My body was tired in that pleasant way that meant I'd had a good, hard workout.

My brain, however, was absolutely wrecked in a very *not* pleasant way. Exhausted from all the upheaval and sensory overload. This was when it went even faster and in even more directions—when I was too tired and wrung out to hold on to a thought.

Eventually, my head slowed down a little, and I went downstairs to the hotel's coffee shop for a triple espresso. My therapist didn't like me using stimulants to calm down, but she understood that there were times when I needed something to quiet the chaos. Coffee wasn't nearly as strong as anything else I'd done, and it didn't make me crave the bad stuff. Plus I didn't actually like it enough to drink it regularly, so my therapist and I had agreed that a super-charged cup now and then was a safe alternative.

In my room, as I continued choking down the bitter drink, I checked my phone or the first time since I'd arrived at the practice rink earlier. To my surprise, there was a text on my screen, and I was relieved to see that it was from one of my old teammates. Tracer—Justin Tracy to everyone else —had always been amazingly supportive. He'd been there when I'd gone through rehab the second time, and he was one of the reasons I'd survived the last relapse. I'd roomed with him for a couple of seasons, too. The man was a godsend; I wasn't sure how I was going to make it through my next inevitable rough patch without him or one of the other guys.

He'd messaged me during practice: *Hey, how is it going in Seattle?*

There were people who asked me questions like that and expected canned answers. Everything was fine. It was going great. I'm good—how are you?

Tracer was not one of those people. He'd told me a long time ago not to bullshit him, and I'd found out he meant it the first time I'd *tried* to bullshit him.

And the chance to be honest was a relief right now, so I texted back the unvarnished truth: *It's fucking rough.*

Unsurprisingly, his response was a Facetime request, and I accepted it gratefully.

Tracer appeared on the screen. He was cleanshaven right now, but that wouldn't last long. While it was tradition for hockey players to stop shaving during the playoffs, he took it to another level. He superstitiously never shaved at all once the regular season started, and he inevitably looked like a Viking by the time the postseason rolled around. It was always jarring to see him like this early on, since it looked like he'd shaved off about fifteen years along with the fur.

I didn't let my mind linger on the fact that I wouldn't be there to rib him about the awkwardly pube-like phase his beard always went through before it became respectably full. God, I missed him, but at least we could still talk.

"Hey man," he said. "Having a tough time?"

As I leaned back against the hotel bed's headboard, I sighed. "Yeah. It's just... It's all new, you know? New team. New coach. New systems."

He nodded and gave a quiet grunt. "That's hard for anybody. It's gotta suck for you."

"It does."

He locked eyes with me through our phones. "Level with me—are you hanging in there?"

I didn't have to ask for clarification. "So far. I've had a few moments of temptation, but...I'm still good."

His lips pulled tight as he nodded solemnly. "You know you can hit up me or one of the boys, right? If you think you're going to..."

I exhaled. "I appreciate it. But it's not like I can just come to your place anymore, you know? Or hang out after practice or whatever."

Those afternoons of playing video games at a teammate's house or kicking back with a movie in someone's hotel room had pulled me out of many, many low points. Even though I'd known at some level that none of that would last forever—hockey careers did have shelf lives, after all—it was seriously terrifying to imagine going forward without it. And intimidating as all hell to imagine developing that kind of relationship with my new teammates. Tracer and the others had seen me at my worst and helped me back on my feet, so they understood what I was up against. It wasn't some abstract, nebulous thing to them. It was very, very real. Hell, they'd seen me relapse, and they'd helped me quietly get back into rehab and get clean without the league ever catching on. *Twice.*

No one in Seattle had been there for any of that.

Well. *Almost* no one.

Tracer spoke again, derailing the train of thought that was about to start on Josh. "Listen, man, we're not on the same team anymore, but I'm still your friend, okay? So are the other boys. You need help? You have a bad night?" He tapped his chest. "You fucking call us. Got it? Don't try to ride it out alone."

"Thanks," I croaked, my throat suddenly tight. "I think I'll be okay. It's just...new, I guess. A lot of pressure."

"I bet. But you've got this."

God, I hope so, I wanted to say, but he wouldn't like that answer. Instead, I just said, "I appreciate it."

I really did. I was so, so grateful for the support, and especially that I still had that support even though we wore different jerseys now. I just hated that I needed it. And that he and the other guys *knew* I needed it.

But they were there. And I was here. Yeah, I had their support, but it wasn't 24/7. It couldn't be. Even when we'd been on the same team, there'd been times when I couldn't reach someone, or when I didn't dare let the less-understanding teammates or staff members catch on that something was wrong. Now there'd be even less opportunity. What if they were flying? Or on the ice? What if I was?

How do I do this alone?

Well, I'd have to cross that bridge when I got to it. In the meantime, I was grateful I had this lifeline. Sobriety was a tough enough struggle without having to go it alone.

Teammates like Tracer had done a lot for me. Saved my life, if I was honest. If nothing else, I owed it to them to keep my shit together and stand on my own two skates.

I had to grudgingly admit that Josh had also saved me. As much as I wanted to hate him—and there were a lot of reasons why I *did* hate him—I couldn't deny that he'd been instrumental in getting my life and my career back on the rails. He'd also abandoned me at the worst possible moment, but shouldn't I give him some credit for getting me into rehab before he'd bailed?

Probably. Yes. But he *had* still abandoned me. When I'd been at the lowest point of my life, he'd shown me that rock bottom had a basement, and that basement was him walking out on me while I was detoxing.

Fresh anger surged through me at that memory. Like hell was he going to see me like that again.

Oh, I'd be fine. I'd be absolutely perfect, because as long as I had Josh nearby to judge me if I relapsed, I was going to stay cleaner than I'd ever fucking been. Not really what my therapist and everyone at rehab had in mind when they said I needed a support system, but if it kept the blow out of my nose, then it worked, right?

Well, hell. Maybe I had support on this team after all.

I mostly managed to avoid Josh, or at least avoid interacting with him, but I should've known that luck wouldn't last. We'd be in too close quarters, especially once the team was on the road, which we would be next week for the first preseason games.

I debated a few times if I should just head him off and talk to him. Didn't know what I'd say or how it would go, but we needed to break this standoff and at least stop with the frosty silence. Get it out on the table, tell each other whatever it was we needed to say, and then do our level best to stay apart when we could.

It was right after practice one morning when we finally wound up face to face. I'd known it was coming, too. We'd been deep in a drill, practicing the butterfly as Kayla and another trainer fired pucks at us, and I'd momentarily forgotten who the other goalie was. I'd called out that his left leg pad looked like it was coming loose, same as I would've with any other teammate. Same as I'd have expected any other teammate to do with me.

When he'd turned toward me, eyes hard behind his mask, I'd bitten back a curse because I'd known we'd have words later. Especially since it turned out the pad *hadn't* been coming loose; he just didn't secure them quite as tightly as I did mine, or as tightly as he had in the past. Apparently he liked them a little bit looser now than he had back then; my old backup goalie had done the same thing. I just wasn't used to seeing Josh do it this way, and he clearly wasn't impressed with me saying something about it. All I could do was hope that when he did get in my face about it, he had the good graces to wait until we were alone.

He did, and when that moment came, it was in the parking garage as we were both heading back to the hotel where we were staying. He cut right to the chase, too:

Glaring hard at me, he demanded, "Did I miss the memo where you're the assistant goalie coach?"

Stopping to face him, I rolled my eyes, mostly because I

knew that pissed him off. "Act like you've never done the same thing with your other teammates if you think their gear is fucked up."

His jaw worked. "You know this is different."

"Is it?" I crossed my arms. "How do you figure?"

"Because one of us is going to be the starter," he said through his teeth. "And every little bit counts. So—"

"So I'm going to give you suggestions to fix your shit?" I barked a humorless laugh. "If I was trying to make you fail, I wouldn't have said anything at all."

"Bullshit. You wanted to make sure Kayla noticed and thought I didn't know what I was doing."

There was no point in even trying to convince him that wasn't the case, though I sure noted it in case he decided to point out one of *my* mistakes or an issue with *my* gear.

Way to tip your hand there, pal.

As much as I wanted to antagonize him and piss him off, I was tired. And like it or not, we did have to coexist on this team. If he wanted to be enough of a dick that Coach or Kayla decided to punt him off the roster, that was his business, but I'd be wise not to take the bait myself when I had so much riding on staying in their good graces.

"Look." I narrowed my eyes. "I don't like this any more than you do, but it's not like either of us has a choice."

"You don't say." His voice was colder than anything I'd ever skated on. "So maybe focus on keeping your own shit together." He stepped close. Not as close as he would've been in our better days, but way closer than he needed to be right now. Eyes hard, he growled, "There's a whole lot riding on you. I hope you understand that."

"You mean like the team?" I snapped. "And my entire damn career? Yeah, I'm well aware."

"Good," he gritted out. "Then does that mean we can trust you not to fuck up and drag us all down with you?"

Fury burned hot behind my ribs, and it was almost enough to mute the shame that wanted to crawl up my throat. I hated him for throwing that in my face. I hated him even more for being right.

"I haven't used in years," I told him, and I was being honest. It was fewer years than he probably knew, but still. Years. "I don't intend to start again now. Especially not..." I flailed a hand at our surroundings, as if that might encompass the shitty situation we were both in.

"I fucking hope not," he said through his teeth. "Because I swear, if I so much as think you're powdering your fucking nose again, I'll—"

"Toss me into rehab and disappear?" I spat. "You don't have to tell me. I know *exactly* what you'll do."

He laughed bitterly, backing off a little and putting some more space between us. "What did you expect me to do? Stick around? After all the shit you—"

"You didn't have to desert me the way you did." I hated how much my voice shook. *Hated* it. He had no right to pull this much emotion out of me. "I almost thought you wanted to help me back then, but obviously you just wanted to wash your hands of—"

"I *did* want to help you." He was suddenly in my face again, and way closer than before. "I *tried* to help you. I tried everything I could think of." Stabbing a finger at me, nearly hitting me in the chest, he added in a low, angry whisper, "Don't you *dare* act like I didn't."

"Yeah. Sure you did." I let the sarcasm drip like syrup. "That's why you bailed while I was—"

"I fucking *tried*, Sol," he snapped, and there was a slight waver in his voice that caught me off-guard, and it only got worse as he kept talking. "If I'd wanted to leave you to the wolves, I'd have walked out long before your ass went into rehab. I'd have called the damn cops instead of getting you help. I stuck around even when no one would believe me about your problem, and I didn't leave until I could walk away without being scared shitless you'd fucking OD. You can tell yourself all you want that I bailed at the first opportunity, but that was far from the first." I swear to God his eyes welled up as he gritted out, "It was just the first chance I had where I didn't think you'd wind up dead the minute I was gone."

He didn't wait for a response. Instead, he brushed past me, nearly clipping my shoulder with his, and stalked out of the parking garage.

And I...

I just stood there. Stock still. Speechless.

What the fuck just happened?

CHAPTER 4

JOSH

I was actually grateful for the white-hot anger from that conversation with Sol. I hadn't been this furious in I didn't know how long, which said a lot, given my shitshow of a divorce. This wasn't a good feeling at all, but it *did* keep me upright and composed (sort of) until I was well out of Sol's earshot. In fact, I made it outside, across the street, and into the hotel before the cracks started to show.

In the elevator, I had to fight hard to keep the tears inside, and I held on to my anger so the hurt wouldn't break loose. The last thing I needed was someone getting in here with me, recognizing me, and then posting to social media that they'd seen Josh O'Brien having an emotional break-down in an elevator. Not that anyone in Seattle probably had half a clue who I was, but whatever—the prospect of being on the wrong end of a camera lens kept me composed all the way to my room.

Finally, I was there, and once the door was closed and deadbolted, I pushed out a breath.

Then I let all the feelings come crashing in.

Anger at Sol for being such a fucking punk. Anger at

myself for letting things get so bad that I was in this stupid situation in the first place. Just everything.

But also regret, and worst of all, that deep, deep hurt I'd buried under miles of resentment for so many years. It seared its way to the surface now, refusing to be ignored and making damn sure I knew that no matter what I told myself, I had deep, unhealed wounds with Sol's name carved all over them.

Wiping my eyes with a shaky hand, I pushed off the door, shuffled across the room, and dropped onto the edge of the bed. I covered my face and tried to pull myself together, but I failed miserably.

It was so damn tempting in a moment like this to say fuck it and tell my agent I wanted out of this contract. Send me to the minors. Send me to Europe. Cut me loose completely. Whatever. I just wasn't going to make it through a season in Seattle with someone who'd torn me apart me like this. Not when I was still so raw over my divorce, and not when all *this* asshole could see was me *abandoning* him.

Our conversation repeated over and over in my head, the words cracking against the inside of my skull like pucks slamming into dashers. God, I hated him. I hated him for throwing it in my face that I'd left after putting him in rehab. I hated that he still held a grudge against me for that. Yeah, maybe it wasn't the best time to leave someone, but I'd been at my absolute breaking point *weeks* before that.

I'd never *wanted* to abandon him. I'd never *wanted* to lose him. I just couldn't keep covering for him and watching him self-destruct, and I'd been exhausted like I'd never been before or since. The fights. The fear. The way his habit had permeated every facet of our lives. The way it had been so inescapable, I might as well have been using it, too, if only so

I'd finally get some of the benefits out of it on top of all the bad shit. If my life was going to be hell because of cocaine, I might as well enjoy the rush alongside the nasty effects, right?

That was when I'd known I couldn't handle any more—when I'd been tempted to start using the drug myself. Because when he was high, he was happy. Utterly blissed out. The sex had been amazing, at least before I'd realized it was the coke, not just him being horny. I, on the other hand, had been miserable, and it had only gotten worse the more I'd begged him to get help.

Sol hadn't wanted help. He hadn't wanted to give up the cocaine. He loved it too much, and no one would listen to me because nothing about him telegraphed cocaine use. By the time the truth had finally come out, I'd been so worn down, I could barely function. Couldn't sleep. Couldn't play hockey. Barely had the energy to work out. I'd very nearly lost *my* career because my boyfriend's addiction had ground me to dust. It was literally in a meeting with the some of our team's brass—one in which they were threatening to punt me to the minors or otherwise discipline me— that I'd finally gotten through to someone.

Threadbare with exhaustion and defeat, I'd told them, "Test him after a game. If it doesn't come up positive for cocaine, you can release me from my contract and I'll never play hockey again."

Even now, all these years later, imagining their wide eyes and startled silence gave me a rush of relief. It was in that moment that I'd known someone finally heard me. That something was going to happen. Sol was going to get the help he needed.

"You're that sure?" the GM had asked. "You'd bet your entire hockey career on a teammate's positive drug test?"

"Yes." I'd swallowed hard, forcing back more emotions than I could name. "And I don't gamble. I only make bets I know I can win."

They'd taken me at my word, and Sol had barely left the ice after the next game before he was pulled aside for a piss test.

The following day, he'd been at breakfast with the team like normal. He'd been on the plane to our next city. But when everyone had come down from our hotel rooms to get on the bus to the arena, he was nowhere in sight. Our third goalie had dressed for the game, acting as backup while I started. Everyone had asked, but no one had an answer: Where was Sol?

The announcement had come out the day after that, with headlines screaming that he'd tested positive for cocaine, would be suspended for twenty games, and had to complete league-mandated rehab before he could resume playing hockey. He'd be subject to random tests for the rest of his career, and if he popped again, it would be a forty-game suspension. A third time—sixty games. After that, he'd be out of the league. There were ominous predictions that he was statistically very likely to relapse, so even if he did make it through this and get back on the ice, it was only a matter of time before he snorted his way right out the door for good.

When it had all come out, I hadn't felt vindicated or smug. I'd been absolutely devastated. Completely crushed and overcome with guilt, relief, and guilt over being relieved. I'd blamed myself, even though I knew I'd done the right thing.

His rehab was in-patient, and I'd asked if I could visit him when we were back in Phoenix. They'd told me I could. That it was good for him to have visitors and support.

So I'd gone.

He'd still been detoxing at that point, and I'd never seen him so miserable and broken, not to mention angry. He was furious with me. Told me this was worse than if I'd cheated on him. His career was quite possibly over; even when he came back from his suspension, there was no telling if any team would want to keep him.

"How could you do this to me?" he'd demanded. "What the fuck, Josh?"

I'd left the facility and sobbed in my car. Fucking *sobbed*. The way I was breaking down right now on this hotel bed had nothing on how wrecked I'd been that day. All these years later, I could still get choked up just thinking about those hellish minutes crying in the shadow of the building where the man I loved was going to hopefully get his life back on the rails.

When I'd pulled myself together, I'd stared at the facility through my tears and windshield, and I'd asked myself when I would come back. How long I should give him. How long I should give myself.

And the answer...

I wasn't coming back. Sitting there in the car, I hadn't really made a decision about whether I wanted to, or if I should, or anything. I simply knew that...I wouldn't. I just wouldn't.

Feeling strangely calm and determined, I'd gone home that night, packed my things, and moved into a hotel room. A month and a half later, shortly before Sol was to rejoin the team, I was traded at my request. After that, we only ever saw each other again on opposite ends of the ice. On the rare occasion we were in the same room, there were too many cameras and hot mics around for us to even look at each other sideways.

Now we were here. In Seattle. On the same roster. And I couldn't fucking take it.

Because deep down, beneath the resentment and the hurt and those wounds that had never healed, the fact was... I *loved* Sol. He'd been everything to me at one time. The love of my life, I'd thought.

Even in the absolute darkest days, even right there at the end, I'd loved him. I'd loved him enough that it had caused tension in my marriage. I still loved him now.

Which was exactly why it hurt so bad to hate him this much.

Eight Seasons Ago

"Good game, rookie." Nils—Gunnar Nilsson—clapped my shoulder as he walked past where I was sitting in the hotel bar. "You stood on your head out there. Do it again next game, and you might be bumping this jackass to backup."

"Hey!" Laughing, Sol flipped him off from across the table. "Fuck you. Maybe he wouldn't have to work so hard if you boys did your job and kept the puck away from him."

Nils waved a hand. "Nah. We don't have to work as hard to keep it away from him because we know he'll actually keep it out of the net."

"Dude, fuck off." Sol was still laughing, though, rolling his eyes as he reached for his beer.

Nils chuckled, and he and a few of our other teammates headed out.

"He's right, you know." Sol's smile held, but his eyes

were sincere. "You killed it out there tonight." Raising his mostly finished beer, he added, "Keep it up."

My face was on fire, though I had no idea why. "Thanks." Idly running my fingers through the condensation on my iced tea, I said, "Feels like redemption after..." I grimaced.

Sol shrugged it away. "If that keeps you going, then run with it. But you're a good goalie. Your first couple of games..." Another shrug. "Happens to everyone." He tilted the bottle toward me. "You wouldn't have made it to this level if the scouts and coaches didn't see something in you."

I knew that. I did. But every time Sol reassured me— God, he'd done that so much since I'd made the Firebirds roster a couple of months ago—it made me feel less like someone was going to realize I wasn't worth the paper my contract was printed on. The coaches, our other teammates, the media, and even the fans had all said the same things, but hearing it from Sol settled something in me. Probably because he was a goalie, too. He understood the pressure that came with being the man between the pipes, and how much a netminder's performance could make or break a game.

He knew what it was like to hear all the sports reporters and commentators emphasizing that a particular team's success or failure came down to their goaltending. He knew as well as I did that a team could have generational talents on every line and D pair (not that that would ever actually happen) and still fall apart because of a goalie. At the same time, a mediocre roster of whatshisname players could soar to a Cup win on the back of a solid goalie.

So yeah, it made a difference to hear encouragement from another goalie.

It had nothing at all to do with the fact that it was *this* goalie, or that my mind short-circuited every time he directed those blue eyes at me. And those smiles? Fuck. I would take it to my grave that the one and only goal I'd let in tonight had been seconds after I'd caught Sol's eye. Sitting on the bench in his pads and a backwards baseball cap, he'd given me a little nod and one of those easy smiles, and suddenly I hadn't stood a chance against the odd-man rush coming my way.

Could've been my first career shutout tonight, I thought as I listened to him telling me about some disaster of a game last season. *But all things considered, I can't complain.*

As we hung out in the bar, we kept talking, the conversation drifting from hockey to the restaurant scene back in Phoenix (which he knew and I was still learning) and what neighborhoods I should think about if I decided to buy a place.

"Eh." I shrugged as I turned my empty glass between my fingers. "I like the apartment the team hooked me up with, honestly. I'll buy something eventually, but I'm not in a big hurry."

Sol nodded. "I get that. I'm not a big fan of change."

"No?"

"Nope." He actually blushed as he added, "I still live in the place the team put me up."

"You—really?"

"Mmhmm." He mirrored my shrug. "It's nice. And I mean, it's just me, so I don't need one of the palaces like Collins has."

"God, that place." I laughed, shaking my head. "Holy fuck. I'd get lost there!"

"I know, right?" Sol chuckled, but he sounded fond. "With that many kids, though..."

I grunted in agreement. Our captain had six kids, and

predictably, they were all high-energy. Came with the territory when both Mom and Dad were professional hockey players. "Yeah, I don't think I need a place that big. But maybe I'll buy something. Eventually."

"There's no hurry." Sol picked up his beer, but frowned, evidently realizing it was empty. Then he looked around, and he straightened. "Are we the last Firebirds here?"

I scanned the room, and sure enough, there wasn't a familiar face in sight. "Holy shit. What time *is* it?" According to my phone—almost 2:30. "Whoa. When did that happen?"

"Again?" He laughed. "Man. We keep closing down the bar like this, Coach is going to kill us."

"Probably." But I didn't regret it. Not tonight. Not any of the other nights where we'd lost ourselves in conversation only to look up and realize it was well past midnight and our teammates were long gone.

Sol sighed heavily and slid off his chair, gesturing toward the bar. "Guess I should close my tab."

"Yeah, same." My tab wasn't bad tonight; I'd only had a series of interestingly flavored iced teas. I'd had that familiar feeling the last couple of days that a migraine might be looming—the vaguest sensation that my head wasn't throbbing but wanted to—and I knew from experience that alcohol could tip that from "maybe migraine" to "mistakes were made." Truthfully, under any other circumstances, I'd have just gone to bed and not bothered hanging out with my teammates in the bar like I did after most away games. Even with the dim lights, the noise could be a bit much, so going to sleep was the best idea.

But I just hadn't been able to resist coming down. Not to hang out with my teammates—to hang out with one teammate in particular.

If I had to guess, Sol had two or three drinks since we'd arrived, but that was spread out over a few hours. He was steady on his feet, not slurring in the slightest, and it wasn't like either of us had to drive—the elevators were about twenty feet from the bar, and our rooms weren't far beyond.

As we stepped into the elevator, I was exhausted—ready to faceplant in bed and hope I managed a little sleep before we had to be up at the crack of dawn to go to the airport. Especially since the low-grade threat of a migraine was still there. But I was also disappointed the evening was over, and somehow not at all surprised we'd lingered in the bar until the wee hours. Again.

Yeah, I'd probably regret this tomorrow when I was barely awake at the airport.

I stole a glance at Sol. Like me, he still wore his suit, though he'd loosened his tie, which made him unreasonably hot.

He caught me looking at him too, and as warmth rose in my face, he offered a tired but genuine smile.

Oh God. I want you so bad.

I yanked my gaze away from him and stared at the numbers above the door. I was sure he was still watching me, but I was too much of a coward to confirm it.

At our floor, we both stepped out. Our rooms were in opposite directions, so we paused, and my heart thumped against my ribs the way it usually only did during overtime.

Sol met my gaze, and there was that smile again. "I'll see you at breakfast?"

Mouth dry, I nodded. "Yeah. See you, uh...see you at breakfast." I laughed, sounding almost as nervous as I was. "Not even sure it's worth going to sleep at this point."

Sol's tired but genuine laugh didn't help my runaway pulse in the slightest. "Might as well grab an hour or two at least." He half-shrugged. "Something, something, we made this bed and now we get to lie in it." The instant the words had left his mouth, his teeth snapped shut, and color bloomed in his fair complexion. "I, uh..."

Maybe I was tired, but it took me a second to realize he'd even metaphorically implied the two of us sharing a bed. The way that flustered him threw me off-balance even more than the comment, which would've flown right over my head had he not drawn attention to it.

Sure my face was as red as his, I choked out a laugh. "Yeah. Guess we, uh, kind of signed up for this."

"Yeah. Kinda."

Our eyes locked. His were unreadable. Should I have grabbed on to the comment and run with it? Tested the waters a little to see if he was just embarrassed that he'd accidentally said something inappropriate to a rookie, or if he'd been thinking some of the same things I had lately?

But I quickly pushed all that away. We were in a hotel with our team. We both had roommates. We had to be at breakfast in like three hours so we could get to the airport. If there was something crackling between us—something that kept drawing him into long evenings with me in hotel bars—this wasn't the time to see what those sparks could ignite.

I cleared my throat. "I should, uh..." I gestured in the direction of my room.

"Me too." He took a small but decisive step toward his own. "I'll see you at breakfast. Good night, Obie."

"Good night."

We held each other's gazes a moment longer. Then, without another word, we continued in separate directions, my heart pounding all the way.

CHAPTER 5

SOL

Present Day

The life of a professional hockey player was nothing if not chaotic. Kind of came with the territory of eighty-four games a year, trades happening fast enough to give someone whiplash, and constant travel. I was as used to it as anyone could be.

But I'd also been spoiled, staying on the same team in the same city for nine years. I'd never envied my teammates who were bounced all over the league, especially those who had to move during the season on a moment's notice. Moving was stressful enough without trying to practice, travel, and play with a brand-new team at the same time.

On top of that, I didn't have a partner. A lot of my teammates over the years had mentioned how much they relied on their partners during transitions. They could focus on jelling with the new team while a spouse handled the logistics of relocating. I didn't have that luxury. Then again, I also didn't have kids, so maybe it balanced out.

Whatever. All I knew was that today was moving day, and the movers were due to arrive at my new apartment forty-five minutes after I'd booked it out of the training facility after practice. I'd had time to shower and stuff a little bit of food into my face, but then I'd had to get my butt to my new apartment.

At least the team staff had helped me nail down a place to live. I wasn't going to buy anything—not in this over-priced town and sure as shit not when I didn't know for sure if I'd be staying with the Sasquatches. For the next year at least, I'd be renting a two-bedroom apartment in Green Lake, a neighborhood a couple of miles away from the training facility. I'd only been down here once—a quick trip to have a look and sign the lease after a staff member had found me a suitable apartment—but it seemed nice. Plus the lake was only a couple of blocks away, and apparently it had a multi-use trail around it. Good for jogging. I'd take it.

For today, there wouldn't be any jogging or exploring— just moving in.

I was still hungry from practice, so I grabbed a sandwich from a café across the street from the apartment. Of course, I'd barely stepped into my kitchen and taken a bite before I heard a big diesel engine outside. Shit, the movers were early. Oh well. The sooner they finished, the sooner I could settle in. Okay, so settling in meant living out of boxes until about two weeks before I moved out, when I would suddenly unpack everything and then regret it because I had to pack it all up again. I'd done that in my condo as well as my house, and I'd probably do it in this place, too.

But at least my stuff would be here.

I took another bite, grabbed my water bottle, and

headed downstairs, washing the food down as I went. Then I stepped outside to see, as I expected, a moving truck parked on the curb. There was a small parking garage beneath the building for residents and guests, but of course, the truck wouldn't fit. I was kind of amazed it was able to park at all until I remembered the landlady had said something about putting up *No Parking* signs to keep people off that part of the street on moving day. Good thing this place thought of everything, because I was lucky I'd had the brainpower to order my sandwich.

God, I couldn't wait for all this chaos to be over. It was so hard to focus on any one thing when there was so much happening.

A phantom itch in my nose reminded me there was a way to quiet everything down and make it all slower and easier to grasp, but I ignored it, same way I did every goddamned day of my life.

Blow will help in the moment, I reminded myself for the millionth time. *It's not worth it in the long run.*

Unaware of me pulling myself together, a burly dude hopped out of the truck's cab. When I flagged him down, he came up to me with a clipboard in his hand.

"Hey," I said with a smile that hopefully hid how absolutely through the roof my anxiety was right now. "You guys are early!"

He shot me an odd look, then shrugged and looked at the clipboard. "Right. Josh O'Brien?"

I froze. "What? No, I'm—"

"Oh, hey!" Josh's voice stopped my breath in my throat, and I turned to see him coming out of the building behind me. "Sounds like traffic was a nightmare!"

The mover chuckled. "Always is in this town. Sorry we're late."

"Nah, it's all good." Josh eyed me. "What are you doing here?"

"I'm, uh…" I glanced at the mover. The truck. The apartment. My ex. *Oh, you have got to be kidding me.* My mouth had gone dry, but I managed, "Waiting for the movers."

Josh's face fell. Mine probably did, too.

The mover pulled Josh's focus back to the paperwork, and I bowed out to get my head together…and wait for my own movers.

We were moving into the same apartment building? Seriously? And this wasn't one of those sprawling complexes with a hundred units spread out over multiple buildings, either. No, it was *one* building. With *six* units.

A memory wormed its way in:

"We got really *lucky with this place,"* Lily, the coordinator who'd handled finding me an apartment, had told me the other day. *"They had three units open up, so we were able to get you a really good price!"*

I'd been so overstimulated and overwhelmed in the moment, so caught up in trying to strategize moving in, learning my way around, getting utilities squared away, and all those other panic-inducing tasks that I hadn't stopped to wonder why the complex might have offered the team a deal.

Now it was painfully clear. Rentals were in high demand in this area. The only way someone was going to get some kind of deal was if they were securing multiple units. It wouldn't have surprised me at all if one of the other new guys on the team was going into the third unit.

So now Josh and I were not only in the same city.

Not only on the same team.

We were living in the same tiny apartment building.

Because of course we were.

My movers arrived shortly after Josh's. Fortunately, being single guys, neither of us had needed full-sized moving trucks, so they'd both been able to fit—if a bit snugly—on the street. I'd had a moment of panic, wondering how two sets of movers would be able to work with one freight elevator, but both crews put their heads together and quickly came to a solution. I wasn't exactly sure what that solution was—I was too scattered and flustered to keep up—but in the end, boxes and furniture were moving quickly and efficiently out of trucks and onto our respective floors.

I was on the second floor. Josh was on the third. Probably just as well this wasn't some enormous high rise or something. I didn't even want to imagine what the crews would have to do to make that work.

Both crews also had state-mandated breaks as well as lunch, during which time they'd sit in their cabs or the backs of their trucks. That worked out well, too, since their different start times meant slightly staggered break times. While Josh's crew was taking a break, mine took advantage of having full access to the freight elevator to bring up some of my larger furniture. His did the same when mine clocked out.

At one point, my guys were having trouble maneuvering my entertainment center, which meant they were holding up the elevator for quite a while. I was sure Josh was going to get pissed, but before he even knew what was going on, his guys started using the regular elevator and taking smaller loads until the larger one was available again.

And before I knew it, everything was done. Josh's crew

left. Then mine did. The landlady took down the *No Parking* signs. Life went on.

In my apartment, I sat on my couch and stared at the sea of boxes. There were things I needed—dishes and cookware, stuff like that—and I'd be stressed out as long as everything was still messy and packed like this. But the thought of unpacking it all... Organizing it all... Making sense of it all in this new space...

I just kind of...froze. I didn't know where to start. Even if I could figure that out, all my energy was gone. Partly from dealing with the move. Partly from the absolute system-shutdown my brain did whenever I faced down a huge task.

Unpacking. Settling in. Adapting to this new city. To this new noise of this new neighborhood. To this new team. To this new life.

I could always call one of those services that would unpack and arrange things. But I knew me. It would be six months before I looked one up. Another six before I made the call. A lot of my current and former teammates swore by those services, but for me they were procrastination with extra steps.

I knew intellectually that if I just got up, popped open a box—any box—and started putting away its contents, then I'd keep going. One piece at a time. One box at a time. One room at a time. I *knew* this.

Executive dysfunction, a therapist had called it. Something about how the brain gets overwhelmed by a task—a big one, or even a tiny one like making a phone call or handling an email—and just...stops.

If I could push past it enough to get off my ass, open a box, and put something away, then I'd get somewhere.

But I didn't. I couldn't.

Goddammit. I hated when I got like this.

It didn't help that somewhere in this very same building, my ex-boyfriend had probably already collapsed a dozen boxes and started hanging things on the walls. The movers had been gone, what? Three hours now? Hell, he probably had at least one room that was reasonably functional and looked like someone lived there.

I closed my eyes and leaned back against the couch. Josh was always so organized. So on top of things. Nothing went bad in his refrigerator. No call went unreturned. No mail stayed unopened. He was everything I'd never been able to be. And what was standing in my way? Me. Me and my stupid, flailing, crash-prone brain that could never seem to decide if it preferred to hyperfocus on something ridiculous or refuse to concentrate on something important. Or do both at the same time. That happened a lot.

Sighing, I wiped a hand over my face. There was a solution. A short-term one, to be sure, but sometimes the calm that quieted my racing thoughts could also snap me out of this inability to fucking move.

I wondered how much better my life would've been if my executive dysfunction had ever kept me from going through the motions of getting powder from a bag and into my nose. I could absolutely shut down at the prospect of making a sandwich or a two-minute phone call, but acquiring some coke, arranging it into lines, and snorting it? Piece of cake. Every time.

Maybe if I'd picked a drug that required more steps, I would've—

No, no. Better not go down that path again.

I opened my eyes and stared up at the ceiling.

I couldn't hear Josh moving around up there, but I had no doubt he was. He'd probably be up half the night making sure his apartment looked like something out of a damn magazine. Twenty bucks said that when I went down to the parking garage tomorrow morning, there'd be a mountain of collapsed boxes and packing materials piled in and neatly beside the recycling bin.

Would he notice that only he had brought down moving stuff? Would he catch on that I hadn't done jack shit to settle in? Would he know I was still just as much of a mess as I'd always been?

Probably not, but something about that—something about imagining him figuring out I hadn't lifted a finger to unpack my apartment—cracked through that wall of executive dysfunction. With a ball of shame and irritation in my stomach, I pushed myself up off the couch, snatched the box cutter off the counter, and sliced the tape on the nearest box.

Two hours later, when I stopped for some water, I'd made a sizeable dent in the sea of boxes, and I had several of them collapsed by the front door, ready to be taken downstairs. Some of the kitchen cabinets were full, and a few framed photos were leaning against a wall so I could hang them later. It was...progress. A surprising amount of progress, fueled by spite and embarrassment.

Guess Josh wouldn't be sneering at my lack of discarded packing material tomorrow after all.

CHAPTER 6

JOSH

I'd spent the last three days unpacking and assembling my apartment in between practicing and working out, and the only thing more wrung out than my body was my mind. I was utterly exhausted but I needed an outlet. Settling into my apartment had been the best available option, and I'd attacked it like my life had depended on it

As a result, there wasn't a scrap of cardboard or bubble wrap left in this place by the end of the third day. I was sore in places that I was pretty sure had come into existence for the sole purpose of hurting after I'd spent three days doing too much.

But I couldn't relax. My place was completely settled, but I sure as shit wasn't.

I tried FaceTiming with Amber, my best friend back in Chicago, but she couldn't talk. We exchanged a few texts— mostly me reassuring her I just wanted to catch up and this wasn't the *I'm-about-to-mentally-implode* emergency it absolutely was. Then she'd had to go, and I'd been left to wander from room to room in my spacious apartment as its walls started aggressively closing in.

A walk around Green Lake, maybe? That was one of the selling points of this place. Except if I made it halfway around the lake before my bitchy body decided it had finally had enough, then I'd still have to drag myself back here.

That was when I remembered that one of the *other* selling points of this building had been the gym on the top floor.

Without pausing to wonder if a workout was even doable, let alone a smart thing to do, I threw on some gym clothes, grabbed a water bottle, and headed upstairs.

There was no one here right now, which was a relief. I didn't need anyone to witness me limping through a simple workout as if I hadn't seen the inside of a gym in five years.

There were two stationary bikes facing out the floor-to-ceiling windows. The view was a nice one—mostly trees enclosed by some high fences. I was pretty sure that was Woodland Park Zoo. I'd heard some of my teammates saying they'd taken their kids there recently, and it was a really nice zoo. Might have to check it out myself.

Just...not today. It was already six o'clock, and anyway, I was basically a shambling corpse held upright by sheer stubbornness and restlessness. No point in paying for the privilege of walking around on concrete until I could actually enjoy it.

I sat on one of the bikes and took a moment to get familiar with the programming. Arenas and hotels always had stationary bikes and other workout equipment, but this wasn't a brand or model I'd used much before. And my brain wasn't functioning much better than my body right now, so I at least made sure I knew how to program a light interval program and didn't accidentally set off an ejection seat or some shit.

With the program rolling, I started pedaling, beginning with an easy warm-up so my muscles could get into the swing of things. After a few minutes of that, I upped the intensity to something that would give me an actual workout and burn off some of this restless energy, but wouldn't have me crawling back to the elevator afterward.

I was ten minutes in when I realized I'd forgotten my earbuds. I only noticed because the radio playing over the gym's speakers had switched to a song my old team had always played during warm-ups, and I didn't like the memories it was churning up. But since I was only running on three mental cylinders right now, I'd forgotten my music, so I was stuck listening to it and letting the past crash through my head. When it ended, it segued into something annoying as hell, and I hummed along with it, grateful it wasn't the previous song.

About halfway through "Dance, Dance, Annoy the Fuck out of Me" or whatever that song was called, the air pressure changed, signaling that someone had opened a door.

I glanced in one of the mirrors beside the window, and if it had been physically possible to crash a stationary bike, that's exactly what I would've done.

Reflection to reflection, Sol and I locked eyes.

He halted. My feet faltered.

The bike gave an entitled little beep, because how dare I stray from the program, and I shifted my attention to the speedometer. It was blinking red, letting me know I needed to pick up the pace. I did, and the lights turned a more tolerant green. Good thing I wasn't wearing a heart monitor this time; I didn't need anyone, least of all myself, hearing what was going on with my pulse right then.

I silently begged Sol to get on a treadmill or start on a

weight routine. Deep down, though, I knew that wasn't going to happen. Not unless his left ankle had magically decided it could handle intervals on a treadmill without complaining. Not unless he was doing two weight routines a day now—he'd been working the kettle ball this morning at the training center.

Couldn't this gym have more than two bikes?

Of course not.

And now both of those bikes were occupied.

I stared straight ahead while Sol started his warm-up. Still, in my peripheral vision, I could sense him moving. Could almost feel his exertion from here. Christ—he was pushing it harder on his warm-up than I was on my program.

Fuck *that*.

I cranked up the intensity. From the corner of my eye, I caught him glancing at me. Oh, he'd noticed. He might've even chuckled to himself, but I didn't let myself look to find out.

I definitely didn't let myself think about all those times we'd jumped on the bikes and let the competitiveness rip. How many miles we'd logged and calories we'd vaporized through a good-natured refusal to be bested by the other. How often our trainers had rolled their eyes and reminded us not to push it so hard we hurt ourselves.

How many times we'd wound up in bed after a workout, laughing like dorks at how sore and tired we were. How often we'd joked about that bed we'd made and had to lie in, dicks rock-hard while our bodies were useless.

How much I missed—

I stood on the pedals and pushed hard through a tough interval, every muscle screaming. I'd pay for this later, but the pain and fatigue was almost enough to mask the pain in my chest. No, not that kind of pain. Not *"I pushed too hard and need an ambulance"* pain. This was pure regret and resentment and frustration and *grief*.

Squeezing my eyes shut and gritting my teeth, I pedaled harder, hating myself for still feeling anything like grief. For caring if I looked weak or slow in front of him.

My divorce hadn't fucked up my head like being in the same room with Sol did.

Or...maybe it had? Maybe I was just projecting my unresolved bullshit over Damon on to Sol because he was here. Except that didn't seem right, because the emotions that flared to life whenever I saw Sol's face or heard his name were familiar. They were just more intense these days because I wasn't seeing him on TV or across the ice in another sweater.

He was *here*.

And I was here.

And suddenly it wasn't my overtaxed body saying, *Josh —enough.*

My head and my heart couldn't take another second of this.

I ended the program. Dismounted onto badly shaking legs. Wiped the bike down with trembling hands. Got the fuck out of there.

In the elevator, I leaned hard against the wall and took in gulps of air. I wasn't out of breath from my workout anymore. The shaking—yeah, that was muscles that were completely fucking done—but my thumping, aching heart and this feeling like I couldn't get enough air? That was something else entirely.

The elevator reached my floor, and I stumbled down the hall and into my apartment. Safely inside, I leaned against the closed and locked door, and I hated myself for all the emotions trying to break loose. In my chest. From my eyes.

We were *adults*. It had been *years*. We were *professionals*. It was *over*.

But somehow, after all this time, I couldn't escape him. Physically. Emotionally. Professionally.

We have practice tomorrow. The preseason starts soon. Traveling. And we live in the same building. He's here and neither of us is going anywhere.

What the fuck am I supposed to do?

CHAPTER 7

SOL

As soon as the gym door had thudded shut, I paused my program and sat back, pedaling halfheartedly as I stared out at the neighborhood and park below.

It had taken a solid hour to convince myself to come up here and work out. The same mental block that liked to keep me from unpacking or making phone calls or otherwise functioning like a normal human being had kept me unmoving in my apartment. I'd known I needed to work out. I'd done weights this morning, but some hardcore intervals would get my conditioning up to where it needed to be.

I'd finally convinced myself to come up here and do five minutes. I knew myself—if I made it that far, then I'd finish a workout. It was just getting out of the apartment and into the gym that was the tough part, and I had to negotiate with myself for that first inch like a parent encouraging a kid to try one bite.

I just hadn't bargained for Josh.

As soon as I'd seen him, I'd wanted to turn tail and walk out, but like hell was I giving him that satisfaction. I wasn't letting him derail any piece of this career I was trying desperately to save, including the workouts that would keep me from getting hurt or just faceplanting on the ice from exhaustion.

When he'd started ramping up his workout, I'd done the same. He wasn't going to derail me, but he also wasn't going to outdo me. Didn't matter how tired I'd be afterward or how sore I'd be tomorrow. Faster. Harder. Until I couldn't fucking move as long as Josh didn't walk away with another reason to think he was better than me.

But then out of nowhere, he'd stopped, and he'd left.

The program hadn't been over—I could see the readout clear as day—but he'd stopped. He'd taken the time to wipe down the bike, and then...

Then he was gone.

And as soon as the door was closed...

I squeezed my eyes shut and ran a hand through my sweat-dampened hair. Who was I kidding? I was done, too. All my energy. All my motivation. All the spite. All the competitiveness. Gone.

I swore and shut off the program. After I'd cleaned off the bike, I went down to my apartment, grabbed a shower, and threw on some sweats. Then I dropped onto my couch and—

For fuck's sake.

I'd had this couch for years. Knew its quiet creaks and semi-firm texture like I knew my mattress and pillows. But suddenly I was on this couch in another time and place, and my chest ached as my mind insistently went there.

"Think one of us will ever go?" Josh had gestured at the screen as the All-Stars intro started.

"Maybe." I'd sat beside him and handed him one of two beers. "I fucking hate three-on-three, though."

"What?" He chuckled as he brought the beer up to his lips. "You don't like OT?"

I groaned and took a deep swallow before I said, "Ugh. *No*. I'm a good goalie, but I definitely prefer playing with five guys in front of me instead of three."

He grunted, tilting his bottle toward the screen. "But at least the other guys only have three. It's when they've got five and we've got three that I want to speak to a manager."

I snorted. "I think Coach is still fired up about that."

"*I'm* still fired up about it," Josh grumbled. "Like, we're already on the penalty kill, and you're going to slash one of their guys *right* in front of the damn ref? What the fuck was Lawson thinking?"

Rolling my eyes, I shook my head. "No idea." I put my beer down and turned to him. "You saved our asses that night, Obie. I know it was bullshit, and that had to be three of the most stressful minutes of your life, but you're the reason we held our lead."

The blush in his cheeks lightened my head more than this beer ever would. So did that bashful smile. "The penalty kill units were awesome. It wasn't just me."

"No, but a great penalty kill isn't worth a damn without a solid netminder to backstop them." I paused. "I mean it— they almost doubled their shots on goal for the entire game just during those penalties." I nudged him gently with my elbow. "The penalty kill can take credit for the shot attempts, but the shots on goal—those are you and only you."

He was scarlet now, and he was so damn cute. Josh's confidence had been through the wringer since the season had started, but he had a solid record under his belt now. He hadn't played a ton of games—I was the starter, after all —but he was good. I hadn't even been offended when

Coach had started talking about switching us to tandem instead of starter and backup. I wasn't about to complain about sharing top billing with a goalie of Josh's caliber.

Josh took a swig of beer, then put the bottle on the coffee table and sat back. "Thanks, by the way. I was a mess earlier this year. Up here." He tapped his temple. "But the pep talks and stuff—it's helped a lot."

I smiled, but whatever I was about to say died on my tongue when his eyes flicked to my lips.

No, Sol. Don't go there.

It didn't matter how many times we'd burned the midnight oil in hotel bars after games. Didn't matter how much we gravitated toward each other in the locker room. On the bus. During meals. He was my teammate. My rookie teammate. My exceptionally hot rookie teammate who found as many excuses to hang out with me as I did to hang with him.

I needed to get a handle on this situation before it got seriously out of control, but Josh spoke before I had a chance to.

"Can I ask you something?" His voice was low and quiet, and something about it had me on edge in a strangely familiar way.

All I could do was nod.

He swept his tongue across his lips. Caught me glancing at his mouth. Fuck. Then, voice still low, he asked, "Is anyone else coming over tonight?"

I swallowed. "Uh. No. Is, um... Is that okay?"

"Yeah, it's fine." He chewed his lip. "Just, um...I guess I was just wondering why you only invited me over to watch the game."

Every molecule in my body stilled.

Oh. *Hell.*

No, that hadn't been my intention. I hadn't even thought twice—just asked a rookie teammate if he wanted to hang out and watch the All-Stars with me.

But I was realizing in the same moment he was that he absolutely had me dead to rights.

Heat rushed into my face. "I, um..." I cleared my throat. "Didn't really think about it, I guess?" It was the complete truth.

"Oh." The single word was hard to read. Didn't sound like disappointment or even relief, but maybe—

He glanced at my lips again.

Fuck me. That was *interest* in his eyes. Nerves, fear, uncertainty, but definitely interest.

Before I realized what I was doing, I licked my lips. And...yeah. He noticed. Jesus H. Christ. I did not think any of this through.

Josh studied me for a long moment, unreadable thoughts rolling over his expression. Then, right before my eyes, fierce determination and confidence broke through the nervous rookie façade. Swallowing hard, he closed his hand around the beer I was still holding. Without thought, I let go.

The click of glass on the marble coaster was barely audible over the sound of commentators on TV and my heart slamming into my ribs, but I jumped anyway.

Josh faltered slightly, hand still on the bottle as he held my gaze. After a few uneasy seconds, he let go of it. Tentatively, he reached for me, and I wondered if either of us had realized before this moment how little space I'd left between us when I'd sat down. I sure as hell knew about it now, and apparently so did he.

Glass-cooled fingertips grazed the side of my neck.

Our position on the ice required us to be extraordinarily

good at reading eyes and body language. I knew—could feel it in my bones—that Josh was reading me right then. Watching and waiting, getting a bead on my response before he moved any farther.

I also knew exactly where he was heading. I was there in his crosshairs, somehow both still and trembling, waiting for him to make a move like I waited for a skater to give away his plan of attack during a shootout.

Except in those moments, the skater and I both tried to hide our thoughts and actions until it was too late for the other to react.

In a moment like this...

I moistened my lips again. Not because they needed them. Because I wanted to tell him yes.

His breath stuttered. His fingers twitched on my neck. For a couple of heartbeats I was sure he was going to back off, but the fingertips against my skin became a firmer, heavier presence, warm and sure. There was still uncertainty in his eyes, though.

I'd forgotten how to speak, so I went with the next best thing and slid my hand over his knee. Josh's eyelids fluttered closed as he sucked in a breath.

When they opened again, he met my gaze with fire in his. His voice sounded rough as he whispered, "This what you had in mind? When you invited me over?"

I found the ability to speak again, and the words that tumbled out startled both of us: "Which answer ends with you kissing me?"

My heart stopped. Josh's eyes widened.

And a second later, I forgot about anything and everything in the world that wasn't Josh's soft, insistent lips against mine or his thick hair between my fingers.

Perfect. This was absolutely perfect. He was an

assertive kisser without being overbearing. Just...perfect. Nothing made me want a man more than if his kiss could melt my spine, and that was exactly what Josh's kiss did to me in that moment.

He touched his forehead to mine, warm breath gusting across my tingling lips. "Whoa."

"Uh-huh." I carded unsteady fingers through his hair. "You, uh... Still want to watch the game?"

His huff of laughter was almost soundless, and the way he tightened his grip on the back of my neck answered clearly enough even before he said, "Forget three-on-three. I'm interested in one-on-one."

I snorted, and we both chuckled, and then we were off and kissing again. One-on-one, indeed.

Several years and over a thousand miles later, I was in the same place I'd been that day. Still on this couch. Still reeling and overwhelmed.

God, I missed him.

I missed who and what we'd been back then. What we were today—Christ, what a mess.

I let my gaze slide to the ceiling. Josh was up there somewhere. Maybe watching TV. Maybe eating. Maybe cursing my name and wondering what he'd ever seen in me.

Wincing, I squeezed my eyes shut. I'd ruined everything.

My brain tried to remind me that Josh had fucked up too, but right here, right now, sitting in the same spot where he'd kissed me in another time and another place—in the same spot where we'd ignored more hockey games and movies than I could count—I hurt too much to be angry. I missed too much of what we'd been before it had all come apart.

No, there was no going back. Too much had been said

and done. The past was in the past, and that was where it had to stay. Here in Seattle, in the present, the absolute best we could be was cordial neighbors and functional team-mates. Maybe friends, someday. We'd both fucked up too much to be everything we'd been in Phoenix.

But if only for tonight, I let myself wish things were different.

I let myself hurt for him.

CHAPTER 8

JOSH

"Sol is starting in the net tomorrow night," Kayla informed us before the last practice ahead of our first preseason game. "Halfway through the second period, you'll switch. Next game, it'll be reversed, and Obie will start. Got it?" Her tone let us know the decision was made and wasn't up for discussion.

I glanced at Sol—we were both putting on our gear in the locker room—then up at her. "Got it, Coach."

"Got it," he echoed.

She nodded sharply, then stepped away, probably to talk to Coach about something or another. I flicked my eyes toward Sol just in time to catch him doing the same. We both immediately shifted our attention to our gear, and neither of us said anything.

What was there to say? In the week and a half since our encounter in the gym, we'd exchanged all of three words at most. Longer than that, honestly—at least since the confrontation in the parking lot. Probably since we'd both arrived in Seattle now that I thought about it.

Whenever the near-silence had started, it was uncomfortable as all hell, but it beat the alternative, and no one else on the team seemed to notice. Kayla probably did. She was way too observant and spent way too much time with us not to be dialed in to the tension thrumming between us. She was also under a ton of pressure to have a pair of functioning goalies, though, so she'd focused on doing her job—putting us through our paces, working on our weaknesses, and making sure we were ready for the season to start.

Tomorrow would be the first of five preseason games. This was where we would prove our mettle...or prove that Seattle really had made a big mistake by signing one or both of us. It was also where Coach and Kayla would likely decide who was the starter and who was backup.

No pressure or anything.

That actually gave me a bit of an advantage over Sol, and just acknowledging that mentally made me feel guilty as hell. Sol could handle pressure sometimes, but he could also crack catastrophically under it. It was part of what had driven his addiction, and I hated myself for thinking it might give me an edge during this preseason.

I'm such an asshole. Jesus.

But he'd been an asshole, too. He'd been the reason our relationship had fallen apart. I fucking hated him, and damn it, I'd take any edge I could get.

"I don't think you actually hate him." My ex-husband's angry, jealous voice wormed its way into my brain as I finished putting on my gear. *"Look me in the eye and tell me you wouldn't jump at the chance to be with him again."*

God, we'd had that fight so many times, and it was so damn stupid.

"I don't want him," I'd thrown back. *"I love you. That's why I married you."*

"Was he an option when you married me?"

I gritted my teeth and banished him from my mind. I needed to focus on practicing and on tomorrow night's game. Not on my marriage. Not on either of my exes.

I glanced up from adjusting a pad, and I found Sol still on the bench on the other side of the room. He wasn't looking at me. He was talking to one of the trainers about something as he pulled on his chest protector. Which absolutely did *not* make his shoulders look broader or his hips narrower.

I don't want him. I jerked my focus back to putting on my padded base layer shirt. *I sure as shit don't love him.*

Okay, fine. I was still attracted to him. I'd allow that much. He was sexy and always had been. But there was nothing about his physique or his smile or his kiss that made up for everything else, and I needed to remember that.

I needed to focus on getting that starter position. On hockey. On protecting the net. On resuscitating my career.

Not on Sol, damn it. I'd already wasted too much time, effort, and heartache on him.

And I was never making that mistake again.

I had to give him credit—Sol had his head together tonight. In fact, he was standing on it. We were playing a lot of young and inexperienced skaters—typical for the preseason —and they weren't protecting the defensive zone as much as they should have. As a result, Portland was absolutely *hammering* Sol with shots. By the time we switched places midway through the second period, he'd allowed a single puck into the net, and I didn't think God Himself could've made that save.

The other team was also young and inexperienced, and

like Sol, their first goalie had stood on his head, but he'd let two goals past him. I was taking over the crease while my team tried to hold—and ideally widen—a one-game lead. Yeah, no pressure or anything.

The thing about a team full of rookies and youngsters during the preseason was that they, much like Sol and me, had something to prove. In their case, they were trying to prove they deserved a coveted spot on the major league roster instead of being sent back down to the minors. Now that they were losing, Portland's young guys were coming out swinging.

Literally swinging—two minutes after I took my position, there was a scrum near the penalty box. Not long after that, a couple of rookies dropped gloves and went at it behind my net. That put us on the wrong end of a bullshit power play, since the refs called both of them for fighting *and* threw in one of our forwards for roughing because he was trying to keep one of Portland's D-men from joining the fight.

The power play was all they needed to tilt the ice. Our penalty kill unit was as young and inexperienced as was expected during the preseason, and it only took fourteen seconds for a puck to get by them and whip past my head into the net. They grabbed the momentum and ran with it, and with our young guys on their heels, Portland made drive after drive for our goal, firing puck after puck toward my net. I was proud of the saves I made, because holy hell, I'd made a lot of them, and some were damn close.

They weren't quite enough, though. Not when I was basically on my own while our defense flailed and our offense kept delivering the puck right to Portland's sticks.

"It's the preseason." Volkov tapped my pads with his

stick in the locker room after the game. "You looked good out there, man. Don't sweat it."

"Thanks." I smiled but didn't really feel it. "Still sucks to lose."

"It wasn't on you." Leclerc, our captain, tapped my pads as well. "You shouldn't have been left unprotected like that."

I winced. I could defend the net, damn it. Yes, protecting me was part of the defensemen's job, but protecting the net was *my* job. I should've made those saves.

And even when my teammates were encouraging me, they *knew* where I came from. They *knew* what my last couple of seasons had been like. All of their *"don't sweat it, man"* and *"it's just the preseason"* had to be lip service. They weren't saying it, but I was sure they were thinking it: *"Don't you dare drag us the fuck down like you did your last team."*

I wasn't going to. No way in hell.

Except tonight...

I swore as I started undoing my gear. Tonight had been a bad one, and it left me rattled and terrified I was going to continue to be a trash fire in the net until someone had the good sense to put my career out of its misery.

There was still time. I could still do this. I knew it was the preseason. I knew it didn't count the way regular season games did.

But much like those kids trying to score spots on the team, I had something to prove. I also had something to lose. After tonight's game, Sol *had* to be edging ahead of me in the fight for the starting goalie position.

There's still time. I can still do this. Sol could still fall apart.

Against my will, my gaze found him in the crowded

locker room. He was down to his base layer, talking to a reporter in that effortlessly charming way of his. That smile did things to me no drug could ever touch, and unwelcome emotions fluttered stubbornly behind my ribs. Not anger or resentment this time. Not even hurt. No, it was nostalgia and even... Fuck. Even affection.

I miss you, my brain said despite everything. *I miss us.*

I quickly turned away. Yeah. I could still do this. Sol could still fall apart.

Or I could just lose my damn mind and make it all a moot point.

Oh God. I am so fucked.

CHAPTER 9

SOL

Seattle was definitely different from Phoenix in one very distinct way—the *crowd*. Despite the team being meh at best, fans turned out in droves, even for the preseason. If the preseason was this loud, I could only imagine what the home opener would be like.

As we warmed up for our second game, fans banged on the glass and waved signs and shouted. The enthusiasm was palpable, and from the high pitch of a lot of the noise, there were quite a few kids in attendance tonight.

There was more light and sound coming from the arena itself, too. Strobes. Music. Flashing ads all along the two parallel bands that ringed the arena between the upper and lower bowls.

So much light. So much noise. Just...*chaos*.

Behind my mask, I took a couple of deep breaths and concentrated on doing some stretching in between skating small circles. Josh was in the net right now while the team did line rushes, so I had a few minutes before it was my turn.

I needed to get my shit together. I was used to this,

damn it. I'd been playing in arenas for years, including the playoffs, which sometimes included actual pyrotechnics. I'd been to the All-Star game, for God's sake, and that had lasers and all kinds of crap.

So I could handle this. I knew I could.

I looked around, trying to absorb all the chaos and adapt to it. Over by the bench, my gaze landed on Colfax, one of the defensemen, right as he waved some smelling salts under his nose and inhaled sharply. He winced, grimaced, and shook himself, then did another whiff for good measure.

I had to look away as my mouth started watering. Smelling salts had never done much except make me dry heave, but watching him go through the motions had me itching for a bump of cocaine. Back in the day, I'd used empty smelling salt packs to sneak blow into the locker room. While my teammates were doing whiffs to wake themselves up, I'd go through the same motions, but get a nose full of coke instead.

"You know you're not supposed to hold them that close to your nose, right?" a teammate had teased. *"No wonder it makes you tear up, dumbass!"*

I'd just played it off as wanting to get the most out of the fumes. The sniffling and eye-watering didn't turn any heads because actual smelling salts had the same effect, and that one small bump would be enough to keep me focused and calm for an entire period—exactly the way I needed to be right now.

No. I wasn't going to use cocaine again. I knew I wasn't. The cravings came, especially when I was stressed or couldn't focus—or in this case, both—but they passed. They always did. Just had to grit my teeth and ride it out. Same as always.

It was bad tonight, though. And this was just preseason.

What the fuck happened when the season actually started? The crowds would be bigger and louder, and so would all the effects and—

"Hey." Josh's voice set my teeth on edge, and I turned to meet his glare as he said, "You gonna be here tonight?"

I glared right back at him. "I'm not the one who let that game-losing goal through, so—"

"Oh, fuck off," he grumbled.

"What?" I let the sarcasm drip. "You can dish it out but—"

"Fucking dick," he muttered, and skated away. I rolled my eyes. I honestly couldn't decide if he truly thought I was going to lose my focus at an inopportune moment, or if he was trying to psych me out so I *would* lose it. Either way, he could go fuck himself. Especially because he was kind of right that my concentration was precarious tonight, though if he really had been trying to psych me out, it had backfired —nothing sharpened my focus like resenting the ever-loving hell out of him.

I pulled my attention from him and continued warming up. Fortunately, thanks to our masks and the noise, no one had noticed the exchange.

Or, well, I *thought* no one had noticed.

"Solomon. O'Brien." Kayla waved us aside as we came off the ice after warm-ups. "A moment?" Once the rest of our team had gone into the dressing room and the three of us were alone in the hallway, she folded her arms over her blue jacket and glared up at us. She was close to six-foot, but we were taller and wore skates, so we towered over her. You wouldn't know it by the way she stared us down like a couple of misbehaving kids, though. "Either of you want to tell me what that was all about?"

I blinked. "What?"

She narrowed her eyes. "Don't play stupid. I saw the two of you sniping at each other. And don't think I haven't noticed the animosity during practice and in the locker room. Hell, any time you two are in the same room at all."

I straightened, and I think Josh did too.

She gave a humorless laugh. "Oh, did you boys think you were being subtle about it? All those dirty looks and going out of your way to not speak to each other?" Kayla scowled. "Nice try." She stepped closer, shifting her glare back and forth between us. "Whatever it is—can it. Focus on the goddamned game and keeping pucks out of our net. Got it?"

I had a feeling this wouldn't be the last she had to say about it, but she probably didn't want to keep us away from Coach's pre-game speech for long. This was the short and sweet version. Tomorrow at practice, I suspected we'd be hearing from her again.

We both nodded and mumbled that we understood and, like a couple of kids who'd been scolded, shuffled into the locker room just in time for the speech. I didn't hear much of what Coach said, but to my surprise, my head wasn't as full of noise either. In fact, I was as laser-focused as I ever was without chemical intervention.

Specifically, on Josh.

Maybe I shouldn't have been surprised. After all, ever since we'd crossed paths again, he'd had that effect on me. Was it healthy to spend an entire hockey season pissed off at a teammate in the name of concentrating well enough to play? Probably not, but it beat the alternative.

Guess I didn't need to take anything after all.

Turned out spite really was a hell of a drug.

Eight Seasons Ago

I wasn't used to sleeping next to someone.

It wasn't that I never spent the night with my hookups or the guys I'd dated briefly—I just didn't sleep. Too restless with someone beside me. Too twitchy in an unfamiliar bed. I was two seasons into my career with Phoenix and I still struggled to sleep in hotels, which could make road trips into a bit of a nightmare.

But last night...

Last night, I'd slept.

As the Arizona sun carved early morning light around the edges of my bedroom's blinds, I was rested. Comfortable. Blissed the hell out, now that I thought about it.

I'd been on the bench for last night's game, but my body ached deliciously thanks to the...postgame festivities. I'd be paying for it all today, especially staying up so late, but that was fine. A slightly groggy day and dragging ass at practice was a price I was willing to pay for a long night in this man's arms. It wasn't our first time together—we'd hooked up a few times since he'd come to my condo to watch the All-Star game—but it was the first time one of us had stayed over.

And I felt... God, I felt amazing. Well-fucked and well-rested.

All those pleasant aches protested when I started to move, but not enough to stop me from rolling onto my side and molding myself to his back. He stirred a little as I kissed the side of his neck.

"Morning," I murmured into his dark hair.

"Is it?" Josh tilted his head, stubble scratching against

the pillowcase as he offered up more of his neck. "Could've sworn we just went to sleep."

"Mmm, right?" I kissed my way along the curve of his neck to his shoulder. "Sleep well?"

"Uh-huh." He found my hand on his waist, slipped his fingers between mine, and pulled my arm around him until our joined hands were at his chest. "Haven't slept that good in ages."

"Me neither." Especially not with someone else in my bed, but I didn't mention that. Nuzzling his neck, I murmured, "We should probably get up and shower. Get some coffee. If we're late to practice..."

His dramatic groan of protest made me chuckle. "Ugh. Practice? Really?" He whined theatrically. "But I was in goal last night. Shouldn't I have the day off or something?"

"Doesn't work that way, baby." I kissed beneath his ear. "Sorry."

He harumphed.

"Hey, look on the bright side," I said. "You're not the one with the sore ass."

Josh snorted, and I buried my face in his neck as we were both overcome with sleepy laughter. When we'd started to compose ourselves, Josh shifted a little, and I loosened my hold so he could roll onto his back. God, he was beautiful—brown eyes tired and happy. Dark hair adorably messy. A silly little smile curling the full lips I'd spent so, so much of last night kissing. I'd had the worst crush on him ever since he'd become my backup goalie. For months now I'd been living for the nights we closed down hotel bars just talking about whatever until fatigue caught up with us. And in the weeks since the All-Star game... Jesus. I felt like a teenager all over again. Completely stupid for this man, and loving every second of it.

Now this? Waking up beside him and drinking in how gorgeous he was when he was sleep-rumpled and satisfied? Perfect. Absolutely perfect.

Some seriousness crept into Josh's expression as he reached up to touch my unshaven jaw. "We have to keep this quiet, don't we?"

My stomach tightened, but not with the same preemptive panic it would have even a season ago. Covering his hand with mine, I kissed his palm. "There's no rules against it, but... Yeah. We should."

Josh sighed. "Sucks, though. I wish we could tell people."

That made me smile. "Me, too. Maybe someday we can be out, but for now..."

He nodded. "But if, hypothetically, it did get out... If people figure out we're..." He swallowed.

"If they figure out we're together?" I tried not to let him feel me tensing up in anticipation of the, "*maybe we shouldn't do this.*"

A blush bloomed in his cheeks, the color standing out against the dark shadow of his scruff. "Yeah. That." He swept his tongue across his lips. "I mean...I'm not talking about broadcasting it or anything, but like if a friend figures us out... Are we, like, together? Or are we just..." His brow pinched and he chewed the inside of his cheek.

Ooh, so *that* was his concern. Not about ending this in the name of avoiding scrutiny—about what we actually were.

"We don't have to give it a name and carve it in stone," I said softly. "We just started seeing each other, so I don't want there to be pressure, you know?"

He nodded, the worry still etched into the creases of his forehead.

I squeezed his hand. "Let's see where it goes. But if you're asking if I think we're just fuck buddies or something..." I shook my head, admittedly nervous as I laid down that card. Even though I got the feeling we were on the same page, it was always a risk to say out loud that there was more going on than sex.

From the way the corners of his mouth turned up, I had nothing to worry about. We were very much on the same page.

This was sex. Seriously *good* sex. But also more.

We were teammates. We were friends. But also more.

Josh grinned as he ran his thumb along my cheekbone. "So...keep it on the DL, but don't freak out if someone trustworthy finds out Cary Solomon is my boyfriend?"

Those words were music. They made my heart do things it never had before. I was Josh's boyfriend. He was mine. We were... God, we were doing this. Here in my bed, after the most restful night I'd ever spent next to another person...

I couldn't believe this was real, but it was.

I kissed him lightly—the most I dared while we both had morning breath—and murmured, "If someone finds out Josh O'Brien is *my* boyfriend, I might freak out, but it won't be in a bad way."

That got one of those adorable laughs out of him. I couldn't wait for more of those. And more mornings like this. And more of being the one who made him laugh, smile, and gasp.

I couldn't wait to fall completely head over skates in love with him.

CHAPTER 10

JOSH

I didn't think anything of it when Kayla told Coach Maines she wanted to work with Sol and me separate from the rest of the team the morning after our second preseason game. It wasn't unusual, and it gave our younger goalies—Sweetman and a recently drafted prospect—a chance to practice with the big guys.

But when she joined the two of us on the practice facility's second rink, I knew immediately that there was more going on. The second she stepped onto the ice, I could see the anger in her eyes.

Aw, fuck. What did we do this time?

She had a bucket in one hand—probably pucks—and a stick in the other, so we would be practicing. But she clearly had something else on her agenda first.

"All right." She dropped the bucket to the ice by her skates with a decisive, echoing *thunk*. "I want to make this crystal clear. I'm not kidding about what I said during the game." Her eyes flicked from Sol to me and back. "Whatever this animosity is between you guys? It's obviously still there, and it's a problem. And you either need to make it *not* a problem, or start talking to the farm team about getting jerseys with your names on them. Because I'm not going to put up with it. If there's a genuine issue—something the front office needs to get involved in—then come talk to me. But if this is just competitiveness over who's the starter, or something completely unrelated to hockey, or—" She waved a gloved hand. "I really don't care. Get it off my ice, and *keep* it off my ice. Got it?"

"Yes, Coach," we both said. No way in hell was I arguing with her, and apparently Sol felt the same way. We could and would deal with our bullshit on our own time. There was just too much on the line to risk more of Kayla's ire.

"All right." She nodded curtly and picked up the bucket. "With that out of the way, you boys need to practice." She dumped the pucks at her feet, and I suppressed a curse.

Despite the animosity between us, Sol and I exchanged grimaces. After all, we could hate each other to hell and back, but there was one thing we'd both despised with a fiery passion ever since our youth hockey days:

White pucks.

Fuck my life.

Don't get me wrong—they were great teaching devices. Nothing helped a goalie practice tracking the puck like tracking one that was barely distinguishable from the ice. I understood and appreciated their value—I just fucking hated them.

"Obie." She pointed at the net with her stick. "You're up."

I very carefully kept my expression from giving away my fondness for white pucks, pulled down my mask, and took my position.

Kayla sent me a few slow, soft shots at first to warm up. The pucks were actually a very light cream color, so they were visible against the much brighter and cooler white of the ice. They were just way harder to see than a black puck. So, the first few she sent to me, I tracked and blocked without too much difficulty. By the time she'd upped her speed and started hitting me with harder and faster shots, I was holding my own. A few made it past me, which was to be expected, but I managed to trap or deflect most of them.

Kayla skated off to the side to retrieve one of the pucks I'd deflected, and I stole the opportunity to squeeze my eyes shut for a second and blink a few times. Because as much as training with lighter pucks had always been a pain in my ass, the biggest problem now was that following them meant more eye strain than following black pucks. That meant headaches. Yay.

When I heard Kayla stop and turn, I opened my eyes and readied myself. Good thing, too—I had about two seconds to focus before she sent a puck flying in from my left. By the time I'd batted that one away, another. Then another.

Finally, Kayla tapped her stick on the ice and called out, "Nicely done." She dismissed me from the crease and gestured for Sol to take my place.

Grateful for the breather and a chance to rest my eyes, I skated out of the way and went to the bench to grab my water bottle. My head was aching a bit, but it wasn't too bad. Nothing that signaled a brewing migraine. I'd be fine.

After I'd taken a few gulps of water, I leaned against the dashers to watch Sol training with Kayla. She did the same routine with him—a few easy shots, then amping it up until he was all over the crease. Much like me, some of the pucks got past him, but most stayed out.

Watching Sol now, I tried to view him as a teammate, not as my ex-boyfriend. That was easier than you might expect—the design on his mask wasn't the same one he'd had years ago, and it was almost impossible to see his face from this angle. Aside from occasional glimpses of *Solomon* across his shoulders when he turned just right, he was just a fellow netminder, not the man I'd loved a lifetime ago.

And I had to admit—he looked good. At one point, he did a windmill save to snatch a puck out of the air, nearly toppling in the process, but he recovered, tossed the puck away, and was poised and ready when Kayla fired another one at him.

About the time Kayla was wrapping up with him, two other players stepped onto the ice: Volkov and Colfax. A forward and a defenseman.

"Perfect timing, gentlemen." Kayla gestured at the net with her stick. "Obie, you're up."

Sol left the crease and I took his place. At Kayla's instruction, Volkov and Colfax set up in front of me. Awesome—now I not only had to track white pucks, I had to do it through a screen of two of our biggest players.

They played their roles well, too—Volkov was trying to block me from seeing Kayla and the puck, and Colfax was trying to get him out of the way. The resulting back-and-forth made it even more difficult for me to track the puck than if I just had a couple of players standing in front of me. Even a black puck was difficult under these circumstances, and using a white one definitely didn't set the game to easy mode.

Unsurprisingly, I didn't stop as many shots this time. Some bounced off the two skaters. Others went right between their skates and sticks, or Volkov would try to tip them in. It was frustrating as all hell, but this was exactly the kind of thing we faced in games, so I bit back some curses and fought hard to keep those damn white pucks from crossing my goal line.

Kayla blew her whistle, and the skaters both relaxed, making some small circles and shaking out their arms. "Well done, boys. Especially you, Obie."

"Man, I'm glad we don't have to practice with these things." Colfax scooped a puck up onto his blade and whistled. "What the fuck."

"Maybe you should." Volkov tapped one toward Colfax's skate. "You'd be better at—"

"Fuck off." Colfax tossed his puck like a hacky sack toward Volkov, who caught it, dropped it, and fired it at Colfax's skate, narrowly missing.

"Hey, hey," I laughed as I left the crease. "Don't hurt him—I need him to keep pucks away from me."

"He's fine," Volkov said dismissively.

Colfax gestured at Volkov, probably flipping him off—it was hard to tell in hockey gloves. I just chuckled and skated out of the way so Sol could enjoy a round of screening with white pucks.

Leaning against the boards in front of the bench again, I watched, and just like when he'd been out there alone, Sol was doing well. Definitely holding his own. I was pretty sure that was supposed to aggravate me. I was trying to grab the starter position over him. He was my competition.

But he was also my teammate. Regardless of who was the starter and who was the backup, we'd each be between the pipes during at least some games this season. There'd be enough games with either of us playing to make a huge difference in whether Seattle had a shot at the playoffs. So I had a vested interest in him playing well.

And I also...

Fuck me, but I also *wanted* him to play well. It was good to see him moving that easily, making saves, and keeping his cool. It was good to see him focused, especially since focus had always been so hard for him, and as near as I could tell, this was the kind of focus he had to work for, not the kind he'd found in a line of white powder.

The fact that we had baggage and issues didn't change any of that. Just made me feel weird about being happy for him when I also had so much animosity toward him.

I *hated* having this much animosity toward him. Sometimes I dated men and after we split, I could barely recall what I'd ever seen in them. Take my ex-husband, for example. Our marriage had crashed and burned so hard, it was difficult to remember a time when we'd *liked* each other, never mind loved each other. I mean, I could remember the good times, but they felt...detached? Like someone else's memories. Or a dream. Something.

With Sol, the good times were crystal clear. I could still feel the remnants of the feelings I'd had for him back then. Losing him had been less like a breakup and more like I'd literally lost him. Like he'd been there one day, and gone the next. Dead, just like I'd been terrified so many times he would be. The man he was at the end was a different person altogether. Not a partner who'd stopped being on his best behavior and let his true colors show—not like my ex-husband—but an entirely different person. The man I'd fallen in love with hadn't soured into a jerk; he'd vanished completely. *That* was the man I'd missed so, so much.

And sometimes, like now when he was practicing on the ice, that man was still here. Still alive. Still playing hockey. Still existing as if he'd never blinked out of my reality like a mirage. That, I decided, was the worst part about being on the same team with him—the moments when I caught glimpses of the old Sol. When the man I'd adored flickered across my line of sight like a ghost dancing through my peripheral vision before disappearing back into the cold, bitter void.

Do you know how much it hurts to miss you so much when you're right here in front of me?

I turned away to put my water bottle down, and I stole that moment with my back to him to push out a harsh breath. I vividly remembered how happy I'd been with Sol before the cocaine. That was happiness I'd been chasing ever since, but had never been able to find. Not even in the best years with Damon.

"If he called you up and wanted to give it another shot," Damon had accused me one night, *"you'd drop me like yesterday's garbage."*

Sometimes I thought he believed that. Sometimes I thought he'd only said it because he knew it would get me right where he wanted me—doing everything I could to prove I loved him and he was the only one for me. Damon hadn't understood. He didn't get why there was still grief for Sol. That it didn't mean I wanted him back—I just missed someone I would never see again. Someone who didn't exist anymore.

The whistle startled me back into the present, and I turned to see Sol, sober and safe, gliding out of the crease, flushed and out of breath behind his mask. Kayla watched me expectantly, and I quickly pushed off the boards, pulled down my mask, and headed toward the goal.

As we passed each other, Sol and I made eye contact for a second, and I nearly lost my edge.

How do I find what we had?

I quickly banished that thought and continued toward crease. This was not the time to be thinking about any of that. My love life. My past life with Sol. My marriage. None of it. The only thing that mattered right now was getting my career back on the rails. Once I had a handle on that, I could think about finding another man.

Another man to fall for, crash and burn with, and then wonder why I'd ever thought it would end any other way.

Yeah. That sounded like a real treat.

Definitely not something I needed to be thinking about right now.

Hockey. Just hockey.

So I positioned myself in goal and focused on the ice, on Kayla, on Volkov and Colfax, and on those infernal white pucks.

The Sasquatches had two preseason games at home, and now it was time to take this show back on the road. Not my first away game with the team, but my first long flight with them, since Portland had just been a brief hop. For this one, we were heading to Denver, which wasn't exactly a cross-country flight, but it was almost three hours.

Having been traded twice before I'd landed in Calgary —briefly to Boston and then spending a season and a half in Chicago—I was familiar with the early adjustment with a new team, where I didn't quite know anybody unless we'd played together previously, and I was still finding my place socially. Like everyone else in the league, the Sasquatches were friendly and welcoming to new guys both on and off the ice. So, unsurprisingly, I was invited to sit with some of my teammates to play cards and shoot the shit.

Normally, I'd have taken them up on the offer, but I politely declined. "Maybe on the way back?"

They'd shrugged and hadn't seemed bothered by it. Even guys who regularly hung out together on flights sometimes bowed out to sleep or read.

I wanted to join in. I missed the camaraderie of my past teams, and I was especially hungry for it now. But I wasn't quite ready to grin and bear it through a card game with Sol. And he probably wasn't ready to do the same with me. It was better for both of us if I sat this one out.

I found a seat near the middle of the plane, across from Darby. He was texting with someone, though he acknowledged me with a nod, which I returned before getting myself situated.

Soon after that, we were taxiing, and as we headed for the runway, I cringed. I wasn't afraid of flying—not that I particularly liked it—but every time a plane took off now, I vividly remembered how awful those first few flights had been after my most recent concussion. The pressure changes had been fucking miserable. These days, it was pretty much normal—as normal as could be for someone prone to migraines—but I couldn't help shuddering at the memory of those nauseating takeoffs and descents, and I still got a little queasy just thinking about it.

As the plane leveled out, I sent up another prayer to the hockey gods for no more concussions.

But not because I get a different *injury,* I mentally clarified. *Or because my career ends for some other reason. Or because I get bounced to third string. A healthy, injury-free career as a starting goalie for as many seasons as I can play with no more concussions.*

The hockey gods did, after all, require specificity.

I chuckled at my own stupid thoughts. I wasn't as superstitious as some of the guys I'd played with over the years, but this was an exception. Ever since the night I'd pleaded for my team to score "one more goal, damn it," and they'd ended up getting an own goal—on *me*, no less—I'd learned to be extremely specific about what I was actually asking of whatever sadistic beings oversaw this ridiculous sport.

My head throbbed a little as the flight went on, but it wasn't too bad. No signs of an impending migraine, which was promising. When the queasiness had ebbed enough for me to read without getting sick, I took out my phone and thumbed through social media on my burner accounts just for something to pass the time. Nothing super interesting going on. Some rumors about trades in the works. Updates on a defenseman in Philly who'd broken his collarbone last night. Fans chirping each other over whose team was clearly going to win the Cup based on their preseason performance.

I had to chuckle at that. The commentators and fans alike always acted like the preseason was the damn playoffs. If a team killed it in the preseason, they were going to sweep the championships. If they blew it, they were bound to not even make the playoffs, and their entire coaching staff needed to be launched into the sun.

In reality, preseason wasn't that serious. Yeah, we played for real, but the rosters were usually full of rookies who were getting the hang of playing at this level and new guys getting used to a team's systems. While the younger guys often had something to prove, the veterans usually eased off the gas a little—they'd knock off the rust and get back in their groove, but they didn't run on all eight cylinders until games started to count. So, the young, inexperienced guys often played better in the preseason than veterans with multiple Cups under their belts. Same thing every year, and yet fans and commentators still had the same dramatic reactions.

Right now, the consensus was that Seattle was doomed, and a lot of that was because of Sol and me. The offensive lines and defensive pairs were pretty solid, but Sol and I had both made some costly mistakes. Clearly, that meant our team was going to finish last in the league, Coach Maines would be fired, and the two worthless goalies would be justifiably sent packing. There were also the predictably sexist remarks about how Kayla needed to be replaced immediately. She clearly wasn't qualified, said all these jackasses who were more concerned with her gender than the fact that she'd backstopped Team Canada to three medals. Oh, right, because women's hockey didn't count.

I rolled my eyes and continued scrolling. Some of the doom and gloom that people were predicting about Sol and me—about the whole team, really—might end up being true, but it was just too early in the year to say for sure. What I did know was that Coach and Kayla both seemed pleased with our performances in the net. Sure, everyone preferred it if we won, but if we were going to give up stupid goals and cost our team games, this was the time to do it.

I kept scrolling, and I found an article about my previous team and how they were predicted to fare this season. They had a promising young goalie who'd been a first-round draft pick—ninth overall—and it looked like he was going to play this season. My former backup, Grainger, was now the starting goalie, and his first preseason game had been a shutout. The Chinooks' previous starting goalie—

I stopped reading at that point. This reporter hadn't liked me when I was on the team, and I doubted she had much more affection for me now. I really didn't care to find out what she said about me when she didn't have to worry about looking me in the eye during post-game locker room interviews.

Instead, I found an article about the absolute shitshow that Vancouver had been turning into over the last few years, and whether or not this would be the year they pulled it together. Especially after they'd had the first overall draft pick, they were in a good position to—

My text app pinged.

Then I saw the name, and my heart stopped.

Damon.

I closed my eyes and pressed my head back against the seat without reading his message. Things were going okay right now. I was feeling great physically. I was playing well, jelling with my new team despite my ex-boyfriend's presence. I was even coexisting with him without too much issue, and pretty much letting preseason doom-and-gloom social media bullshit roll off my back.

The last thing I needed was to hear from my stupid ex-husband.

Ugh. Maybe it was some loose end from the divorce. Or maybe the house had finally sold. Except any of that would go through our lawyers or our Realtor. Damon really had no reason to contact me directly anymore.

Curiosity sent me back to the phone, and I pulled up the text app.

Looks like you're going to be in Chicago soon. Any chance you want to meet up?

Oh, for fuck's sake. We'd met back when I'd played in Chicago, and I'd forgotten he'd moved back after the divorce since his family lived there and he couldn't stay in Canada. He was right, too—we had an away game there very early in the regular season. Wonderful.

And as for his question, the answer to that nonsense was a resounding *hell no* even before I reached the second message, which was just two emojis: the eggplant and the sploosh.

I grimaced and put my phone down as my stomach roiled. The last time we'd been in the same room, we'd barely been able to look at each other. Now he thought I wanted to hook up with him? What the hell?

Anger cut through the nausea. I'd had it with his shit. The breakup had been messy, and the divorce itself was even messier. Unless he was texting me to let me know he was joining a monastery and taking a vow of silence that included electronic communications, I didn't want to hear from him.

Ah, but here he was, thinking I actually wanted a piece of him. Divorce really was the gift that kept on giving, wasn't it? Like a sentient case of herpes. Jesus fuck.

My gaze landed on Sol, who was a few rows up, laughing at something one of our teammates had said.

My stomach curdled all over again. Fucking hell. *Why* did I have such toxic taste in men?

Closing my eyes, I swore under my breath and wiped a hand over my face.

Fuck dating. Fuck everyone. I was going to focus on hockey for the foreseeable future. Maybe an anonymous hookup here or there when I was too horny to take care of it myself. But that was it. I didn't even like casual sex, but that had always been way less complicated for me than any of my sorry attempts at love. Somehow I was pretty good at finding guys to fuck—those who had reasonably good hygiene and were fun to fool around with—but whenever I tried a relationship, I eventually wound up walking away from a smoldering crater and wondering why the hell I'd ever given them the time of day.

Okay, that wasn't entirely true. I could see, clearly and

objectively, what had drawn me to both Sol and Damon. I could remember the good days without needing to filter them through rose-colored glasses. Because both relationships had started out great. There hadn't been any signs—none that I could see then or now—of what was to come.

The changes had come slowly. Sol's addiction, Damon's manipulation—they'd crept in like mold inside the walls: quietly eating away at everything, making my life miserable, until one day the whole place was infested and I couldn't breathe anymore.

That might not have been the best analogy, but close enough. And I'd done my part in my marriage unraveling, though it was hard to tell where my sins ended and Damon's gaslighting began. Like okay, I admittedly hadn't been the best about focusing on him when I was home briefly between games, and I owned that. I'd neglected him, and I shouldn't have. But him fucking those other guys? That had been his choice. I might not have been great at making him happy, but I also hadn't made him swipe right and drop trou.

It also wasn't like I'd signed up for long and bumpy recoveries from various injuries. I hadn't volunteered for that awful, protracted period of struggling just to be a human being again, never mind a husband or a hockey player. Like, dude, I get it—it sucks ass to try to accommodate a partner whose balance is off, cognition is recovering, and migraines won't stop, but it wasn't a picnic for me, either. And unlike him, I couldn't walk away from it all.

In sickness and in health, my ass.

I'd eventually gotten better, fortunately, though odds were I would never be a hundred percent recovered. My marriage? God, we'd been a mess. It hurt like hell when he left, but if he couldn't stick with me while I was going through something like that, then he could fuck off.

And he thinks I want another taste of that? Ugh. No.

I opened his text again and wrote back, *No, thanks.*

As soon as I sent it, I regretted it. I should've just ghosted him. He would absolutely get the last word in, and I needed to stop giving him opportunities to do it.

Sure enough, a few minutes later, my text notification went off again.

Yeah, I figured. Knew as soon as I heard he was signed to Seattle that you were done with me.

The surge of anger almost drove a string of curses from my lips that would've had the whole team staring. Somehow, I managed to stay quiet, though. Didn't even slam my phone down. Or throw it. Because goddamn, if I'd been alone, I'd have hurled the damn thing into the wall and cursed his name every way I could think of, noise complaints be damned.

Not here, though.

This isn't about Sol, I wanted to tell him. *This is about you bailing on me. You cheated on me. You left me. Don't try to put this on him.*

But there was no point in engaging. After thinking it through for a solid fifteen minutes, I wrote back with unsteady hands, *We're done here. You have anything else to say to me, go through our attorneys.*

Then I blocked him. Keeping him unblocked would've given me ample evidence to show my attorney that he was harassing me, but I was way more concerned with just not hearing from him again. I was so, so done. I didn't want to hear any more about how I was supposedly still in love with Sol, and how the divorce was my fault, and how I was a terrible husband but a passable piece of ass. I was just...*done*.

At least Sol never blamed me for everything.

The thought hit me in the chest like a slapshot. Opening my eyes, I found Sol, and I watched him as he listened intently to something Volkov was saying. When he laughed, my heart fluttered in the same instant a sharp bolt of regret cut through me.

We were so good together.

We really had been. And then we weren't. All because of that stupid white powder.

No, Sol had never blamed me. Not for his addiction, anyway. For leaving, yes, but something told me Damon would've found a way to add the cocaine to the list of things I "made" him do by being such a shit partner.

Maybe I *was* a shit partner. Sol's addiction had been beyond my control, but I *had* abandoned him at rehab. Even if it didn't justify cheating, I *had* left Damon alone more often than not. I hated Damon for deserting me while I was recuperating from injuries, but hadn't I left Sol while he was in rehab? Was my divorce karma coming to bite me in the ass for how I'd abandoned Sol?

Maybe. Maybe not. At least I'd never cheated on Sol. And I'd tried to help him, for God's sake. He'd hated me for that. Damon...he'd just gotten sick of our lives being ruled by the unpredictable and ongoing effects of my concussed brain.

Pressing back into the airplane seat, I rubbed my forehead. I sucked at relationships. No way around it. Either because of the men I chose or the way I handled the relationships themselves, I sucked at it.

Definitely needed to stay single for a while.

I'd just focus on hockey. If I couldn't redeem myself as

someone worth dating or marrying, then at least I could be the one thing I'd always been damn good at—a goalie.

I gripped the armrest and pushed out a breath.

I don't care if it's preseason. I'm getting a shutout tomorrow.

CHAPTER 11

SOL

I would never admit it out loud under torture, but I was relieved that Coach had Josh in the net on opening night.

Oh, I still wanted that starter position, and I was still going to fight tooth and skate to get it. Absolutely. For tonight, though, I wasn't going to complain about sitting here in a chair beside the bench, wearing a backwards base-ball cap instead of my mask, doing pretty much fuck all for the entire game. If Josh was injured or Coach pulled him for whatever reason, I'd be put in, but that was pretty rare. The backup goalie usually spent the entire game right here.

On most nights, even without my asshole ex-boyfriend between the pipes instead of me, I'd be twitching and squirming the entire time. I'd never been good at sitting still or being bored, and I was even worse at twiddling my thumbs when I could be out there helping my team.

Tonight, I'd take the twitchiness and the boredom over the alternative. I'd get my chance out there on home ice soon enough. This game would give me a much-needed opportunity to get used to my surroundings.

Because holy hell, a hockey game in Seattle was an *experience*.

I mean, I'd been overwhelmed during the preseason, but this? The season opener? Holy fucking hell.

Despite the Sasquatches being historically terrible, the game was sold out. Apparently losing teams were kind of a thing in this town, and Seattle fans were the farthest from fair weather fans you could find. They supported all their teams through the worst years (which accounted for most years when we were talking about the Mariners or the Seahawks), and during those precious good years, they put every other fanbase to shame. Someone even told me that during that run when the Seahawks finally won a Super Bowl, fans were so loud and raucous they registered on the Richter scale at the nearby university.

I'd kind of thought all of that was an exaggeration. We'd had a decent crowd for the preseason games, and they'd been loud and enthusiastic, but preseason crowds were usually made up of kids, their parents, and a whole lot of drunk-ass fans. They were *always* loud in their own way.

Tonight? Oh my God.

If anything, my teammates had undersold just how wild —how literally seismic—Seattle crowds could be. There was an ass in every seat in the house, everyone was shouting from the tops of their lungs, and all those strobe lights and cinematics from the preseason had barely been a glimmer of this reality. The place was already vibrating from the music and the excited fans. As our starting lineup was read, I didn't hear a word the announcer said over the deafening roar of seventeen thousand people pushing their vocal cords to their absolute limit. This was playoff-level overstimulation. Oh God—what would this crowd be like if the Sasquatches defied the odds and actually made the playoffs?

My head swam. The noise and the lights yanked my focus in every which direction until it all blurred together.

I played with the edge of one of my leg pads, focusing on the texture of the material and the stitching. Yeah, good thing I wasn't out there tonight. I could spend this game just getting used to it all—as much as I ever got used to anything like this—before I had to cope with it *and* mind the net.

On the bright side, when it was my turn out on the ice, I probably wouldn't be able to hear opposing players chirping at me over all the noise. I could usually ignore what they were saying, but I was that guy whose head turned at every sound or flicker of light. You know that kid who gets distracted by something shiny or because a car drove by? The one people jokingly jangle their keys in front of to get his attention? Yeah, that was me, and I hadn't gotten any better as an adult.

At least I'd mostly learned to focus on the puck and on keeping it out of my net, and I could ignore chirps the vast majority of the time, but once I started getting distracted, it was an uphill struggle for the rest of game. The less I heard, the better.

Not much I could do about all the noise or the flashing lights and colors, though. Jesus.

I closed my eyes and exhaled. The season opener always overwhelmed my senses. I'd gotten used to it in Phoenix, and I'd get used to it here, even if Seattle took it to an entirely new level. I could do this.

But yeah, thank God Josh was handling things tonight.

I looked out at the ice to watch my team. Seattle's offense had been weak for the last couple of seasons, and apparently the forwards and defensemen alike had listened when Coach Maines said they weren't doing that shit again this season. Someone had mentioned on the plane that our

GM was threatening to trade the hell out of anyone who wasn't pulling their weight, and by the looks of it, nobody wanted to test how serious he was about that.

We were against New York tonight, and they couldn't get the puck into our defensive zone to save their lives. Halfway through the first period, we were already up two-nothing. They tried, though, I'd give them that, but our guys just weren't giving up an inch without a fight. Three break-aways in a row were broken up before the red line. One had Seattle heading back into the offensive zone, but it was stopped by a whistle. Offside. Of course.

That was something that could kill momentum, but it didn't. Instead, it gave our guys a chance for a much-needed line change and a rush on New York's net. One of their forwards—a center who was young and small but fast as hell —grabbed the puck for yet another breakaway.

He didn't get far. Colfax mugged him in the neutral zone, then sent it screaming by two forwards in a beautiful pass to Darby, who was wide open thanks to half of New York trying to cover Volkov at once. Darby took full advantage and made a run for the goal that had the entire stadium —myself included—on their feet, screaming, "Go! Go! Go!"

New York's netminder was crouched and ready, paddle and trapper up as he twitched side to side, trying to antici-pate where Darby would shoot.

With a good fifteen feet between him and the goal, Darby wound up for a slapshot, and in the same second the goalie moved into position, Darby tapped the puck to Volkov, who was now unprotected. The goalie realized his mistake a heartbeat too late, and he tried to correct. At the same time, Volkov must've realized he had two players closing in on him, because he tapped it right back to Darby.

That goalie didn't stand a chance.

The roar that filled the stadium drowned out the horn. Standing in the net, the goalie let his head fall back as he was bathed in the red glow of the goal light. Even from here, I could feel the frustration coming off him in waves, probably because I'd been there myself. It was not a good feeling. And while I fist-bumped Darby and Volkov when they came by the bench, while I cheered for the goal and our team's early and growing lead, I did feel sorry for the guy. Three-nothing before the end of the first? Yeah, that sucked.

A lot of that was because his team wasn't defending him well, and they weren't moving the puck into our zone enough. Hell, New York only had a single shot on goal while Seattle had seventeen already. The fact that he'd already made fourteen saves said a lot more than the fact that he'd let us score three times; the ice being tilted *that* hard wasn't the goalie's fault.

But every goalie knows how it goes—when the score is that lopsided, the blame falls on the man in the crease.

I shuddered as I took my seat again and the skaters set up for another faceoff. It was only a matter of time before New York yanked the goalie. Probably not much time, either—from where I was sitting, I could see his backup moving around and doing some stretches.

Pulled in the first period? Ouch.

He ended up lasting through the buzzer, though. That third goal had lit a fire under New York's ass, and they finally pushed into our defensive zone. After seventeen minutes of having to do next to nothing, Josh was suddenly in constant motion. As the shot counter ticked up, he made save after save, including an absolutely glorious windmill to just barely clip a puck that was destined for the top shelf. The collective gasp followed by roaring applause said that everyone had been sure that shot was going in. If Josh didn't get one of the stars tonight for that save alone, I'd eat my mask.

The period ended, and Josh skated off the ice, drenched in sweat and out of breath as our teammates tapped their sticks on his pads. Coach met him in the locker room with a firm clap on his back, and from the tired smile on Josh's face, Maines must've given him some kind of enthusiastic encouragement. Well-deserved, too. I didn't have to like Josh to respect him as a goalie or to be impressed by that last save.

And I didn't have to be on the same team to feel sorry for the guy in the other net. All goalies had rough nights, and the best we could hope for on those nights was for our offense and defense to make up for it by keeping the puck away from us in the first place. Sometimes...well, sometimes it didn't work that way. A floppy defense, a lazy offense, and a goalie having an off night made for the kind of game that was talked about for *years* after the fact.

This kid was not having a bad night. Not in terms of his technique and focus, anyway. He was playing just fine, and in fact he'd made some damn impressive saves. He was just out there on his own without nearly enough support.

But he'd be taking the fall on social media. That was just the way it went.

Been there. Done that. Poor kid.

My gaze drifted to another goalie who was having a perfectly good night, but who actually had a team supporting him enough to make his efforts worthwhile.

As we all sat through Coach's intermission speech, my mind wandered back to my second season in Phoenix. To one of those nights that still lived in infamy on social media, YouTube, and sports bar conversations.

In the locker room that night, I'd sat beside our rookie

netminder after the reporters had cleared out. He'd been staring at the towel he'd just used on his face, and his cheeks were still bright red. I'd suspected that was a combination of the game and his shower, but mostly from having cameras and microphones in his face when he'd just wanted to go somewhere and die of embarrassment.

"Hey. It's one game." I'd touched his arm. "There's still seventy-something left to play. You'll be fine."

He'd looked up at me, dark strands of sweaty hair hanging down over his big brown eyes, expression full of that absolute certainty that he was never coming back from this. It had, after all, only been his second start at this level.

"I fucked us." Josh had sounded even younger than his twenty-two years that night. Like he was back in his youth days. "God, I'm such a mess."

"No, you had a bad night." I squeezed his arm again. "We all have them. It doesn't stop just because you're in the majors now."

His brow pinched, and I swore his eyes were begging me to make that real and not just a platitude. Except it *was* real. This was only my second season playing at this level, and I knew of what I spoke.

"You know Tad Northam? Starting goalie until he retired last season?"

Josh nodded slowly.

"Okay, well, he had some spectacularly terrible games his last year." I laughed dryly. "The guy won the Xavier the same season he allowed eight goals in one game."

"Really?" Josh's eyes lost focus. "Oh. Yeah. That was... what? Five years ago?"

"Yeah. And the only time anyone ever mentions that stupid game is like this—when they're telling you he was a spectacular goalie who still had occasionally terrible games just like the rest of us lesser mortals."

That brought a halfhearted chuckle out of Josh. One that had done things to me I'd known even in that moment it shouldn't. He was a teammate. Wanting a teammate was a bad idea. But goddamn, he'd been so adorable. So freaking cute.

Then the laughter had died away, and as he rubbed the back of his neck, he sighed. "I haven't exactly done anything to make up for nights like..." He gestured toward the hallway leading out to the ice.

"How many games have you played at this level?"

"Two. And they've both been terrible."

"Nah, the other night wasn't bad. You only let two goals in."

"Uh-huh. While the other guy got a shutout."

I shrugged. "He was a brick wall that night. It happens. So do nights like this." I gently bumped my shoulder against his. "You'll be fine."

Josh chewed his lip and avoided my gaze.

I wasn't good at stuff like this. I didn't take platitudes or encouragement very well, and I sucked at giving them. I racked my scattered brain, looking for a way to show him that having a crap night was just part of being a goalie.

An idea came to me, and I said, "Stay right there." Then I went to my stall, dug out my phone, and came back. He watched curiously over my shoulder as I pulled up YouTube, and it only took a second to find the video I was looking for.

"Here." I put the phone in his hand. "Watch this."

He glanced at me, then focused on the phone and hit play.

The video started with an absolutely awful clip—one that

would never stop making me cringe—of me losing an edge right when an opposing player dumped a puck into our defensive end. It hadn't been intended as a shot—just a dump so they could do a line change—but it was coming dangerously close to my net, so I'd moved to deflect it. In the process, I'd lost my edge, and when I'd stumbled, I had indeed managed to deflect the puck...away from its harmless trajectory toward the boards and straight into the back of my own net.

"Oh wow," Josh said with a cautious laugh. "I think I remember this."

"Yeah. I'm still shocked they didn't trade me after that. Keep watching."

A title rolled across the screen:

Two straight minutes of proof that Cary Solomon is paid way too much.

"Holy shit," Josh breathed. "That's kind of...mean."

"Eh." I shrugged as another of my greatest failures appeared. "Comes with the territory."

To his credit, Josh didn't watch the entire video. After three horrible save attempts, he paused it and handed it back. "Thank you. I don't want to be happy that you've got shit like that out there, but it's nice to know I'm not a hopeless train wreck."

"Nah, you're not. You didn't wind up here by mistake, and no one is going to wake up tomorrow and realize you don't belong here."

"As long as I don't fuck up like that again?"

"You will," I assured him. "Trust me. But you'll have good games, too. I've seen the way you play. You'll be fine."

Oh, fuck me—that smile returned to his face, sweet and shy and so damn cute.

"Thanks," he said again. "Next game, I'll do better."

"I know you will."

And he had—his next game was a three-two win. The one after that? His first career shutout.

In the present, sitting here in the Seattle Sasquatches locker room several states and a lifetime removed from that night in Phoenix, I pulled my gaze away from Josh and swallowed the sudden lump in my throat.

Josh was a far better goalie now than he'd been back then, and that said something. It was one of the reasons his slump had been talked about so much—because he was *so damn good*, and then he wasn't. If tonight was any indication, he was on his way back to that level, and I hoped he was. Even if I still wanted that starter position over him, even if I still resented him, I hoped—just like I quietly had for all these years when I'd followed his career from a distance—that he'd be the goalie I'd known he could be. That the potential I'd seen in that rookie who wasn't much younger than me came to fruition.

It had. Slump or not, he'd carved himself a permanent place in this sport's history.

And we'd been strangers for most of that. That night I'd sat there with him in Phoenix all those years ago, if someone had told me how things would go, I'd never have believed them. Maybe that we'd wind up in bed—I'd felt that sizzle of two-way attraction even then—but not that I'd fall so hard for him. Not that I was mere months away from the first taste of his perfect kiss, and several more away from another first taste that would start me down the road of addiction. Not that I'd lose Josh.

Not that we'd wind up on another team together as both estranged lovers and total strangers.

Realizing how much had happened between that night

and this one—fully grasping, maybe for the first time, how much I'd had and lost—took my breath away.

Movement around me told me everyone was getting ready to head back out to the ice. Intermission was nearly over. Time to sit on my ass and watch Josh do what he'd proven year after year he was damn good at doing.

Time to wonder where the hell everything went wrong, and where we'd both be today if I'd never taken that first whiff of white powder.

Fuck.

As I followed my teammates down the tunnel, I was starting to think that, when it was my turn to tend the goal, the lights and crowd weren't going to be the problem for my easily overstimulated brain. It probably wouldn't even be those persistent cravings for blow.

It was going to be the man sitting quietly on the bench in pads and a ballcap.

CHAPTER 12

JOSH

"Goddamn, O'Brien!" Leclerc knocked his helmet against my mask seconds after the buzzer sounded the end of the game. "You're getting first star tonight. No doubt."

I laughed, still out of breath but relieved as all hell that the pressure was off now. "I don't know—Darby's hatty has to put him in the running for first star. I'll take second or third."

He chuckled. "Fine. Second star." He whistled as we started toward the bench. "Amazing, man. Fucking amazing game."

Smiling, I shrugged under my pads as I took off my mask. Our teammates quickly descended on me with stick taps and fist bumps. I was relieved as hell, that was for sure. The game had been a long and brutal one. I'd barely had to lift a finger for most of the first period, but New York had been relentless after we'd scored that third goal.

They'd come out with their backup goalie in the second period, and both the offense and defense were determined to do whatever it took to stop the bleeding. A good chunk of the second period centered around the neutral zone, with both teams barely able to get into an offensive zone, never mind stay there. Then a one-timer from the blue line had made the score four-nothing, and between Seattle's momentum and New York's frustration, the game had turned physical. Lots of checks. Two scuffles. A fight in the dying minute of that period. In between, New York managed to draw a couple of penalties, and they'd used their power play chances to fire everything they had toward my net.

Then, thirty seconds into the third period, they finally got one past me...

Only to have it called back after Coach Maines challenged it for offside.

If they'd been frustrated before, they were pissed now, and they were out for blood. It was a combination of desperate drives for the goal to try to close our lead, and attempt after attempt to goad my teammates into fighting. They were trying to get us to fight for multiple reasons—to try to draw penalties, because they were losing their tempers...and because fights were, much like dirty hits, a way to get key players off the ice.

They miscalculated that last one, though, because when someone finally succeeded in injuring a player, it backfired spectacularly. Instead of drawing a penalty, they took one, because the defenseman wasn't even subtle about charging that forward. Worse for them, it was a five-minute match penalty, since it was a high hit with intent to injure.

But the thing that turned the Sasquatches from a solidly performing team into a collective force to be reckoned with was the sight of our youngest player—Järvinen, the rookie winger on the fourth line, laid out and not getting up. The fans booed furiously as the replay showed, in excruciating slow motion, Järvinen taking a shot, and a second later, that asshole ramming into him elbow first, cracking the kid in the head and sending him first into the glass, then crumpling to the ice.

The trainers were at the rookie's side before the replay had even finished. A full minute later, the whole crowd breathed a sigh of relief and applauded as Järvinen was helped to his feet. He couldn't quite stand up straight, but he was able to skate off the ice with help from a couple of teammates. There was blood on his face, though I couldn't tell if it was from his mouth, his nose, or both.

The ice crew came out to clean the blood off the ice while the refs announced the penalty, which resulted in a roar of approval from the crowd. I watched my on-ice teammates exchanging glances, and there was no mistaking what was passing between all of them:

Those fuckers made the rookie bleed. Now we make them pay.

And oh, wow, my team definitely made New York pay.

I did about as much in the last ten minutes of the game as I did in the first—basically nothing. Seattle took full advantage of the five-minute power play and scored twice. When New York was at full strength again, it didn't make much difference. The collective rage among fans and teammates alike may as well have been an additional player out there with us for all New York could gain—never mind keep —control of the puck.

By the time the buzzer sounded for the final time, the score was seven-zero.

Following my teammates back into the dressing room, I was absolutely flying. Even if I hadn't actually had to do much, a shutout was a shutout, and it was exactly the kind of redemption I'd been craving. Not enough to counter my recent disaster seasons, but enough to make me think the tide might be turning.

The dressing room was full of back slaps and happy chirps. Our team had a toy version of one of those belts they give out at WrestleMania, and after every win, it went to the player who'd had the best night. It had gone to Volkov after our last preseason game, and after hat tips to me and some of the other guys, he gave the belt to Darby, much to the raucous applause of everyone in the room.

"Third career hat trick." Volkov smacked Darby on the shoulder. "Well done."

Darby grinned and, as was tradition, put on the belt over his sweaty base layer. "Thanks, Volks. Great game tonight, guys. Let's keep it going."

"What he said." Coach Maines nodded sharply. "That's how you play against a team like that. Well done. And before we let the reporters in..." He motioned toward Dr. Armstrong. "We've got an update on Järvinen."

Instantly, everyone sobered, and the room was suddenly still and silent.

Dr. Armstrong cleared his throat. "He's being evaluated at the hospital for a concussion and a possible fractured jaw, but he's conscious and alert. We don't have any updates yet, but at this point, it's mostly precautionary, so I'm anticipating good news."

Relief rippled through the room. Deep down, I think we'd all known the kid was *probably* fine, especially after he'd been able to leave on his own power, but head injuries were weird and could turn ugly in a hurry. Getting confirmation that he was good definitely let everyone breathe easier.

Coach finished up his postgame speech, and we all

continued getting cleaned up so the reporters could be turned loose on us.

As I stripped off my gear and showered, I kept thinking about the rookie. Having had my life upended by a head injury, I was seriously relieved he was good. Hearing that he'd gone to the hospital definitely turned my stomach, even if I knew that was a fairly routine thing. Plenty of players went to the hospital after on-ice injuries just to be absolutely sure there was nothing serious—been there, done that myself—and most of the time, there wasn't. The league just didn't like taking chances.

Though I knew the league's concern was anything but altruistic, I appreciated them erring on the side of caution when it came to our health. Especially after one of my teammates in Calgary had been taken in "just to be on the safe side" with what seemed like a moderate concussion. The CT found a small bleed that had been, in the words of our team doctor, "very much working toward becoming a *big* bleed." It had ultimately been the end of my buddy's hockey career, but considering it could've ended his life, he didn't complain. Well, okay, he *did* complain—he was too much of a rink rat not to be upset over early retirement. He just didn't bitch about the doc making him go to the hospital that day.

From the sound of it, Järvinen was going to be hating life for a while, but he'd be okay. If the concussion was minor, he could be back on the ice in as little as a week or two. A broken jaw could mean eight weeks or more, depending on how bad it was and how well it healed. Hopefully he didn't lose any teeth; that was a risk when you played hockey, but it really could add injury to injury.

At the very least, no one in the know seemed concerned that the rookie was in any danger of long term or career-ending problems, though only time would tell what kind of lingering effects he'd have to deal with. Didn't I know it. Still, just knowing he would be released from the hospital and was likely to continue playing hockey was enough to let me breathe easy for now. I'd shoot him a text when I got back to my locker, just to check in and tell him I hoped he was okay. And probably give him hell for not beating the shit out of that defenseman, just because we were hockey players and couldn't resist a chance to chirp at each other. That was how you knew you were *really* hurt—when your teammates *weren't* talking shit.

After my shower, I headed back into the locker room. As I passed by the sinks, I caught a glimpse of Colfax. He was dabbing at his nose and sniffling.

Cold water trickled down my spine. *Christ. Another one?*

But I quickly dismissed that thought and kept walking.

I was imagining things. Sniffling was a perfectly normal thing that perfectly normal people did. Especially perfectly normal people who'd been using smelling salts for half the night; my nose ran sometimes just from catching a whiff when a teammate used those foul fucking things nearby.

I was just jumping to conclusions because of past experience.

It was hard to let go of that conclusion, though. And hadn't I noticed Colfax working his jaw during a stoppage earlier tonight?

Even that didn't mean much, though. He wore a mouth-guard, and a lot of the guys who wore them constantly played with them while they waited for their next shift.

But they didn't usually do that side-to-side grinding motion that became incredibly conspicuous after you'd seen it in a few people. That hard movement that made every muscle in their face tight, and made me wonder how I couldn't hear their teeth grinding from ten paces away. I'd never completely understood it; something about how cocaine's simulant properties caused involuntary muscle movements, and that came out in teeth-clenching and jaw-working. Whatever it was, I could spot it from a mile away these days.

Still...people who didn't use cocaine ground their teeth. People who'd never touched the stuff sniffled. Jaw movements and sniffling didn't mean anything.

Except when it did.

I shook the thought away. I'd keep an eye on Colfax, but even if I figured out he was using, what the hell could I do? Be the new guy who was already on thin ice narcing on the generational talent? Rat him out to people who might very well decide they were fine with him using as long as he kept getting results, and oh by the way, you can pound sand because our rookie goalie is suddenly ready to come up after all?

Hello, rock. Meet hard place.

One step at a time. Figure out if there was actually a problem. Then figure out if the powers that be would be receptive to hearing about it. That second thing was harder than people realized. I would know.

But I'd cross that unpleasant bridge if and when I got to it.

In the meantime, all I could do was keep my head down and try not to lose my last chance at a hockey career.

I trudged back to the dressing room. Even my relief over Järvinen being okay and my elation over tonight's shutout couldn't quell the sick feeling in my stomach. The league had a problem, and after all this time, I'd given up hope that it would ever acknowledge that problem, never mind do something meaningful about it.

I hated the helplessness. I hated sitting back and watching the same progression happen over and over, season after season, with teammate after teammate, because nothing I or anyone else did ever seemed to stop it.

Some guys functioned all right, just like there were some who could—at least for a while—maintain their lives and hockey careers alongside a drinking problem or a painkiller addiction. I was pretty sure it was an open secret when guys like that were using, but as long as they didn't get caught, didn't cause any trouble, and didn't fuck up on the ice, everyone looked the other way. By the time the substance abuse became a problem, they were usually already deteriorating on the ice, which made it a lot easier to give him the boot under the pretense of "getting him help."

If someone was still valuable enough to a team, no one was going to rock the boat. Not when the ten-million-a-year superstar forward is putting up a hundred points a season. Not when that beast of a defenseman is breaking years-old team and league records. Not when that goalie is moving at superhuman speed to make highlight-reel saves.

As long as they weren't popping for steroids on their routine random drug screenings, and as long as no one actually saw them using, nothing came of it. Nobody pushed very hard for cocaine to be added to the list of substances included in those routine screenings, either. Couldn't imagine why that was.

In the locker room, I found Sol talking to a couple of reporters off to the side. Just the sight of him sent a surge of frustration through me. That was quickly followed by guilt.

Yes, he was the reason cocaine use was on my radar like

this. Why I was so quick to notice it. Or think I was noticing it. But he was hardly the only person who used.

Just the only one who ever managed to hurt me in the process.

I tore my gaze away from him and focused on getting dressed. I was decent—reporters had no qualms about approaching us when we were in our skivvies, so I always made sure I at least had on a pair of sweatpants when I came back from the shower. Good thing, too. I'd barely put down my shower kit when half a dozen microphones were thrust into my face.

I'd expected that much. First regular season game as a Sasquatch. First shutout in a long time. How did I feel about my performance? What did I think about the team's chemistry? Was it good to be back with a former teammate from when I was a rookie?

I was pretty proud of my ability to answer that last one without so much as a wince. "That's kind of how the sport works, you know? People you play with come and go, and sometimes you end up with guys from the past." I nodded to a stall three down from mine. "Leclerc and I played a season together in Chicago, too." With a smile that I hoped was convincing, I added, "Always good to be teammates again." With Leclerc, at least, that wasn't a lie.

They asked a few more questions, then left me to continue getting dressed so I could go shove some food into my face. I was starving after that game.

Starving, but still queasy enough that food didn't sound appealing in the least.

There *might* be a cocaine user on this team. There was definitely a recovering addict who *might* still be tempted to pick it up again if it were readily available. Say, if a teammate invited him to go party like that one forward had so many years ago.

And there wasn't a damn thing I could do about it, especially without any actual proof beyond a gut feeling.

Fuck. *Fuck!*

Between Colfax and Sol, I didn't feel anything like a goalie who'd quite possibly just broken his two-year slump with the best night of his career.

I'd never used cocaine in my life. I barely drank. I hadn't even smoked pot as a kid because I'd been terrified of getting kicked off a hockey team. I was so straightlaced in that department that it had become yet another source of conflict between me and my ex-husband.

"It's the off season," he'd bitched one night, still offering up the joint I'd refused. *"And this is Alberta—it's legal! Christ, Josh. Lighten up a little."*

No, I'd never touched anything besides alcohol.

But you sure wouldn't know it by how much that shit interfered with my life.

CHAPTER 13

SOL

I did my level best to coexist with Josh as the season got rolling. That mostly consisted of avoiding him as much as possible, which wasn't as difficult as you might think; even at practices, we were only on the same side of the ice when Kayla was working with us on something. Otherwise, we were usually on opposite ends of the sheet for scrimmages or offensive and defensive drills.

We'd both settled into groups of teammates we hung out with on the bus or the plane. Sometimes those groups would meld together, especially at bars after games, but then there'd be enough people for us to stay reasonably far apart without being conspicuous about it. As far as I could tell, no one had caught on that there were any issues between us, and even Kayla hadn't said anything about it in a while.

Good. As long as we were staying out of each other's way and not disrupting the team, we'd be fine.

Tonight, we'd played a hell of a grind in San Jose. Now some of us were cutting loose at a bar close to our hotel. It was the usual—some fans asking for selfies, a few puck bunnies looking for hookups, but mostly the guys just chilling at a table with beers. Or water, in my case.

Colfax was the ringleader tonight, which I was quickly learning was normal. He was usually serious and didn't say much in interviews, and he was a beast on the ice. Pushed far enough, he had no qualms about dropping gloves, which usually resulted in the other guy regretting his life's choices.

When Colfax was dressed down and there were no cameras around? He was charismatic and fun. Usually the loudest in the group, and the most generous with buying rounds for the whole place. He also welcomed the new guys, too, whether they were recently acquired veterans like me or the rookies. Tonight was no exception.

"Yo, Eggs!" Colfax beckoned to someone across the room. "Come hang with us!"

The redheaded kid who emerged from the crowd smiled shyly, looking seriously starstruck as he joined us at the table. "You guys don't mind?"

"Not at all." Colfax gestured for a server. "First drink's on me." He put an arm around Axel's shoulders and herded him onto a barstool right beside him. "Join the party!"

Axel stared wide-eyed at him, then around the table. True to his word, Colfax bought him a beer, and the rookie looked like he was about to fall off his barstool as we all clinked our glasses against his.

I chuckled behind my water glass. Oh, I'd been there. Being a rookie surrounded by veteran players was surreal as hell. Plus Axel had been a little untethered ever since Järvinen got hurt; they'd been close throughout their time in major juniors, and he was probably desperate for camaraderie while his buddy was out.

Wouldn't be long before he was one of the veterans taking rookies under his wing. I could feel it. This kid was going places. Axel Egillsson was a left winger who'd been drafted from a top major juniors team, and he'd made the team's roster after a single season in the minors. He was cute—a few freckles sprinkled across fair skin, red hair that was always either curly and sweat-darkened or perfectly arranged, and brown eyes that were going make the fans lose their minds.

His reputation preceded him, too. I'd heard about him in juniors when people had started speculating about up-and-coming talent. Axel—Eggs, as he was nicknamed—was quite possibly a generational talent, and he'd been drafted sixth overall. Apparently the kid had emigrated to Canada from Iceland as a kid, and much to his parents' chagrin, had quickly fallen in love with hockey (I was pretty sure they'd gotten over that, especially once their son had become a star). On the ice, he was an absolute demon, but in person, he turned out to be quiet and maybe even shy. It was hard to tell if that was who he was, or if he was still just starstruck by some of his teammates. Time would tell. He'd stayed close to Järvinen since day one of training camp, but that kid was out for at least another six weeks thanks to his concussion and fractured jaw.

So, Axel was on his own, and as he joined our group, he was a little quiet. Slowly, though, he was getting into the groove, laughing and joking with everyone. As he was listening to Darby tell a story, though, Axel absently rubbed his shoulder and winced.

Colfax noticed. Pointing with his chin at the kid, he asked, "Hey. What's the matter with your shoulder?"

Axel dropped his hand and folded his arms on the table.

Shrugging a little gingerly—and without moving his left shoulder at all—he said, "Eh, it's fine. Just slept on it weird on the plane." He groaned. "How the fuck do you guys stay awake enough to play cards when we fly? I swear to God, if I'm not wearing my gear, I'm trying to sleep."

"Get used to it," Darby said with a gruff chuckle. "Lack of sleep is part of the game."

"No shit." Axel laughed. "I've been playing since I was four. Just...it's a lot more at this level."

That got him some sympathetic grunts and nods. The regular season was not for the faint of heart, and I still struggled with it sometimes. There just weren't enough hours in the day to sleep as much as I needed to in between traveling, training, practicing, working out, eating, and playing. And then there were all the media obligations on top of it; Axel had been featured in a bunch of articles and stories about rookies lately, so that had to be cutting into his downtime too.

I felt for the kid, that was for sure. I'd been like him in my rookie season too, and this year, though I was a veteran, I was on an entirely new team. I wasn't starstruck this time— just a fish out of water.

That was getting better, though. As I'd started getting to know my teammates, I'd found a groove with most of them. Hockey players made friends quickly, especially since we all usually either knew each other, or we knew someone who did, so we fell into friendships pretty easily.

When I'd first moved to Seattle, I'd spent a lot of my downtime alone just because I'd been too overstimulated and too stressed, but I was finding my footing more recently. Now that I'd settled in with this team and the chaos of the regular season, I'd started socializing more outside of practices and travel. Especially with how weird things were with

Josh, I tried to put some space between us by getting more involved with our other teammates.

Tonight was the first time I'd had really sat down to get to know Colfax. He'd turned out to be hilarious—the kind of guy who could make anything into a joke, but poked fun at himself and situations instead of other people. He had the rookie laughing and relaxing into the conversation. Definitely the kind of guy every team needed, since he made everyone feel welcome and like part of the group.

And the longer I hung out with him tonight, the more certain I was that I needed to stay as far away from him as I could without disrupting the team's chemistry.

I'd had an inkling. Something in the back of my mind that said, *"Danger!"* But I'd been so hungry for social interaction, and I'd been missing the camaraderie of a team so much, I'd ignored my internal warnings. Now, sitting at that table, listening to him and Darby telling a story about something from last year's All-Star game, there was no ignoring that unnervingly familiar knot growing in the pit of my stomach.

I didn't hear much of what he said. Didn't really catch what had happened at the All-Stars that had him and Darby in stitches. No, I was more focused on the way Colfax was talking. How fast his words came tumbling out. Clear and enunciated, but rapid fire—nothing like when he was talking to reporters or Coach, or to the younger guys during practice. Closer to the way he talked during games, now that I thought about it, except that was usually more sharp-edged, like a man holding on to his temper by his fingernails. This was a happier version of the defenseman who would, with relatively little provocation, beat the holy hell out of a player with fifty pounds on him, and who'd still be talking shit with blood running down his face on his way to the penalty box.

Fast-talking. Twitchy. Short-tempered. Aggressive as all hell.

No one else at this table or on the team probably noticed the signs, but I did. I couldn't miss them. I especially couldn't miss them when they were coupled with the constant sniffling. Plus there was the way his jaw worked from side to side whenever he wasn't speaking or eating, and I'd noticed more than once how much worse it was during games. There was the nonstop drinking, too—not alcohol, just water, but he was always taking sips as if his mouth were dry. Anyone else at the table might've thought the sheen of sweat on his forehead had to do with the spicy wings he'd been eating, but that wasn't the whole story. I could feel it in my bones.

Oh, yeah. This was *just* what I fucking needed—a teammate who was also a gregarious, friendly cocaine user.

Colfax was exactly the kind of guy who could put an arm around someone's shoulders and introduce them to blow like it was the most amazing thing ever. I knew because that was exactly the kind of guy who'd given me my first taste.

My mouth started watering at the realization of how easily I could probably get my hands on some cocaine right about now, and I quickly took a drink and forced myself to focus on what Darby was saying.

I didn't want to think about that drug. I couldn't. Not now. Not ever. That train of thought always led to seriously terrible decisions. But it was even more important to not get swept away by those thoughts right now because there was something else I needed to focus on—the rookie.

Because it was becoming clearer by the minute that

Axel was completely enamored with Colfax. And Colfax had noticed how tired Axel was. It was only a matter of time before, *"Hey, I've got something that'll help."*

It also made me nervous having an active user on the team because everyone—and I mean *everyone*—knew my history. If the powers that be decided to test someone, I'd wind up getting called in for a test, too. Didn't matter if anyone actually had reason to believe I was using. I had a history, and therefore I was immediately under suspicion if someone else was doing blow. Plus, a condition of my return after rehab was that I was subject to drug tests at any time for any reason, including no reason at all, for the rest of my career.

I wasn't worried I'd pop positive. I'd been sober for almost three years. No, what I was worried about was the rumors. If it got out that Colfax was getting tested and so was I, then suddenly the rumors would start flying that I was using again. If I tested clean, people would say I'd just gotten lucky. That the cocaine had been out of my system by the time someone got around to getting a sample from me. It only took a couple of days, after all, unless they did a hair test, and even that might be inconclusive, because it could show up years after the fact. If I came up negative on a blood or piss test, that would only be conclusive proof that I hadn't used within the past few days. Or that I wasn't using heavily enough for it to linger in my system beyond that. If someone on the team was using or suspected of using, then it would take nothing short of divine intervention to convince the league and the fans that I hadn't been involved.

There would be no convincing anyone that I hadn't been using before that brief testing window had closed, and I couldn't refuse the tests or even object to them. Even if I could, that would just put me under more suspicion, or it might result in me suddenly getting traded under bullshit pretenses like salary cap issues. I didn't have the goodwill or the leeway with Seattle that I'd once had in Phoenix. I couldn't afford the scrutiny, because I sure as shit couldn't afford to become a liability—a real one or a perceived one— to a team that might drop me at the end of this short contract.

Helplessness churned in the pit of my stomach. What the hell was I supposed to do? Because I doubted anyone else was going to do a damn thing. After all, the league had an enormous blind spot when it came to cocaine use. Honestly, I could've named at least a dozen players off the top of my head who I was *certain* were active users. But it wasn't listed as a performance enhancer (even though it absolutely was in this sport), so the league just sort of ignored it right up until they couldn't. When there was no pretending they didn't know someone was using, then there'd be tests, suspensions, rehab, and all of that, but for a hockey player, getting caught with coke either meant you were extraordinarily reckless (which happened when the addiction got out of control) or it meant someone turned you in. Not that I knew *anything* about that second option.

So Colfax probably wouldn't have to worry about a thing since I doubted anyone else on the team was as quick as I was to recognize the signs of cocaine use. As long as his performance on the ice didn't suffer and he didn't do anything stupid *off* the ice, he could keep snorting his paychecks to his heart's content. No one would test him. No one would test me out of an abundance of suspicion. Err, caution.

He would keep playing, I would keep being the pariah

with no credibility, and no one would catch on if Colfax started hooking up the rookie with our drug of choice.

So...what did I do?

I could go to Josh. As much as I'd hated him for ditching me in rehab, I couldn't deny that of everyone on our team, he was the one I could bet on most certainly knowing who to talk to and how to get help for an addicted player. He took it seriously, and regardless of the bad feelings he had for me, if he thought any of our teammates—especially the new kid—needed help, he'd help.

Except, no, I couldn't go to him. That would mean outing the rookie as a user before I had any kind of proof that he'd done more than hang out with Colfax. It would quite possibly mean putting a target on his back that could follow him through his entire career, all because I'd jumped the gun and assumed that since being around Colfax tempted *me* to use, then clearly Axel was using. I didn't even have hard evidence that Colfax was using (though if he wasn't, then I was the King of England). Plus, I couldn't put this all on Josh. Whatever our past issues, he hadn't signed up for another round of dealing with a cocaine-addicted teammate (or two). And who would even believe me, anyway, especially without actual evidence that any of them were using?

All I could think to do at this point was stick close to Axel and try to redirect him if the need arose. Even if that meant I had to stick close to a man who, I had absolutely no doubt, had some of that sweet white powder on his person.

I am so fucked.

The party stayed fairly low-key tonight, fortunately. We

did, after all, have to be at the airport tomorrow morning. Everyone needed to get as much sleep as we could, so we all just had a few drinks before heading back to our hotel, which was a block or so away.

As we all walked from the bar to the hotel, I glanced back to make sure everyone was accounted for, and something in me froze solid. Colfax was a few paces behind the group. Walking close beside Axel. Speaking low to him.

Oh. Shit.

The only thing missing was the arm around the kid's shoulders. Or maybe they were just friendly teammates and I was projecting. But what if I wasn't?

Panic surged through me. I thought fast, then pulled up my phone and did a quick search. When I found something that would get the job done, I fell back and sidled up beside Axel. Smiling and as casual as could be, I asked, "Hey, did guys you see this?" Then I pushed my screen in front of them.

Axel instantly grinned, either oblivious to or ignoring Colfax's irritated look—not to mention his thousandth sharp sniffle of the night—and all three of us halted.

"Oh, damn," Axel said. "Is this from last game when— hey, Darby! Did you see this video of you falling on your ass the other night?"

A groan came from up ahead. "For fuck's sake. Really?"

"Yeah!" Axel snickered. "They even put music to it! Ha! This is beautiful!"

I chuckled along, relieved that I'd derailed their conversation for the time being. Thank God for hockey media— there was *always* something hilarious freshly posted to YouTube or some other site.

Darby joined us, and after he'd watched the video too, the rest of the walk back to the hotel was filled with chirping about bad falls everyone had taken. Someone even brought up that embarrassing wipeout I'd done last season that had gained our opponent a critical goal. They could make fun of me all they wanted as long as nobody was actively buttering up the new kid to try something. I didn't even know if Colfax was suggesting anything quite yet. Hell, I didn't even know if he was really going to. Maybe he'd just been talking discreetly with him about something he'd seen on the ice. Something the kid could adjust. Everything else was quite likely all in my head.

Again I questioned my own perception. And I definitely questioned the wisdom of doing anything other than distancing myself from Colfax for my own sake.

But his cocaine use—I was as certain of that as if I'd witnessed him snorting a line with my own eyes. There was a Colfax on every team, and I *had* to err on the side of caution to protect my own sobriety, which meant staying the hell away from him. I *had* to put as much distance between us as I could without our teammates or coaching staff catching on.

Except I kept circling back to that plan's one teeny, tiny flaw: Axel.

I needed to stay away from Colfax for my own protection, but what about the rookie?

Fuck. It was absolute torture being around someone who clearly had access to cocaine. If I asked, he'd hook me up. The users always did—they were hardly going to rat themselves out, and they never pressured anyone if they knew what was good for them, but it was *always* more fun to use with someone else. Made it less shameful when it was a shared vice.

Alone with Colfax, a vulnerable rookie—especially one who was desperate for friendship while his buddy was on

LTIR—was more likely to be tempted. Ditto with the struggling addict who was trying to stay clean while trying like hell to cope with the never-ending mental maelstrom that cocaine just *happened* to be *really* good at quieting.

So where the hell was the line between surreptitiously protecting the rookie and tempting myself beyond the point of no return?

CHAPTER 14

JOSH

I tugged at the lapel on my suit jacket as I stepped out of the elevator. I loved this suit—it was a dark gray with silver pinstriping, and it fit like a dream.

Something about wearing a suit always put me into the headspace I needed for a game. Probably because if I was putting on a suit, I was nearly always en route to a game—either boarding the plane or, like now, getting on the bus to head to the arena.

I stepped out of the elevator with Volkov, Colfax, and Tim, one of the assistant coaches. We strode across the lobby toward the side door and our bus waiting beyond it.

Chicago was brisk this time of year, and as soon as I stepped outside, the chill air smacked me in the face and woke me up a little more. It wasn't quite as cold and sharp as I remembered from living here; probably because while I'd spent the better part of two years here after I left Phoenix, I'd lived in Calgary longer, and that place had changed my perception of what cold really was. I wondered how long it would take for Seattle to make Chicago's weather bite like it used to. In fact, I'd decided I already liked that about Seattle—after living in areas with extreme climates for my entire career, I was finally in a mild, temperate place. Such a nice switch from—

"Josh!" The voice stopped me in my tracks so suddenly that Tim almost ran into me.

He muttered what I thought was an apology as if it had been his fault, but I didn't catch it. I was looking around for the source of that voice.

As if I didn't know.

When my gaze landed on my ex-husband, my blood turned colder than a Canadian winter. How the hell had he found me?

But as he came toward me with a huge smile on his face, I remembered. How had I forgotten that he knew this was the hotel the league used for visiting teams? That we'd stayed here together when Calgary had come to town after I'd been traded and Damon hadn't yet moved to Canada to join me?

Of course he remembers. We've fucked here.

And he wants to do it again.

My stomach lurched, especially when I saw the look in his eyes.

"Josh!" he said again, arms wide. "My God, it's good to see you."

Oh, that son of a bitch expected me to smile and give him a big hug? Out here? Seriously?

Yeah. He did. Because he knew I'd been too well media-trained to shove him away or cold-shoulder him. Not with so many eyeballs and lenses around to notice if I made a scene. He knew exactly what he was doing.

I forced a smile and returned his embrace. At least he had the decency not to grab my ass or do something lasciv-ious out here; spouses, too, were media-trained to a certain degree, and he knew all too well that groping me in public after our equally public and messy divorce would earn him some unflattering scrutiny. No, he was just going to draw attention to us being friendly and a little affectionate in public. That way I'd look like a serious asshole if I so much as hinted later that things were still frosty between us.

After we'd performed our ridiculous reunion, I pulled away. I couldn't say anything, though. Not out here. There were too many people milling around on the sidewalk, including my teammates, some starstruck fans, and a handful of hotel employees, so I took Damon by the elbow and led him back inside. Since there were people in here, too, I found the nearest hallway and herded him toward a secluded spot between what looked like a storage room and a door with *Employees Only* on it. No one else was back here, and I didn't see any cameras either. Perfect.

As soon as we were out of everyone's sight, I released his arm and whirled on him. "What the fuck are you doing here?"

I couldn't believe those innocent eyes had worked on me in the past. Looking back now, it was impossible to imagine ever falling for his charm, just like it was impossible to imagine falling for his gaslighting. I had, and I knew I had, but it didn't seem real. Not when I was standing in his crosshairs now and could see, plain as day, that he was full of shit.

"I came to see you." Damon's voice echoed the fake innocence in his eyes. "You didn't return my texts, so I—"

"I did," I snapped. "I told you that I didn't want to see you."

He rolled his eyes. "Josh. Come on." He smiled in that condescending he always did. "We can be adults about this."

I tightened my jaw. I had four inches on Damon, but he could always make me feel two inches tall with just a look, and he was doing it now with that puppy-dog expression.

Like hell was I falling for it this time.

"We *are* being adults," I said through my teeth. "We're being a couple of divorced adults who are going our separate ways. I'm moving on with my life, and so should you."

"Yeah, we're moving on from all our past bullshit." He shrugged so flippantly I wanted to throw something at him. "So why not put it behind us and enjoy a little time together for old time's—"

"For fuck's sake," I hissed. "Stop. Just stop. It's *over*. I don't want to sleep with you. I don't even want to see you. What's it going to take for you to get that through your head?"

He studied me for a long moment, expression hard. Then he shrugged again. "All right, baby. If that's what you want." He reached out and gave my shoulder a squeeze that made my skin crawl under my suit. "Have a good game tonight, Josh."

Then he turned to go, leaving me standing there like an idiot. And that was when I realized why he'd come here.

Yeah, he did want to sleep with me, but he knew—and had known since our last text exchange—that I wasn't interested. If he'd really, truly wanted a shot at getting in my pants, he'd have come last night. It wasn't exactly a state secret when teams arrived, and fans were always sharing info on social media about if we were at our hotel or if players were at a particular bar. Damon knew well how to find me when there was a whole night ahead of us.

But no, he'd come *today*. Literally minutes before I boarded the bus to head to the arena for tonight's game. Tonight's game, which *I* was starting.

He knew sex wasn't going to happen, so he went for the next best thing—fucking with my mind just before I played hockey. If I had to guess, he was on his way to the arena right now, if not to a sports bar, to watch me absolutely blow it while he quietly gloated about still knowing how to get under my skin.

Fuck him. Fuck him! God, what had I ever seen in him?

With fury boiling in my veins, I headed out of the hallway to go get on the bus. I was still shaking. Badly. Seriously, fuck him. Fuck him for showing up. For getting under my skin. For still being under my skin after all this time. For knowing exactly how to screw with my head and hit me in the places it hurt the most.

Would Coach let me suit up as a defenseman instead of a goalie tonight? Because I suddenly felt the need to check someone into the boards. Or maybe drop gloves and fight.

No, I'd be fine. By the time I was on the ice for warm-ups, I'd be fine. I had to be. I refused to give Damon the satisfaction of seeing me lose my mind and screw my team.

At least my teammates had pretty much cleared out of the lobby. A few were in the small store, likely buying some munchies or water before getting on the bus. Otherwise, all but one had vanished outside and onto the bus, which would be leaving in, according to my phone, fifteen minutes.

The one teammate who remained in the lobby?

Sol.

Sol, who was looking right at me. As if he'd been waiting for me.

My hackles went up. I was so not in the mood to face him of all people. Talking to him was a step up from talking to Damon, but that was a *low* bar.

But much like Damon had outside, Sol approached, and

there was nowhere to go. No pretending I didn't notice him or telling him I wasn't interested.

Sol stopped a couple of feet from me. "Hey." His blue eyes were full of obvious concern. Then he glanced in the direction that Damon must've gone, and he asked, "You all right?"

"What the fuck do you care?" almost rolled off my tongue. But again...out in the open. Too many ears. Too many cameras. And I got the feeling that unlike Damon, Sol at least seemed to be genuinely concerned about me, rather than angling for something he wanted.

So I just said, "I'm good."

The pinch of his brow suggested he didn't buy it.

"We should get on the bus." I started past him, but he stepped in front of me.

"Wait," he said, voice gentle and so quiet it wouldn't carry far at all.

I halted, gritting my teeth.

"Before we go," he said, searching my eyes, "Do you want me to start in goal tonight?"

Fresh rage cracked through the hurt and frustration. Really? *Really?* He was going to pick *now* of all times to try to nudge me out of the way to—

"Josh." He inclined his head and held my gaze, expression completely serious. "I'm not doing this for my benefit."

I blinked. "You...you started in Seattle." That had been the night before last, so this wouldn't be a back-to-back, but still.

"Uh-huh, I did," he acknowledged. "And I know you want to be the starter as much as I do."

Damn. He'd always been able to read my mind, and apparently he still could.

"I'll be fine," I insisted.

His eyebrow arched, the unspoken skepticism coming across so loudly it made my ears ring.

Anger flared in my chest. Really? Seriously? I'd never known him to be this much of an opportunist, but apparently—

"Josh." He put up his hands. "This has nothing to do with our bullshit, or with me trying to get the starter position."

I set my jaw but didn't say anything, instead waiting for him to elaborate.

He slid his hands into his pockets and shifted his weight the way he often did when he was on edge. "Remember your rookie season, when I was on a hot streak, but Coach put you in because I'd gotten some bad news about my grandfather?"

Okay, I hadn't anticipated the conversation taking *this* turn. Sol had seemed all right that night, and in fact he'd been pretty pissed that Coach put me in. Later, though, he'd admitted that he was worried sick about his grandfather, and given that he struggled to concentrate on a good day, he'd been in no shape to be in the net.

"Yeah," I said quietly. "I remember."

"Right. Well. Tonight's kind of the same thing. We both know that if I'd played that night, I'd have broken my streak and probably taken a few games to recover. But instead, I took the night off, and by the time I played again, I had my head together." He held my gaze, and a cautious smile took form. "So consider this me returning the favor."

Oh. Huh.

He sighed, glancing around as if to make sure we really were alone. Then he met my eyes again. "Yes, I want that starter spot. We both do. But that's not why I'm offering tonight." He put up a hand again as if he heard the counter argument I hadn't even spoken yet. "If I wanted to sabotage you, I'd let you play tonight."

I straightened. That...was not what I expected. "What?"

"Come on. There's no way your head is in the game. No one's head would be in the game after"—he motioned in the direction Damon had gone—"*that*. So if I really wanted to screw you over and snag the starter position, I'd just let you go out there tonight and blow it. Because we both know that's exactly what'll happen."

In that instant, my emotions tried to drag me in polar opposite directions. Anger, because I was sure he really was being an opportunist, and also because he clearly thought I couldn't keep my head together after a sixty-second encounter with my asshole ex-husband.

And a mix of hurt, shame, and defeat, because he was absolutely right.

And on top of that came guilt, because I'd been such an asshole to him since we both came to Seattle.

Do you have any idea how hard you're making it to hate you?

I couldn't hold his gaze, but I did nod. "Yeah. If you can... Yeah. Thanks."

"All right." He squeezed my arm, which didn't make my skin crawl like the same gesture from Damon had. "I'll talk to Kayla and Coach."

Mute, I nodded again.

"Come on." He brightened a little. "Let's go get on the bus before someone sends a search party."

I managed a quiet laugh, though my heart wasn't in it. We crossed the lobby and joined everyone aboard the bus. Since I wasn't at all in the mood for conversation, I put in some earbuds and listened to music while the bus pulled away from our hotel. A lot of guys did that while they gathered their focus before a game, and I sometimes did it too, so no one thought anything of it.

I didn't hear my music at all, though. Instead, I just stared out the window at the familiar city that had once been, however briefly, my home.

At one point, I glanced up ahead and saw Sol talking to Coach and Kayla. Kayla glanced my way, concern etched across her face. She'd probably want to talk to me once we were at the arena. That would be fun. I didn't want to talk about this with anyone ever again. Not Sol. Not Damon. No one. But she deserved an explanation, and she'd probably want to hear it from me to confirm that Sol was taking over for me tonight, especially since she was aware of the tension between us.

I wondered if it crossed her mind that he might be exploiting this opportunity to look good. I kept trying to tell myself that was what it was because I didn't want to admit what I knew damn well was the truth: that Sol cared about me. Whether he saw me as a teammate, a friend, or an ex-boyfriend he didn't hate as much as he let on, he cared.

"If I wanted to sabotage you," he'd said, *"I'd let you play tonight."*

I was seriously raw from that encounter with my ex-husband. And I suddenly caught myself missing Sol more than I should, which didn't make sense. It wasn't like I wanted him back just because he was taking one for the team, so to speak. But him stepping up right now definitely melted some of the ice between us. Because he was taking the pressure off me tonight? Because he understood my head wasn't in the game, and he was giving me a chance to pull it together instead of letting me fall on my face in front of our team and coaches?

I closed my eyes and pressed back against the seat.

Whatever his motives, he definitely knew me, and he knew I would be a mess tonight. Even if this did earn him some points from the coaches, not to mention improve his goalie stats, it would prevent me from going out there and showing the world how fucked up I was right now. Sol knew, and Damon knew, but no one else would know. At the very least, they wouldn't get to watch it affect my performance.

I had to be grateful to Sol for that, no matter how much I stubbornly wanted to be anything but. I was still clinging to my anger and resentment over our past, but I had to admit, that was getting harder and harder as time went on. Sol was clearly putting it behind him, at least enough to prioritize our team over our bullshit.

It was probably long past time for me to do the same.

"To the netminders!" Leclerc called out several nights later, raising his beer.

That prompted a cheer from all our teammates who were crammed into this hotel bar with us. Leclerc bumped my shoulder and clinked his beer bottle against my Coke glass. At another table, several guys fist-bumped Sol or clapped his arm.

I smiled and raised my glass as some heat bloomed in my cheeks. This was a nice switch, having a team who was thrilled with my performance. I didn't even mind that I was sharing that spotlight with Sol. Honestly, he'd earned it.

A week after Sol stepped up for me in Chicago—earning us a four-three win after a spectacular shootout—we were on the road again. Tonight and last night, we'd played back-to-back games in Anaheim and Los Angeles, and we'd won both. Decisively. Between us, Sol and I had allowed three goals. He'd blocked thirty-nine of forty shots against Anaheim last night. Tonight, I'd let in a pair in Los Angeles, but that was out of forty-three shots on goal, *and* our teammates had scored six times, so I was hardly going to lose sleep over it. Plus that second goal had been after a couple of bullshit penalty calls had given L.A. a five-on-three power play. Our penalty kill unit had put up a good fight, but they were down a key player against the third-best power play in the league. Definitely not losing sleep over that goal.

The team was happy, too, especially since they'd been a mess before we'd arrived, and they'd fully expected Sol and me to be disasters, too. They weren't shy about telling us that, either.

"Not gonna lie, Obie." Leclerc gestured at me with his bottle. "When they signed you and Sol, I thought we were fucked. But..." He whistled, shaking his head. "You guys are proving *everyone* wrong."

I laughed and shrugged. "Motivated, I guess."

"Well, whatever's motivating you," Meyer said, "keep it going. Because you're both killing it."

I chuckled, hoping it didn't sound as halfhearted as it felt. I appreciated the acknowledgment, and I was pleased with my performance too. I just didn't like brushing up against the reason I was playing as well I was right now. Or why I suspected Sol was playing so well.

I mean, how was I supposed to tell my teammates I was playing my heart out because I didn't want to be my ex-boyfriend's backup goalie?

They didn't know Sol was my ex, for one thing. Everyone knew we were both openly gay, but we'd kept our relationship a secret because the hockey world had been very different back then. Even now I wasn't quite sure how people would react to a couple of teammates dating.

And that was a moot point where we were concerned because I didn't need anyone knowing about our relationship, its horrible ending, or the weirdness between us now.

I surreptitiously watched Sol from across the room. He was oblivious to me, engaged in an animated conversation with Darby, Colfax, and Volkov. Life of the party, just like always.

A rush of nostalgia had me smiling sadly into my drink. So many nights of sitting back and laughing while Sol told wild stories or bantered with our teammates until we were all choking on our drinks and nearly falling out of our chairs. Those were some good times.

Good times that ended in the worst times.

I sighed and took a drink. I was so tired of this emotional roller coaster. I swore the way I felt about him and our past changed from minute to minute, almost giving me whiplash. Sometimes I resented him. Sometimes I wanted him. Then I'd be on the verge of breaking down because of how bad it hurt to be this close to him. A second later, because it hurt to be this far away from him. I never wanted to see him again. I missed him. I hated him. I loved him.

Sometimes, just the sight of him filled me with so much anger, it was a genuine miracle I could contain it. Other times, the slightest glimpse of him made my throat tighten with the threat of tears. There was very little in between, and there was no rhyme or reason to where the emotional roulette wheel would stop in a given moment.

Tonight, it was that second extreme—I fucking *hurt*. I missed him. Us. What we'd had. What we'd been. Every fucking thing that had existed in that perfect world of ours before the snow came. I'd been this raw ever since my encounter with Damon. Something about facing off with him and then having Sol come to my rescue had pulled our dynamic into sharp focus. It had reminded me that Sol was, and always had been, a good man.

We'd been good together. The cocaine was the problem. The addiction. Our relationship hadn't been flawless—no relationship was—but it had been a good one, and as I sat here now, I had to wonder what that relationship would look like in the rearview mirror had cocaine and addiction never entered the equation. Would we have found some other reason to split up? Most relationships ended eventually, so...probably.

And we'd been kids. Inexperienced with love, life, and everything that wasn't hockey. Maybe we would've found a way to mess things up just by being young and immature. But apart from lack of maturity, I couldn't put my finger on anything that would've derailed us back then had the drugs not been an issue.

We had such a good thing before the cocaine.

And tonight, I realized how much it hurt that I would never know what we could've been had Sol stayed sober.

Exhaling, I tore my gaze away from him and took a long drink, letting the cold and the carbonation distract me. It worked, but only for a minute or two.

Damn it. I missed when things were simple with him and the only worry we'd had in the world was flying under the radar of our teammates and coaches. That all seemed so far away now, it didn't even feel real. Except it had been real, and more and more, I had to wonder if my feelings for him had not, in fact, died beneath that mountain of resentment I'd piled on top of them.

Pressing my elbow into the table, I pushed my hand through my hair. Was this how Sol's mind was all the time?

Ping-ponging between thoughts the way mine was bouncing between emotions? Christ. No wonder he'd needed a chemical to quiet it down. Nights like tonight, I was sorely tempted to order something strong or even illegal just to numb everything a little.

I wonder how much I'd be drinking these days if I'd never watched Sol fall apart.

I froze with my soda halfway to my lips. Damn. That was a thought, wasn't it? I'd never been a binge drinker or anything, but I'd definitely been a heavier drinker back then. These days, I couldn't remember the last time I'd been drunk or even lightly buzzed, only that it had happened sometime before that day I visited Sol in rehab. I'd very nearly drunk myself stupid that night, but I'd been too sick with worry and heartache, and I'd also found myself terrified that the alcohol would become for me what cocaine had become for Sol. Instead, I'd just knuckled through that hellish night, stone-cold sober and feeling like shit. To this day, I rarely had more than a single drink in a night.

"Dude, it's the Cup!" Hunts, one of my long-retired former teammates, had shoved a bottle of champagne into my hand. *"Get fucked up!"*

I'd laughed, and I'd taken a swig. I'd also drunk a little from the Cup because it was tradition. But even that night—the night we'd won the Cup after a dramatic comeback from a horrible start to our season—I hadn't let myself drink too much. Couldn't then. Couldn't now. All because of...

I found Sol in the crowd again and let the contradictory emotions roll through me. They were probably going to do that for a while. Maybe for as long as we were teammates. Might as well get used to it.

And on that note, I was done celebrating with the team.

Under the pretense of being tired from tonight's game—

not something anyone ever questioned from a goalie—I paid my portion of the check and bowed out.

My ears rang as I stepped out into the mostly quiet hotel lobby. Hands stuffed in the pockets of my suit, I rolled my tired shoulders and strode toward the alcove where the elevators were located. There was no one else here. Fine by me.

Except that didn't last.

The elevators in this hotel took their sweet time, and wasn't it just my luck that before one had arrived at the lobby, someone joined me to wait.

I glanced up without thinking about it. Somehow...I knew. Even before I met those familiar blue eyes, I knew. I'd felt it.

"Hey." Sol acknowledged me with a subtle nod.

I responded in kind. Both the nod and the non-committal, "Hey."

We stood in uncomfortable silence, because we had no idea how to do anything else these days. It was weirdly similar and wildly different from all those times we'd waited for elevators after closing down the bar together in our past life. When I'd been a nervous, twitchy mess, wishing I could put my hands on him—early on, unsure if he'd want me to, and later, all too aware that he wanted to do the same but couldn't until we were behind closed doors. Tonight, there *definitely* wouldn't be one of those long, secret kisses before we left for our separate rooms.

The elevator opened, and I had a flash of irrational optimism that maybe he'd go down. To the parking garage? To the basement? To hell?

Naturally, though, he joined me in the car, and as the doors slid closed, he pushed the button for the sixteenth floor. "Which floor?"

I gestured at the glowing number. "Same."

Another nod. More silence.

The elevator began its slow ascent, and we both stared straight forward, a good three feet of space between our shoulders.

I was honestly surprised he was calling it a night already. I wasn't surprised, though, to see that he was anything but still—turning his keycard between his fingers, rocking on his feet just enough to make his dress shoes creak. He definitely wasn't high, that much was clear.

Does this mean you're really staying sober?

Maybe. But I didn't have the balls to ask. I didn't want to fight with him again. Anger could carry me through a lot, but when I was this brittle and raw over him, I was as likely to wind up in tears. Neither of us needed that tonight.

The elevator stopped at our floor, and we both stepped out. His room was apparently to the left, and mine was to the right, so we went our separate ways without a word.

Or, well, it started out that way.

"Josh."

I turned around, eyebrows up and trying to seem casual and not like my heart had just jumped into my throat. "Yeah?"

He moistened his lips. "Tonight—that was a great game. You, um...you looked really good out there."

The comment caught me off guard. Sol wasn't one to dispense bullshit, and there was no sarcastic edge. Nothing to indicate this might be a backhanded remark, or that there was a "maybe try doing that *every* night?" waiting to drop.

"Oh. Uh." I cleared my throat. "Thanks. And last night —you were great. The game, I mean. The..." I squeezed my eyes shut as heat rushed into my cheeks. Way to shove my foot in my mouth and give him the perfect opportunity to tell me he knew I meant the game. There would never again be any other context for me to say he'd been great last night.

To my surprise, he didn't grab the accidental double entendre and run with it. Instead, he murmured, "Thanks. I'll, uh... See you at breakfast?"

I met his gaze, and I found sincerity in those beautiful eyes. No sarcasm. No subtext.

Do you have any idea how much I miss you?

I quickly shut down that line of thinking, and I nodded. "Yeah. See you at breakfast."

Then I hightailed it to my room before either of us could make the moment any more awkward. Thank God, my roommate was still in the bar, and he hadn't looked like he was thinking about wrapping it up any time soon, so I probably had a little while to pull myself together.

I got as far as undoing my tie before I sank onto the bed, leaned forward, and rubbed the back of my neck with both hands. I was a mess, and I couldn't even explain how or why. Just that my world had been off-kilter ever since Sol had walked back into it, and nothing I felt or thought made sense anymore.

I briefly considered calling Amber. We'd both been so busy, moving in so many different directions, we hadn't been able to connect beyond a few texts and emails since the summer. I hadn't even had a chance to tell her about Sol and me being on the same team, never mind the absolute hurricane of confusion my mind had been since training camp. I could've used her advice right about now, though I wasn't sure what she could tell me that I didn't already know. I could almost hear her voice in my head:

"You dumbass. Have you forgotten everything he put you through? Jesus, the only thing you should be asking right now is whether you should put some bail money aside for when

you inevitably whack him over the head with your stick. Yes, by the way. You should."

I tried to laugh, but I didn't have the energy. I was just too fucking drained and confused.

On top of everything, I didn't want to read too much into that awkward encounter Sol and I had in the hallway, but I knew him too well—knew *us* too well—to think it was just stilted small talk between exes who'd dated a lifetime ago.

Sol was reaching out and trying to smooth things over. I couldn't begin to guess if he just wanted us to coexist as teammates, or if he wanted us to be friends, or...

No. He didn't want to go back to that. And even if he did, we couldn't. When we were good together, we were amazing. We'd had the kind of relationship I'd never been able to find again. Not even in the best days with my ex-husband. The kind of intense, deep devotion I'd been looking for ever since I'd lost Sol.

If I could have that back without the shitshow at the end, I'd jump at the chance. No hesitation.

The problem was, that shitshow at the end had happened. There were two sides to the coin of Sol and me. The bright, shiny side full of love and bliss couldn't be separated from the darker, tarnished side, and I just couldn't sign up for that. Not again.

So how do I shut off all these feelings for him before they drive me insane?

It occurred to me then that Sol had never had any issues with casual sex. Not like I had. I didn't have some moral objection to it—just wasn't my cup of tea. Sol, though? He'd had plenty of hookups both at home and on the road before we'd gotten together. I'd actually thought it was kind of hot back then; how many nights had I spent, rock-hard in a hotel room imagining what Sol was doing in some other bed?

He was single now. Had been for a long time, as far as I knew. And he was a rich, hot athlete with a gorgeous smile and a mind-blowing kiss. I had no reason to believe he didn't still have his pick of men to sleep with, or that he wasn't enjoying the hell out of that whenever he had the opportunity.

I didn't know if I could handle that now. He wasn't mine—he'd never been a possession or something I owned—but he was someone who still had a fistful of my emotions without even knowing it. What was I going to feel the first time I saw him shuffling into a team breakfast with dark circles under his eyes and a satisfied grin on his lips? Or walking through our apartment parking garage with his arm around another man's shoulders?

Squeezing my eyes shut, I groaned into the silence of the empty room. I had to get the fuck over whatever the hell it was I felt for him. He was a teammate, and if tonight was any indication, a teammate who wanted things to at least be cordial between us. I needed that, too.

But we weren't going to get there as long as just laying eyes on him was enough to make my heart react like a sold-out crowd roaring their approval of a hard-won goal or booing furiously over a piss-poor penalty call. I had to get a grip, unfuck myself, shelve all these stupid feelings and regrets, and learn to coexist with him as a teammate. *Maybe* eventually as a friend. Nothing more.

Even if I had no idea how I was going to pull that off.

CHAPTER 15

SOL

Another night, another win.

I grinned all the way back to the locker room, riding the absolute elation of adding another game to my eight-game point streak. We hadn't won every game I'd started recently, but our only two losses with me in the net had been overtime, so...still points. Best streak I'd had since my career had started falling apart. I probably wouldn't break my all-time record of thirteen—I'd only come near that three other times—but the longest streak I'd had in my previous two seasons had been three. Eight and counting? I'd fucking take it.

The mood in the dressing room was just as celebratory. Everyone was happy, thrilled we were doing better than the analysts had predicted for Seattle *or* its goalies.

Almost everyone was happy.

On the other side of the room, Axel shoved his skates into his locker and tossed his chest protector on top of them. He was pissed tonight, and I didn't think it was just because of that goal he'd missed. The one near the end of the third period that would've given us the win instead of sending us into overtime. Sure, we all would've liked that shot to have found the back of the net, but when all was said and done, we'd still won. Our opponents had come away with a point, too, but they weren't even in our conference, never mind our division, so it wasn't a crucial game. Plus our place in the standings was solid enough already that another team grabbing a point wasn't going to hurt us. We were fine.

Still, his frustration was visible from space. He'd been fine this afternoon and even during warm-ups, but then his mood had taken a dive sometime in the first period. His concentration was off. He was clearly spoiling for a fight by the time the puck dropped for the second period, and he almost got one. Fortunately, Darby had intervened, using a celebratory bear hug to congratulate Axel on his assist, which had diverted the kid from dropping gloves with a scrappy defenseman who'd been on his last nerve. Darby's efforts worked, but Axel was still pissed for the rest of the game.

Then he'd missed that shot. He'd made it halfway to the locker room before he'd utterly demolished his stick on the corner of a wall. Hopefully no one had caught that on camera, but these days, that was unlikely.

"Jesus Christ," Hamilton muttered as he stripped off his gear in the stall next to mine. "What is up that rookie's ass tonight?"

"Fuck if I know," Leclerc muttered as he pulled off his chest protector. "But he'd better get it together." Our captain wasn't joking—he had no patience for people bringing their personal issues onto the ice. Of course it happened. Hockey required a lot of emotion, and if your emotions weren't in a good place when you hit the ice, well...shit happened. But professionals had to know when to rein it in, and Leclerc didn't put up with teammates who couldn't control their tempers. Especially after a win, for fuck's sake—if Axel was this volatile after we'd won, what would happen when we got absolutely stomped? Because it was bound to happen at least once in a season.

Something told me if Leclerc tried to talk to Axel about it tonight, though, it wouldn't end well.

Because I had a feeling I knew *exactly* what had our rookie on edge.

Time to do some damage control.

I thought quickly, and I managed to come up with a reason to pull the kid aside before he went off to the showers and before the media came in. We were both sweaty and disgusting, but I couldn't risk letting Leclerc, Coach, or—worse—a reporter beating me to the punch.

"Hey, Eggs." I gestured for him to follow me out into the hall.

He shot me a sour look, and I could almost feel the *"What the fuck do you want?"* on the tip of his tongue. He glanced around, though, and seemed to remember where he was. Jaw working, he followed me out.

As soon as we were alone, he growled, "What?"

"I won't keep you long." I kept my voice low. "But listen..." I glanced around, then lowered my voice a little more. "Can you do me a favor, and stick close to me at the bar when we get back to the hotel?"

Surprise lifted his eyebrows, but then defensiveness darkened his expression. "Why? You think I need a fucking babysitter or—"

"No! No, it's nothing like..." I sighed, shifting my weight. "If anyone does, it's me."

Axel blinked. "Huh?"

I swept my tongue across my lips. "Come on. Everyone knows about my history."

He avoided my eyes, some more color blooming in his

still-flushed cheeks. He also sniffled. I wondered if he knew that I noticed.

"Some nights are hard," I admitted. "I really want to, but..."

Axel looked at me through his lashes. "So...what? You just want me to hang around you? Make sure you don't...uh..."

"That's all." I shrugged as casually as I could. "You don't have to do anything or say anything. Just...hang out. Stick with me until everyone calls it a night."

The kid swallowed. Sniffed again. "But...why?"

I avoided his eyes this time, maybe laying it on a little thick how uncomfortable I was and how embarrassed I was. It *was* uncomfortable and it *was* embarrassing when cravings actually hit me, but tonight—this was an act. And somehow, it felt even more critical to sell it than all those times I'd tried to convince everyone I was sober and had never touched an illicit substance in my life. I needed Axel to believe I was craving blow so bad tonight that it warranted having someone close by just to keep me from indulging. Good thing I had experience with that playing out for real.

"Sometimes, just having someone there is enough to keep me from going out looking," I told him honestly. "Keeps me accountable, I guess. If there's someone sitting there who will ask where I'm going and call me out when I try to lie, I'm a lot less likely to, you know, go looking."

Axel hugged himself as he watched me. "I thought you didn't use it anymore."

"I don't." My voice came out as barely a whisper. "I haven't in..." I hesitated, not sure how far to tip my hand. "It's been a long time. But it's hard. It's really fucking hard."

He was silent for a moment. "Some of the guys say they

won't take pain meds. For anything. Is this…is this the same kind of thing?"

I nodded. "I won't take anything no matter how much pain I'm in."

"Really?" Axel furrowed his brow. "But you weren't hooked on those, were you? I thought it was just meth."

"Cocaine," I whispered.

He jumped. Subtly, but noticeably. "Oh. It… That's what it was?"

I nodded. "Mmhmm. And it was absolute hell getting off it. Staying off is…" I rolled my shoulders and pushed out a breath, not even having to fake how absolutely drained I was just thinking about it. "It's fucking hard. Every damn day. I don't dare take chances with getting hooked on anything else." Just the thought of a two-pronged addiction made me want to curl up on the floor and sob. Holy fuck. I'd met some heroin and opioid addicts in rehab who avoided painkillers and anesthetics because they were too close to their drugs of choice. Kind of like how I would've avoided things like Adderall even if the league allowed them. For me, the avoidance of painkillers was fear of a secondary addiction. God, that would destroy me. Fuck.

Axel fidgeted, and he swallowed. "It's…really that hard? Getting off cocaine?"

I met his gaze, and I was glad to see some real fear there. I was getting to him, just the way I'd hoped, and I prayed like hell it stuck. That he wasn't so far down this rabbit hole that he couldn't stop without help. "It's incredibly hard. There's help. Good help. I'm grateful like you wouldn't believe for the staff and my teammates, not to mention the rehab therapists. It's not impossible, you know? But it's so damn hard, and it gets a million times harder if I actually give in." I didn't have to fake the shame as I quietly added, "That's why I'm asking for help."

His Adam's apple bobbed. He sniffed again, then looked away, a renewed blush darkening his fair skin, as if he'd realized I could probably see the signs in him. Cautiously meeting my gaze again, he asked, "Why me?"

"Because we hang out after games," I said with a shrug. "You don't drink as heavily as the other guys. I can trust you to pay attention because you're sober."

I felt a little guilty for his wince, but only a little.

He ran a hand through his sweaty red hair, then met my gaze again. "Okay. Sure. Yeah. Just, uh... Let me get changed when we get back to the hotel, and I'll meet you in the bar."

I smiled. "Okay. Perfect." Then I gestured at the locker room. "Speaking of changing, we should probably..." I wrinkled my nose as I tugged at my base layer.

That got a laugh out of him. "Yeah. Seriously. I smell like an equipment bag."

"Eh, comes with the territory." I motioned for him to go ahead. "Let's go get cleaned up."

He nodded and headed back in to where our teammates had mostly finished stripping down. Leclerc and Coach eyed us, and I had a feeling they'd both been ready to tear into Axel for his attitude tonight. Even from across the room, though, I could see them registering that he was more subdued now. Coach pursed his lips, then turned away to look at something on his phone. Leclerc met my gaze and gave me a subtle nod.

As I continued cleaning up after the game, I stole a few glances at my young teammate. He was definitely rattled now. The anger from earlier was a distant memory, and he avoided everyone's eyes as he shakily undressed.

Hopefully I had shaken him up. Given him a peek into what that drug could do to someone.

Is this the future you want, kid? Needing a babysitter just to keep yourself from hunting down an eightball?

Because if you keep snorting that shit, it gets a hell of a lot worse than this.

CHAPTER 16

JOSH

I froze, still on my knees in the crease. The puck was somewhere on or under me. I'd felt it hit me. and I was pretty sure I still had it, but I couldn't see it or feel it now. I just stayed still, because if I slid back, I could carry it right over the line and score an own goal. So I didn't move, kneeling on the ice and fending off sticks and skates and bodies, hoping the puck really was wedged in or under a pad and safely out of the goal.

The ref finally blew the play dead, thank God.

Everyone backed off, and I released my breath. They'd all shoved me back several inches into the net, and there were shouts from the crowd and players alike that "It went in! It went in!"

Had it? Oh fuck.

The light hadn't gone on, but the Detroit players were going to their bench for fist bumps. The scoreboard hadn't changed.

So was it...

Had it...

Slowly and carefully, I stood, and as I straightened up, I felt something move near my left knee. A second later, the puck landed on the ice by my skate. It *had* been in my pads. Question was...had it gone over the line while it was in my pads?

Please, please, tell me it didn't go over the line.

The crowd was roaring, and several Detroit players were shouting at the refs that the puck had crossed the line. My teammates were shouting that it absolutely had not.

Finally, the officials announced that the play would be reviewed, which I expected. They retreated to the penalty box to watch the video, and the footage was put up on the big screen for everyone to see.

Above us, in ultra-slow motion, the puck sailed into the crease, just missing my glove before it wedged into my left pad. In the flurry of activity, everyone had indeed shoved me backward, but only my right knee had crossed the line. I'd ended up twisted slightly, and by the skin of my teeth, kept my left knee—and the puck—out of the goal.

I breathed a sigh of relief. They hadn't announced the call yet, but there was no way they could fuck this one up, and thank God it would be no goal. We didn't need an own goal when the score was tied with eight minutes to go in the third period. If they were going to score on us and win this one, they were going to fucking *earn* it, damn it.

Eventually, the linesman took off his headset and skated out to center ice. "After video review," his voice echoed through the arena, "the puck did not cross the goal line." The mix of thunderous boos and raucous cheers from the crowd drowned out the rest of his voice, but the motion of his arms—similar to a baseball umpire declaring someone safe—conveyed the message: no goal.

"Nice one, Obie." Volkov tapped my pads with his stick. "That could've been ugly!"

I chuckled. "Well, keep it away from my net, and we won't have any ugly, yeah?"

He just laughed and skated away.

The puck dropped again, and my team broke away, barreling toward the offensive zone. Just past Detroit's blue line, though, someone snatched the puck away, and suddenly the action was coming toward me again. They'd caught our defense off-guard, too—now it was a three-on-one rush, which was never good. Fuck.

I was poised and ready, though, focus trained on the skater's eyes and movements, not to mention the puck as it whipped left, right, left again. Every muscle in my body twitched with anticipation of the save I was inevitably going to have to make—just had to figure out if I needed to go left, right, up, or down.

One of our defensemen caught up enough to keep the shooter from making the shot, and they both came around the back of the net. Suddenly everyone was in motion in every direction in our defensive zone. The puck zipped back and forth again as my guys tried to take it away. Players from both teams formed a screen in front of me— Detroit trying to block my view, Seattle trying to block any attackers' shots. I still managed to keep an eye on the puck, though.

The forward passed to my left. He was looking right at me, but he wasn't as good at faking as he thought he was, and his body language gave him away—instead of shooting, he did a no-look pass to the right, and I was ready for the one-timer that came my way.

Or, well, I would've been if a defenseman hadn't

toppled into me, knocking me on my back and sending both of us well out of the crease.

The red light came on before the whistle blew.

Immediately, the whole arena was in chaos again. The crowd booed with fury. Colfax helped me to my feet while Johnson had to be held back from beating the shit out of that defenseman. Leclerc was having some words with one of the linesmen, gesturing furiously at me, the scoreboard, me again. Coach Maines was having a similarly heated exchange with one of the other officials.

From the way the officials were shaking their heads, they didn't think it was goalie interference. Bullshit it wasn't. Fucker didn't just hit me *in* the crease, he knocked me *out* of the crease. If that wasn't goalie interference, then I didn't know what the fuck it was.

Finally, a ref announced that Coach Maines was challenging the goal for goalie interference. Good. I didn't like that he'd had to make that call—that the refs hadn't reviewed the goal on their own—but I was confident that once they actually reviewed the film, there was no way they'd miss it. That, and Maines didn't challenge goals unless he was absolutely sure he'd win; as much faith as he had in our penalty kill, no coach in his right mind *wanted* his team to wind up shorthanded.

The crowd was already super pissed after the last non-goal, and they wouldn't be happy if this one was waved off, too. It would be, though. It had to be.

Except I didn't like how long it was taking the officials to review the goal. From both experiencing it and from watching the replay over and over on the big screen, I couldn't begin to imagine how anyone could look at that and not see goalie interference. How many times did they have to rewatch it to be sure? Or did they just get a kick out of seeing that defenseman send me sliding across the ice like an upended turtle?

A ref skated to the red line, and everyone went quiet.

"After reviewing the play," he began, same as a few minutes earlier, "the call on the ice is confirmed. There is no goaltender interference—we have a good goal. Seattle, minor penalty, delay of game."

The cheers were *deafening*. Coach Maines flailed his arms, and even from here, I could read the words *"Are you fucking kidding me?"* coming out of his mouth.

The worst part about a failed coach's challenge like that —especially one that was such brazen horseshit—wasn't the resulting penalty. It was the simultaneous blow to our morale and uptick in the other team's. When I couldn't stop that wraparound from sneaking the puck in past my right skate, scoring them a power play goal and gaining them the lead, the polarization of team morale worsened.

My teammates fought like hell to claim a lead or at least tie things up so we could go into overtime. Unfortunately, we were collectively no match for Detroit tonight. They had both the boost of morale and the crowd on their side. We managed to score again, making it a one-goal game, but that didn't last. When I was pulled in the final two minutes so we could have an extra attacker, Detroit took full advantage and scored on our empty net. Heart heavy with defeat, I went back out to the goal to at least stop the bleeding.

In the end, despite our best efforts, they beat us six-four.

It happened. I knew it happened. It was impossible to win every game in a season, and it was rare for a team's winning streak to extend beyond seven or eight games. And, I reminded myself over and over, we were more than secure in the standings. Way higher and more solid than anyone had predicted over the summer. We were fine and so was I.

But it still sucked.

"Don't beat yourself up." Leclerc smacked my pads as I skated toward the chute. "This wasn't on you."

I smiled as best I could. It wasn't on me, and I knew it, but in a way, losses were always on the netminder to some degree. Every fuck-up from my own team could be negated if I didn't let the other team score. I was the last line of defense against everything from penalty kills to odd man rushes to unlucky bounces. Even the empty net goals felt like failures on my part—if I did more during the first fifty-eight minutes of the game, Coach wouldn't have to pull me for the last two so we could make a desperation play to tie things up.

It all came down to the man in the net, and tonight, like so many nights, that man was me.

So every loss was heavy on my shoulders. I'd almost become numb to it over the past couple of seasons because I was such an absolute mess in the crease, but this year, I was killing it. Every time we lost while I was between the pipes, it hit hard in tender places that were still convinced my career was hanging by a fraying thread.

As I stepped off the ice, I was startled to see one of my teammates waiting for me.

Sol was wearing his gear except for his mask. Instead, he had on a backwards Seattle Sasquatches baseball cap. Seeing him there wasn't so much a surprise. It was the lack of smugness or snark on his face. In his beautiful blue eyes, I found nothing but sympathy and kindness.

"Good game." Sol's pat barely registered through my thick pads. "They definitely can't pin this one on you."

Though Leclerc had said the same thing, the words hit differently from Sol.

"I..." I swallowed as I started down the tunnel with him

on my heels, memories of rookie pep talks echoing in my ears. How many times had Sol talked me out of my own head and reminded me I was doing just fine? And he was still doing it now? Over my shoulder, I murmured, "Thanks."

"I'm serious." His footsteps stopped behind me, so I halted too, and I faced him. His expression was still gentle and understanding. "You've been killing it out there. And you blocked thirty-nine shots tonight."

"Those weren't the problem," I muttered. "It was the six I let in."

"Five," he corrected.

I shrugged under my pads. I didn't need to explain to him how much those empty net goals weighed almost as much as the rest, or why.

"It wasn't on you," Sol insisted. "That one goal absolutely should've been goaltender interference. They shouldn't have had a power play, and..." He tsked and shook his head. "Just...it wasn't on you, okay? They had four extra men on the ice wearing black-striped shirts."

I managed a laugh at that. "How come those guys never play for us?"

"I know, right?" Sol rolled his eyes. Then he motioned for us to keep walking. "Come on. Grab a shower and get some food. The next game will be better."

"Because you'll be in the net?"

He gave my shoulder pad a smack. "Shut up. You know what I meant."

I laughed as we continued into the locker room. Yeah, I knew what he meant. I appreciated it, too. Especially with as weird as everything had been with us lately, I appreciated him reaching out like this instead of letting me spend the whole night blaming myself.

Maybe that meant everything past and present was water under the bridge. Or that it was on its way to being water under the bridge.

That, or Sol was just trying to pretend it was so we could coexist.

Whatever it was, I'd take it, especially on a night like this.

CHAPTER 17

SOL

Oh my God, I want a line so fucking bad.

I paced around my half-unpacked apartment, trying to expend some energy and pull my thoughts into order and just *breathe*. My head was too scattered to concentrate on anything. I had more energy than I knew what to do with, but just the thought of tackling some of the boxes still piled all over my apartment almost paralyzed me. I couldn't stop moving, but I also couldn't *do* anything, and it was making me insane.

We'd had game after game after game recently with flights and bus rides in between, and now we were in Seattle for a homestand. One that left us with multiple nights of no games, no commitments. Without the frenetic pace and pressure, I was unmoored. Restless. Flailing.

I wanted to calm the hell down and quiet my mind, and I hated that I knew exactly how to do that.

What's the harm?

When I'm high, I'm a hell of a lot better than when I'm like this.

I need to sleep. If I do a line, I'll sleep so well.

I closed my eyes and rubbed them hard, as if I could somehow chase away that voice that was always there to remind me how much I'd loved cocaine. These were the most dangerous moments—when I found myself missing the days when I'd just give in to the craving. When I remembered how fun it had been and how calm and collected I'd felt. When I didn't spend so much energy—physical and mental—resisting, and instead just indulged until I felt amazing. When I was in this simultaneously scattered and hyper-focused frame of mind that cocaine had always been able to soothe.

I was pretty sure it would've been easier to resist if I hadn't enjoyed the high so much. If it hadn't felt so damn *good*. I'd known people who drank too heavily or did harder drugs, and they'd cling to the memories of misery when they were trying to sober up. Because there were always some side effects—getting sick, blacking out and realizing after the fact that they'd done something they couldn't undo.

Me, I didn't have a lot of those memories. Detoxing, sure—that had been hell—and I hadn't enjoyed the constant sniffling or the way my jaw ached sometimes, but those had been minor compared to the absolute euphoria that came whenever I did a line or a bump. I remembered my mind slowing down to something more manageable. Thoughts coming into focus. Noise in my head quieting. I remembered nights on the ice where I was so present and in the moment, effortlessly following the puck as if everything were happening in slow motion. I remembered sex that seemed to go on forever, with every nerve ending lighting up with the bliss of another man's touch. Sometimes I hadn't been able to come or even get it up, but it was still amazing and sexy.

The worst part besides detoxing? This. Craving it.

Needing it.

Wanting it.

I missed the high. I missed the calm. I didn't miss the hunger for more, especially when I'd run out and needed to go *find* more, but everything else... God, I'd loved it.

It made me do stupid shit, though. I may not have gotten as wired and agitated as most people did on coke, but I did feel ten feet tall and bulletproof. I felt immortal. I could do anything, and I'd be fine. Like that one night when a few of us were high as fuck, and someone got the bright idea to do lines off the blade of a hockey stick. Looking back now, I could only imagine what *else* I'd been inhaling, especially when we'd all gone back to try to get every last precious grain out of the tape. Same with the time some teammates and I did bumps off the puck one of them had used to score his first pro goal earlier that evening. In some of my highest, hungriest moments, I hadn't given any thought at all to what I was snorting off, so God knew what kinds of things had gone up my nose alongside the blow.

But the bliss...the calm...the *quiet*...

All the feelings I never wanted to end...

The aftermath, I reminded myself. *Remember the aftermath.*

I thought hard about the lows. Those periods when I'd been out of cocaine, or when I hadn't been able to use for whatever reason. The detoxing at the end. The absolute shambles of my professional and personal lives. Giving in tonight would just sign me up for more of that misery, and I didn't want to go there again.

At least this wasn't a craving like I'd had in the early days of trying to get sober. Back then, it had been more of a chemical craving. Withdrawal.

No, this was completely mental. It was what happened

when I got into a spiral about something, or when my mind absolutely wouldn't calm the fuck down so I could concentrate, and that little voice in the back of my head started reminding me how much the cocaine helped. The calm. The focus. How everything felt good, and how I could keep doing bumps for hours or even days to maintain that high. Or, during games, when I'd ostensibly start each period with a whiff of smelling salts like some of my teammates did, except the stuff I kept on me was something much stronger and better.

Point was, I was damn good at using in plain sight without anyone catching on.

Anyone besides my ex, anyway.

The thought of Josh sent a rush of fury through me that didn't help me calm down one bit. It also didn't do a damn thing to make the cocaine less inviting.

I knew intellectually that cocaine was not a solution. Not to this. Not to anything. It never had been and never would be. I knew it always sent me down a spiral that started costing me dearly, and not just financially. I knew that every line and bump I did was ruining my life.

The problem was that I also knew how unaware of all that I'd be with a nose full of cocaine and a head full of mellow bliss. I knew how many times I'd been able to come down easily afterward and function like normal—well, "normal" for someone with ADHD—without any ill effects, which made it really hard to convince myself that if I got high now, I'd regret it later. Even though I knew damn well I would.

I dropped onto the couch, leaned forward, and rubbed my eyes with the heels of my hands. God, I was a mess. I needed...

No, not cocaine. I did not need cocaine. And no coffee,

either. Sometimes that could settle my brain, but when I was like this—when I was this painfully hungry for blow—caffeine didn't do much. Even if it did, it felt too much like feeding the demon instead of fending it off.

I needed...

Help.

That was it. I needed help.

Sometimes I could ride this out myself. In fact, most of the time, I could and did. But I never knew until it was too late if I was going to be able to hang in there on my own, so I'd had guys I could call. Teammates, like Tracer and Petrovich. It had been especially easy when I'd roomed with Tracer because he'd be right there more often than not. No one would notice that he was sticking close to me.

But Phoenix was playing tonight. If they weren't on the ice right now, they were getting ready, and the last thing any of them needed was me crashing their pre-game routines with a long-distance mayday call.

Which meant...

Fuck. I was on my own. I had no one on the Sasquatches. No one who knew. Well, everyone *knew*—it wasn't exactly a big secret that Cary Solomon had been suspended for cocaine use. But no one here knew me. I definitely didn't know any of them well enough to call someone up and ask them to help me ride this out.

There was Axel. I was pretty sure I'd rattled the shit out of him the night he'd watched me, he thought, riding out a craving like this. But that had been an act. This was the real deal. I needed someone here who wasn't a user himself. Because if I had Axel here and we both wound up in a vulnerable moment at the same time—me giving in to my craving and Axel wanting another taste of cocaine—then we'd both be in a world of hurt.

I couldn't do that to him. I could fake it to scare him out of using, but there was no way in hell I was risking his sobriety for mine.

So who the fuck else could I call? I needed a support system, but I hadn't been on this team long enough to know who'd be supportive, who'd think I was a junkie loser, or who'd suggest we go drinking and get fucked up (yes, I'd had teammates like that).

I had no one on this team. I was completely alone.

Except...

I squeezed my eyes shut and wiped a shaky, clammy hand over my face. No. I couldn't go to him. Yeah, he was here in the same building, and yeah, he was familiar with my addiction, but he hadn't been there for anything past that initial detoxing.

On the other hand, it wasn't like I needed him to *do* anything. I just needed someone to be there with me. Even if he didn't say a word or do a thing, it went a long, long way for me to have someone in the room. I couldn't go hunt down an eightball without explaining to the other person why I was leaving. That meant concocting some kind of bullshit story, and it meant coming up with a reason why I needed to go alone. If they were sitting with me to ride out a craving, they'd know better than to buy it, and they'd either insist on going with me wherever I went, or they just wouldn't let me leave. That was almost always enough to keep me from even trying.

Fuck it. If ever there was a moment to swallow my pride and reach out, this was it. I couldn't afford not to. All I could do was hope that Josh said yes.

I pushed my feet into a pair of sneakers, grabbed my keys, and headed up to his apartment. A moment later, I was at his door. After taking a second to compose myself, I gulped, pushed my shoulders back, and knocked on his door.

As soon as I did, it occurred to me that I could've texted. Everyone on the team had everyone else's number. Then again, maybe if he saw with his own eyes what a wreck I was, he'd realize I was serious. And he wouldn't have texts he could screencap and show to—

The door swung open. On the other side, Josh eyed me, gaze full of suspicion, but no surprise. He must've had a Ring or something and already knew I was here.

Before he had a chance to tell me to pound sand, I blurted out: "I need help." My voice was shaky, my shoulders heavy with shame.

Josh peered at me. "With what?"

I swept my tongue across my parched lips. Whatever thoughts hadn't already been scrambled by this overwhelming craving scattered as the suspicion and resentment in my ex's eyes filled me with shame. Why had I come here? I remembered—I knew what I'd wanted to beg for—but what in the world had possessed me to think this man would actually help me?

Do I have any other options?

That pulled some of my focus, and I managed, "I still... Even after rehab, I still get cravings." I swallowed hard. "Bad ones."

Josh's eyebrows rose with obvious alarm. "Drugs?"

Heat bloomed in my cheeks as acid rose in my throat. I couldn't hold his gaze, so I stared down at our feet and nodded. "Yeah."

Neither of us spoke. After the silence had lingered for a few long seconds, I chanced a look at him, and I couldn't begin to read his mind. Some of the alarm still hung on in his eyes, but there was more. Resentment, maybe? Disgust? Frustration? It was hard to tell.

Then his features hardened, and the alarm vanished as he glared across the threshold. "You didn't want my help before. Why the fuck do you want it now?"

The words lanced through my ribs. "Josh, I just—"

"I *tried* to help you back then," he growled. "And you've hated me for it ever since. Find someone else to use."

Before I could respond, he shut the door, and the emphatic click of the deadbolt echoed through my chaotic head.

I closed my eyes and pushed out a breath as a wave of queasy hurt washed over me. Seriously? *Seriously?*

Panic surged up through the hurt. Oh God. Now I had to ride this out alone? I hadn't had to ride out a heavy craving by myself in a long, long time, and I—

No. I *was* going to ride this out. I was *not* going to give in. I'd been sober for going on three years. Would've been almost seven if not for that relapse. Well...four. Because of that *other* relapse.

Now I was trying *real* hard to relapse again tonight.

And you can't even be bothered to help me, you jerk.

Anger flared hot in my chest, and to my surprise, it actually tamped down the craving. Fuck Josh. Fuck him for abandoning me back then and turning his back on me now. He'd probably be thrilled if I gave in to my craving, got fucked up, and lost my position on the team. He'd get that starter spot he so obviously craved.

No. Not happening.

I was *going* to ride this out. I was *going* to make it without giving in.

Because I was not giving that asshole the satisfaction of watching me break again.

CHAPTER 18

JOSH

Leaning against the door, I listened to Sol's footsteps fading down the hall. My anger dimmed with the sound, and I closed my eyes as shame took its place. Too many emotions churned inside me to even begin to name them all.

Damn it, Sol. If you'd asked me for help back then, I'd have done anything.

But you're asking for help now.

Yeah, I'd been pissed at his audacity, coming to my door to ask me of all people for help. But now that he was gone...

Shit.

The thing was, I'd been carrying a ton of resentment for a long time, and none of that was going away overnight. Not after everything he'd put me through all those years ago. And my God, I was so tired. The fatigue pushing down on my shoulders reminded me of the days late in our relationship when I'd been close to my breaking point. Ready to just throw up my hands and say, "Fuck it, I've done all I can."

I *had* done all I could for Sol back then. If he wanted to

fall off the wagon and use again now... I mean, I hadn't been able to stop him when he still loved me. What made me think I could stop him now that he hated me?

But I couldn't lie—I was torn.

Even if he hadn't been clearly trying to bridge the gap between us recently, even if he hadn't been trying to smooth things over enough for us to be civil, he *was* a teammate. What kind of man would I be if I let a member of my own team fall apart just because I was bitter about our jacked-up past? It didn't matter if I wanted to help Sol. I needed to help the Sasquatches. Like it or not, that meant stepping in to keep one of our guys from hunting down a hit of cocaine and spiraling downward again.

And fuck me, but resentment and anger aside...

I *did* want to help Sol.

"Goddammit," I muttered, and grabbed my keys off the hook. Then I stalked out of my apartment and half-jogged downstairs to his.

I was almost there when it occurred to me he might not have come back after I'd told him off. He might've gone down to his car or out on foot in search of the drugs he was craving. I might've already screwed this up beyond repair.

Well, I'd start here, and if he wasn't home, then I'd go looking for him.

With my heart in my throat, I pounded on his door.

The sound of a deadbolt had never given me so much relief, especially not in the same moment it filled me with so much apprehension. And suddenly there we were, standing on opposite sides of a threshold again, this time with him in his apartment and me out in the hallway, hoping I didn't get a door slammed in my face.

Sol regarded me with suspicion, but also some...hope?

Relief? Anger, too, and I supposed I didn't blame him for that. God knew what he was going to finally say to me—if this would turn into a screaming match that got the cops called on us, or if he'd quietly step aside to let me in—but I didn't give him a chance.

"I'm sorry," I blurted out. "I... If you need help, then..." I ran out of words. Guilt over rejecting him and worry about his state of mind had me too tongue-tied to say anything coherent. All I managed was to repeat, "I'm sorry."

His eyebrows went up. Understandable—it had been a long, long time since he'd heard me apologize for anything.

He dropped his gaze and stood aside, gesturing for me to come in. "Thanks."

Maybe it was just as well that neither of us could say much right now. The more we said, the better the odds of one of us saying something we couldn't claw back.

I accepted the invitation and stepped into his apartment. The carpet beneath my feet seemed firm and solid, but I still couldn't shake the certainty I was walking out onto precariously thin ice. When the floor creaked softly under my weight, my spine prickled as if the surface of a pond had just signaled it was about to give.

Too late now. I was already here, and if this ice was going to splinter, it wouldn't matter if I was coming or going —I was still going down.

The door clicked shut.

Heart pounding, I turned to face him. These apartments were decent-sized, all things considered. The living area was slightly larger than a high-end hotel suite, which was more than enough for a bachelor pad. That much space should've meant plenty of breathing room with only two of us in here, especially when we stood a few feet apart, but I swore I could feel the walls pushing us together. The one behind me was a good five feet away, but I was sure it was nudging against my shoulder blades like the goal's crossbar letting me know I couldn't back up any farther.

And was that the same couch he'd had all those years ago? God help me. There were a lot of memories on that thing that I did *not* need to be remembering right now.

Silence hung between us, emphasized by the hum of the refrigerator and the mumble of traffic on the street below.

Now what?

Well, I'd come here for a reason. The same reason that had brought Sol to my door. Maybe if we focused on that, we could break this awkward little standoff. Except that topic was its own minefield, so I had to tread carefully, starting with my tone. I didn't want him to hear all the bitterness and resentment, but I also didn't want him to hear how much it hurt to be here at all. I tried to tell myself this was just all those raw emotions carrying over from my divorce, but...no. No, these were feelings that had Sol's name all over them.

I wasn't about to let him catch on to any of that, so I tried to keep my voice as neutral as possible. "What do you need from me?"

Sol exhaled and broke eye contact. "Just be here. You don't have to do anything. Just..." He leaned against the door. "Be here."

Those words hit me in places that were more tender than I expected. I didn't think he meant it that way. He was too folded in on himself right now. Too preoccupied with a battle inside his mind that I couldn't begin to imagine. When he was like this, I doubted he had the wherewithal to deliver a barb that would dig itself into that raw spot in my conscience that had been there since I'd driven away from the rehab facility. The one that had needled at me all this time that I could've at least stuck around until he was through the program.

I couldn't have. I'd been too destroyed to handle one more day of us. I'd made sure he was someplace safe and on a road to recovery, and then I'd bailed to save myself. And he'd never forgiven me for it.

Now, like then, all he wanted was for me to be here.

With a lump in my throat, I shifted my weight. "Okay. I'm here."

He didn't meet my eyes, and his voice barely reached me across that short distance as he whispered, "Thank you."

Silence descended again. I still had no idea how to fill it. Or if I should fill it.

"Do you, um..." He pressed his palms against the door, and the quiet but rapid tap-tap-tap of his nails on the wood hit my nerve endings like water dripping from a leaky faucet. Abruptly, he pushed himself off the door and moved toward the kitchen, motioning for me to follow him. When he spoke, he spoke fast, the way he did when he was nervous or agitated. "Do you want something to drink? I don't have a whole lot of variety, but I've got—"

"Water's fine." I deliberately kept my voice soft and measured, since that could sometimes help to settle him. As much as anything did, anyway. Anything that wasn't a chemical like the one that had him so wound up in the first place.

Sol busied himself pulling down a couple of glasses and filling them with the pitcher from the fridge. His hands were unsteady. Though he managed relatively simple tasks, they took work, and I could only guess how much of his shakiness was from his ADHD, from the cocaine craving, and from nerves because I was here.

It hurt to see him like this. I hated him. I loved him. I missed him. I never wanted to see him again. All of those feelings converged into total misery as I watched him struggling.

I'd wondered how bad this must've been for him to come to me of all people. Watching him now... I got it.

After I'd accepted a glass of water from him, we leaned against opposite counters in the narrow kitchen. I sipped mine, then studied him and quietly asked, "Does this happen often? The, um...the cravings?"

Some color rose in his face. He didn't get defensive like he had in our past life. Back then, he'd blow up at me if I so much as hinted that he had a problem. As hard as it was to see him like this, I admittedly would've killed for it back then. To see him acknowledging that it was a problem and clearly fighting *so hard* to stay clean.

He seemed to consider my question before he shrugged. "Kind of? Sometimes I'll go months without really wanting it. Then it'll be a couple of weeks of feeling like this off and on. Then nothing for a while. It's..." He exhaled, running a hand through his hair. "It's weird."

"Stress?" I suggested.

Without looking at me, Sol nodded. He took a deep swallow of his water before putting the glass aside. Resting his hands on the counter's edge, he drummed his nails again, and he kept his gaze focused anywhere but on me. "I'm always afraid I'm going to fall back into it again. It's..." He wiped his hand over his face. "It's fucking terrifying."

The vulnerability made my chest hurt. And renewed

guilt twisted in my stomach. He'd been so scared of giving in to this craving, he'd swallowed his pride and come to me of all people. And what had I done?

Well. I was here now. Hopefully that redeemed me at least a little bit.

"You've stayed sober this long," I said softly. "That has to count for something."

To my surprise, Sol's shoulders slumped, and he exhaled. "No. I haven't."

My heart fell into my stomach. Didn't matter how well I knew that a relapse was almost statistically guaranteed—the admission made me sick to my stomach. "You're still using?"

"No, no. Not..." He shook his head but avoided my eyes. "I'm sober now. But I've relapsed before." He swallowed hard as a blush darkened his fair skin, and his voice was full of shame and regret as he quietly added, "Twice."

"I..." Jesus. I had no idea what to say. "I didn't know. I thought... This whole time..."

Sol swept his tongue across his lips as he shook his head again. "No. We managed to keep it off everyone's radar, so—"

"We?"

His gaze flicked up to meet mine, but only for a second. "Some of my teammates back in Phoenix. They knew about... I mean, they were the ones I'd go to whenever I was like this." He gestured at himself. "So they knew how bad it could be. And when I..." He closed his eyes and sighed. "When I started using again, they caught on, and they got me into rehab without the club or the league finding out."

The sense of relief that he'd had that kind of support—I couldn't even describe it. All this time, it never occurred to me that he might be fighting his addiction demons on his own, and I was glad to hear he'd had people in his corner who'd made sure he got help.

"How did they keep it quiet?" I asked, barely whispering.

"The first time was easy—it happened during the off season. It was easier to hide a relapse then, but it was also easier to hide the stint in rehab."

"And the second time?"

Sol rubbed his neck. "I, um..." He cleared his throat as he shifted from foot to foot, and he finally met my gaze. "Did you happen to hear about when I was out for a couple of months for concussion symptoms?"

I nodded slowly. It had definitely caught my attention.

He swallowed. "Okay, well, my teammates knew I needed help, and we all knew I'd be fucked if I got busted a second time. That's a forty-game suspension, *and* my contract was coming up for renewal. I couldn't risk anyone finding out." He lowered his gaze, and he sounded sheepish as he said, "So, my buddies told the staff they'd noticed some concussion symptoms in me. We all knew the symptoms that the concussion spotters look for, so..." He shrugged.

I blinked. "You...you faked a concussion in order to go to rehab without anyone finding out?"

"Yeah," he whispered. "I'm not proud of it, okay? And please, don't say anything to anyone. It's—"

"Sol." Why was it so hard to resist closing the space between us and putting a hand on his shoulder? "I'm not going to say anything. And honestly, I... Hell, you had a lot on the line, and I can't think of any other way you could fly under the radar for something like that. It's... I mean, it's kind of brilliant, to be honest."

"Maybe," he said almost soundlessly. "And I'm trying. I

am. I swear. The relapses—I got help before things got out of control like they did the first time around."

That much was a relief. It gave me a lot of hope that, whether relapses happened or not, he was committed to staying sober.

"You're asking for help now," I whispered. "So I believe you."

Sol studied me. Then he exhaled and pressed back against the counter. "I've been good, you know? Even with my performance going to shit and everything, I stayed sober. Two years now. Almost three." His shoulders sagged. "But I guess everything lately has been getting to me. The move. My career being up in the air. It's..." He sighed and shook his head. "It's been hard. Especially since there's that little voice that keeps telling me this will all be easier if I do a line or two."

"You know it's lying, though. Right?"

"Except it isn't." He met my gaze this time, but there was no anger in his eyes or his voice. If anything, he looked and sounded on the verge of breaking down. "That's the problem—it *does* make everything easier. I can think more clearly. I can concentrate. Get shit done." He shoved a hand through his blond hair and pushed out a harsh breath. "I know it'll blow up in my face if I go down that road, but God, it would be so much easier to resist if I didn't also know how much it helps me in the short term." He let his head fall back against a cabinet and stared up at the ceiling with tear-filled eyes. "I don't want to use again. But it's so fucking hard."

I couldn't speak. I could barely breathe. Back in the day, I'd have given anything to see him push back against his addiction like this. I'd have sold my soul to hear him, just once, say he didn't want to want the cocaine.

There was no vindication hearing it now. It just hurt. It cut me right to the bone, seeing him in this much pain.

All I ever wanted was for you to get better. I didn't want you to hurt like this.

I had no idea what to say or do, but standing here while he was on the verge of crumbling—I couldn't do that. Forget our past. Forget all my resentment and all the reasons I'd hated him for so damn long.

Without a word, I pushed off the counter, stepped across the space between us, and wrapped my arms around him.

Sol had two inches on my six-three, and we had about the same narrow, lean build. Stereotypical goalies and all that. But as I held him in his kitchen, he felt small and brittle. He buried his face against my neck, and he trembled, and I closed my eyes as I stroked his hair and wished like hell there was more I could do for him.

Some bitter voice in the back of my mind grumbled that we'd both be a million times better off if something like this had happened seven years ago, but I pushed it back. The past couldn't be changed. Right here, right now, Sol was broken, and it didn't matter how much of that had been his own doing.

"I'm sorry," he whispered.

I didn't know if he meant he was sorry about our rocky past, or about leaning on me right now. Either way, I just held on and whispered, "You're going to get through this."

He sniffed sharply. "I know. You're here."

I squeezed my eyes shut, trying to hold back my own emotions. "You've got this even without me."

"Yeah. I do." He loosened his embrace and straightened. "But it's a hell of a lot easier with help."

I nodded as we drew apart. "Just tell me what you need."

Our eyes met.

And everything stilled except for my suddenly pounding heart.

I had no idea what he needed in that moment, but it was undeniably clear what he wanted. Or maybe that was just me, because one look at him up close like this, and good God, I had never—not even in our brightest days—ached so much for his mouth on mine.

Sol swallowed. His gaze flicked to my lips. Then back to my eyes. "Josh..."

I didn't think my heart had ever slammed this hard into my ribs. Not even in the critical moments of a playoff game. Memories poured into my mind of who we'd been before everything went off the rails, and I was so off-balance, I wasn't sure I could've let go of Sol if I wanted to.

I was absolutely sure that I *didn't* want to, though.

Either he saw the same fire in my eyes that was burning in his, or he was just braver than me, but Sol lowered his chin and closed that sliver of space between us, and...

Oh. *God.*

Soft, insistent, familiar lips against mine. Strong arms around me. A stutter of breath across my cheek. Tight, powerful body fitted to mine like we were both made for this exact moment.

The tiny kitchen spun around us. I could maneuver quickly and precisely over ice on thin metal blades in my sleep, but standing here with my feet flat on solid ground, it was a genuine miracle I didn't fall right to the linoleum.

Sol kept me upright, though, holding on even as his languid kiss made the world list under my shaking knees.

He broke the kiss and touched his forehead to mine.

"Jesus fuck, Josh," he panted, trembling fingers trailing down my cheek.

"Uh-huh," I breathed. "Something like that." I drew him back in, swallowing his low moan as we sank against each other again.

Fucking hell, I'd forgotten how much I loved kissing him. More memories flooded in of the two of us when we were younger, grabbing every opportunity we could find to fool around. As much as I'd refused to let myself think about any of it, I'd never forgotten how playful he could be in bed. How relaxed and carefree the sex was. What it felt like to be the reason he was begging for more, right on the edge, almost crying as he pleaded with me to take him there, holding on to me for dear life as he came. How far into bliss he could drive me, whispering, "Baby, you're so sexy," all the way.

We'd started out gentle this time, but this kiss was hot and hungry now, and he dragged his fingers through my hair the way he always had in the past. Denim separated our matching erections, but not by a lot; there was only so much twin layers of fabric could do to mask all that heat and desire. Holy fuck, we needed to get all this out of the way so we could—

Sol abruptly broke the kiss. "God, I'm sorry. We—Jesus. We shouldn't... I can't do this."

I froze. Then I stepped back, lifting my hands off him. My mind was still whirling, still trying to catch up and make sense of the situation, but he'd said no, so of course I backed off.

"I'm sorry," he said again, refusing to meet my gaze. "I can't."

"Okay. Okay, we won't." I was out of breath, dizzy, and confused. What had changed? Why was—

Oh.

Oh fuck.

My mind cleared enough to land on the reason I was in his apartment in the first place.

As soon as my brain touched on that, I opened up some more space between us. "Shit. You're right." The words *I should go* sprang to the tip of my tongue, but I quickly remembered that I couldn't leave him. Not now. Because if I knew him, he'd be struggling even harder after this. So would it be worse if I stayed or if I left?

I swallowed hard. "Do you, um... Do you want me to go?"

Sol chewed his lip, avoiding my gaze. "I can't... We can't. I'm not going to use you as a distraction just to get through this."

It hurt to realize he'd only kissed me because I was the nearest warm body and sex was a great way to pull his focus away from his addiction.

That sting only lasted a second, though, because reality set in fast. Nothing about the way he'd kissed me said his cocaine craving was the whole story. I'd been with Sol in the past when he'd been high, or when he'd *wanted* to get high and couldn't. I'd also been with him when the drugs weren't a factor and he'd only wanted me, and the way he'd kissed me tonight had taken me back to *those* nights.

Somewhere deep down, Sol still wanted me.

And maybe not so deep down, I still wanted him, too.

Not tonight, though. Not like this.

"We don't have to do anything," I whispered. "What *do* you need from me right now?"

He looked at me through his lashes. "Would it be too much to ask for you to stay?"

Some part of me wanted to say that, yes, it was absolutely too much. We'd just reignited a whole lot of feelings I didn't want to have, and that was going to start pulling at some wounds that didn't need to be reopened, and staying here with him wasn't going to help with any of that.

But leaving him alone wasn't going to help him stay sober. Especially now.

"I can stay," I said.

His shoulders sagged with obvious relief. "Thanks. I, um...I'm sorry. About..." He gestured at the two of us as color bloomed in his face.

"It's okay. It took two." I shifted, sliding my hands into the pockets of my jeans. "We've got a complicated past. It's..." I shook my head. "Don't worry about it."

From the pinch of his brow, he was absolutely going to worry about it.

"It's fine," I insisted. "Let's just..." I motioned toward his living room.

"Okay. Okay, yeah." Sol took a deep breath. Then he gestured at the flatscreen TV. "I think Philly is playing Long Island. Want to watch the game?"

I couldn't have cared less about either team—or, in that moment, about hockey—but I nodded anyway. It was something to focus on besides each other, and that might actually keep us both sane while he rode out this craving for blow.

We picked up our barely touched water glasses and moved into the living room. Fortunately, that familiar old couch was a big one. Kind of necessary for someone as tall as he was, and it left a ton of breathing room between us. Breathing room that hadn't existed in the past when we'd nearly always wound up on the same cushion. Together. Touching. Kissing. Anything and everything two men could do on a couch, we'd done on this one. Even the faint, familiar creak as we sat down had memories crashing through my head like a tribute montage when a player returned to his old arena after leaving for another team.

In silence, we sat with a wide cushion between us on that memory-filled couch, and we drank, and Sol pulled up the Philadelphia-Long Island game, which had just started. I wondered if he was following the action any more than I was. At this point, a player could've grown wings or a portal to hell could've opened up at center ice, and I didn't think I'd even notice. He probably wouldn't have either.

After what seemed like hours of watching a game neither of us cared about, Sol broke the silence: "I'm sorry."

I swallowed. "For what?"

Sol chewed his lip and stared into his water glass. Then he shook his head and leaned back against the couch, fixing his gaze on the opposite wall as if he couldn't make himself look at me. "For what happened in..." He nodded toward the kitchen. Voice laced with shame and regret, he whispered, "And I'm sure you've got better things to do than babysit me while I ride this out."

Guilt needled at me from the inside, because if he'd said that when I'd first walked in, I probably would've agreed with him. After seeing just how much he was clearly hurting, how hard he was fighting to stay sober, even when it meant swallowing his pride and coming to me...

"Our past is..." I considered my words. "It is what it is. But let me help you tonight."

He turned to me then, his eyes pleading with me to mean that.

"I *want* to help," I insisted.

He held my gaze for a moment. Then he nodded, and we kept quietly watching the game. It felt like there was more that needed to be said, but I doubted either of us knew how to navigate this conversation. I sure as hell didn't.

And it didn't help that I was still a mess from that incredible, disastrous moment in his kitchen.

I wondered what it said that I'd come here to help him fight off a craving for cocaine, and now I was the one who could barely sit still because I wanted *him*.

What did it say that I wouldn't have stopped if he hadn't? If Sol hadn't hit the brakes, we absolutely would have gone too far, and I'd probably be hating myself for that right now instead of sitting here wishing his hands and mouth were on me again. I knew how bad he was for me, but one look...one kiss...

If Sol hadn't whistled the play dead, things would've gotten as out of hand as I wished they could've. We'd have fucked each other senseless, then come up for air and realized it was a mistake, but holy hell, the sex would've been amazing. Almost amazing enough to make the heavy, nauseating regret afterward worth it.

Do you have any idea how much I still want you?

Another wave of memories came crashing in. Nights—and mornings, and afternoons, and really any time of day when we had a few minutes to ourselves—tangled up with Sol's lean, powerful body. Not when the cocaine had started joining us like an unwanted third person, but the early days when I couldn't get enough of the way he kissed me and touched me. When he was high, he just wanted to be overwhelmed with sensation, and it could've been anyone in bed with him while he was that fucked up.

When he was sober, though? When it was just the two of us? Fuck, no one had ever held a candle to Sol in the bedroom when he was sober. He could be anything I wanted in a given moment—rough, gentle, frantic, tender. Sometimes he was begging me. Sometimes he whispered harshly in my ear, "Tell me what you want, baby," and then he'd do all that and more.

To this day, the sexiest memory I had was him riding me from behind while he kissed my neck. He was one of the few guys I'd been with who was tall enough to do that with me, and even now, I could still get myself off by imagining his soft lips and rough stubble on the back of my neck while he moved slowly inside me.

I shivered, masking it by shifting on the couch as if I couldn't quite get comfortable.

I also hadn't bottomed in a long time. I mostly topped, but I did like switching things up sometimes, and it had been *ages*. The last guy to top me was the one I'd dated before I met Damon. Damon never, ever topped, and he didn't even like using toys on someone else.

Sol had never objected to being on top, though, and holy hell, what I wouldn't have given for the world to be right enough us to be naked, right this minute, with his dick buried inside me.

The world wasn't right enough for that, though, and I reminded myself for the millionth time of all the reasons why we hadn't worked out. Including the reason I was here in his apartment in the first place.

I had to give him credit for backing off. He could have easily used me as a distraction.

I was spooked by how much I'd wanted us to keep going. Less than an hour ago, I'd slammed the door in his face, because fuck him—I wasn't interested in helping. I was done with him. I didn't care about him. Then guilt had driven me to his apartment, because yes, I *did* care about him.

As soon as he'd kissed me...oh my God. So many emotions had tumbled through me in that moment. Even now, as I watched the Philly-Long Island hockey game without half a clue what was happening on the ice, I was almost shaking with need for him.

Because I'd never stopped wanting him. I understood it was his addiction that had ruined everything. Once that had taken hold, he hadn't been the man I knew anymore. There were glimpses of him. Moments when I could almost forget about the drugs because he was so sweet and so amazing. Even when he was in the throes of withdrawal, or when he was so high that the only thing that mattered to him was *staying* high, he was still Sol, and I'd still loved him.

As much as I wanted to hate him now, I couldn't deny that I still cared for him. I could tell myself all day long that I was just here because a teammate needed help, but that was bullshit. Yes, I'd have done this for any member of the Sasquatches who asked, but I wouldn't be this invested. I wouldn't hurt this much.

I wouldn't be wishing so hard that we hadn't stopped at kissing.

But we'd had to stop. Reality was what it was, and I couldn't separate him from his addiction. Being with him had meant being with the cravings, the highs, the lows, the withdrawals.

Even now, when he was—as far as anyone knew—sober, the addiction was still here. He was still struggling.

He was trying *so hard*, though. In ways he hadn't back then. The denial was gone. The absolute conviction that he knew what he was doing and he could handle it—gone. Sol had his pride, but still, he'd come to my apartment. He'd asked me of all people for help.

Because he *wanted* to stay clean. Yes, he was still fighting against his addiction, and he probably would be forever, but the fact that he'd shown up at *my door* to ask for help rather than give in...

I couldn't help seeing him in a different light. He wasn't weak. He never had been, but the man sitting here now was so much stronger than I'd ever realized. And fighting a much bigger and uglier battle.

"Are you going to be okay?" I asked.

Sol turned to me, a hint of surprise lifting his eyebrows. "What do you mean?"

"I mean..." I chewed my lip. "The craving—you said this happens sometimes."

He dropped his gaze and watched his fingers playing at the edge of the remote. "They happen, yeah. Not too often. Not as often as they used to, thank God. And usually I can just ride it out. But sometimes..." He closed his eyes and pushed out a breath. "I can't even explain it. Just...sometimes it's bad, and I get so scared I'm going to give in."

The fear in his voice was real, and it was heartbreaking. His stubbornness and recklessness in the past had driven me insane with frustration, but it had never occurred to me that this was the alternative. This was the part that had to come out if he was going to break free of his addiction. As much as anyone ever could, anyway. Yeah, this was necessary, but Jesus fuck, it was hard to watch.

Sol moistened his lips. "Listen. You're helping me today. A lot. And I appreciate that." He looked right in my eyes. "But tell me honestly. If this happens again... *When* this happens again..." His brow furrowed as he swallowed hard. "Would you rather I didn't come to you?"

Holy shit, was that a question with a ton of layers. I avoided his eyes as I considered my answer. Because today had already been an excruciating roller coaster, and it was going to take me days or more to sort out all the emotions we'd churned up since the moment he'd shown up at my door.

"I'll understand if the answer is no," he said softly. "Seriously. We've got a messy history, and you've already done more to help me get sober than I've ever had any right to ask anyone."

I locked eyes with him, startled to hear him acknowledge that.

He swallowed again. "I'm still figuring out who I can go to in Seattle. But it's... There's consent, you know?" He half-shrugged. "I don't want to lean on people who didn't agree to take on that weight."

My throat tightened around my breath. How different would our worlds be if he'd come to me like this seven years ago? I didn't relish seeing him metaphorically on his knees, laying himself bare and making himself so painfully vulnerable to me of all people, but it also gave me hope that he really, truly was fighting harder than I'd ever thought he would to stay clean.

I couldn't say for sure if I had the capacity to see him through cravings like this, even if they only happened once in a blue moon. But I knew without a doubt that no matter how ugly our past, I couldn't turn my back on him.

I spoke slowly, making sure I considered each word before I said it. "We need to keep the lines clear. What we are. What we aren't. The past is messy, but neither of us can afford for things to be messy right now. Stuff like"—I gestured toward the kitchen, hoping he understood what I was referring to—"is just going to make things complicated."

Sol nodded without speaking.

"But we're teammates. And I do..." My voice caught, and I had to clear my throat. "I do care about you." I was afraid he'd ask for clarification—if I just cared about him as a teammate—but he didn't, and I was thankful for that. "If you're struggling like this..." I paused to give it some more thought, just for a few seconds to make sure I was sure, before I whispered, "Yeah. You can come to me."

The relief on his face and in his posture didn't do much for my resolve to keep from touching him. The urge to wrap my arms around him again and reassure him that he wasn't alone—that was almost irresistible. But if I did, then we'd...

Yeah, that would get out of hand again, and no matter how amazing it would be if it did, we couldn't.

My neutral voice was harder than ever to maintain now: "I mean it, Sol. I'll do whatever you need to keep you from losing your sobriety. But not..." I swept my tongue across my lips and tilted my head toward his kitchen. "Not that. I can't."

Please, please don't ask why. Don't make me explain that I still want you, but not like this.

Sol winced. "Yeah, I know. I'm sorry we went there. I knew it was a bad idea, but I just couldn't..."

I was kind of glad he didn't finish that sentence. Something told me he'd just stopped himself from saying he couldn't resist, and I needed to hold on to the illusion—however flimsy—that he had the self-control to keep us from crossing that line. God knew I sure didn't.

"So we'll keep it like this," I said. "Platonic. I can live with that if you can."

He nodded slowly. Then he looked at me again, and the tiniest of smiles cracked through and damn near broke my heart *and* my resolve.

"Thank you," he said almost soundlessly. "It, um... It means a lot. I try to do this on my own, but sometimes..." He shook his head.

"You don't have to do it alone. I've got you. So does the rest of the team."

Sol pushed out a breath. "Thank you. I really do appreciate it."

I just smiled back, and we kept watching the game.

I knew he appreciated it.

And I would help him with this. Anything he needed.

Anything but that.

No matter how much I suddenly needed that like air.

CHAPTER 19

SOL

Lying alone in the early morning light, I couldn't decide if I wished yesterday had been real or a dream. It felt like both. And I knew it had been real. Even now, my head was still foggy, my thoughts lethargic the way they always were after I'd spent a few hours trying like hell to resist giving in to cocaine. Nights like that left my brain feeling like an overly taxed muscle—weak and fatigued.

I closed my eyes and rubbed them. I wished people understood how hard it was. How it might've been as simple as "just say no," but there was nothing easy about it. Not for an addict.

Especially not for an addict looking for more than just a high. Cocaine was great for that, but what I craved was the *relief*.

An old teammate of mine, Hartford, had struggled with a painkiller addiction after a series of hip and knee injuries. He'd gotten a handle on the addiction, same as I had, but it hadn't been easy, especially as he'd continued playing hockey.

"It sucks," Harts had admitted to me one night while

he'd iced his knee. *"Because when I come off the ice and I'm hurting like this, I know there's something that'll help. And the pain is so fucking bad sometimes, it's almost enough to make me stop caring about what else will happen if I take some damn pills."*

I got it. Holy shit, I got it.

His words haunted me. They always came back to me when my sobriety was hanging by a thread, and sometimes they were the only thing that kept that thin, fraying thread from snapping.

About six months after we'd had that conversation, Harts had been racing a defenseman for the puck. He'd lost an edge, gone down, and slammed into the boards at a bad angle. The impact left him with a broken shoulder. The pain drove him back into a bottle of pills. He was suspended from the league before he'd even come off LTIR, and he'd been sent to rehab again. Three weeks in, he bailed. A few days later, he nearly died from an overdose. We all tried to offer as much support as we could, but he stopped responding to any of us, and a few months later, his wife— our one remaining connection to him—took the kids and left. No one blamed her. And to this day, a little over three years later, no one knew where Harts was or if he was even still alive.

I shuddered as I dropped my hand onto the mattress beside me. I had to stay sober. I *would* stay sober. The thought of spiraling down as hard as Harts did, especially when he'd had even more support than I did now, terrified me. His wife had done everything she could. His parents and in-laws helped as much as possible. The team rallied around him. And still...his addiction had ultimately won.

I had former teammates I could call or text...sometimes. I had current teammates who seemed to like me and might have my back. My parents... Well, my family had been the type that often created addicts—volatile, unforgiving, unstable. They'd mellowed some over the years, but ironically, they didn't have a lot of patience for addicts, and there was a reason a number of therapists along the way had encouraged me to remain low- or no-contact with them.

"Their anger and blame will only make your struggle harder," a therapist had told me.

"What they see as tough love," another had gently laid out, *"is actually toxic and counterproductive."*

"Firm boundaries are certainly necessary when dealing with an addict," my most recent therapist had said, *"but there's a big difference between enforcing boundaries and kicking you while you're down."*

So my parents were mostly out of the picture.

The resources in my support network were limited to say the least.

I have Josh.

That thought had me closing my eyes again and swearing into the silence.

Last night, we'd been about the most peaceful and cordial since we'd arrived in Seattle. I'd stayed on the rails despite that nearly irresistible craving, and Josh deserved a ton of credit for that.

But things had also gotten...complicated. And though he'd left my apartment at the end of the night with a gentle hug and a whispered, *"Text me if you need help,"* I had a feeling things weren't going to stay that easy. We had too much baggage. I didn't need to read his mind to know that last night had been hard for him, and not just because he'd had to be in the same room as me. As much as he wasn't one to wear his heart on his sleeve, I'd watched all those emotions rolling over him while we'd both pretended to watch that hockey game.

If I knew him as well as I thought I did, then I knew that once he'd gone home and had some time and space to himself, he'd let the whole night come crashing in. He'd let all those emotions dig in. Put names on them. Put *blame* on them.

If I knew Josh—and I did—then he would be one of two things when I saw him again.

One, he'd be frosty toward me. All that anger and resentment would be back with reinforcements now that he'd seen how truly pathetic and helpless I was in the face of the addiction that had ruined our relationship. At best, I'd get a cold shoulder until he couldn't keep his feelings to himself anymore. After that, let's just say I'd had enough fights with Josh in our past life to know it wouldn't be pleasant.

The second option was a hell of a lot less appealing: he'd be *hurt*. I wasn't stupid—I knew he didn't like seeing me struggle, not even when he didn't like seeing me in the first place. And there was also that moment in my kitchen...

God. What was I thinking? I'd known even as I gave in to temptation and moved in for that kiss that it was a mistake, but since when had I ever been able to say no to Josh? In that instant when he'd loosened his embrace and our eyes had met, I'd gone back to our best days, and the hunger in his expression had matched my own.

I hated myself for that. Josh had been there to help me, not to be a crutch or a distraction. I refused to use him. He deserved better than that.

So if, when I walked into the locker room today, I was met with angry or hurt-filled eyes, I fucking deserved it.

And I wished for the millionth time that I'd just ridden out last night alone.

Even if I'd given in and lost my sobriety, at least I wouldn't have hurt Josh.

Again.

With my heart in my throat and my stomach full of unpleasant butterflies, I walked from the parking garage into the training center.

Some of our teammates were already here, the chatter and the sounds of movement and equipment echoing up the hallway from the locker room. I hadn't seen Josh's car in either parking garage—here or below our apartment—so I had no idea if he was here yet. Maybe he had a maintenance day?

Well, only one way to find out.

I stepped into the locker room, and I was both frustrated and relieved that he wasn't here. Damn. Now I didn't have to face off with him, but that also meant I still didn't know how things were going to be between us.

All through practice, I wondered if maybe this was just in my head. Maybe we'd actually put some things to bed last night, and things would be better going forward. We could be teammates and even something like friends.

Or not.

Because Josh showed up just as I was getting dressed after practice—he'd been at some media thing with the PR director, I guess—and he was talking to Kayla and Diaz, one of the trainers. Dressed in a suit, too. Goddamn. I'd seen that gray suit before, but it looked even sexier on him today. Because my whole body was still vibrating with need for him after that kiss in my kitchen? Because I was sure he was a million miles farther out of my reach now? Because I was insane?

It didn't really matter, because when we made eye contact across the locker room... No, we were definitely not in a better place than we'd been yesterday.

In fact, when I'd decided there were two possible versions of Josh I'd encounter today—one angry, one hurt—I'd overlooked an even worse third option:

Both.

In that moment, I would've given anything to have his expression ice over like it had when we'd first crossed paths in here before training camp. I'd have sold my damn soul for him to glare at me like that again today. That would've been so much better than catching that subtle crack in his composure. The way his lips tightened and his eyes narrowed. How his jaw worked when he looked away, and how quickly he found a reason to get the hell out of here.

Sighing, I dropped onto the bench to put on my shoes.

I really should've just knuckled through the craving yesterday instead of making things worse with Josh. In fact, I was seriously starting to think the one thing I did better than play hockey was fuck up things between me and Josh.

Was it too much to ask for one of us to get traded sooner than later? Ideally before we drove each other insane?

Yeah, it probably was, given why we were both here in the first place.

I closed my eyes and rubbed the back of my neck. This wasn't a hockey team. This was Purgatory. And I had no idea how long we both had to stay here until the hockey gods decided we'd duly purged our sins. Hooray.

After I'd put on my shoes, I debated staying to eat with my teammates, but decided I didn't have it in me to socialize today. I could eat at home. For now, I needed to get the hell out of here.

Oh, but the universe wasn't done with me today:

As soon as I walked into the parking garage, my usually scattered focus zeroed in on Josh. Who was watching me. Waiting for me. With his arms folded across his chest. As he leaned against my car.

This conversation is going to be fun, isn't it?

I stopped with some space between us. "I'm guessing you want to talk."

He pursed his lips. "I think we *should* talk. Don't know if that means I want to."

Ouch. Damn.

Swallowing hard, I shifted my weight. "Okay. What's on your mind?"

Josh locked eyes with me. "Last night, we..." He flinched and stared at the concrete between us. From the way he tightened his arms across his chest and fidgeted, he was less angry and more uncomfortable. Nervous, maybe. Pinching the bridge of his nose, he exhaled. "I want to help you stay sober. I really do." He dropped his hand and looked right at me, all the anger and hurt falling back to reveal the fatigue. I suddenly wondered if he'd slept at all. Voice heavy, he said, "But it can't go down like it did last night. It can't."

"I know," I whispered. "I'm sorry. I... That wasn't why I went to you. You were just the only one I could go to."

He nodded, posture eroding slightly under that exhaustion he could no longer hide. "I want you to come to me again if you need to. Honestly. I meant it when I said you could." The hurt crept back into his expression as he held my gaze. "But I need some distance, too. We *cannot* cross that line again."

"We won't. That's... I mean, I put a stop to it because I'm not going to use you for... That wasn't what that was about, but I didn't want things getting blurry, you know? Why I came to you, and then us ending up..." I shook my head. "I wanted your help, but I wasn't going to use you. If we were going to hook up—and I'm not saying we are or we were—it isn't going to be like that."

"We're not going to hook up," he said flatly.

Why did that hit me in the gut? What had I fucking expected? I was lucky he was giving me the time of day, and damn lucky he hadn't bailed on me last night. Hooking up was not and never would be in the cards.

"I know," I said.

Josh stared at the concrete between us again, and he gave another slow nod. "Okay. Because that's not us anymore, you know?" He swallowed before looking at me again, and his voice was just hard-edged enough to *almost* hide the hurt. "I'm your teammate. And I'll help you stay sober. But I'm not *that* for you anymore."

Ouch again. Jesus.

I just nodded mutely. It wasn't like I didn't know. We'd been over for a long time, and it was still a wonder he hadn't shoved me away last night. The way he'd looked at me, kissed me, held on to me—that didn't tell the story he was telling now. But this was what he wanted, and I wasn't going to push him. He was done with me. Full stop. Couldn't say I blamed him.

"How often does that happen?" he asked, and then stiffened as if the question hadn't come out right. Cheeks coloring, he cleared his throat. "Cravings like that. You said they don't happen much. But...how often are we talking about?"

"It's kind of hard to predict. When it gets bad enough that I need help—that's once in a blue moon." Kind of a lie, but I'd already promised myself I wouldn't go to him again unless the situation was dire.

"Okay." He searched my eyes. "And you're committed. To staying sober."

"Absolutely," I said solemnly. "I know I fucked up back then. And last night. But I don't want to go there again. That's why I came to you." I swept my tongue across my suddenly dry lips. "I promise—I'm committed."

He studied me for a long moment as if he were searching for tells that I was lying. Few people could probably find those tells as easily as he could, but I doubted there were any for him to see this time. I wasn't lying. I *was* committed.

Finally, he exhaled, loosening his folded arms. "All right. And the rest of the time... I mean, we have to coexist. The past is the past, but whether we like it or not, we're in this together." He gestured around us.

"I know." I swallowed. "We just have to be teammates. We don't have to be friends."

My own words made me wince.

I wish we could *be friends.*

Avoiding my gaze, Josh nodded. "Okay. So we just... keep doing what we've been doing, I guess. Stay out of each other's way. Do our job." He shrugged tightly and looked at me through his long lashes. "Be teammates."

"Exactly."

We locked eyes for a moment longer.

Josh set his jaw and squared his shoulders. He tugged at his suit jacket as if he needed something to do with his hands. "All right. So. Teammates."

"Yeah. Sounds good."

We held eye contact for a moment before he smiled in that practiced way we all did when reporters wanted upbeat answers after a demoralizing loss. "All right. Well. I'll see you at the game tonight."

"Yeah. See you then."

With that, he walked away, leaving a clear path between me and my car as the *snap* of his dress shoes on concrete echoed above my heartbeat.

I got into my car on autopilot but didn't make it any farther than that before I had to close my eyes and process our conversation.

So things were weird between Josh and me. Again. Still. Whatever. I wasn't surprised—hell, I'd have been shocked if they weren't weird at this point—but it was still hard to swallow.

I felt like such a damn tool. He'd been there for me when he didn't have to be, and I'd let nostalgia and all my lingering desire for him take over at the worst possible time. Honestly, I was damn lucky he hadn't shoved me away last night, stormed out, and left me to weather everything myself. I was still surprised he hadn't done that. I kind of wished he had, if I was honest; that sounded less painful than this. Because seriously, this arrangement hurt more than sniping and not being able to look at each other. Especially when I swore I could still taste that long kiss in my kitchen. The one that had been *anything* but one-sided.

Maybe this hurt because it meant everything was resolved now. We'd settled our past, and we'd agreed to move on in separate directions. Continuing to butt heads would've meant something had to give eventually, which would've meant a shot—however slim—at things getting better between us. A resolution that meant us being closer. Friendlier.

Something had given, and this was the resolution. Distance. Neutrality. Something like numbness where all those emotions—for better or worse—had been. I didn't even feel that pull to compete with him for the starting spot on the team anymore. Just...emptiness and resignation.

Josh and I were on the same team. We lived in the same building. We were in each other's lives for the foreseeable future.

But even in those horrible months right after our breakup...

He'd never been this far away.

CHAPTER 20

JOSH

Solomon-O'Brien Skeptics Eating Crow: Seattle Sasquatches Close to Number One Spot in Pacific Division; Goalies in Contention for Xavier Trophy

SEATTLE – Netminders Cary Solomon and Josh O'Brien are having spectacular comeback seasons in Sasquatch sweaters, leading many to change their tunes about the questionable preseason acquisitions.

Just a few months ago, Solomon and O'Brien were believed to be on their way out, with save percentages lower than ever and shockingly terrible goals against averages. Now their team is close to knocking Portland out of the top spot in the Pacific Division while both men are already favored to be strong contenders for the league's prestigious Cam Xavier Memorial Trophy honoring the season's top goalie.

O'Brien currently leads the league with a 0.925% save

percentage and 2.22 goals against average. Solomon is close behind, boasting a career high 0.920% and 2.31.

Head coach Heath Maines, who recently announced O'Brien and Solomon will be operating as tandem goalies rather than a starter and backup for the foreseeable future, admits he was "unsure about" the pair when they were signed. He mentioned previously in multiple interviews that he would be focusing on strengthening Seattle's defensive pairs, leading many to believe he had little confidence in the men who'd be backstopping his team.

Hedging his bets by focusing on Seattle's D-core has paid off: Maines now has one of the most difficult teams to score against. If a player can make it past Maines's defensemen, he'll find himself up against one of the two unexpected best goalies playing hockey today.

Scott Harmon, first-line center for Montreal, commented after last week's two-one overtime loss, "There must be something in the water in Seattle. O'Brien was Swiss cheese last season, and now he's a [expletive] brick wall."

Colorado defenseman Mark Somersby spoke similarly of Solomon after a six-zero loss to Seattle: "Used to be a shutout from him would be embarrassing. This time I had a text from [Minnesota's Aaron Wilson] saying, 'Welcome to the club, man.'"

When asked about his thoughts on playing Seattle this week, Houston forward Owen Davies said, "Whichever one is in the net, I just hope to God we don't end up in a shootout with them." Both Seattle goalies have blocked every shot in Seattle's three shootouts this season.

Seattle Goalie Coach Kayla Rooney stated, "They were both solid goalies. Everyone knew it. Sometimes people get into slumps or go off the rails." With a smile, she added,

"Everyone else wanted to give up on these two, and that's their loss and Seattle's gain."

Indeed, Seattle seems to be reaping the rewards of giving Solomon and O'Brien second chances.

I read the article a couple of times before I put my phone down.

I was playing my ass off these days, but outshining Sol was going to be easier said than done. I had to give credit where it was due—he had been playing well. Really well. I wasn't shy about saying that I had been, too. Coming to Seattle had breathed new life into both our careers. How much of that was competitiveness between us, fear of what would happen to us professionally if we didn't get our shit together, or just pulling ourselves out of slumps, I didn't know. But coming here had been good.

I still wasn't sure how I felt about us being tandem goalies. In a way, it was kind of a relief, and it eased some of the tension between us. The competitive tension, anyway. That, and it meant sharing the workload more than we would as starter and backup. If one of us was on a hot streak, Coach would keep us in the net for a few games in a row (back-to-backs notwithstanding), but in general, he alternated us pretty regularly. That gave us both time to recover between games, which I liked.

At first, I'd worried we'd both start slacking off now that we weren't trying to outdo each other in the name of scoring that starter position. That hadn't been the case, though. I wasn't about to be the second-best goalie to him or anyone else. Also, I was far too happy with my performance this year to let off the gas, and my career still felt way too precarious to take anything for granted. If I knew Sol as well as I thought I did, he was probably thinking along the same lines.

And all of that boiled down to one undeniable bottom line: if we kept performing like this, the Seattle Sasquatches would most likely want to keep us. Which meant we'd either have to keep working together or hope another team made one of us an offer we couldn't refuse.

I had no intention of leaving if they offered me an extension. Knowing how much this move and adapting to a new team had fucked with Sol's head, I doubted he was going anywhere if he had a say in the matter.

So...we could be stuck together.

For *years*.

What was I supposed to do with that? I couldn't even walk into the locker room without my emotions going haywire, and that had only gotten worse since we'd touched in his kitchen. One minute, I wanted to fall at his feet and offer him everything in the world. The next, I wanted to let fly all the hurt and anger I'd been carrying for seven years. And the next after that, I just...wanted him.

At least the hostility had mostly faded. Yeah, my anger and resentment sometimes kicked in, but for the most part, it was just awkward and uncomfortable. Less like we didn't want to be in the same place, and more like we didn't know how.

Maybe that was a good sign. We weren't trying to kill each other, so maybe we could do this. Put the team first. Coexist. Work together for the good of our team. Get along like adults who could move on from our messy past. Maybe not even go insane in the process.

I rubbed my eyes and groaned.

What is wrong with me?

Maybe I needed some outside advice. Ideally from

someone who already knew most of the story, since spelling it out all over again sounded exhausting.

Fortunately, I had someone who'd been there for all the highlights and disasters of every relationship I'd ever had.

And even more fortunately, after months of schedules refusing to line up, Amber was available for a FaceTime call.

"Hey you!" My best friend smiled at me from my screen. "Sorry it's been so long! How's Seattle? Is it as wet as everyone says it is?"

"Nah, not really. I mean, it's pretty gray right now, but it's winter. I'll take this over Calgary."

She made a face. "Ugh. Winter in Calgary is just inhumane."

"I know, right? This is way less miserable."

"I bet it is." Wrinkling her nose, she added, "Probably helps that you're not living with that douchenozzle anymore."

I tried to chuckle, but it came out sounding even more halfhearted than it felt, and I couldn't look her in the eye. "Yeah. That... Good thing. Good thing."

Instantly, Amber's expression turned serious. A second later, it hardened, as did her voice. "Joshua Keith O'Brien. Do *not* tell me you're getting back together with that pathetic excuse for a husband. I swear to God, I will fly out there and—"

"No, no." I shook my head and met her gaze on the screen. "We're not getting back together."

She blew out a breath. "Thank fuck. I was worried there for a second."

"Nah, you don't have to worry about that." I rolled my eyes. "In fact, he showed up in Chicago and thought we should hook up for old time's sake or whatever."

"Did you tell him to shove a cactus up his ass sideways?"

A genuine laugh burst out of me. "See, this is why I need you around all the time. You think of the best come-backs." I sighed. "No, I didn't tell him that, but I did tell him to get lost."

"Good." She nodded sharply. "Because fuck him. Or, well, don't fuck him. Ever."

"I won't. Don't worry about that."

Another nod. Then her brow furrowed. "So what's going on? Because you seem kinda..." She pursed her lips and studied me as if she couldn't find the word.

I sighed. "Have you been following the team at all?"

She grimaced sheepishly. "I mean, a little? You know I don't do hockey."

"Oh, I know." She'd been to some of my major games, like when I'd won the Cup, but she just could *not* get into hockey. That was fine by me—it was nice to have people in my life whose lives didn't revolve around the sport. I rolled my shoulders. "Okay, well, have you seen who's on the team with me? The other goalie?"

Amber shook her head.

I exhaled. "Any guesses?"

Her brow furrowed. "How the hell would I know? I don't know who all the players—" I swore I *felt* when the piece clicked into place. Her eyes went huge and her hand went to her lips. "No way. Josh. No. You can't be serious."

"I'm serious."

"Holy. Shit." She stared at me, then spoke as if she were gingerly asking me for details of a horrific car crash: "How, um... How is that going?"

"It's..." I closed my eyes and deflated, leaning back on my couch. "It's been tough."

"Yeah, I bet. If I venture into hockey news, am I going to find an article about Seattle's goalies getting into a brawl with each other?"

That drove another real laugh out of me. "No, it's not *that* bad. I mean, I've thought about it a time or two, but..." I shook my head. "No."

"So...?" She raised her eyebrows.

I tilted my head back against the wall, took a deep breath, and filled her in, being completely candid about what happened in Sol's apartment and how much he'd been distracting me lately.

"I've spent my whole life not even noticing naked guys in the locker room," I said, letting my exasperation come through. "You play hockey, it becomes a non-issue, you know?"

Amber nodded. She probably remembered when I came out in high school, and guys worried I'd be checking them out in the locker room. It had taken a while to convince them that I was far too busy putting on my forty billion pounds of gear to grab an eyeful of teammate ass.

I ran a hand through my hair. "I'm not kidding, I've been finding reasons to show up a few minutes late to practices. Like, not late enough I'm late to get on the ice, but getting there when I know Sol will be dressed or mostly dressed. And I've been hanging out for a few extra minutes on the ice to give him a chance to get out of the shower and start getting dressed. I... Jesus Christ. I never look at guys, but just knowing he's there is driving me insane!"

"Maybe because you've never stopped being attracted to him?"

"You think?"

"I mean, I don't blame you. You've got the *worst* taste in men, but that one..." She made a chef's kiss gesture.

I rolled my eyes. "You're not helping."

"I'm just saying!" She put up a hand. "I'd be distracted by him, too!"

"Okay, but he's not just eye candy for me! We've got..." I flailed my own hand. "History. Ugly, complicated history."

Amber sobered. "That's an understatement."

"Right?" I scratched the back of my neck. "So now I have to coexist with him, which is a million times harder after he fucking kissed me, and..." I shook my head, and I sounded pathetic as I whispered, "I don't know how to do this."

Her expression was full of sympathy. "I'm not surprised. That history is long and complicated, but I don't think you ever got over him completely."

"No," I admitted softly, "I don't think I did." I gnawed my lower lip. "So what should I do? Because unless one of us gets traded—and I don't see that happening any time soon—we're stuck together at least through the end of this season."

"What do you want to do?"

"Probably the opposite of what I should do."

She arched an eyebrow.

I sighed. "I want him, okay? I told him we have to just be teammates, nothing more, but..." I made a frustrated sound. "*Ugh.* There are days when I can't even look at him, but then I can't look anywhere but right at him, and..." My shoulders drooped. "I want him.

"Maybe that should tell you something." She must have seen the protest in my expression because she put up her hand again. "Hear me out. You called me for advice, so shut up and let me give you advice."

I shut up.

"If you feel this strongly about him," she said, "then maybe you shouldn't ignore that."

"But I was with him. And he's an addict. Isn't there some saying about doing the same thing over and over and expecting different results?"

"You mean like telling yourself over and over that you don't love him when you clearly do? That kind of thing?"

I pressed my lips together.

Her voice was both gentle and firm as she said, "Don't try to tell me you don't love him, Josh. Because you do. We both know you do."

Avoiding her gaze, I nodded. I didn't want to still feel this way about him, but I could no more stop it than I could stop my hip from being sore after games sometimes. I could ignore it, I could try to soothe it, but I couldn't just will it to not exist.

"I do love him," I admitted almost soundlessly. "But what am I supposed to do with that?" I groaned. "It was so much easier when I hated him."

"Was it, though?"

I didn't answer. I probably didn't need to.

Amber took a deep breath. "Listen, maybe you need to think about who you and he are now versus who you both were back then."

"What do you mean?"

"It's been, what, nine years now?"

"Seven," I said quietly.

"Okay, and that's a long time."

"Is it?"

"It's long enough for you to meet someone, fall in love with him, marry him, and divorce him, isn't it?"

I winced. "Touché."

"Right. The point is, you're not the same person you

were back then." Her voice softened. "He probably isn't the same person he was either."

"He's still an addict," I whispered.

"He always will be. But you said yourself he's trying to stay sober. I mean, coming to you even while things were so tense?" She whistled. "*That* is a man who is *committed* to staying clean."

Chewing my lip, I nodded. Hadn't I thought the same thing? "That doesn't mean we can be a couple again, though."

"No, but it doesn't mean you can't, either."

"So what do you think I should do?" I moistened my lips. "Besides getting together with him, since apparently that's..." I rolled my hand in the air.

"Oh, it's absolutely what I think you should do," she said unrepentantly. "But maybe start by trying to be friends with him. Be teammates. Be friends. Then see what happens." She inclined her head. "And by that I mean, let things progress naturally instead of being a stubborn butthead about it."

I laughed, though I didn't really feel it. "I just feel like if we let things progress, I know exactly where they'll progress *to*. And I'm afraid of that."

"Because you're teammates? Or because of your past?"

I swallowed. "Both."

"Reasonable," she acknowledged. "But maybe it keeps trying to happen because it needs to. Because it's right."

I cocked a brow.

She shrugged. "Think about it. Would being with him now really be the same as being with him before? He's been through rehab. He's not in denial about his addiction anymore. You've both had years to mature. I know you've grown up a lot in those years, and if he's still holding on to his career, he must've sobered up and matured during that time, too." Her voice and expression softened again. "Look, I've seen you through a lot of relationships and breakups since we've known each other. And no one—not even that thing you married—has ever made you hurt as much as Sol. I don't mean when you guys broke up. I mean how much you love and care about him. It's been years, and you still get that sad look in your eyes whenever someone mentions him."

"Isn't that a red flag that he might be toxic for me?"

"Maybe," she said with a slight nod. "But it could also mean you've got stronger and deeper feelings for him than anyone else. His addiction threw things off the rails, but what if this—being on the same team and in the same city— is a second chance to get things right?"

There weren't words to describe how much I wanted that to be true, and how afraid I was that it *was* true.

"What if we fuck it up again?" I asked quietly. "I don't think I can handle losing him again."

She grimaced. "It's a risk. Every time you're with someone, there's a risk of things going south. But would you rather try and fail? Or spend the rest of your life wondering what might have been?"

"I'm not sure which is worse in this case. I've spent the last several years wondering what might have been had he never become a cocaine addict."

"Fair. And that's not something either of you can change. But he's clean now, and he's obviously trying to stay that way. You're both older and more mature. You've got a chance to, at the very least, put your friendship back together." She half-shrugged. "If you try, you might lose him. If you don't try, then he's already gone."

Ouch.

I kneaded the back of my neck and sighed again. "Okay. I'll, um...I'll try the friends angle and go from there. I guess we'll see what happens."

Why do I feel like we won't stay platonic for long?

And why do I feel like that'll be an even bigger disaster than before?

CHAPTER 21

SOL

I needed to get laid.

All my chaotic and jumbled thoughts kept leading back to that.

I'd been home from practice for a good two hours, and I still had too much energy to burn. Too much going on in my head. And we had a game tomorrow night—I needed to pull it together, and some good (or mediocre, if I was honest) sex could sometimes restart my brain enough to quiet the static.

It wasn't just the need for a sweaty distraction, though. For as much as Josh and I had agreed to coexist, to not go there again, I wanted him. God, I wanted him so bad. One kiss... One hot embrace in my kitchen... One brush of his hard-on against mine...

I was losing my mind now. Especially since I had to see him nearly every day. Worse, I had to see him in the locker room. I'd been playing hockey long enough not to think much of seeing guys in various states of undress, and I was respectful enough not to stare, no matter how hot a particular teammate was.

Josh, though. Fuck. I'd catch a glimpse of him on his

way to or from the shower. See him out of the corner of my eye as he stripped down to nothing. It was actually worse when he was in his base layer. That snug black material clung to places that my fingers and mouth vividly remembered. It emphasized his lean torso, his powerful arms and shoulders, and that ass.

Putting on his pads didn't help, either. The big pads made us basically look like blocky cartoon characters, but the smaller pieces like the chest protector and the padded pants could definitely draw the eye to regions I'd have sold my soul to run the tip of my tongue or finger over again.

Here in my apartment, safely away from my hot-as-hell ex-boyfriend, I sighed and raked a hand through my hair. It hadn't helped that we'd kissed, and then promised not to fool around again. That kiss and that promise had only pulled my focus to how much I wanted to do unwise and unprofessional things with him, and it was all driving me out of my mind. I definitely needed to go get laid, if only to expend some of this frustration that built and built every time my gaze landed on the man who'd been justifiably voted Sexiest Goalie in the league twice in his career.

He probably had his pick of men, especially after his very public divorce all but screamed "Gentlemen, Josh O'Brien is now single!" to every corner of the damn continent. God help me if I could ever hear him through his floor and my ceiling, because Josh was not quiet in bed, and I didn't imagine any man experiencing his ministrations would stay quiet either.

I shivered, swearing aloud. Yep. Definitely time to get laid. Like...now. *Tonight.*

This was a new town, though. An entirely new scene. Back in Phoenix, I'd gotten a feel for the places to go, not to mention the places *not* to go, either because the men were unsafe or the drugs were plentiful. I'd had a handful of guys I could text for a booty call if I was in town, and sometimes they'd hit me up, too.

Here? Well. It was back to square one. Time to go looking and see if I could find a hookup. No boyfriend—not yet. The regular season was no time to start an actual relationship. I'd either focus too much on hockey and neglect him, or the reverse, and disaster was inevitable.

Sex, though—I could handle sex. Find some sober and reasonably attractive guy (or two) who understood consent, and a fun night could be had by all.

The question was...where?

Clubs were awful, especially when I was this stressed out. The pressure to perform this season had made arenas and even practices into massive sensory overload, and a club would be even worse. But where the hell else was I going to meet someone? Because overstimulated or not, I wasn't going to magically develop the patience or concentration to deal with apps. Just the thought of sifting through profiles to find someone I might match with was enough to make my brain short circuit.

That wasn't to say I never used apps. There were stretches where I'd laser focus, constantly tweaking my own profile and looking through dozens or hundreds of profiles, obsessively checking in case a new one had popped up that I hadn't swiped right or left on. I'd make connections and chat with guys, but whenever I went to actually meet one, I'd sweat over if I was overlooking someone else who might be a better match, or missing a message from someone, or—

Yeah, my brain and hookup apps were a bad combo, whether I was hyper-focused or had the attention span of a squirrel.

Clubs...ugh. They were always a nightmare, but at least

I could usually get results, even if those results amounted to making out on a dancefloor or screwing in a bathroom stall.

You can rationalize it all you want, some voice in my head told me, *but you know clubs are a bad idea.*

I shut down that line of thinking. As long as I didn't drink, I'd be fine, and I didn't drink anymore. I could also spot another cocaine user from a mile away and avoid him like the plague. Stay away from the users and don't order any alcohol—yeah, I'd be fine.

So what the hell was I waiting for?

Fuck it.

I showered, dressed, and then scrutinized myself in the mirror. I doubted anyone in this town would recognize me; that sometimes happened in Phoenix, but I hadn't been here very long, and I also made a point of not wearing my usual backwards baseball cap when I was out on the prowl. That was almost always enough to keep anyone but the most devoted fan from picking me out of a crowd.

I kinda didn't mind if someone did recognize me tonight, if I was honest. I'd been out for years. Someone had once sold a tabloid a story about hooking up with me, and literally no one had cared aside from a handful of homophobic hockey fans, and they could go fuck themselves anyway.

Another time, someone had snapped a photo of me sipping what looked like a cocktail, and they'd posted it to social media. Again, there was the usual bitching from homophobes, but otherwise, it didn't really register on anyone's radar. Our PR guy happened to see it, and he'd just laughed it off, because who the hell cared about me being in a club?

I'd had a moment of panic when I'd seen the photo, though. The drink in my hand hadn't been alcoholic, but everyone thought it was, and...no one cared. A hockey player? Drinking? So what?

Fortunately, one of my teammates at the time, Cans, had discreetly pulled me aside about it.

"Is everything good, man?" he'd asked. "I saw that picture of you in the club, and..." He'd pantomimed drinking something, then raised his eyebrows.

"I'm fine." I'd shaken my head. "It was just a soda. No booze."

He'd been a little dubious, but I'd eventually convinced him I hadn't actually been drinking any alcohol. Still, he'd watched me for a while after that whenever we hung out with the team. He'd scrutinized me for, I assumed, signs of a hangover or something when he knew I'd been out the night before.

It had irritated me at the time. Now...

Fuck. Now I kind of wished I had someone on my team who'd keep me honest like that. No, I hadn't slipped up in a long time, but I would be the first to admit that one of the things that kept me from drinking was knowing that my teammates were keeping an eye on me.

In Seattle, everyone knew about my past with cocaine, but no one knew that drinking led me to using again. I'd *loved* the way alcohol and cocaine went together, and I couldn't drink without getting a nearly irresistible craving for blow. So I didn't drink. Even when I went to clubs like I planned to tonight, I didn't drink. Ever.

But tonight, no one would be looking over my shoulder. No one would be peering at me at tomorrow's morning skate to see if my eyes were bloodshot. If someone got a picture of me with a drink in hand, even if it was undeniably alcoholic...no one would care.

I closed my eyes and inhaled deeply. Held it. Let it out.

No, I didn't have my old support network anymore. I could go to Josh if I had a craving and was *really* desperate, but I wasn't itching for cocaine tonight, and even if I had been, I didn't want to wear out that tenuous welcome. Besides him, I didn't have people ready and willing to hold me accountable for the subtle slip-ups that those unfamiliar with my addiction wouldn't recognize. I could, I realized in this moment, absolutely get away with a drink and a line tonight, and no one would know.

But I'll know. I looked at myself in the mirror. *I'm* not *going down that road again.*

I don't want a drink.

I don't want a line.

Just sex.

A memory flashed through my mind of some of the absolutely *spectacular* sex I'd had while high, but I tamped it down. That wasn't what I wanted. Not anymore. Yes, it had been amazing at the time, but it had come at a cost I was no longer willing to pay. Not even in those moments of weakness when I convinced myself the cocaine was what I needed to be the hockey player who actually held on to his career.

A fleeting thought occurred to me that going to the club at all might be a bad idea. All that sensory overload with alcohol flowing all around me and—undoubtedly—someone in the room with cocaine they were willing to share. Maybe even someone who wanted to do some lines *and* hook up, making irresistible little suggestions as they grinned through the flickering lights and spoke over the backbeat of noise and chaos. That was all way too much temptation to back-slide on my sobriety.

Sheer stubbornness and fierce determination pushed those aside, though. I was not going to hide from my addiction. I was not going to let it control me anymore. I was absolutely capable of walking into that club, ordering something non-alcoholic, and walking out with a willing partner for the night. Sure, I wasn't going to find the kind of calm or bliss I'd had when I was still using, but I *would* find release, and tomorrow, I'd have my head together for practice and the game.

No, I didn't have any teammates who could hold me accountable anymore. I had myself, though, and damn it, that was enough. I'd made it this far. I'd stayed sober even when I'd wanted to do anything but. A lot of people thought I was a junkie, a relapse waiting to happen, and if anything, the need to prove them wrong was stronger than my desire for chemical bliss.

Fuck them.

I strode out of the bathroom, found my wallet and keys, and left.

Time to go get laid.

CHAPTER 22

JOSH

Ugh. Finally.

I pulled into the parking garage below my apartment complex. I'd gone to the neurologist after practice, and I'd spent part of the afternoon talking to a Realtor. Both had gone well enough, but it had been a long day, and I'd capped it off by spending a solid hour in Seattle's legendary traffic. To say the least, I was glad to be home.

I shut off the engine and rubbed my eyes. The neurologist appointment had just been an introduction to the new doc who'd be keeping up on my concussion symptoms going forward. She'd reviewed my records from my previous doctor, and she was pleased with my progress. She'd also suggested a different medication to help with the migraines. Not a bad visit.

The Realtor had been a little more depressing. I'd wanted to get a general idea of the market in this famously expensive area. I wasn't going to be buying any time soon— not until I had more than a one-year contract and felt like my position was a bit less precarious—but it didn't hurt to get an idea of what I'd be getting into if and when that time came.

Million-dollar postage stamp condos and shoebox apartments, that was what I'd be getting into. Ugh. I already didn't get paid nearly as much as some of the superstars in the league, and I'd taken a pay cut when I'd come to Seattle. The sprawling place I'd had with Damon in Calgary—I couldn't touch anything like that here. A one- or two-bedroom condo outside the city was probably the best I could hope for, at least until Damon and I sold our place.

Ah, well. I had an apartment, and it was a nice one. I had a contract, even if it was a short one. For now, that would have to do.

With a sigh, I collected my phone out of the cupholder and got out of the car.

And wouldn't you know it? I wasn't the only one in this garage right now.

As I started toward the elevators, Sol was coming the opposite direction, staring at something on his phone as he walked, and he...

Oh, hell. He looked good. The black pants were so snug, they might as well have been leather, and something about the way that belt sat on his narrow hips made my breath stutter. His white T-shirt wasn't much looser than his pants. When he was dancing or sitting, he knew exactly how to position himself so clothes like that would show off the abs I'd once left a bite mark on. Fuck, he was hot.

The way he was dressed also left zero doubt about where he was going, and a mix of fear and fury turned my blood to ice.

Before I could stop myself, I growled, "Seriously?"

His head snapped up and he stopped dead. Then his expression darkened. "What?"

"You're going clubbing."

His eyes widened for a second, as if he were startled, but then he must've remembered that *we* used to go clubbing together. I knew exactly how he dressed when he wanted to look good on the dancefloor. When he wanted to be noticed. No, the outfit wasn't exactly flashy, particularly not in the clubs we'd gone to, but he had the body to make it unbearably sexy, and he knew how to use it. No way in hell he didn't intend to go out and use it like that tonight. He was undoubtedly going out to get something. I just couldn't tell if he was after something to go in his ass, his mouth, or his nose.

Sol stepped closer, glaring hard at me. "I'm sorry, am I not allowed to go out?" He gestured at me with his phone. "Do I need to bring you along as a chaperone?"

I faced him fully and crossed my arms. "That depends."

"Does it, now?" He gave a caustic laugh. "On what?"

I set my jaw. "On whether you're out on the prowl for a piece of ass, or if you're looking for a hit of—"

"Oh, fuck off, Josh." He rolled his eyes. "That was years ago. And a lot of *rehab* ago, not that you'd fucking care."

That hit below the belt, which caught me by surprise. The words *"No, I* don't *fucking care"* desperately wanted to come flying off my tongue, but they didn't. I couldn't say it. He'd done enough lying for the both of us while we'd been together.

I didn't *want* to care, but fuck me, I did. And after that night I'd helped him through a craving, he fucking *knew* I cared, just like we both knew there was a part of him—a very convincing part—that still wanted cocaine.

Keeping my voice even, I said, "It hasn't been that long since you had a bad craving for—"

"And I'm good now. I wouldn't be going out like this if I wasn't."

I pressed my lips together. "We also have a game tomorrow. And *you're* starting in the net." I gestured at him. "You really going to be in any shape to—"

"Go fuck yourself," he snapped. Then he shoved his phone into his back pocket and came closer, eyes narrow and lips pulled back across his teeth. "Why do you even give a shit, huh? Because if I go out and fuck myself up the way you obviously think I will, then Coach will drop the tandem goalie shit and you'll get the start, won't you? Isn't that what you want?"

Rage boiled in my chest, but I kept it back as much as I could. "I want to *earn* the starting position. Not get it because you fell off the goddamned wagon and couldn't stay on your skates."

Sol's bark of laughter was frosty and humorless. "Is that it, then? You want me to keep my shit together so you can win because the victory just isn't as sweet if you only got it because I fucked up? Am I close? You want to beat me instead of letting me fuck myself up?"

"That's not it at all," I growled. I didn't even think we were really arguing about hockey at all. "Christ, what the hell is wrong with you? You're my ex, but you're still my damn teammate, and no, I don't want you to get fucked up." I swallowed, and damn if my voice didn't try real hard to crack as I added, "I don't have to like you to want you to be okay."

He blinked, but then rolled his eyes. "Yeah, you care about me as far as I can benefit you as a teammate. Typical Josh."

I stared at him. Oh, we were doing this, weren't we? Right here, right now? After that night I'd spent losing my damn mind in his apartment? After I'd been going insane because I'd said we could only be teammates while every part of me was *screaming* for more? "Is that—are you fucking kidding me? Is that really what you think?"

"I think it's giving you a lot more credit than you deserve."

"What the hell is that supposed to mean?"

Another sharp, bitter laugh. "Oh, come on. I may have been out of it there at the end, but I'm not stupid. As soon as you got the team to throw me into rehab, you bounced. Completely washed your hands of me. Once I wasn't a liability to—"

"That is *not* what happened," I snarled through the sudden sting in my eyes. "Not even close, you son of a bitch. And you *know* it."

I would never lay a hand on someone if we weren't on the ice, but I wouldn't lie—there was a momentary compulsion to backhand that smug skepticism right off his fucking face. I couldn't have done it even if I really wanted to, though, because my legs also suddenly felt like they weren't going to hold me up for much longer. As if the unspoken *"we both know you didn't care about me"* in his expression was enough to knock my knees right out from under me. Hadn't I convinced him otherwise? Apparently not. Jesus Christ.

Somehow, I found enough breath to grit out, "I didn't just walk away for kicks, you know. It fucking *hurt* to see you like that."

"So you just bailed?" he demanded. "Things got rough, so you got out before—"

"I could've bailed a long, long time before that." I stepped closer, glaring right up into his eyes, and damn if even the rage could keep my voice steady. "I tried to help you for *months*, Sol. Fucking *months*. If I'd just been looking out for myself, I'd have been gone long before you ever saw the inside of that facility."

"You couldn't do that, though, could you?" Sarcasm dripped off every syllable. "Not until I was suspended and couldn't fuck up the team any more than I already had. We both know it's true. You—"

"It's *not* true," I hissed. "I tried to—"

"I needed *help*," he snapped. "From people who knew me and loved me. You made it clear as day that you didn't when you—"

"Don't you dare say I didn't love you," I snarled. "Don't you fucking dare, Sol."

He blinked.

"I loved you," I said, voice even shakier now. "I did everything I could think of to help you, even when you didn't want help and when no one believed me. I put my goddamned *career* on the line to save you."

He laughed bitterly. "Bullshit."

"It's not bullshit. You never knew this, but Coach and the GM sat me down and threatened to send me to the minors because I wasn't playing for shit. And I told them exactly why I wasn't playing for shit—because you were an addict and no one would listen to me, and it was tearing me apart." I swallowed hard, determined not to lose my composure as I ripped open this years-old wound for him to see. "I told them straight out to test you, and that if you didn't pop positive, they could release me from my contract and I'd never play hockey again."

Sol stared at me in utter disbelief. Oh, I had his attention now.

My voice still threatened to crack as I said, "I literally bet my career on you testing positive, because it was the only way I could convince someone to help you. And by the time they did..." I gritted my teeth and swallowed again, struggling against that lump in my throat. "Your addiction didn't just hurt you, Sol. That year? All that time I spent trying to save you from yourself and get someone—anyone— to help you? That fucking destroyed me, okay? It broke me. I had to watch the man I loved self-destructing, and by the time I finally got you some help, I could barely stand on my own two feet anymore." My eyes burned, and at this point, I didn't even care if he saw how raw and hurt I was. Hell, I *wanted* him to see it. "Don't you *dare* tell me I didn't love you. I fucking *still* love you, and I hate myself for that because all it's ever gotten me is the worst pain I've ever known."

Sol's lips parted, shock written all over his face. Finally, voice barely a whisper, he said, "You...you still..."

"Yes," I gritted out. "I never *stopped* loving you. Not even when I wanted to."

More shock. More silence.

When his paralysis finally broke, though, he didn't say a word.

He just stepped closer, grabbed my neck in both hands, and kissed me.

I was too startled to shove him away, and by the time the shock wore off...

Fuck. Who was I kidding? I wanted him. I always had. If I had one weakness on this earth, it was Cary goddamned Solomon, and his sudden, needy kiss made me want to drop to my knees in front of him. I was way more raw and off-balance than when we'd kissed in his kitchen, and I wanted to cry with frustration, relief, need, and hell if I knew how many other emotions. I wanted everything Sol's kiss offered and then some.

And just like that moment in his kitchen, I couldn't resist him. I didn't want to. Consequences and regrets be damned—I wanted him so bad I could barely breathe. When I did manage to breathe, I caught the intoxicating scent of that cologne he'd always worn. How many times over the years had I smelled it and thought of him? One hint of that familiar sandalwood tinged with something faintly citrusy, and my mind was instantly fixed on him. And that was when I *wasn't* holding on to him and losing myself in that kiss that I couldn't deny I'd been missing all these years.

When we came up for air, we were both shaking. Both panting. My fingertips trembled on his cheek. His ragged breath gusted across my lips. Just like it had in his kitchen, the whole world was spinning around us, and I was pretty sure Sol was the only thing keeping me upright. That might've been mutual.

I was a wreck. Physically. Emotionally. My cheeks were damp. Something in my head screamed that this was wrong. Something else screamed that it was more right than anything had been in a long time. Years, even. And there was a little part of me that said being with me meant Sol wouldn't go out to the club, and then he wouldn't...

But I didn't just want to keep him away from any threats to his sobriety. Right now, *he* was *my* temptation— the habit I thought I'd broken but desperately wanted to dive into without caring about anything else.

Sol touched his forehead to mine. His voice was soft now, and unsteady: "I love you, Josh. I've... God, I always have."

Fresh tears rolled down my face and my throat was too tight to speak, so I did the next best thing—I kissed him again. The quiet moan he released took me back to some of the hottest, sexiest nights of my life, not to mention some of the sweetest and most romantic moments. Sol had been there for some of the worst—he'd been the catalyst for all kinds of hell—but no matter how much I'd tried to tell myself otherwise, he'd played a crucial role in so many of the best, too. So many moments and feelings I hadn't realized I'd been missing this much.

He broke the kiss with a gasp and met my gaze with eyes full of fire I hadn't seen in years. "My place?"

Two words. That was all we needed. We both knew what he meant and exactly what would happen if I said yes.

That voice in my head told me I'd hate myself for this later. Maybe I would. No, I *definitely* would.

But right now, that didn't sound so bad in exchange for a little while—even a few minutes—of feeling good like only Sol had ever made me feel good.

So I nodded. "Y-yeah. Your place."

CHAPTER 23

SOL

Our clothes may as well have been goalie pads for all they let me feel Josh's body, so I was pulling his out of the way as soon as we were through my apartment door. He was doing the same, panting between kisses as he shoved my shirt off and fumbled with my belt.

When he dragged me down on top of him in my bed, there was nothing left between us but body heat and unrelenting need. It had been years since I'd been naked with Josh, but goddamn, we picked up right where we'd left off, kissing and touching like we still had each other's turn-ons committed to memory. As if I could ever forget anything about being in bed with this beautiful, responsive man.

As we made out and wound each other up, my mind was going a million miles an hour. Even more than it usually did, and way more than it did when I was in bed with someone. So many feelings. So much that I wanted and needed. And wasn't there some reason we weren't supposed to do this? Or, like, several reasons?

Probably.

Yes.

Fuck it. Josh's hands... His mouth... His body... The way he held on to me like—

No, seriously. We said we couldn't do this. And there were reasons for that. Big ones. A lot of them.

Somehow, I talked myself into breaking the kiss, and I met his gaze. Oh, God, the fire in those gorgeous brown eyes. Took me right back to those nights when we—

"We said...we said we weren't going to do this again."

"I know." Josh swept his tongue across his kiss-swollen lips. "But we're..." He shook his head. "I fucking want you. I can't help it."

"Same, but after last time—"

"Are you using me as a distraction from cocaine?"

I blinked. "What? No! Absolutely not."

Josh drew me in, grinning, and just before our lips met, he murmured, "Then this is something else."

His kiss silenced everything. I was pretty sure the situation wasn't as simple as he was making it out to be, but whatever. I couldn't think when Josh's tongue was in my mouth.

So...I didn't.

This was hot, and familiar, and overwhelming, and I completely lost myself in it. In *him*. I still knew in the back of my mind that this didn't solve a damn thing, and it was a terrible idea for a million reasons, but...

But I just couldn't help myself. Not with eager hands sliding all over my body. Not with deep, hungry kisses stealing my breath and turning my whole body to pure fire.

Josh nudged me, and we shifted positions so he was on top now, his lips never leaving mine until I'd landed fully on the pillow. Then, and only then, he started down my chin and over my jaw. He kissed up and down my neck just like he always had in the past, and I squeezed my eyes shut as I tilted my head back to offer up more of my throat. The soft skate of his lips and the warm rush of his breath had me arching off the bed and ready to go out of my goddamned mind.

"Jesus, Josh," I murmured, dragging my nails up his back. "You know exactly...exactly how to turn me on."

A breath of hot laughter rushed across my neck. "You make it sound like you're hard to turn on."

Under normal circumstances, I could banter and be witty in bed, but this wasn't normal circumstances. This was Josh O'Brien kissing my throat and turning me to absolute jelly. Fuck banter and wit—I just wanted him and all the heat and promise in his touch.

At the edges of my thoughts, alarm bells were going off, trying to pull my focus away from Josh and on to all the reasons this was a terrible idea. All the reasons we said we wouldn't do this. We were a mess. We had history. We had bullshit we needed to sort out—bullshit we'd been throwing in each other's faces right up until the second my lips had met his. None of that was going away just because we turned each other on too much to think about it, and there *would* be fallout from this.

My mind didn't—couldn't—linger on any of that, though. Josh held my focus like few things in this world ever could, and those alarm bells were muted by soft moans, shuddering sighs, and the creak of the mattress under our combined weight. Whatever happened afterward, I let Josh be the center of my universe for right now.

I don't care what happens next.

I dragged my palms down his sides as we explored each other's mouths with all the confidence of longtime lovers, and still with the wonder and reverence of the first time we'd ever touched.

All I want right now is this.

He sat up over me, and for a moment, I just stared at him, raking my eyes up and down that beautiful, powerful body.

All I want right now is you.

I was so caught up drinking him in, I almost didn't hear him when he breathed, "You have condoms?"

Oh, fuck yes.

I nodded. "Uh-huh. You want to be on top?" We were both as vers as they came, and although I'd topped him plenty of times, we'd usually gravitated toward him topping me. Not for any reason that I could put my finger on—it was just the groove we'd fallen into and both seemed to like.

So I wasn't ready when he murmured, "Actually...I haven't bottomed in ages."

A zing of need ran down my spine. "You want me to fuck you?"

The heat in his eyes answered loud and clear even before he rasped, "Yes. *Please.*"

Instantly, my mind was full of a pornographic film reel of topping him from every imaginable angle, in every position we could managed.

"Hell yes," I whispered.

He grinned, then claimed a kiss that had me wondering if I'd even get the condom out of the drawer before I came. Had I ever been this turned on before? Maybe, maybe not— the only thing I could say without a doubt was that if I *had* been this turned on before, it was with Josh. No one had ever taken me higher than he did, and I was overcome with a feeling that had become deliciously familiar during our relationship—that dizzying desire for a single night to last forever.

"Get the condoms," he rasped, the words halfway between a plea and a demand.

"Let me up."

He did, and I rolled toward the nightstand. I barely had my hand in the drawer before he'd molded his hot body against mine, and his lips traced up the back of my neck, scrambling my thoughts and making me tremble all over.

"Josh..." I closed my eyes and let my forehead touch the mattress. "I can't..."

He laughed softly and kissed the back of my shoulder. "I love making you shake like this."

Was I shaking? Oh, yeah. I was. All over.

"Let me get the condom," I panted, "and I'll make *you* shake."

His breath stuttered across my skin. Another kiss on my shoulder, and he released me. The coolness where we'd been touching was so jarring, it scrambled my thoughts for a couple of seconds. I almost forgot what I was doing, but my fingertips found the edge of a condom packet, and my focus came back.

I sat against the headboard, and as I put on the condom, I glanced at Josh, who was on his side, lazily stroking his dick as he watched me. "How do you want it?"

He licked his lips, then met my gaze through his long, dark lashes. "From behind. Fucking love it like that."

Dozens of memories suddenly vied for centerstage, every one of them focused on me riding Josh from behind. Sometimes sitting up with my hands on his hips. Sometimes laid out over him, driving him into the mattress. So, so many times of drinking in his scent as I kissed his neck and rocked into him until he was begging—almost sobbing —for me to make him come. *So* many orgasms, his and mine, that left us both a trembling, panting wreck afterward; all those sexy memories had me steel-hard right now.

From behind? Oh, baby, you don't have to ask me twice.

I shakily got the condom into place and murmured, "Turn around."

Josh grinned. He sat up and paused to kiss me, drawing it out until I was dizzy and out of breath all over again, and then he got on his hands and knees.

In our past life, he could usually bottom without a lot of prep, but he said it had been a long time. I also didn't want to take for granted that all the tension between us hadn't translated into physical tension, so I erred on the side of teasing him open until he was losing his mind.

"Sol," he rasped after I'd fingered him for ages. "For fuck's sake, would you just—oh, God. Yes."

I bit my lip as I pressed into him. I was already dizzy with need, but now that I was inside him—especially as I found the slow, steady rhythm that had always driven him out of his mind—I had to hold on to his hips just to keep myself upright. When was the last time sex had thrown off my balance and my equilibrium like this? I didn't know, but I had a feeling I knew who it had been with.

Sliding my hands up and down his sides, I watched myself sliding in and out of him. I missed the days when we did this bareback—missed that unfiltered contact—but I couldn't ask him to do that. Not now. And the muted sensation with a condom was still mind-blowing; it was impossible *not* to be on the verge of losing my mind when I was moving inside this man.

God, I missed you.

The thought dropped into my head without warning. It made me lose my rhythm for a few seconds, but I recovered, and hopefully Josh didn't notice.

I leaned down and wrapped an arm around his midsection, letting my lips skate along the back of his neck.

Josh shivered hard. "Oh, fuck..."

I kissed just below his hair. "Yeah?"

"Y-yeah..." He arched under me and clenched around me. "Love...love when you do that."

"What? This?" I brushed another kiss across his skin, and the shuddering gasp answered even before he murmured an affirmative.

"So good." His voice was strained. He let his head fall forward, and he rolled his hips with mine. "Slow like this. It's... God, Sol."

"Anything you want," I breathed. "I want to make you crazy."

The response was a whimper I'd heard so many times in the past. That sound that meant he was too far gone to articulate anything coherent. I loved it when he was like this. Loved the way he sounded. Loved the way he felt. Loved...

Loved him.

I squeezed my eyes shut and picked up some speed, reveling in his helpless moans. Distantly I was aware of silence where mental alarm bells had been clanging earlier, and if I focused, I could probably still make sense of the nebulous artifacts of whatever had had them going off in the first place. I didn't, though. I concentrated on the only thing in the universe that mattered—Josh.

"You're so damn hot," I purred in between kissing the side of his neck. "Josh, baby... My God, you're so sexy like this." He moaned in response, and I kept talking, but I didn't even know what I was saying. Hopefully he understood how much he turned me on, how hot he was, how perfect he was. If the words weren't coming out fully formed, hopefully he caught the meaning anyway.

Rocking in and out of him, I was on the verge of losing my mind from both ecstasy and frustration. I was so damn close, I knew for a fact that a few deep, hard thrusts would take me there in seconds. The bliss and relief were right there, frustratingly out of my reach but so, *so* close, but I couldn't stop this slow, fluid motion. I couldn't get enough of Josh. His body. His heat. His moans-bordering-on-sobs as I steadily pushed him closer and closer to his own release. I'd do this all night—frustration and exertion and everything —if I could just feel and hear him slowly unraveling in my arms like this.

I grabbed the headboard with one hand for balance, and with the other, I started pumping Josh's dick. That got me the choked moan I knew from our past. Breathless, slurred curses rolled off his tongue, and he rolled his hips to drive himself into my fist, which also drove my cock into him a little faster, a little harder. His hand joined mine on the headboard, and we both took advantage of the extra leverage. Faster. Harder.

"Sol," he murmured. "Please."

I closed my eyes and buried my face in his neck. So close. So fucking... Jesus, I was right there. I didn't even know if I could speak coherently, but I tried anyway: "Come, baby. Take me with you."

Then, just like he had every time I'd whispered that to him in the past, he shivered hard. Gasped. Cried out.

And in an instant, everything was just bliss and heat and release.

When the smoke cleared, we'd both sunk down to the mattress. I had the presence of mind to keep enough weight off him that he could still breathe, but mostly, I slumped over him as we both trembled and took in gulps of air.

Those alarm bells were ringing again. Distant, quiet, but getting louder like approaching sirens.

I closed my eyes and buried my face against Josh's neck again.

All the reasons why this was wrong—those could wait.

For right now—if only for this moment—everything in my world was perfect.

CHAPTER 24

JOSH

There were very few constants in the world. The sun rising and setting. The tide going out and coming in. The inability of the Cleveland Ice Sharks to make the playoffs even with generational talents on their roster.

And among those constants—the way Sol could, with a look or a kiss, ignite desire in me that no one else ever had. Didn't matter what we'd been through—what he'd put me through—I had always been putty in his hands, and tonight was no exception.

Was that healthy? Probably not. But the second he'd kissed me in the parking garage, I'd needed him too damn much to think, and giving in to all that desire had felt a million times better than everything else I'd been feeling right then, so...fuck it. And in the moment, it had been amazing. Spectacular. Not just because Sol could drive me wild like no one else in the world, but because I'd been over-whelmed with the need to be touched at all. That moment in his kitchen when Sol'd kissed me and backed off had been a painful reminder of how long it had been since I'd felt an affectionate touch at all, and I'd been hungry for it ever since.

Tonight, Sol had given me everything I'd been aching for since... Hell, since my marriage had started unraveling, now that I thought about it For a little while, I'd been lost in someone. I'd been *desired*.

And now...

Oh God. I was going to be sick.

I didn't know if it was because I'd had sex with Sol, or because I'd enjoyed it so much, or because I physically ached to do it again, but either way...I was going to be sick.

I hated myself for wanting him so badly, and for giving in to that temptation even though I'd known all the way to my fucking bones that I'd regret it afterward. Nothing ever ended well between us, no matter how good it was in the moment.

Standing at his bathroom sink, staring at my reflection as a few water drops slid off my hair, I let that regret roll over me. For not pushing Sol away when he'd kissed me. For not saying no when he'd suggested taking this upstairs. For not putting a stop to it once the clothes had started coming off. For being here in Seattle at all.

"Goddammit," I whispered into the silence, and wiped a hand over my face, brushing away some of the cold water I'd just splashed on it. If I'd just worked harder to get back on my game after the concussion. If I'd kept it together through the divorce. If I'd kept my stats up. Kept my place on the team that had become home. I knew most of that wasn't possible—head injuries healed on their own time, and I defied anyone to get through a divorce like mine without crumbling—but I was still kicking myself. I could've done better. I could've done more. I could've picked up an extension in Calgary, or been signed elsewhere, but no, I'd fallen the fuck apart and wound up here, and how fucking poetic was it that my downward spiral had landed me in my ex-boyfriend's bed after I'd *sworn* we wouldn't do this.

Amber had encouraged me to just do it, and I'd hemmed and hawed about it, but now I knew it was a mistake. After the fact, of course. Christ. At this rate, I might as well text Damon and ask if he was still interested in hooking up, because what was one more in an ever-growing list of self-sabotaging fuck-ups?

Except...no. I didn't want Damon. I never wanted his hands on me again. The thought of him kissing me made my stomach turn in a very different way. That was revulsion, not regret.

Sol didn't have that effect. Maybe life would be easier if he did.

I inhaled deeply through my nose, and fuck me, but I could still smell his familiar cologne. I didn't even know what brand it was, only that it was popular enough for me to catch a whiff of it now and then, and it always made me think of him. This time, it had been on him and so was I, and I'd let myself get high on that scent while I got drunk on him.

I may as well have killed a bottle of tequila for all I was paying for it now. I wasn't getting violently sick, but it wouldn't take much to get me there.

What was I thinking? Goddammit, what was I thinking?

And now that I could think again...what was I supposed to do next?

Oh, I knew exactly what I needed to do. The worst part of still being in love with Dr. Jekyll was knowing I couldn't be with him because of Mr. Hyde. And there was no separating the two.

So. Yeah. I knew what I needed to do. First things first,

get dressed and get the hell out of here. There was no way I was getting my head together while I was still in Sol's apartment with my clothes all over his bedroom floor.

I gave myself one more look in the mirror, took a deep breath—fuck that cologne—and headed out of the bathroom.

Sol was lounging on the bed, the sheet draped partly over him. For a second, he was the very picture of satisfaction—heavy-lidded eyes, a faint grin, the lingering flush in his face and neck—but as soon as our gazes locked, he tensed. Sitting up, he swallowed hard.

The sex had cooled the anger from earlier, but now the hurt was coming through. All the memories of when we'd touched like this in the past. Back before things had gotten complicated.

Back before Sol—

No. No. Now wasn't the time for that. Yes, I still blamed Sol for destroying our relationship. And yes, he was the one who'd kissed me in the parking lot and lit this fuse. But I'd made the choice to follow him up to his apartment. Hell, I'd made the choice to be confrontational instead of just walking past him like any sane person would have. When he'd kissed me, when I'd come up here with him, when I'd taken off my clothes and his, when I'd pulled him down onto his bed—I'd been well aware of what I was doing and with whom. I mean, fuck, he'd even tapped the brakes because we'd promised we wouldn't do this, and I'd said, "Let's go." I could blame him for a lot of things, but the blame for this fell squarely on my stupid head.

I should've said no. It wasn't just that I shouldn't have said yes—I shouldn't have *wanted* to say yes as badly as I had in that moment.

"I need to go," I said without preamble.

"Josh." Sol put up his hands and held my gaze. "Wait."

"For what?" My mouth had gone dry and my voice sounded raw. "I shouldn't even be here."

He winced. "We should talk about this."

Right then, he was a mix of two sides of him I'd known all too well in the past. The sex-tousled and satiated version who'd shared my bed, and also the pleading and apologetic version who'd convinced me time after time that he was done using. I knew that second part wasn't what he was doing now. As far as I knew, he was clean these days. This wasn't about his addiction—it was about us.

Except there was no "us" without his addiction. Looking back, there probably never had been—I just hadn't been aware of it until he couldn't hide it anymore.

"Josh," he pleaded. "Talk to me."

I swallowed past my emotions as I shakily pulled on my jeans. "We said we wouldn't... We *can't* do this, Sol."

"It's better than the alternative, isn't it?" He sounded like he was trying to keep the comment light—*almost* making a joke, but not quite. "Barely being able to be in the same room?"

"I don't think... This is going to make that worse, isn't it?"

He chewed his lip. "It doesn't have to."

"But it will. You know it will." I cleared my throat, and my voice refused to stay steady, but whatever. Sol had seen me cry before. "We're bad for each other. We can already barely coexist as teammates. We can't afford to be messy, and even if it's fun in the moment, this"—I flailed a hand, encompassing us and the bed we'd thoroughly rumpled —"*isn't* going to help with that."

"We still have to coexist," he acknowledged quietly. "And...I mean, we do like each other better when we're in bed." He shrugged, and there was a hint of a cautious smile on his lips as he ventured, "Maybe this is what we need."

The absolute avalanche of emotions almost knocked me off my feet. I fucking hated that so many of those emotions were in favor of his stupid idea. I had missed him. What we'd been together. What we were like when the clothes were gone and nothing mattered but each other. I still missed that, and his suggestion made me ache for it. The idea that we could have that again—even if it was just a fraction of what we had before—made me want to grab on to him and not let go.

But those feelings—the ragged remnants of love, some pathetic nostalgia, all of it—were buried under the rest of the avalanche.

"Are you insane?" I hissed, narrowing my eyes at him. "You think we should keep sleeping together? *Regularly?* Because—what? So we can maybe fuck away the awkwardness and coexist on the team without killing each other?" I made a disgusted sound and shook my head. "Fuck off, Sol. I'm not screwing you just because it's better than hating each other."

God, that hurt just to say out loud. Sex between him and me was too good to be the lesser of two evils. Way too good to be something we just did because the alternative was miserable and career-threatening. His suggestion... Ugh, it just made everything that had ever existed between us feel cheap and scummy.

Sol exhaled hard. "Do you have any better ideas? Because we're both stuck here, and—"

I laughed bitterly. "Oh, yeah, that makes it even *more* appealing. Let's pretend you didn't destroy our relationship and—"

"I never suggested pretending I didn't." His voice was

suddenly laced with anger, but there was a tremor that made me think the anger was shielding some feelings that hit closer to the bone. "I've *never* forgotten it, Josh. Never. But we're both stuck here. Both of our careers are hanging by a thread, and us being able to coexist plays a much bigger part than I'd like in whether that thread snaps or not." He spread his hands, the anger fading in favor of the hurt he'd obviously been trying to hide. "So maybe I'm just out of goddamned ideas for getting through the rest of the season."

I looked away, grinding my teeth so hard they hurt. "We shouldn't. We can't."

"What else do you have in mind?"

Begging the GM to trade me to the East Coast, effective immediately, that's what. Send me to fucking Cleveland. Just get me out of here.

I didn't say that, though. I didn't say much of anything except, "I need to go."

"Josh..." He let that soft plea trail off, and he didn't follow it with anything else. Maybe there was nothing to say right now. He'd already put it out there, what he thought was our best solution.

Neither of us spoke while I dressed. He didn't follow me out of the bedroom, and I was grateful for that. I let myself out of the apartment, locking the door behind me, and then went upstairs to my own place.

As soon as I was inside, I leaned against the door, swore into the silence, and let our conversation knock around in my head like a couple of oversized defensemen duking it out on the ice.

Keep hooking up? Because that was better than hating each other while we were stuck on the same roster? Fucking seriously, Sol?

I hated him for suggesting it. For thinking I'd want to be

his casual lover or fuck buddy or whatever he'd had in mind. For thinking sex was the answer—the thing that might soothe some of the resentment between us so we could function as teammates and maybe even be friends. I *hated* him.

But most of all...

I hated myself for wanting all that and more.

———

I was a mess. No two ways about it. Truthfully, I hadn't been okay in a long time—having your health, career, and marriage implode all at once kind of has that effect—but ever since that night in Sol's apartment, I'd been a goddamned wreck. *That* night? Hell, *those* nights. The one where he'd been trying to fight off a craving for cocaine, and the one where we'd both given in to this craving for each other. We were a disaster, and we both needed some space to get our heads right.

I hated this distance between me and Sol.

We could barely look at each other, which seriously sucked when we couldn't *avoid* each other. One minute I hated myself for not hating him enough to say no that night. The next, I wondered how I'd ever thought resisting him was an option.

At least no one else seemed to notice. If nothing else, we were getting better at keeping our bullshit out of everyone's sight. Especially Kayla's, since she'd made it clear she wasn't having it.

I sure knew about it, though. I couldn't concentrate on anything. I couldn't sleep. I'd almost run a red light on the way home from practice yesterday. I'd been rattled because I'd spent the whole practice struggling to focus. During a scrimmage, I'd wanted to stride across the sheet, grab him by the arm, drag him someplace private, and fuck again until we were a sweaty, shaking mess. I'd also wanted to face off with him and demand to know what right he'd had to put me through all that hell back then and all this hell now.

And on top of all that...

Sol wasn't the only member of the Sasquatches who was on my radar. During that brief window when things had been good between Sol and me, I should've taken my mouth off him and jumped on the opportunity to bring up one of our *other* teammates.

Colfax.

That man *had* to be a cocaine user. There was no way he wasn't. And he and Sol had been awfully friendly lately.

On the other hand, what if Sol hadn't noticed? If I pointed it out to him, would that make him put some distance between himself and Colfax? Or would it make him get even friendlier in hopes that our teammate might hook him up?

What was the right thing to do in this stupidly complicated situation? Because while throwing up my hands and screaming sounded the most appealing, I was pretty sure that wouldn't actually help.

For today, I'd try to do the thing I usually did best: play hockey. We had a game tonight, one that I was starting, and I needed to be sharp. Seattle was on a hot streak—we'd gone 7-2-1 in our last ten games, and both of the regulation losses had come down to a single goal. Team morale was good. Kayla and Coach Maines were both pleased with how Sol and I were tending goal. I needed to do my part to continue that trend.

Our morning skate was optional, and unsurprisingly, the crowd in the locker room was sparse. Sometimes I bowed out of the optional skates. They were kind of a pain in the dick, especially since it meant putting on and taking off all my gear multiple times in the same day. On the other hand, having the opportunity to attend optional morning skates in the first place meant I still had a hockey career, so I did attend them more often than not.

Like this morning. My hips were also a little stiff today, which happened sometimes—goaltending was *not* kind to the hips—so I wanted to skate a bit and do some light practicing just to loosen up all the bitchy muscles and tendons. As I put on my gear, my back had some complaints, too, so yeah, being here was definitely a good idea.

On my way to the ice, the sounds of pucks cracking against the boards and the glass echoed up the tunnel along with voices. Was I late? No, I wasn't late. Some teammates getting an early start, I guessed. Usually the first goalie on the ice for practice or a morning skate was the starter for that night, but sometimes people showed up early if they wanted to get in some individual work. Or if they were injured and skating alone as part of their rehab.

Lo and behold, I stepped out onto the ice to find Järvinen skating with a trainer. The kid was wearing a full face shield and a no-contact jersey, so he was probably still week-to-week at best. At least he'd been cleared to skate so he could keep up his timing and conditioning. There was some talk about him rejoining the team for practice before too much longer; that was promising. Fingers crossed—he'd missed most of the season already.

His frustration was evident, too. He'd been a cheerful and chill kid at training camp, but today, he was on the spicy side. When a puck pinged off the iron, his shout of "Fuck!" reached the rafters.

I winced on his behalf. Poor kid. Being injured sucked. I

wasn't surprised to see him *or* his anger out here before practice.

What I *hadn't* expected was to see Axel and Sol out here already.

At the opposite end of the sheet from where Järvinen was working (and swearing), it looked like Axel was practicing getting into close quarters with the goalie. He'd been a little timid about getting right up to and even into the crease, so Sol was helping him out before practice started. Axel worked on shooting from just outside the crease, snagging the rebounds before they were out of reach, and battling to squeak pucks past Sol's pads from inches away. Being well-practiced and fearless at close range like that could separate a good forward from a spectacular one, and Sol was a great goalie to work with if someone wanted to hone those skills. He'd always been a force to be reckoned with when opponents brought the battle right to his front door, and I'd aspired for years to be as good as he was in that department.

Axel would learn a lot from Sol. I could say plenty about Sol, but he'd always been one of those goalies who could elevate the play of any skater who worked with him.

As I was getting warmed up, other players joined us on the ice...including Colfax.

That in and of itself didn't raise any red flags. He came to most of the optional skates. No, there were two things that had my heart pounding with worry.

One, the way he immediately zeroed in on Sol and Axel. He seemed to be best friends with everyone on the team, but I really, really didn't like how much he gravitated toward Sol. How well those two got along. How much time they spent hanging out on and off the ice.

Because the other thing that bothered me right now?

The conspicuous way Colfax kept sniffling and wiping his nose.

Dude. It's not even noon. Are you fucking serious?

But I knew he was. Because I knew that snorting a line first thing in the morning wasn't exactly out of character for a cocaine user. Because I'd witnessed it myself. With the man who was currently leaning on the goal with his mask pushed up on his head, laughing with Axel at something Colfax had said.

I swallowed bile as I skated a few slow circles, ostensibly to warm up instead of expending this nervous energy that was suddenly crackling through me.

This was bad. Seriously bad. Even if Sol's sobriety was on the rails right now—and I had every reason to believe it was—there were moments when he was holding on by his fingernails. I'd witnessed one of those moments with my own eyes.

So what the hell happened when he hit one of those weak moments at the same time Colfax started arranging white powder into tidy, tempting lines? Or casually asked him if he wanted to partake? Or hell, Sol caved in on his own and asked Colfax to hook him up?

What are you doing, Sol?

He of all people had to know how dangerous it was for a recovering addict to hang around an active user. They must've warned about that in rehab, right? Seemed like common fucking sense to me.

And yet, there he was—still fighting his own addiction, still struggling with the occasional nearly irresistible craving, and still hanging out with an obvious cocaine user.

Plus, he and I weren't exactly friendly right now. Maybe not as hostile as when we'd first arrived in Seattle, but the air between us was...off. That made me one less person he'd feel like he could come to if he had another rough night.

Guilt prodded at me, but also frustration with him. I knew him, and I knew he'd be wary of reaching out to me right now, and yet he was *still* putting himself so close to an obvious cocaine user.

How the fuck did he think this was going to end?

And what the fuck could I do about it?

CHAPTER 25

SOL

I swear to God, the next time he does this, I'm going to lose my shit.

I gripped my water glass so tight, it was a miracle it didn't splinter in my fist as I watched Josh and Colfax laughing at something on Josh's phone.

I'd been sitting at a table in the hotel bar with Colfax, Darby, and Axel, when Josh had appeared, insisting Colfax had to see this video that had just posted of someone they'd both been teammates with at different points in their careers. Something about him getting into a fight with a defenseman twice his size and getting his ass handed to him. I didn't catch much more than that—I was too busy being irritated that, yet again, Josh had materialized while I was in the same space as Colfax. It was getting conspicuous, and I didn't like it.

The video ended, and Colfax and Josh laughed and joked about it for a moment. Fortunately, Josh didn't stick around this time, though he did pause as he was wandering away.

"Oh, hey, Eggs?" he said to Axel, who was beside me. "Good game tonight, kid."

Unaware of the annoyance simmering in me, Axel grinned. "Thanks! I'm gonna get that first goal yet."

Josh chuckled. "Give it time. You're racking up the assists, though."

Axel beamed. Josh's eyes flicked to me, and his smile faltered. Only for a second, though. Then he was gone.

Conversation at my table resumed, but I didn't take part. I was too busy fuming.

The thing was, people drifted in and out of each other's orbits when we were hanging out like this. I did it. Everyone did it. It was just part of being social with the team.

No, what annoyed me was that this was the *fifth* time in as many days that Josh had found his way into a conversation I was having with Colfax. Once, it had been toward the end of practice, when Josh had suddenly needed a defenseman for something he was doing with Sweetman and Kayla. Then on the plane, a card game had needed another player, and Colfax could never say no if the game was Uno.

After that, Josh always seemed to notice exactly the kind of women who piqued Colfax's interest. We'd all be hanging out, and Josh would appear and whisper something to Colfax, and suddenly Colfax would be gone—off to chat up the girl Josh had spotted. Colfax had even commented one morning that Josh was the best wingman he'd ever had.

Now this. What the fuck?

I wanted to know, and my opportunity to ask came when I saw Josh step out of the bar to take a call. A short one, fortunately—probably his agent, judging by the snippets I heard—and when he turned around to come inside, I was waiting for him, blocking the door like it was a goal.

He stopped, looked me up and down, and set his jaw. "What?"

I cut right to the chase: "Is there a reason you keep insinuating yourself into my conversations?"

He eyed me coolly. "Is there a reason you're sticking so close to Colfax?"

I laughed humorlessly. "What? Do I have to run it by you before I make friends with my teammates? Or is this second grade where I can't be friends with someone who's also your friend? Am I getting warmer?"

His glare hardened. "It's not that, and you know it."

"No, actually, I don't." I stepped closer to him, and through gritted teeth, I demanded, "What exactly is your fucking problem?"

"I don't know, Sol." He glared right back at me, not backing down at all. "Maybe I know you too well to think you should be hanging around a fellow cokehead."

My lips parted. It took several seconds for me to fully process what he'd said. What he was implying. Even still, I asked, "What the fuck are you talking about?"

He narrowed his eyes. "Don't play stupid. We both know Colfax is—"

"We don't know shit about him," I growled, even as my stomach dropped at the realization that Josh had picked up on the same thing. "And it doesn't matter if he is because I'm *not*. I'm *done* with that crap."

"Are you, though?" He cocked his head, suspicion and sarcasm coming off him in waves. "You said yourself you've fallen off the wagon before."

My teeth snapped together. "You're really going to throw that in my face? Seriously?"

He waved his hand sharply, as if he were batting away my disbelief like an errant puck. "I'm not throwing anything in your face. I'm acknowledging reality. This team is relying on you, and here you are, flirting with temptation."

God, the audacity of this fuckhead.

"You make it sound like I don't have anything on the line here," I threw back. "You really think I want to risk my last chance at a hockey career with—"

"You didn't think twice about risking what we had," he hissed. "Why should you start caring about anything now?"

The words slammed into me like a skater crashing my goal. It was a genuine miracle I didn't need to take a few steps back just to regain my balance. Somehow, though, I stayed rooted to the spot, staring at him.

"If you want to fuck yourself over," he went on through clenched teeth, "then do it. But this whole team is relying on you. If it's not too much to ask, don't fuck us over." He narrowed his eyes, and his voice dropped to a furious growl: "Haven't you and your habit done enough damage?"

It took so, so much self-control not to lose my temper and blow up at him. I was acutely aware that we were in public, though, even if we'd stepped out where there weren't so many people around. Staying as calm as I could, I said, "I know I did a lot of damage. No one knows that better than I do. I'm not about to do that again."

His lips thinned. "You sure about that?"

My temper again tried to surge through, but I just gritted out, "Eat a dick, Josh."

"Tell me I'm wrong to worry that might be—"

"You *are* wrong." The words came out louder than I meant, but fuck it. "If you want to make assumptions about me using, then fine. Go right ahead." I swallowed my own shame and fury. "But I try every goddamned day to stay sober. I don't want to go through that hell again, and—"

"Yeah, you say that, but we both know it's only hell

when you're sober. When you're using, you're all about getting high and staying that way." Josh gestured sharply. "Fuck everyone and everything else as long as you can get fucked up."

"I'm done with all of that." I stepped up close, right into his space, and glared down at him. "I know what I did back then, and I'm not doing it again. I'm sure as shit not dragging the team down—"

"Bullshit," he snapped. "You can say that now, but don't act like you'll be singing the same tune if you start using again." He stabbed a finger at me, and his voice wavered slightly as he snarled, "Because you had no problem dragging me into your fucking addiction with you, even if you never offered me a single goddamned line."

I blinked.

"You had no problem fucking me over with it," he went on, anger and hurt coming through equally loud and clear. "So how am I going to take you at your word that you're not going to do it again when your drug of choice is *right there*? Huh? Tell me, Sol, because all I have to go on is your history, which happens to be *our* history, so forgive me if I don't buy that you give two shits who you destroy as long as you get that high you're always missing."

My throat tightened around my breath. I wanted so badly to lash out at him. How dare he throw my addiction in my face like that? But at the same time... Fuck. He wasn't wrong. When I was neck deep in cocaine and high as balls, I didn't know or care who I was hurting. Who I was taking down with me. I didn't care about anything except getting high, staying high, and getting higher.

Voice quieter but no less hurt or angry, he said, "You're a different person when you're using. We both know that. And staying sober is hard for you. It is for anyone, but I've seen how hard it is for you, even now." He exhaled. "I want you to stay sober, Sol. For the team, and because I *do* care about you."

I winced. I believed him, which was part of what made this conversation so damn hard. For all the reasons I'd given him to hate me, I believed him when he said he gave a shit about me. Barely whispering, I said, "I know."

Josh pointed at his face, his hand shaking ever so slightly. "Then look me in the eye and tell me you're not courting disaster by being so goddamned friendly with someone we both know is using. And don't fucking lie to me."

I swallowed past the sudden lump in my throat. He had every right to make that accusation and to demand that truth from me. He had every right to want to protect our team and himself from me.

"I'm not lying." I spoke slowly, carefully, and honestly. "Yes, I have weak moments, but I'm staying sober. Period. I have way too much on the line."

Josh's eyes were full of icy disbelief.

Suddenly exhausted by everything, I shrugged heavily. "If you think I'm fucking up, then..." I spread my hands. "Fine. Do what you have to do."

He studied me while dozens of emotions rolled across his expression. My heart pounded. I was all but daring him to go to our coaching staff and say there was a cocaine problem in our locker room.

Do, it Josh. You're braver than I am.

You have more credibility than I do.

You know how to get people to listen better than I do.

After a painfully long moment, he gritted out, "Fine. Keep it that way, all right?"

Then he stalked off, and I wavered on my feet.

I was torn. I wanted to grab Josh by the shoulders and tell him he was absolutely right—that it was incredibly dangerous for me to be hanging around Colfax. Because it was. Every time I was in the same room as that guy, I could hear the siren's call of that delicious high. Every time he came back from a restroom or down from a hotel room with brighter (not to mention dilated) eyes and a conspicuous sniffle, the words *"Do you have any?"* would dance on the tip of my tongue, and I *knew* that he would know exactly what I meant. That he would say yes.

Josh was right about me, and he was right that I should stay the fuck away from that particular teammate.

The part I couldn't explain was that I hung out with Colfax to try to keep him from being alone with Axel. I didn't see potential prey in Axel—I saw *myself* in him. Saw the eagerness for acceptance. The stress at trying to adapt to pro hockey life. Not the ADHD or the need for calm— nothing about Axel made me think neurodivergent, though that didn't necessarily mean anything. Point was, I could see young me in Axel, and I was terrified of how deep those similarities ran.

It was entirely possible that I was wrong. Axel probably had his head screwed on straight enough that he'd taken my message for what it was, and he'd never touch cocaine again. At the very least, he was probably smart enough that nobody was going to *pressure* him into using again.

The problem was that that kind of pressure *wasn't* an issue. With drinking, yes, because good God, most people could not accept "I don't drink" without grilling the person about why, pushing them to try something different, or otherwise making it weird.

With the hard drugs, though, it was a whole other story. The peer pressure of using with teammates wasn't the same as what we were taught to look out for as kids. It wasn't a group of people cornering someone up and telling them they wouldn't be accepted, they wouldn't be cool, or they were a chicken. It was nothing like that. I'd never been pushed to use. It wasn't like when someone was pushing me for sex and took a rejection personally or kept applying pressure because they couldn't engage unless I did. With cocaine or any other substance, the polite *"no"* was nearly always accepted with a shrug and a *"No sweat—more for me!"* and that was the end of it. Sometimes they even asked if I minded them using when I didn't, or they'd plead with me not to rat them out.

The peer pressure we learned about in drug resistance programs in school just...didn't happen, in my experience.

No, in my experience, when there was pressure to use, the call almost always came from inside the house. It was a voice in the back of the mind that saw the offer to "party" as an invitation to be part of the group. Refusing wouldn't get a person ostracized, but accepting would get them pulled in close.

I'd worked my whole life to be a professional hockey player, and once I'd made it, I'd been desperate to be *in*. To be one of the guys. To feel like I was one of their peers instead of an imposter who was one bad game away from everyone realizing I had no business here. The more I fit in off the ice, the more I belonged among these men *on* the ice.

So my deepest fear with Axel was that he would see others using, and out of desperation for their approval and camaraderie, he'd join in, no matter how many klaxons were blaring in his head and telling him it was a mistake. It was so easy to say he could just not use, or that no one in their right mind would volunteer to join in, but I'd been in that position. I was scared to take for granted that Axel had the kind of willpower that would've saved me years of heartache. Especially now while his closest friend on the team was still out with an injury and would be for a while.

And I wanted so, so badly to spell that all out to Josh. I wanted to tell him everything so he'd understand why I was sticking close to Colfax's little clique. But how did I do that without fucking over the rookie? I had no way of knowing if he'd used again, if he was *going* to use again, or anything. He probably had more brains and willpower in his little finger than I did (which was, granted, an incredibly low bar), and he'd been duly rattled the night he thought he'd watched me struggling that hard with my addiction.

But there was a *chance*.

Colfax could say all the right things. He could catch Axel on a night when he was exceptionally vulnerable. Axel could be that desperate to be part of the group. He could convince himself, just like so many addicts did (myself included), that it wasn't a big deal and he could stop any time. There was no telling what would happen if and when he found himself with a straw in his hand and a line of white powder laid out in front of him.

The best I could do at this point was stay in his and Colfax's orbit as much as possible, and to do whatever I could to intervene if I saw Colfax leading Axel down that familiar snow-covered road.

As for Josh...

I hated that cocaine had driven us further apart than the night in bed had. Sex had made things complicated between us, but cocaine always had and always would be the biggest wedge. He still saw me as an addict—a liability to this team and a danger to our young teammates.

I wanted to ask him for help so we could work together to protect Axel, but I didn't know how. I didn't know what to tell him, or if I should tell him anything, or if I should just let him keep thinking I was barreling toward my next relapse. He probably wouldn't listen to me anyway. He'd just assume I was throwing Axel under the bus to justify hanging out with a teammate who could get me cocaine.

I had to protect Axel's career and future. If someone busted Colfax—if Josh or I ratted him out—then there was a good chance any players who hung out with him regularly would be tested too. I'd be fine, but I couldn't be sure that Axel would. His life and career could get upended by a positive test, even if he'd already managed to stop using. Especially if someone decided to do more than a blood or piss test, which could pick up traces from even weeks earlier.

No, my best bet right now was to keep being a presence when Axel was around Colfax. Be there so he'd remember what I'd told him the night I'd begged him to help me through a craving. Be there so I could divert him if someone —Colfax or anyone else—started breaking out familiar paraphernalia.

Yes, spending time with Colfax meant putting myself at risk. It was only a matter of time before we were in a situation where he felt comfortable breaking out the coke in plain sight. All I could do at that point was hope like hell I had enough willpower to abstain, and I knew from past experience that my ability to resist went down dramatically if I was in the same space as cocaine.

If I could see it...

If I could see and hear other people using it...

If it was so close I could taste it...

I closed my eyes and took a few deep breaths. I could do this. If Colfax used in front of me, I could and would resist the urge for a single line, because I knew one line turned into three, and three lines turned into bump after bump after bump to maintain that calm, quiet high. I could and would resist.

Because like hell was I letting Axel go down this miserable road.

CHAPTER 26

JOSH

"Is there something I need to know about?" Kayla flicked her narrowed her eyes between Sol and me in hallway from the ice to the locker room. "Because you've both been off your game the last few nights." She crossed her arms over her blue suit jacket. "I thought everything was resolved between you. Was I wrong?"

"We're good." Sol pointedly looked at her, not me. "Just a rough stretch, but we're good."

Speak for yourself, I wanted to snap, because I wasn't good, and I hadn't been good since that night in his apartment. My stats left no doubt about that.

But I wanted to stay professional (not to mention professionally employed), so I nodded. "Yeah, we're fine. I've just been a little off. I'll get it together."

"I would hope so." She gestured over her shoulder toward the dressing room where Coach was probably already laying into our teammates. "Because they're a mess, too, and you're our last line of defense."

Sol and I glanced at each other this time, exchanging

nods, and then turned to Kayla again. "Will do, Coach," we said.

"Good." She jerked her head toward the dressing room. "Go get your shit together."

Thank God for that. I didn't enjoy getting chewed out, but I was also desperate to take off some of my gear for a few minutes and suck down some electrolytes. Because regardless of the tension between Sol and me, this game was a shitshow, and that wasn't entirely on me. In fact, if we managed to win, my teammates had damn well better be buying me dinner after, because I was standing on my goddamned head while they kept turning over the puck and taking penalties. For as much as I hadn't been playing my best, I *had* kept the puck out of the net except for the two power plays. I was good, but there was only so much I could do when Vegas brought out their power play unit, especially during that unfortunate forty-five seconds where we'd had *two* guys in the box.

The score would've been a lot worse had the cross bar not made two saves. Both had left my ears ringing, but I didn't complain because those deafening pings sounded a hell of a lot sweeter than Vegas's goal horn.

Kayla was right—I really needed to get my shit together and protect this damn goal. I could lose my mind over Sol later. For sixty minutes a night (more if we went into overtime), I had to be able to turn off our bullshit. Even if I could see him from my goal, and even if he was right there whenever I skated to the bench for a drink during a commercial break or when I stepped off the ice during a delayed penalty.

Hockey, I reminded myself over and over. *Not Sol. Deal with him later.*

At least Vegas's goalie wasn't doing so hot, so we'd

managed to get two past him. Now, as we returned to the ice for the third period, the score was tied. Both sides cranked up the heat to break the tie. Our second line was up, making drive after drive on Vegas's net, and from what I could see, they very nearly succeeded before the goaltender slammed his trapper down on the puck and stopped play.

Our guys took advantage of the stoppage for a quick line change. Thank God—the defensemen had been out for over two straight minutes, and they looked ready to collapse.

The fresh players set up in Vegas's defensive zone. I was surprised to see Johnson, Leclerc's left winger, entering the faceoff, but I was admittedly relieved, too. Leclerc hadn't been doing so hot on the faceoff dot lately, and we really couldn't afford to let Vegas have the puck more than they already did. Hopefully Johnson had been practicing.

The puck dropped, and—damn it. Vegas had it. Passed it. One of our defensemen made a solid effort to get it away, but then a wave of gold-and-white jerseys were skating full tilt toward my end of the ice.

I was ready. Watching the puck. The players. Their eyes. Their skates. Their sticks.

The player with possession faked, but I expected it, and I kept my eye on the puck as he sent it to one of his teammates. The other guy caught it on his stick and—

Oh. Fuck.

I knew what was coming, but there was nothing I could do except brace: that wiry forward was coming in hot, flailing to keep control of the puck, and when he tried to make the shot, he threw himself off balance. Momentum kept him sliding forward, and in a heartbeat, he slammed into me and we both tumbled into the goal.

Everything went white for a split second when the back of my mask hit the crossbar, but I recovered before I'd fully hit the ice. I was already scrambling to my feet, frantically searching for the puck, when I realized the ref had blown the whistle. Everyone stopped.

Thank God. Didn't need the puck sliding past me while I was—

The ice listed hard, and I grabbed the crossbar as I dropped to my knees. Then onto my free hand. When had I let go of my stick?

Everything spun around me.

Cotton filled my ears. Noise. Undiscernible noise. More spinning.

"Obie?" A hand landed on my shoulder. "Hey man, you okay?"

I nodded, shakily pulling off my mask. I lost my grip on it, and it tumbled to the ice with a sharp *crack* that sent another thunderbolt through my head.

Vaguely, I was aware of booing and activity around me. I was conscious, just dizzy in that way that made everything else blur together. It would clear. Just needed a minute. Needed to take a few deep breaths.

Al, one of the trainers, was suddenly by my side. "Obie, look at me."

I blinked a few times, then lifted my head to meet his gaze, which made the stadium tilt again.

He studied me, nodded sharply, and told someone, "Concussion protocol."

Aww, fuck my life.

I wanted to argue and insist that I was fine. This wasn't a concussion. It was just a lingering effect of the *last* concussion. Which...I had some hazy inkling that that was actually worse. Something about secondary impacts, though I was pretty sure I was long since past the window for that to happen. The fact that I couldn't quite remember made me think twice about arguing with Al about concussion protocol.

Someone helped me to my feet, and I was vaguely aware of Sol coming out to take my place in the net. As I skated toward the bench with help, renewed booing went up all around us. What the hell? Were they booing their own guy for taking a penalty? *Had* he taken a penalty? I'd lost track.

But when I glanced up at the screen, I realized what was happening. On the replay, I got up, then went back down, and that prompted more booing and shouts of disgust.

Oh, shit. They thought I took a dive. On the screen, it looked like I had. Like I'd suddenly realized I could draw a penalty by appearing hurt so the player who hit me would go to the box. A goalie on my last team had done that, and he'd taken a penalty for embellishment. From the way Vegas's coach was shouting and gesticulating, I suspected he wanted the same for me. I could only imagine what the TV commentators were saying.

I wasn't embellishing, though, and the refs knew it. Vegas's coaches and crowd didn't like it, but the refs weren't going to penalize me.

Al and the team doc took me into one of the side rooms away from the dressing room. I wasn't sure if this was the designated quiet room, or if it was just a conveniently quiet and distraction-free space. Whatever. I couldn't think too hard about much of anything, so I just sat down and leaned my head against the wall as I waited for the room to stop spinning.

Kayla and Al helped me take off my pads and skates, and someone shoved a water bottle into my hand. Then Doc ran me through the usual questions and tests. I thought

I did okay; my head was throbbing and I was still dizzy, but my mind felt more or less clear. When he asked me things like what city we were in and what day it was, I had to think about them for a second, but that was mostly because the dizziness was so distracting. It was hard to think about anything when I was concentrating so hard on not tumbling out of my chair.

"I'm good," I told Doc. "Just..." I gestured at my head. "Dizzy."

"Is it getting any better?"

I thought about that, too, then slowly and cautiously nodded. "Yeah. I think it just rang my bell a bit, but it's not like the last time."

God, that had been bad. I'd actually lost consciousness for twenty or thirty seconds, and there were few things scarier than waking up to skull-splitting pain, frantic voices, and stadium lights. I'd been a wreck after that one.

I felt like crap tonight, but it was definitely better than *that* disaster.

Doc ran me through a few more tests. He also watched the replay video a few times on his iPad. After he was finished, he gave a slight nod. "You're going to be off the ice for at least forty-eight hours. We'll reevaluate tomorrow to see how you're feeling, and each day after until I'm satisfied you're safe to play."

"Do you think he needs a CT?" Kayla. Jesus, I'd forgotten she was even in the room.

Doc shook his head and twisted around to look at her. "We'll keep an eye on symptoms for the rest of the evening and into tomorrow, but this appears to be a very mild concussion."

Well, that was a relief. And the longer I sat here, the better I felt. The water helped. So did the quiet. The adrenaline had long since eased off, which definitely made a difference. My head hurt, though it wasn't bad, and I was still a little dizzy and my balance wasn't quite normal, but they were better. So was the fear of a worse injury; funny how much it helped when that started to subside.

The game had ended at some point. I'd heard some of the noise and activity outside, but it was distant and muted. I couldn't even tell if we'd won or lost. Now that Doc was done with me, though, and just had me sitting in here while a staff member went to get me some food, I was curious. Kayla grabbed my phone out of my locker for me, and I pulled up social media, since that always seemed to be the place for up-to-the-minute commentary.

Somehow, we'd won. I'd definitely have to watch some of the recaps later, because we'd gone from tied to a four-three win. Sol had made a number of saves, apparently, and he'd only let one puck get by him. On a power play again. Christ, how had we taken so many penalties tonight?

Well, we were walking away with two points, so I wasn't going to complain. Coach would probably have words with everyone, but at least we'd won.

I scrolled through my feed just to see if there was any commentary on the goals or penalties. Apparently the media had already interviewed several players about the game, because there were tweets containing quotes and video clips. My alleged embellishment was getting a lot of airtime, too. And I was already becoming a meme; several people had suggested I give up hockey and try out for the Olympic diving team. Great.

I was happy to see that a few of my teammates had been quoted as saying I hadn't taken a dive.

"I saw him up close right after he went down," Darby told a reporter. "That glassy-eyed look? You can't fake that."

I mean, you could. It actually didn't take much. But I appreciated the faith.

Leclerc had also apparently been close by when it happened, and he said, "I think it was the opposite of a dive. He tried to get up and keep playing when anyone else would've stayed down."

Others had said the same, but one post caught my eye, and I had to wonder for a second if Doc needed to redo some of those cognitive tests.

Sasquatch goalie defends teammate: "Josh O'Brien doesn't embellish. He didn't f*cking dive."

I blinked. Was...was *Sol* of all people defending me? And swearing at the media in the process? Okay, this I had to see.

I tapped the video, which showed Sol sitting on a bench in the visitors' locker room, his face still flushed and his blond hair sweaty and tousled. Several microphones were in his face; that had never been his favorite thing, but he was always charming and polite. As a reporter asked him about one of his saves in the third period, he was his usual friendly, smiling self.

Then someone said, "There's a lot of talk of O'Brien embellishing after that hit in the second period. What do you have to say about that?"

Instantly, Sol's expression darkened as if someone had just insulted his ancestors. "If anything, Obie's the guy who will keep playing while he has blood in his mouth. He doesn't just give up, and he does *not* dive for penalties. That's not him. If he went down, then something went wrong, and anyone who knows him knows that." He leaned a little closer to the mic, and he seemed to be glaring right in someone's eyes as he added, "Josh O'Brien doesn't embellish. He *didn't* fucking dive."

The video ended, and I stared at the static image that remained.

Then I watched it again, just to make sure Doc really *didn't* need to readminister all those tests.

Nope. It was real. Sol really did defend me.

I wouldn't have expected him to throw me under the bus. No matter how much he didn't like me, we both knew damn well that you didn't shit talk your teammates around cameras or hot mics. Still, he could've given a noncommittal, canned answer like, "You'd have to ask the medical staff" or "I wasn't on the ice, so I don't know what happened." There were any number of ways he could've dodged the question, or he could've just blandly said he had faith in his teammates.

But the vehemence? The way the question seemed to infuriate him? That was unexpected. Unprofessional, too; he was probably getting reamed out right now by our media person for snapping at a reporter and swearing on camera.

I didn't even know what to make of what he'd said, and it wasn't the head injury screwing with my ability to think.

I just had no idea how to process Sol going to bat for me like that.

Josh definitely didn't look so hot when he came down for breakfast the next morning. It was hard to say if his glazed eyes were from the concussion or from what was probably a sleepless night, but either way, he looked miserable.

And people think he took a dive? Jesus Christ.

I mean, I got it. Some goalies did dive, and that infuriated fans and players alike. I didn't blame them, because it was bullshit.

Josh, though—that hadn't been a dive. I'd watched it happen, and I'd watched the replay several agonizing times, and if I was honest, I was surprised the concussion wasn't any worse, or that he hadn't jacked up his neck or something.

That, and I knew Josh. His rookie season, someone had crashed his net, and Josh had continued playing through a period and a half until the end of the regulation, plus two minutes of overtime before our team had finally scored. It was only after he'd limped back to the locker room that anyone realized he was hurt, and the staff had been furious with him after an X-ray revealed he'd played through a fracture on his left foot. A mild one, sure, but it had hurt like hell, and he'd had tears in his eyes when he'd pulled off his mask after the game.

A few seasons later, he'd tried to keep playing after an opposing forward and one of his own defensemen had tumbled into him. The teams had been ready for a faceoff in his zone, the ref a split second away from dropping the puck, when Josh had suddenly taken off his mask. Everything had stopped, and Josh had left the ice. Turned out even in a guy as stubbornly determined to play through anything, there was no such thing as knuckling through a fractured collarbone.

So no, I didn't buy for a second that he'd taken a dive last night. Sitting here now, surreptitiously watching him, I struggled to eat my breakfast because just the memory of last night had me ready to get sick. Twelve hours later, I could still feel the cold panic in the pit of my queasy stomach. I'd been concerned when he'd been hit. Scared when he'd gone down. When he'd *stayed* down?

I shuddered hard and shifted my attention to the food I needed to eat. Even now, the worst-case scenarios kept flickering through my head. Another broken collarbone? A severe concussion? A neck injury?

Then he'd tried to get up, and the trainers and everyone else around him had told him to stay down. That had made me feel a little better—he'd been with it enough to try to power through his injury—but I'd still been worried about what the trainers had seen that I couldn't.

Anger surged through me as I shoved some eggs into my mouth. Fuck everyone who thought he'd embellished last night. Every last one of them.

I stabbed my fork into a home fry.

"Josh O'Brien doesn't embellish," I could still hear myself growling. *"He didn't fucking dive."*

Our PR director, Dave, had had some words with me afterward. Reminded me about cursing on camera. And I got it. I was media-trained to hell and back, but I hadn't been able to keep my anger from surfacing. The nerve of that reporter. The *audacity*. Dave could bitch me out all he wanted—I wasn't going to just smile through someone talking that kind of trash about Josh. Least of all on camera.

Coach would probably update the hockey world on Josh's status during his next media availability, and he'd probably update the team before that. Maybe on the way to the airport or something.

I wasn't about to wait that long. After I'd bused my plate, I searched the room and found Josh, still at his table with his own plate still in front of him. He was eating alone; that didn't surprise me. Sometimes after an injury— especially a head injury—the last thing anyone wanted to do was socialize or listen to other people socializing. If anything, I was a little surprised he was down here at all; the aftermath of a migraine always left him with a massive aversion to food, and the one time I'd seen him post-concussion, he hadn't wanted to eat either. I didn't know if he was queasy, or if he was just too miserable to think about anything beyond existing. Either he was more or less okay today, or someone had persuaded him to at least try to eat.

Cautiously, I approached his table. Recalling the time I'd spent with him during migraines and head injuries, I kept my voice soft. "Hey."

He looked up at me, then blinked in surprise, which made him wince. "Oh. Hey."

I fought the urge to fidget or tap my fingers on the

table's edge. "Just, uh... How are you feeling? After last night?"

He shrugged tightly, as if every muscle in his upper body were steel-tight. They might've been—after all, the head-injury bone was connected to the neck-injury bone. Every concussion I'd ever had included some bonus fuckery in my neck, shoulders, and upper back.

"I'm okay," he said. "Fucking hurts, but it sounds like I'll be okay." He grimaced. "You're, uh...probably going to have to start in Phoenix."

My stomach dropped. Oh, Jesus. I hadn't even thought about that, but he was right. We played in Denver tomorrow night, and two nights after that, we'd be in Phoenix. The plan had been for me to start tomorrow and for Josh to be in the net in Phoenix.

So much for that.

Well, it couldn't be helped, and Josh needed to focus on recovering, so I waved it away. "I'll be fine. I have to play against them eventually."

He sighed. "That's going to be rough."

Oh, it was. Phoenix's fans had been done with me well before the team had put me on waivers, and I doubted they thought any better of me now. I fully expected to skate out onto the ice to an earth-shaking chorus of boos.

"It'll be fine," I insisted. "I've been booed before."

That got the faintest laugh out of him, and he looked down as he poked at some otherwise untouched scrambled eggs with his fork. "Haven't we all? Fans are brutal."

"They're passionate." I shrugged. "This is the other side of that coin."

"True. Kind of comes with the territory, doesn't it?"

"Yep."

The conversation wasn't as awkward as it could've been

between us, so that was a plus. Wasn't the most comfortable, either, but this was probably the best I could ask for these days.

The whole time, I couldn't shake the feeling I'd had when I'd seen him laid out on the ice last night. When he'd been up after the crash, and then he'd gone down. That absolute bone-deep terror when reality had sunk its teeth in —he wasn't getting up. He wasn't playing any more that night. I could still feel the way my hands had shaken as I'd grabbed my mask and paddle, because it had suddenly been all too real.

Right now, it should've been sinking in that he was okay. Yeah, he'd be on concussion protocol for a while. He'd be feeling like shit for a few days at least. But he was okay. He'd left the ice on his own power, even if he'd needed help. No stretcher. He was fine.

While half of hockey had speculated that he'd embellished and taken a dive, all I could think—during the game and right now—was that it could've been so, *so* much worse.

What do I do if something happens to you?

That thought almost had me dropping to the banquet room floor like Josh had fallen to the ice last night. He was my ex. My teammate at best. There was way too much baggage and resentment between us for anything more; my God, we'd learned that the hard way after we'd fallen into bed together and then clashed over my friendship with Colfax.

But that didn't mean I didn't have feelings for him, and those feelings included not being able to breathe if I so much as thought about him getting hurt.

I masked a shiver. "I, um... I should let you eat. I need to go pack."

Josh nodded, still chasing a piece of egg around on his plate. "Yeah. Me too. Thanks for checking on me."

"Don't mention it."

Silence set in, and hell if I knew how to fill it, so I made good on what I'd said—I left him to his breakfast.

I'd only made it a couple of steps, though, before:

"Sol?"

I turned around, and I found an expression that was a mix of pain and sheepishness. "Yeah?"

"I saw your interview last night."

My spine straightened. "Oh. Yeah." I laughed nervously. "Dave wasn't happy about that."

Josh's laugh was almost soundless. "I bet he wasn't." He sobered, staring down at his plate for a moment before meeting my gaze again. "Thanks, though. For saying what you did."

I shifted from foot to foot. "We both know you don't dive."

"I know. But I appreciate you having my back like that."

"Of course I have your back," I said. "You're my teammate."

He held my gaze. I held his.

I had no idea what to say, and apparently neither did he, and if we stayed like this a second longer, I was going to lose my mind. I mumbled something else about needing to pack, left him to his breakfast, and hurried out of the banquet room.

Safely alone in the hallway, I stopped to gather my thoughts.

I hated what I'd said. Not defending him or swearing into a microphone—I'd stand by that until the end of time— but the part about doing it because he was my teammate. I mean, yes, that was true, and I'd have come to defense of anyone else wearing the same sweater as me.

It just wasn't the whole story here. Not even close.

But how the hell was I supposed to tell anyone the truth? Just come right out and tell a hot mic that I'd never have this much respect for a player who embellished like that? Look a camera in the eye and ask if they were sure they wanted to talk that shit about the man I loved?

God, I was a mess.

I wanted Josh to be respected. I wanted him to be okay.

And fuck me...

I just wanted him.

CHAPTER 28

JOSH

As the clock ticked down to warm-ups in Phoenix, I settled into the press box high above the ice. Bosco and Mars would be joining me after warm-ups, since they were both healthy scratches, but for now, I was the only player up here. Järvinen hadn't traveled with the team; though he was physically almost ready to be reactivated, he was on LTIR, and he wouldn't be eligible to play until after this road trip.

So for the moment, I sat alone, though there were a few people milling around in the box. I didn't pay any attention to them. I had on a Sasquatches toque even though it wasn't as cold up here as it was down by the glass. The hat was just a convenient way to mask the earplugs I was wearing. People wore hearing protection all the time at games, but I'd learned last time I was out with a concussion that it could spark all kinds of questions about my recovery, if I was being plagued with headaches, if I'd be able to handle the noise once I returned to the ice. Better to just hide them. And it wasn't like people looked twice when they saw a hockey player wearing a toque with a suit.

My head *was* throbbing already tonight. Coach had

given me the option of sitting out the road trip, since I wasn't likely to play before the team returned to Seattle, but I was too stubborn for that. I'd had worse concussions; I would be back out there practicing before too long, damn it.

The horn sounded, announcing that warm-ups were about to start. Seattle came out first, and unsurprisingly, there was booing. A lot of fans at various arenas booed when the opposing team skated out for warm-ups. It was just one of those things that happened at hockey games.

Phoenix's fans weren't usually *this* emphatic about it, though. I'd played here plenty of times, both for and against Phoenix, and they were as loud and enthusiastic as hockey fans ever were, but the booing wasn't usually too crazy.

Tonight, though? Holy fuck. The second my teammates started skating out onto the ice, the crowd exploded into boos. I hadn't heard a crowd this angry since one of my former teammates—a total shitbag—had played in Philly a month after he'd been suspended for a seriously dirty and dangerous hit on their rookie forward. It was the kind of thunderous booing that made my head pound and had players glancing around in case fans started throwing things onto the ice. That happened rarely—people were asking to be kicked out and banned if they threw anything that wasn't a hat for a hat trick—but it was still smart to keep your head on a swivel when the crowd was that pissed. And seriously, the game hadn't even started yet, but the fans were already *heated*. What the hell?

But then my concussed brain caught up.

Oh. Right.

Sol.

People banged on the glass when he stopped near it. Any time there was a puck on his stick, the booing got even louder. When one of our teammates chipped a puck past him during line rushes, the crowd cheered.

And then the chanting started.

"Solomon sucks! Solomon sucks! Solomon sucks!"

I craned my neck and tried to get a bead on him, but from here, I couldn't see him very well. I did see a few of our teammates skate up to him and tap his pads with their sticks. They did that anyway—it was good luck, after all—but they were breaking away from their warm-up routines to do it this time. Probably giving him words of encouragement, too. God knew he needed it.

Jesus. This crowd *hated* Sol. That hadn't been a big secret, but I could only imagine what it was doing to his head to hear his own former fans booing him that hard.

There would be no video tribute for him tonight. Not like other longtime players often received when they returned with different teams. Fans knew that trades happened and so did free agency, and sometimes beloved players wound up wearing different sweaters.

But sometimes players left on less than great terms, and the fans didn't let them forget it. There'd been an incredibly talented forward on my last team who'd been an absolute dickhole to the team but acted sweet as could be around fans. Then he and a defenseman had gotten into a knock-down drag-out fight at practice. The defenseman had lost a tooth. The forward? He'd lost his place on the team, especially after stories and videos had come out revealing that he was a locker room cancer who'd talked shit about fans and teammates alike. He'd been promptly shipped off to Calgary in a lopsided trade for a couple of third round draft picks. Fans had literally posted videos of themselves burning his jersey, and when we'd played on their ice again? Holy shit. They'd booed him *hard*.

Sol hadn't done anything like that. He'd had a couple of rough seasons and left when he wasn't at the top of his game. Yes, he'd cost his team the playoffs, but that shit happened.

I had a feeling that playoff loss had just been the straw that broke the camel's back. He'd been a league punchline ever since people found out he'd gone into rehab, and commentators and fans alike loved to remind him that he was on thin ice (so to speak) because of that mistake from years ago.

As I watched the Zambonis running over the ice after warm-ups, I sighed. I should've been in the net tonight. Or Sweetman, but Coach and Kayla had both decided he wasn't ready to start against this team. Sol was a much faster and more solid goalie...assuming he didn't let the crowd's vitriol get under his skin and into his head.

Oh, please, don't let them get under your skin and into your head.

You've got this, Sol.

I wished there was time for me to run down to the locker room to give him a pep talk, but it was too late for that. The Zambonis were gone. The refs were out. The pre-game montage was on the screen. I'd never get down there in time.

Damn it.

Seattle's starting lineup was announced, and I didn't hear a thing after Sol's photo appeared between our top defensive pair. More booing. I doubted any Phoenix fans would have voices by the time this game was over.

The teams came out on the ice, and both starting lineups did some skating to loosen up before the national anthem and faceoff.

Leclerc skated up to tap Sol's pads, but he stopped and

put a hand on Sol's shoulder. They exchanged a few words, then they each nodded. Leclerc leaned forward to bump his helmet against Sol's mask, tapped his pad with his stick, and skated toward center ice. A moment later, one of the alternate captains, Johnson, did the same.

Alone in the net, Sol leaned over and seemed to take a few deep breaths.

You've got this, I wished I could tell him from here. *Ignore the fans. Watch the puck. You've got this.*

In fact, now that I thought about it, Leclerc and Johnson had probably told him something to that effect. I hoped they had.

After the national anthem, the game started. And my God, it was not a boring game. Especially when it became clear that Phoenix's fans weren't the only ones who had it out for Sol tonight.

After Sol made a save, a Phoenix forward "accidentally" crashed the goal, sending both Sol and the net sliding across the ice.

Immediately, one of our defensemen—I couldn't quite see who from here—dropped his gloves and went at the forward, but the refs quickly broke up the scrum. Or, well, they tried to. While they were focused on the instigator and our D-man, a fistfight started by the glass, and someone else threw gloves.

In under a minute, the whole thing was over, ending with a yard sale all over our defensive end, three people heading to the box (two of theirs and one of ours), and Volkov going to the locker room for—if I had to guess—stitches. The power play lasted for about forty seconds before Darby scored, but each team was still down a player while the remaining two finished their five-minute majors.

The crowd seemed happy that they got to see a fight,

especially one that early in a game, and that Sol had taken a hit, but they were pissed about the penalties and the resulting power play goal.

Our teammates were out for blood now. That wasn't a surprise. Nobody took kindly to another team fucking with their goalie, even when it was accidental, and it was painfully obvious that the hit Sol had taken was anything but accidental.

It was also painfully obvious that it had jacked up his concentration. During the last five minutes of the first period, he tried to play the puck and whiffed it, sending it like a gift right onto the stick of Phoenix's first-line sniper. Only an absolutely miraculous play by Leclerc behind Sol kept the puck out of the net. Not thirty seconds later, after one of our defensemen lost an edge in the same moment Phoenix broke away and headed for our end, Sol was suddenly alone in the defensive zone. Any other night, I was sure he'd have made that save, but tonight... Fuck.

Even from here, I could feel the defeat coming off him as the goal horn sounded. How the hell was he going to make it through forty-two more minutes of hockey tonight?

Fuck it. I needed to talk to him.

Without saying a word to anyone, I got up and hurried down to ice level, aided by a security guard who knew the arena's layout better than I did. By the time I reached the dressing room, my teammates were filing in, sweaty and aggravated. No one seemed to be directing it at Sol, though. Leclerc smacked him on the shoulder and told him he'd done great. Darby jokingly told him he owed him a beer. Most of the frustration in the room was at the Firebirds for targeting Sol.

"They hit the goalie again," Axel declared as he angrily

retaped his stick, "I'm taking the match penalty. I don't give a fuck."

That prompted cheers from our teammates, and Sol even cracked a halfhearted smile.

"How about we keep them away from the net *and* the netminder?" Coach Maines took his usual spot in the middle of the room. "We're not losing players to suspensions over a team that's five spots down from us in the conference standings, all right? Especially not when we're up against Pittsburgh and Edmonton this week, and we need all hands on deck for those games."

There was a general murmur of reluctant agreement, and nods all around the room.

Coach went into his usual speech, then left everyone to retape sticks, hydrate, and otherwise prep for the second period.

By the time I had my opportunity to talk to Sol, only four minutes remained in the intermission. I made my way across the crowded room, and I gave one of his shoulder pads a firm tap. "Hey. Don't let them get in your head, okay?"

He looked down—he was a lot taller than me when he had his skates on—and met my gaze with sad, frustrated eyes. "Easier said than done. You know that."

"Yeah. I do. But I also know they'd be chanting your name in an entirely different tone if you were in a Phoenix sweater and putting up the stats you have right now."

Sol's eyebrows rose.

"Come on, dude." I laughed softly. "People are already making noise about you winning the Xavier Trophy this year."

"They..." He blinked. "Oh. Shit."

"Right? So all that bullshit out there?" I gestured toward

the hallway that led out to the ice. "They're just trying to psych you out, but the proof is in the numbers. You've got this. Okay?"

He studied me skeptically, and I thought he might try to push back. Instead, though, he relaxed a bit beneath his bulky pads. "Thanks."

I flashed him a quick smile. "Get out there."

He gave my dress shoe a gentle tap with his stick, then headed out to the ice.

After he'd left, I went back up to the press box, making it to my seat about ninety seconds into the period. The game continued to be a wild one. There were a few more scrums—one of which landed a guy from each team in the box for roughing—but nobody dropped gloves. Probably just as well. As satisfying as it was to watch some asshole get a well-deserved beatdown, it also sometimes landed much-needed players on the injured list. Not good.

Leclerc scored, putting us in the lead. Phoenix answered in under a minute, and by the end of the second, the score was four-four.

Two and a half minutes into the third, we regained the lead again, and this time we held it. Phoenix was pissed, their fans rabid with rage over the score, over Sol, and over a couple of penalties that even I thought were questionable. The Firebirds hammered Sol with shot after shot, rocketing their shot count from twenty-one at the beginning of the period to forty-three.

"You've got this," I whispered to Sol as he made save after save. "Come on. You've got this."

He did, too, standing on his head as the rest of our defense and offense alike tried to get the puck out of our defensive zone. Finally, they managed to shift the momentum and take the fight to the other end of the ice, giving Sol a much-needed breather.

Seattle scored, but it was ruled offside and pulled off the scoreboard. Though we still held the lead, getting a goal yanked could really fuck with morale, and Phoenix took full advantage. Their defenseman stole the puck from Nichols, sent it to their rookie forward, and the kid barreled toward Sol as the announcer was saying there was one minute left to play.

Seconds later, that rookie squeaked the puck under Sol's pads, and the score was tied.

Despite a valiant fight after that, Seattle couldn't answer the goal.

Oh fuck. Overtime.

Overtime was a grind, but Sol—despite or maybe because of the cacophony of boos raining down every time he moved—wouldn't let anyone score. Unfortunately, the other team's goalie wouldn't either.

I was on the edge of my seat as the shootout started. Those were stressful as hell on a netminder anyway. On a netminder whose confidence had probably been taking hits all night thanks to a crowd who hated him?

God, I didn't envy Sol in the slightest.

The first and second shooters came up empty for both sides. Our third almost got it in, but the puck bounced off the iron, prompting raucous cheers from the hometown crowd.

I held my breath as Phoenix's third shooter took the puck on his stick. Sol was poised and ready, so focused on the shooter and the puck that I could feel it from here. The shooter faked. Sol didn't fall for it. Another fake. Still didn't fall for it. Then the guy wound up for what looked like a high shot, and Sol rose up just a little in anticipation...

leaving just enough room for the tapped puck to slide through his five-hole.

I felt Sol's heart drop a split second before the red light went on. The crowd went ballistic, celebrating their team's hard-fought win, and there was also some distinct taunting thrown his way as he skated toward the bench.

I couldn't get down to the locker room fast enough. By the time I made it in there, reporters had already been turned loose, and four were hovering around Sol.

He was a mess. He had on his well-practiced media face, smiling and answering questions like a professional, but in his eyes—oh my God, it was like tonight's game had broken something in him. All the barely contained fury from the other night? When he'd snapped at the reporters about suggesting I'd taken a dive? It was gone now. Nothing but defeat and shame, as if he'd just singlehandedly ruined the entire season instead of taking one of many losses a team was statistically guaranteed to endure. An *overtime* loss, no less, so we still got a point! Plus he'd hardly been the only one on our team who'd made mistakes tonight. He was the reason Seattle had made it into overtime in the first place instead of losing in regulation.

But the fans had been brutal.

The reporters weren't cutting him any slack.

And I could tell from here that he was completely blaming himself.

CHAPTER 29

SOL

Nights like this were some of the hardest. Cocaine didn't just calm me down and focus me—it also made me feel good, and right now, I craved anything that could pull that off. The consequences didn't even matter as long as it broke through this miserable funk.

As I showered after that awful game in my old arena, I didn't want cocaine. I just wanted to feel good. If cocaine was the answer to that, then bring it the fuck on. Bring on *anything* to make my mood suck less.

At least the reporters had finally moved on. They'd gotten their sound bites. I was sure they had videos of me all over social media, and I'd be a meme by tomorrow morning. Sad Solomon. There'd be a picture of me next to the word "defeat" in the dictionary. Or maybe "failure." "Disaster."

Or "snowman."

I shuddered as I turned around to let the spray beat on the stiff muscles between my shoulders.

"Hey, Snowman." Carver had grinned at me as everyone else started setting up for a faceoff in our defensive zone. *"This yours?"* He'd tapped his stick next to some

snow on the ice that formed a long, straight line. Whether he'd done it with his stick or it had just happened naturally, I didn't know, but he'd been incredibly pleased with himself about the joke.

Tracer had overheard it, and he'd shot Carver a venomous look, but there hadn't been time to say or do anything. The puck had dropped. The action started again. Seconds later, everyone was at the other end of the ice.

Later, I'd caught sight of Tracer and Carver exchanging some sharp words on the bench. Whether it was about the snowman comment or Carver's terrible giveaway, I didn't know. I told myself it was the former.

Or not, since Carver snowed me during his next shift. It hadn't been enough to keep me from seeing and stopping the puck, but it had been enough to set off Colfax. Fortunately, the refs had seen Carver laughing about it before Colfax had face-washed him, and they decided the snow had been deliberate. They sent him to the box for two minutes for unsportsmanlike conduct...which would've given us a power play had Colfax not wound up in the box, too—in his case, for roughing Carver.

Now, as I washed away the sweat, shame, and fatigue, I couldn't even muster up the energy to be pissed off about him snowing me. It happened sometimes, even accidentally, when a skater stopped suddenly in front of the crease, and quite frankly I'd rather catch a face full of ice chips than have the player topple into me like the one who'd concussed Josh or who'd crashed my goal in the first period of this game. It annoyed me, especially when it was deliberate, but it wasn't that big of a deal.

When it came from a former teammate who'd taken to calling me Snowman?

I sighed and rubbed my neck. He wasn't the first. He

wouldn't be the last. Opponents who really wanted to get under my skin loved to throw that one out there, and they knew that *I* knew what it meant. It just hurt to hear it from someone who used to be...maybe it was generous to call him a friend, but apparently my fall from grace and ultimate departure from Phoenix had left more bad blood than I'd realized.

Awesome. And I still can't fuck up without people bringing my addiction into it.

If everyone's going to be such a dick about it, maybe I should just go buy some and—

No. No. *Absolutely not.*

I was not listening to that insistent voice. I sure as shit wasn't going to give anyone any more reason to define me by the powder I'd stupidly put into my nose. The powder I really, really fucking wanted to put in my nose right now.

I wouldn't. But I wanted to.

I can stop giving in to it. When will I stop being defined by it?

Didn't have answer for that.

Still feeling like shit, I shut off the shower, toweled myself off, and shuffled back out to rejoin my team. I'd been in there for a while, so I wasn't surprised to see that the locker room had mostly cleared out. The media was gone. Our teammates had showered, dressed, and left to find food.

In fact, only one other person besides me remained: Josh.

He hadn't needed to change clothes or shower—he was still in the suit he'd been wearing earlier—and the press wasn't all that interested in him tonight, so I couldn't imagine why he'd linger. I wanted to be annoyed with him, too; didn't he realize I'd been dawdling so I could have a few minutes to myself?

"I heard the cooking staff is making tamales tonight." I put my towel on the bench and reached for my bag. "Might be some left if you hurry."

"I'm good." He made no move to leave. Damn him.

With my back safely to him, I closed my eyes and exhaled. So help me, if he was here to tell me how awful I'd been out there, or worse, give me a pep talk, I was going to—

"I'm sorry the fans were so rough on you."

I tightened my jaw. His tone was gentle, not the least bit patronizing, and the words prodded at a dam that wasn't doing such a hot job of holding back my emotions.

"I didn't expect them to be happy to see me," I ground out, busying myself with pulling on a pair of gym shorts and a T-shirt. I'd put on the suit before I left for the hotel, but I wasn't dressing to the nines for my post-game meal. Assuming I could stomach anything. Ugh, food sounded awful, and just going through the motions sounded like—

"My old team probably won't be much better." Josh laughed dryly. "They were booing me while I still wore a Calgary sweater."

At that, I faced him. "They were?"

"What can I say?" He offered a tight shrug. "I was a mess."

I broke eye contact and sat on the bench to put on my socks and sneakers. "You had a head injury and a..." I hesitated, glancing up at him. "The shit you were going through ranks a little higher on the list of understandable problems, you know? No one thought you should be booted out of the league or sent to prison or something."

"I mean, the people who don't like gay guys playing hockey or marrying other gay guys had some opinions about that."

I looked up at him again, and the corner of his mouth

rose in a cautious smile, as if he was trying to make me laugh but would understand if I didn't. It wasn't that funny, but it did kind of take me back to the days when we'd both use our dark senses of humor to help each other through shitty moments. *That* made me chuckle a bit, if only from the nostalgia.

My humor only lasted a moment, though. I stared down at the sock in my hand, and I tried to swallow the lump in my throat. "Your old fans and teammates aren't going to give you grief for your addiction."

Josh sat beside me on the bench, leaving some space between our shoulders. "No one should be giving you grief for yours."

I glanced at him and offered up a wet, bitter laugh. "Has that ever stopped anyone?"

He was quiet for a good minute. Then, "You have fans, Sol. Seattle goes nuts every time you're out there. Our team-mates—they respect you. We've seen how you perform. Yeah, you're gonna have some bad nights. So am I." He laughed. "Hell, I had a bad night get capped off by a concussion, and people still think I took a dive."

I met his gaze. "They're still busting your balls for that?"

He half-shrugged. "It comes up. Probably will for a while. But have you looked at your stats recently? You're killing it, and so am I. Phoenix is probably just pissy that their goalies' stats look like rookie numbers next to yours."

That admittedly did bring my spirits up a little. "Tonight won't help those numbers."

"No, but you've mostly been on a hot streak this season. And tonight wasn't a regulation loss, so you've still got a point and so does the team."

I exhaled, my shoulders sinking as some weight slid off them. "I guess that's true. It just felt so..." I shook my head and flailed a hand, then resumed putting on my socks.

"I don't think it would feel good for anyone. And maybe you won't feel good tonight. It's probably going to be a sucky night for you."

I turned to him, and I found nothing but sympathy and understanding in his eyes.

He put a hand on mine and squeezed gently. "Sometimes things ruin your night, you know? And then you sleep it off, and it feels better the next day. This is probably one of those things." He paused. "Or maybe you'll feel better once you've practiced with the team or played another game. This kind of funk—it sucks, but we both know from experience it doesn't last forever."

I nodded. It was amazing how often I needed to be reminded of that. Misery always felt immoveable. Pain, sadness, illness—hell, a mosquito bite—it all felt in the moment like it was going to last forever, but before I knew it, it was gone.

"This too shall pass," I whispered.

"Exactly. And it might help tonight if you ate something." He motioned toward the hallway that led to the room where everyone was eating. "You must be starving."

My stomach growled in agreement. I was always famished after a game, and this game had gone into overtime. "Yeah. I am." Sighing, I rose. "Thanks for the, um... I don't know if *pep talk* is the word, but..."

He stood too, and a soft smile materialized on his lips. "You looked like you needed it."

"After that shitshow..." I laughed bitterly and nodded.

Josh's face fell. "I'm sorry." He touched my arm. "I should've been out there tonight."

"No." I shook my head. "You need to recover, and

anyway, I *need* to be able to play against them. And in front of those fans. I'll have to sooner or later." I let my gaze drift toward the tunnel leading out to the sheet as acid burned in the back of my throat. "Just...didn't realize how much they hated me."

"They'll get over it. And even if they don't, you will. Your career is back on the rails, and they're probably mad it's benefiting another team."

I laughed quietly. "Yeah. Probably." Without thinking about it, I stepped closer and hugged him, and without hesitation, he returned the embrace. Holding him close, I whispered, "Thanks."

"Any time."

He drew back, and our eyes met.

And fuck me, but the way he looked at me right then— smiling at me like I was the only other person on the planet —was heartbreakingly familiar.

And then, to my surprise, he put a hand on my waist, closed what little space remained between us, and pressed his lips to mine. Softly. Briefly. Lingering just long enough to let me know he meant it, but not so long that we'd get caught. When he drew back, there was that smile again.

That, too, was brief. As he sobered, he broke eye contact. The rush of color into his cheeks probably wasn't arousal, just like the rush of heat to my face definitely wasn't. I mean, I couldn't help but be turned on when Josh touched me, but mostly there was this dawning horror that we'd just undid any progress we'd made toward coexisting as teammates.

"Shit," he whispered. "I'm sorry. I shouldn't have—"

"It's okay."

"No, it isn't." He shoved a hand through his hair. "Damn it. I just wanted to... I don't want things to be weird between us, but we were..." He squeezed his eyes shut and pinched the bridge of his nose.

"Most of the time we've been in each other's lives, we were together," I said softly. "It's...I guess it's almost a habit."

He lowered his hand and seemed to consider that. "Maybe? I..." He shook his head. "I don't think it's quite that simple, but maybe something like that. I don't know. Just...I'm sorry."

"Josh." I touched his arm. "We've both said it—we have a complicated history. Lines are a little blurry. I promise, I'm not reading too much into this."

He studied me, brow furrowed.

"It's okay," I whispered. "I'll... Hell, I'll take an awkward minute or two over the way things have been, so..." I half-shrugged and offered up a cautious smile.

He held my gaze, then relaxed into a smile of his own. "Okay. I'll, um, try to remember where the lines are."

Fuck the lines. Let's go back to the hotel.

I kept that to myself, though. Things were way too delicate with Josh, and I'd already learned the hard way how awkward and weird it could get if we threw caution to the wind. We *had* to function as teammates. We'd be better off if we could be friendly, too. Things had been rough in that department, but now we were supporting each other in ways we both desperately needed after our most recent seasons.

Sex and love would only complicate that, and we couldn't afford complicated, no matter how deliciously tempting it was.

So I just said, "I'll remember where the lines are, too. And, um... Thanks. Everything you said. I needed that."

He smiled again, and then he left me to continue getting

my shit together in the now deserted locker room.

Alone, I sank onto the bench again. My knees were shaking too damn much to hold me up, and I needed a minute to collect my thoughts. Not from tonight's shitshow of a game—that barely registered in my mind now—but from that exchange with Josh.

Some part of my brain was still stuck on the idea that Josh hated me. That I hated him. After that recent conversation about Colfax, I'd pretty much convinced myself he did.

With the way my lips tingled, though...

With the way my heart was still going wild...

With that knot of shame absent from my stomach after he'd reassured me that tonight wasn't the end of the world...

Oh God. He doesn't hate me.

And I...

Closing my eyes, I leaned forward, elbows on my knees as I raked both hands through my hair.

Yeah, I loved him. I'd known that for a long time. But I'd also known, and so did he, that we had to keep some distance between us. We fucking had to.

I didn't want to, though. I missed him. I missed when leaning on each other was what we did instead of a novelty. I missed knowing we could always find some way to make the other laugh even when the situation didn't warrant much humor.

"*Hey, it could be worse,*" I'd deadpanned to him one night, gesturing at the cast on his foot. "*You've got ten toes, so breaking two is like...twenty percent shitty, you know?*"

"*So you're saying I half-assed it?*"

"*Not really. Half-assing it would've taken out at least five. This?*" I tsked and shook my head. "*Not even a quarter, dude.*"

A laugh had burst through his depressed, pain-filled

expression, and he'd rolled his eyes and shaken his head. "*Fuck you.*"

"*Maybe when your foot doesn't hurt so much.*"

He'd quirked his lips and seemed to give it some serious thought. "*I mean, my toes are broken, but I'm pretty sure my dick still works. And I know yours does.*"

"*You're pretty sure?*"

"*Pretty sure.*" A wicked grin. "*Maybe we should check?*"

We had, and it had, and tonight, I missed everything about who and what we'd been back then.

I want us back so damn bad.

Some part of my mind tried to tell me this was another addiction. That I kept gravitating back to him. That he was something that felt good enough to draw me back again and again—for a taste, just a little taste—only to blow up in my face like it had every time before.

That part of my mind was wrong, though. Josh wasn't an addiction. He never had been. *He'd* been hurt by my addiction. By me. He and our relationship had been collateral damage. Letting myself indulge in Josh wouldn't hurt me the way cocaine or some other drug would.

If anything, *he* was the one who'd get hurt.

My heart fell into my stomach. That was the bitter truth, wasn't it? All those years ago, if Josh had jumped ship sooner than he had, he could've walked away mostly unscathed. Maybe thought I was an asshole and a junkie, but moved on with his life. He'd been through hell because he hadn't been able to just let go of me. And tonight, even after all of the shit I'd put him through, some part of him *still* couldn't let go of me.

I closed my eyes and exhaled into the stillness.

When it came to Josh, he wasn't the drug.

I was.

CHAPTER 30

JOSH

Finally, after three long weeks, I was off concussion protocol. It wasn't as bad as the one that had knocked me out of
the game for half a season, but any absence made me
twitchy.

I put in some extra practice time with Kayla to get my
conditioning back up, and before long, I was ready to return
for a game. Coach Maines told the press after practice that I
was a game time decision but that he anticipated me starting, and suddenly my name was trending everywhere. My
teammates were giving me shoulder smacks in the locker
room after practice, telling me they were glad I was back.

"Oh, man." Sweetman fell into step with me on the way
out to the practice facility's parking garage. "It's been great
playing up here, but Kayla's right—I am *not* ready for this
quite yet."

"Nah, you've held your own. Don't sell yourself short."

"Dude, we lost three of the five games I played."

"And one of those was in a shootout." I chuckled as I
took my car keys out of my pocket. "I've been doing this for
years, and I still struggle with those."

With a groan, he admitted, "I fucking hate shootouts."

"You and me both." I gave his shoulder a squeeze. "You did good. Seriously. And with some more practice, you'll be doing this in your sleep. Don't sweat it."

He offered a shy smile, then continued toward his car. I felt for the kid. I'd been there, done that—coming up from a farm team to his level was a much bigger leap than a lot of people realized. That first game was inevitably a baptism by fire.

"Kid's a good goalie." Sol's voice spun me around, and I found him a few feet behind me. How long had he been there? I hadn't even realized he was behind us on our way out.

I cleared my throat. "Yeah. Yeah, he's... Another season or two, and he'll be ready to make the jump permanently."

Sol nodded. "Definitely. He's going to go places. Just doesn't know it yet."

I nodded too, and awkward silence hung between us. We weren't arguing, and in fact we'd gotten along pretty well lately, but there was always this discomfort. It was like I couldn't be around him without constantly feeling like there was a rock in my shoe—a persistent annoying presence. Better than gnashing our teeth at each other, I guess? But still frustrating.

We definitely shouldn't have slept together.

And I definitely shouldn't have kissed you in the locker room.

I suppressed a wince. Yes, there was less hostility now, but more of...this. Sometimes I didn't know what was worse.

Sol shifted his weight. "Anyway, I, uh...I'll see you at the arena." He smiled, and it seemed sincere, if uneasy. "Sounds like you'll be starting."

The reminder that I was getting back between the pipes

tonight sent a rush of elation through me that almost made me forget about the metaphorical rock in my shoe. "Yeah. Guess so. It'll be... It's good to be back."

His smile warmed a couple of degrees, taking my body temperature with it. The usual cascade of emotions tumbled through me. I was relieved we were talking and being cordial. That he seemed to care that I was all right and that I was coming back off the injured list.

But I still missed him. Hated him. Wanted him. Loved him. Knew we weren't good for each other. Wished we could erase the past and give a future a try.

When will I stop being such a mess for you?

I realized then that we'd been standing in silence for a few awkward moments, and I spun my keys on my finger as I cleared my throat again. "Well. Um. Guess we'll find out in a few hours how ready I actually am."

The laugh that broke through screwed with my equilibrium more than any concussion had ever aspired to. With a shrug, he said, "I mean, you timed it pretty well. Ottawa has been at the bottom of the league in shots per game, and they're like third to last in the division."

I chuckled. "And you just jinxed me, asshole."

He actually managed to look sheepish, but there was still a devilish glint in those beautiful blue eyes. "Yeah, I probably did. But since when do you like easy games?" He started past me, and he gave my shoulder a pat as he did. "I just jinxed you enough to keep you from getting bored."

I laughed, which fortunately masked the fact that his brief, platonic touch had made me forget how to breathe for a beat or two. "Thanks, Sol. You're a real pal."

He turned around and offered a cheeky wave before he continued walking, and I just stood there with my heart racing and that imaginary rock digging into my heel.

It was progress, right? Moving past our history together. Moving past that night we'd spent that I wished hadn't been a mistake, and the night we'd had it out over Colfax. Sol had gone to bat for me when reporters had suggested I'd embellished my fall, and he'd checked on me the next day. He cared. About a teammate. Because that was all I was now, and maybe...

Maybe that was for the best. Teammates now. Friends, if we played our cards right. More than that just wasn't a good idea for us.

No matter what my heart did whenever we were in the same space.

Stepping out onto home ice for warm-ups felt amazing.

Getting a roar of applause as fans pressed *Welcome Back* #32 signs against the glass? Wow. That was something. Calgary fans had been pretty much done with me for the last couple of years, so I'd forgotten what it was like for people to be happy to see me. I could get used to that again.

Warm-ups went well. I fell into the team's usual routine, and goddamn, it felt incredible to be out there again, knocking away pucks while my teammates ran line rushes. Even when I skated off to the side to give Sol a chance to warm up, my heart was pounding, but in a good way this time. It was all excitement and anticipation of the game. No nerves or frustration.

Okay, some nerves. What if I'd lost a step? What if I needed more time after all? What if everything people said about me last season was true, and it really was time to hang it up and stop pretending I still belonged at such an elite level?

I shook those off as best I could. I'd come back from injuries before, and even if the first game or two weren't my greatest performances, it never took long to find my stride. I'd be fine.

My coaches had faith in me. So did my teammates. So did the fans.

My gaze drifted to the net, where several of the forwards were playing keep away with Sol, something they always did with the backup goalie during warm-ups. As I watched him laughing and trying to stop seven skaters from scoring on him, my heart did a little flip.

Sol had faith in me.

When we'd first come to Seattle, he'd been my competition, and I knew damn well that feeling had been mutual. But everything he'd said in the parking garage...

He *did* have faith in me.

Somehow, that soothed away most of those nerves.

I was back, and I could do this. I *would* do this.

The horn sounded, announcing one minute remaining for warm-ups. I left the ice along with most of my teammates while a few stayed behind to round up pucks and finish their pregame routines.

Shortly after that, we were back out on the freshly resurfaced ice. Two national anthems later, the puck dropped, and we were off and running.

I was pretty sure Sol did jinx me, too. Ottawa usually wasn't great at shooting. They'd get the puck into the zone, then pass, pass, pass, until an opposing player snatched possession and broke away.

Tonight?

Jesus fuck.

I made my first save after a one-timer from the point, and when the ref came to retrieve the puck from me, I glanced up at the clock. 19:46. Fourteen seconds into the game, and they were already shooting? Hell.

After that, it was more of the same. Either Sol truly had jinxed me, or their coaches had gotten on their asses about how the object of the game was to put the puck into the net, but whatever the case, they were coming at me from all directions tonight. Ten minutes into the first period, I was drenched in sweat and already had a dull ache in my shoulder from a windmill save that I still couldn't believe had worked. During a commercial break, I skated to the bench to towel off my face, and I threw Sol a look.

"They don't shoot at the net, huh?"

That mock innocent shrug was far more endearing than it had any right to be. "Maybe they've been practicing?"

After I'd taken off my mask, I held up my glove and narrowed my eyes. "You can't see it, but I'm giving you the bird."

He wasn't wearing his glove, and he brought up his hand to rub his eye with his middle finger.

I laughed, rolled my eyes, and muttered, "Jackass."

"Yeah, yeah." He nodded toward the net. "Get back to work."

"Bite me." I didn't wait for a response, pulled on my mask, and headed back to the crease, chuckling to myself the whole way.

The second half of the period was more of the same, though my team finally found their footing and tilted the ice enough to give me a bit of a break. With four minutes left before the buzzer, Axel *finally* tapped in his first goal of the season, sending the crowd to their feet and making the whole place shake with cheers and applause. The kid was absolutely beaming as he skated past the bench for fist bumps. He was going places—I could feel it—especially now that he was finding his confidence.

After that, Ottawa tried like hell to answer his goal with one of their own, and I fended off several shots in the final minute of the period.

Finally, though, the buzzer sounded, and we retreated to the locker room to rest, regroup, and hydrate.

Sol met me at the entrance to the tunnel. "You look good out there. Haven't lost a step."

The rush of warmth almost made me lose a literal step right then and there. I managed to keep my skates under me, and I flashed him a quick smile. "Thanks."

Then we continued down the tunnel.

Little exchanges like that had seemed impossible just a few short weeks ago. Every time we had one now, it gave me more hope that we could coexist after all. Apparently all we'd needed to break the metaphorical ice was for one of us to get hurt and the other to go to bat for him. Who knew?

Now if I can just stop crushing on you, I might actually stay sane.

I shook that thought away, stripped off some of my gear, and dropped onto the bench to pour some water down my throat.

Coach gave his usual motivational speech. The team reporters came in and asked a few people questions about how we thought we were doing so far tonight. One asked me if I was pleased with my performance.

"Definitely," I said with a smile. "It's always hard, coming back after a long absence, but as soon as the puck dropped, it felt like I'd never left."

There. Now they had something quotable to put all over social media. And if we lost tonight, I could eat some crow. Eh. Whatever.

As I was pulling my gear back on, a flash in my peripheral vision made me flinch. Probably one of the overhead lights reflecting off someone's phone or something.

It made my eyes hurt, though, so I rubbed them without thinking about it.

And there was the light again.

While my eyes were closed.

Instantly, there was a cold ball of dread in the pit of my stomach.

Oh.

Fuck.

As soon as I recognized it, the rest of the auras followed —the Christmas lights across the left side of my vision. The nauseating throb inside my head. The way my balance wobbled even while I was sitting down.

There was no mistaking what this was, and I had about ten minutes to get someplace dark and quiet.

I called out to Diaz, the nearest trainer, and something in my expression must've clued him in because he hurried over. "What's up?" he asked.

I swallowed. "Migraine."

His eyes widened, but he was only frozen in surprise for a second before he took charge. "Solomon—you're in net."

That probably had every head in the room snapping toward us. Every conversation quieted and equipment stopped rattling, but I didn't look to see who was watching me. I didn't even have enough brainpower to think too much about how disappointing it was that I wasn't going to finish my first post-injury game. I was too busy closing my eyes and trying to knead away the building storm through my temples.

"What's going on?" Kayla was suddenly there.

"He's got a migraine." Diaz put a hand on my shoulder. "Talk to me. What do you need?"

"Dark and quiet," I gritted out.

My thoughts were already too scrambled to guess where he'd be taking me. I just followed along as he helped me to my feet and led me out of the room—not an easy task when I was six-three *and* wearing skates while he was five-nine in sneakers.

When he helped me into a chair, I chanced a look around. The trainers' room. Not surprising. That was where I'd ended up the night of my concussion, since it was the designated quiet room for exactly that purpose. It worked great for this, too, especially when he shut off the fluorescent lights.

Voice low, he asked, "Do you want total dark? Or should I leave the door cracked?"

I had to think about that, which wasn't easy. "Dark as I can get."

"You got it." The door clicked shut. A moment later, something covered the crack at the bottom of the door.

"You think of everything," I said dryly.

"My daughter gets migraines." Ah. That explained it. "Can you move enough to get out of your gear?"

"Eh." That was more noncommittal than anything. The pain hadn't set in yet, but I was getting into the stupid phase, as I'd jokingly called it after the second or third time. Where I was completely lucid, but someone had replaced my brain with...with...

With something that wasn't brain. That much I knew. And I also knew I needed to get out of my gear, but the auras had made enough of a mess of my ability to think that I honestly didn't know whether I could or couldn't maneuver out of everything I had to pile on to do my job.

Diaz chuckled. "Let's at least get your leg pads and skates off."

I had no idea how he managed it in the dark. By touch and memory, I guess. One way or the other, he unfastened my leg pads, and a moment after that, he was sliding my skates off. I took out my contacts, too, since I knew myself—I'd be rubbing my eyes a lot until this was over, and I didn't need a scratched cornea on top of everything else.

Eventually, I was down to my base layer. Diaz left to get me some regular clothes, not to mention a towel to get rid of the sweat. A shower would be ideal, but the showers here were too brightly lit. It would have to wait until I was home and could stand under the spray in total darkness.

Diaz returned a moment later. I had just enough time to change clothes and lie back before the auras delivered on their promise of pain. So much fucking pain.

Everything around me was gone. Nothing existed except blinding pain on the left side of my head, like my skull couldn't decide between exploding or caving in, or maybe finding some impossible way to do both at the same time. I shut my eyes—careful not to squeeze them shut, because *ow*. I barely breathed, because every time I exhaled, a groan tried to escape with it, and the vibration alone made everything hurt worse.

The door opened again. I sensed the change in air pressure but didn't dare open my eyes.

"Obie?" Diaz whispered. "How you doing?"

I made a miserable sound in response.

"I've got something that might help." He touched my shoulder, then felt his way along my neck, probably orienting himself to me in the dark. Something cool and damp touched my forehead. It was heavy, but not uncomfortably so; a towel, I guessed. Another joined it, this one covering my eyes, which... Oh God, that felt good.

There was a muffled crinkle. Something cold pressed to one side of my neck. Then the other. I exhaled as the cold brought some relief. It wasn't enough to kill the pain, but it helped, and I'd take whatever I could get. It also soothed some of the nausea that was starting to creep in. There was no escaping that part completely—my migraines only ended one way—but I wouldn't bitch about something taking the edge off for the moment.

"This okay?" Diaz asked.

"Yeah. Feels... Thanks."

"Don't mention it." He squeezed my shoulder. "Hang in there, kid."

I didn't respond.

"You need anything else?"

"Nah. This is... It's good. It's helping a lot. Thanks."

He gave my shoulder another squeeze. "Don't thank me. Thank your buddy in the net."

My brain was too fucked up to make sense of what he'd said until long after he'd left the room. Slowly, though, through the bright red cobwebs filling up my mind, the truth emerged.

Thank your buddy in the net.

Sol.

I swallowed against the nausea. Vague memories surfaced with as much clarity as a migraine ever allowed.

"I'm sorry," I heard myself croaking in another lifetime. *"Completely blew our evening."*

"It's okay." Soft voice. Softer touch. *"Give me a minute, and I'll get your icepacks and the cold cloth."*

Moments later, the same cool touch I had right now—a couple of damp dishtowels across my eyes and forehead, a pair of icepacks tucked against my neck. Then there was dark and quiet, punctuated by the occasional silent touch—his way of telling me he was there and asking if I needed anything without any sounds to worsen my pain.

Sometimes I'd just take his hand and hold it, grateful for his company and his closeness. There was nothing fun about watching someone ride out a migraine, but I'd always deeply appreciated that he didn't leave me to ride it out alone. Not unless I asked him to, which I sometimes did. Even when I hit that last phase where the nausea took center stage, he'd stay close if I wanted him to, and I couldn't count the number of times he'd gently kneaded the soreness out of my neck and shoulders after I'd puked.

Even as my skull tried to crack open and my brain short-circuited, I remembered those hungover mornings after. Waking up feeling like I'd been through the wringer. That certainty that I'd feel like that forever.

I remembered Sol drinking hot lemon water instead of coffee and only eating cold cereal until he was absolutely sure I could handle strong smells again. I remembered him wearing headphones so he could listen to music without disturbing me, but always keeping one earbud out in case I needed him. I remembered lounging on the couch against him while he stroked my hair as I knuckled through the hangover.

And all these years later, even as he had to shift his attention to taking over the crease for the remaining two periods of the game, he remembered what I needed when a migraine kicked in. He'd taken the time to tell Diaz.

Through the pain and queasiness, a lump rose in my throat.

Sol remembers.

And he cares.

CHAPTER 31

SOL

It only took me a second to find Diaz when I left the ice after the game. Still drenched in sweat, still wearing all my gear, I clomped across the dressing room to where he was talking to one of the other trainers.

"Hey," I said. "How's Obie?"

Diaz grimaced. "He's pretty miserable. But he said the cloth and the icepacks are helping, so..."

"Good. That's good." I hadn't expected much more than that. I knew all too well that there was no stopping one of Josh's migraines—just mitigating it as much as humanly possible. "Let me know if I can help, okay?"

"Will do." He gestured at my gear. "Why don't you get showered, kid? You smell like the bottom of a locker."

I laughed and moved to my stall to start peeling off my gear. The rest of the team was in good spirits, and Axel got the wrestling belt from Nichols, who'd gotten it after our last win. There was the usual chirping and encouragement to keep our winning streak rolling.

"And hey, hats off to Sol." Axel gestured at me with the belt. "Way to step in, man!"

That warranted some applause and shoulder smacks from my teammates. I just smiled and shrugged. "Hey, Obie got things rolling. We all just kept his momentum going."

The tone in the room dipped a little, with worry crossing everyone's expressions as they exchanged glances.

"How is Obie, anyway?" Nichols asked. "I thought he was good after the concussion."

"Obie is fine," Coach Maines said over the worried chatter. "He's got a migraine, but he and Dr. Green both expect him to be back to normal by next game. Nothing to be concerned about."

That relaxed everyone slightly, but some of the worry lingered.

"My son gets migraines," Volkov said as he peeled off his chest protector. "They're awful."

"Yeah," Nichols said. "They knock my wife on her ass for a couple of days at a time. Fucking sucks."

There were some grunts of acknowledgment throughout the room, and some expressions of sympathy. I didn't say anything, mostly because I didn't want to tip my hand about how well-acquainted I was with migraines. Specifically, with Josh's migraines. Most people would probably brush it off because we'd been on the same team for a while. You got to know your teammates' quirks and health issues, and I suspected anyone who'd played with Josh for any length of time was well aware of this one.

But somehow, I was sure if I said anything, they'd all see right through to long, sleepless nights of trying not to roll over or otherwise jostle him in bed.

That was probably all in my imagination. There was no way in hell my teammates would be able to read that much into me being familiar with Josh's migraines. Didn't stop me from being paranoid about it, though, and I just kept my thoughts to myself as I continued stripping off my gear.

I kept them to myself when the reporters asked me about him, too. I said I hoped he felt better, and that it was always hard to watch a teammate go down suddenly. I told them that when I was the backup, I was always ready to step up and fill in for the starter, whether because he'd been pulled or injured, and that Josh absolutely did the same for me when the roles were reversed.

It was all the usual canned answers that kept our PR director from getting pissy with me. It also kept anyone from catching on that I was worried sick about him, or that I wished someone would let me step into that dark, quiet room and ask if he needed anything. Untying my skates gave me the perfect diversion so no one would somehow catch on that my fingers itched to run through Josh's hair while I silently reassured him that I was there.

God. This was hell.

But Josh would be okay. I knew from past experience that he'd be fine. It would be a huge relief to see him upright and smiling again, and we'd all move on as a team, and everyone would forget all about this until the next time.

The next time.

When I still wouldn't be able to do a goddamned thing for him.

It was tough to get into the spirit of celebrating at the bar tonight. The game had been great, and I was proud of my team and of my own performance.

I was just worried about Josh. Even though I knew migraines were very rarely worse than just a miserable ride, it sucked knowing what he was dealing with right now. I'd hated the powerlessness back then, and I hated it now.

Is he alone? I drummed my nails rapidly beside my untouched soda. *Is anyone staying with him?*

I didn't even know which he'd prefer. Sometimes he'd wanted to curl against me and hold on while he rode it out. Other times, he'd recoiled from any kind of contact as if the slightest touch hurt. Once in a while, he'd just wanted to be alone until the misery passed. Whatever he'd wanted, I'd given it to him, whether it meant sitting quietly in another room in case he needed something, holding him in a dark shower, or helping him stumble to the bathroom so he could heave his guts out.

Tonight, there was nothing I could do, and I had no idea if he had anyone else. Diaz and Kayla had assured me that someone was going to get him home, but what about after that?

I fidgeted in my seat, turning my glass between my fingers. Should I check up on him? Except, no, I couldn't. If I texted, called, knocked, rang his doorbell—any one of those sounds could have him on the floor begging for sweet death.

I rubbed my eyes and sighed. This had been so much easier back when I'd had a key to his place.

Shame I blew that one, huh?

I could text Diaz. He would know what was going on. I could make sure—

"Hey, Sol." Axel nudged my shin under the table with the toe of his shoe, pulling me back into the present. "You still with us?"

"Huh? Yeah. Yeah." I shook myself and picked up my drink. "I'm here."

He cocked a brow. Then understanding seemed to dawn. "Obie?"

Pursing my lips, I nodded. "Yeah. He got migraines like that when we played together in Phoenix back when he was a rookie." I whistled, shaking my head. "Just sucks, you know?"

"It really does. Poor dude. And there's nothing anyone can do? Like meds or something?"

I shrugged and sipped my drink. "You'd have to ask him. He did have a pretty bad concussion a couple of seasons ago, and there was that one recently, so..." I trailed off with another shrug.

"Oh God." Axel made a face. "Can concussions cause that shit?"

"I don't know if they can *cause* it, but apparently they can make it worse."

He shuddered. "Fuck that noise."

"I know, right? Like we don't get knocked around enough in this business."

He grunted in agreement and took a swig of beer. "I already creak and crack as much as my grandma. I don't need *that* bullshit."

"Just wait." Darby elbowed him. "The broken bones really keep things interesting."

"Pfft." Axel rolled his eyes. "You say that like I haven't broken any before. They didn't just yank me out of Pee-Wees and toss me into the majors, you know."

"Oh, they stopped doing that?" Darby deadpanned. "Guess Nichols got lucky, then."

Nichols turned away from the conversation he'd been involved in, eyes narrow with suspicion. "How did I get lucky?"

"Because the rookie here"—Darby tilted his beer bottle

toward Axel—"says they aren't drafting out of the Pee-Wees anymore." He toasted Nichols. "You dodged a bullet, my friend."

"Oh, fuck you, Darbs." Nichols flipped him off. "The Pee-Wees wouldn't even take you now."

That prompted an "ooh!" from the group, and the jokes kept flying.

Normally, I'd join in with the trash-talking, but my heart wasn't in it tonight. Not even after I'd texted Diaz and he'd replied that Josh was home and doing all right.

He got sick right after he got home, he told me. *My daughter usually feels better after that.*

Well, that was a relief. Like Diaz's daughter, Josh almost always felt a million times better after that particular phase of the migraine. It was awful in the moment, but everything started to relent afterward. Chances were, he'd crash, sleep it off, and feel more or less human—if hungover —in the morning.

He was home. He'd be fine.

And eventually, I'd stop worrying about him.

Not enough to get into the swing of celebrating a win with my teammates, though, because when everyone started settling up tabs, I was seriously relieved. Get me the hell out of here.

"Hey, Sol?" Colfax put his empty beer bottle on the table. "We're all going to hit up a club in the U-District. You coming?"

The thought of going anywhere but home—and doing anything but checking on Josh again—had me suddenly wishing I could collapse right here and go to sleep. Hitting a bar this late? After a game? When I was this wound up? No, thanks.

But then I realized Axel was putting on his jacket and

discussing Ubers with Darby and Järvinen, and ice water shot through my veins.

On second thought...

"Yeah. Sure." I forced a smile. "Count me in."

I was absolutely ready to collapse. Not even a little bit in the right headspace to be partying. All I wanted to do was go home and go to sleep.

But no way in hell was I letting the rookie out of my sight with Colfax.

Guess it's gonna be a long night after all.

CHAPTER 32

JOSH

The migraine left me with a hell of a hangover. A dull throb that felt like someone prodding a fresh bruise. My throat raw from the really fun part. My neck, shoulders, and ab muscles aching from the same. And I was just tired as all hell—completely wrung out like I'd just played back-to-back games. Good times.

I vaguely remembered someone driving me home last night. Kayla? I was pretty sure it was Kayla. Or maybe Diaz. Both of them?

Well, whatever. I was coherent today. Hungover and still vaguely stupid, so what I really needed to do was stay home and veg until I felt human again.

Hockey was a harsh mistress, though, and the Sasquatches had an away game tomorrow night. That meant a flight early this afternoon.

Fuck. I rubbed a hand over my face and sighed. Okay. Okay. I'd... Fine. I'd start with a shower. Then get dressed. Then coffee.

Those went well enough. Showered, dressed, and en route to being caffeinated, I leaned against the kitchen counter and racked my sore brain for what my next step should be.

Packing. That was easy enough. After this many years of pro hockey, I could pack a suitcase in my sleep, though I did triple check everything since I didn't *quite* trust my memory this close on the heels of a migraine. Good thing, too—I'd completely forgotten to pack my toiletry kit. Whoops.

All right. Packed. Now what?

Getting to the airport, that was what.

Just thinking about that worsened the already crushing fatigue. I'd almost forgotten to pack some essentials, barely remembered how to operate the coffeemaker, and had erred on the side of not bothering to shave this morning in case I accidentally trimmed my jugular. Now I was supposed to drive.

We all left our cars at the training center when we traveled, so it wasn't like I'd have to navigate the freeway through downtown Seattle. The side streets could be a little hairy, though. Narrow. One-way. Kids and dogs. Other people who were perfectly coherent but distracted by phones.

I drummed my nails on the counter. I really didn't like admitting defeat. I hated admitting when I couldn't do something, and I especially didn't like erring on the side of caution when I was almost certain I *could* do it.

But pride wouldn't mean much if I caused a wreck. Though I was *probably* okay to drive, I didn't want to take the chance. My reflexes were a little sluggish and my peripheral vision still seemed vaguely wonky on my left side. Neither of those things were particularly alarming anymore—they just didn't bode well for driving safely.

Bottom line? If I wanted to join my team on this road

trip and maybe even start tomorrow night's game, I had to be a responsible adult.

So, I swallowed my pride, bit the bullet, and sent a text asking if I could bum a ride from someone. And in the interest of not making any of my teammates go out of my way, especially the night after I'd had to bail on them in the middle of a game, I chose someone who lived in my building.

No problem, Sol wrote back. *How's your head?*

Still attached, I replied. *Just hungover.*

He responded with a thumbs-up.

Why was that such a relief? He'd helped Diaz make sure I had what I needed last night, and he'd always been amazing in the past when a migraine knocked me on my ass. We were cool these days, even if things could be rock-in-the-shoe uncomfortable sometimes. If nothing else, I was his teammate, so yeah, he'd help me out.

And yet, I was still surprised.

You know exactly why, a little voice in my head muttered, *and it has nothing to do with Sol.*

I ignored that thought and went hunting for my dress shoes. They were, of course, by the front door. Exactly where I always left them.

Yeah, getting a ride was definitely a good idea.

About ten minutes later, there was a quiet tap on my door. Who the hell? It took until I checked my Ring app to remember Sol had been on his way down. Wow, I was a mess.

"Hey." I stepped aside. "Just need to get my stuff and we can roll out."

"No rush." He slid his hands into the pockets of his pressed blue trousers. "How are you feeling?"

I kind of wanted to ask him the same thing, because he

looked exhausted. There were dark circles under his eyes, and he wavered a little on his feet as if it took all he had to stay upright. He was kind of pale, too, even for him.

"I'm better than I was last night, that's for sure." I cocked a brow. "What about you?"

"I'm good." He gestured dismissively. "Long night."

That had my Spidey senses tingling, because I knew what "long night" had meant in Sol's past life. He just seemed tired right now, though. Not even hungover, and definitely not dragging like he'd spent a night doing blow. His eyes were no more bloodshot than anyone else's would be if they'd just had too few hours of sleep, as opposed to staying up unnaturally late thanks to some chemical help.

Something told me I could take him at his word, at least this time, that it really had just been a long night.

So, I let the subject go. I picked up my garment bag, then grabbed the handle on my suitcase. "Good game, by the way. I didn't get a chance to watch the highlights, but it sounds like you killed it out there. Thirty-nine saves in two periods?" I whistled, shaking my head. "Nice."

He laughed softly, some color blooming in his cheeks. "Would've been easier if you hadn't pissed them off in the first."

"What? How did I piss them off?"

"By shutting them out!" He scoffed as we stepped out into the hall. "Rude."

"Hey, that meant we were ahead when you got out there. You basically played two-thirds of a game and started with a one-goal lead." I shot him a pointed look. "You're welcome."

"Yeah, yeah."

As I locked the door, I said, "And don't forget, you're the

one who jinxed me by saying they don't take many shots. So...you kinda brought that on yourself."

"I'm sorry, what was that?" He cupped his ear and craned his neck. "Did you...did you say you wanted to walk to the training center?"

"You want to tell Coach you ditched me while I wasn't fit to drive?"

He tsked and rolled his eyes. "Whatever. You need me to carry something?"

I looked down at my stuff. I didn't have much, so I just shrugged. "Nah, I'm good. Where's yours?"

"In the car."

"Well, in that case..." I shoved the garment bag at him. He took it with a laugh, and we headed downstairs. Though the day was overcast, I pulled on a pair of sunglasses. No point in aggravating my already bitchy eyes and brain.

"Still feeling it?" Sol asked as we left the garage.

"Yep. You know how the hangovers go."

"Uh-huh. I remember." He paused. "Does this happen a lot?" He glanced at me. "I mean, I thought you had meds that helped."

Not very long ago, I'd have suspected he was sniffing around for a weakness. Something to give him an edge so he could snag that starting position over me. It was wild how much things had changed.

"I do," I said. "And the contact lenses help a lot."

"Wait, when did you start wearing contacts?"

"A few years ago. I just wear them during games. They filter out some of the light that triggers migraines."

"Oh. Damn. That's some cool tech." He glanced at me. "And they really do the trick?"

"Most of the time, yeah." I sighed, rubbing the back of my stiff neck. "Between the meds and the contacts, I was good for a long time, but after that bad concussion while I was playing in Calgary..."

Sol sucked in air. "Yeah, I guess head injuries wouldn't help that, would they?"

"Not really, no. At least they started tapering off after a year or so."

"That's good." He glanced at me, brow pinched. "But last night... Do you think it's going to be like this for a while? Because of that last concussion?"

"God, I hope not," I said on a groan.

"Me too. We need you."

I stared at him.

He glanced at me again. "What?"

"You..." I almost shook myself but thought better of it. "Just..." Aw, fuck. I wasn't so sure I could backpedal this one on a good day. On a day when my brain had been replaced with stick tape and ice shavings...

Pressing his elbow under the window and rubbing his neck, Sol sighed. "You're not my competition, Josh."

I blinked.

"We're teammates." Another glance my way before he navigated a turn onto another side street. "Yeah, we've got history. And it's messy. But right now..." He shrugged, resting one hand on top of the wheel. "We're good, right?"

"Yeah," I whispered. Then, with a cautious chuckle, I added, "Trying to best you for the starter spot *did* make me play a lot harder, though."

Sol laughed, which did things to my head that the migraine never aspired to. Unaware of how dizzy I suddenly was, he said, "Well, I mean, we can still compete against each other if it keeps our stats as hot as they are right now."

"Oh yeah?"

"Well, yeah." He offered a sly smile. "Forget the starter spot—I'm coming for the Xavier Trophy."

"Ooh." I wagged a finger at him. "Those are fighting words, my friend."

He cackled. "You think you can beat me?"

"Are you kidding?" I snorted. "You're toast, buddy."

"Bring it."

We exchanged playful glares across the console, then both laughed. My God, that felt amazing. Flirting with him would be the best thing ever, but I could take good-natured chirping. It was as close to our old normal as we could safely get.

The conversation faded to a natural lull, and the only sound was the engine idling as we sat at a red light. When the signal changed, the engine whined a little as he continued driving us toward the practice arena.

My mind drifted back to last night. Kind of hard not to, given the persistent throb on one side of my head. Through the memories of lying there in horrible pain, there were moments of Diaz coming in. Of something cool on my face and beside my neck.

"Thank your buddy in the net."

I inhaled deeply and turned to Sol. "Thank you, by the way. For everything you told Diaz to do last night."

He looked at me briefly, brow pinched. "Did it help?"

"A lot, yeah."

"Good." He blew out a breath, and from the drop in his shoulders, he was genuinely relieved. "It's been a while, so I couldn't remember everything you used to need."

"No, no, it was...it was great. Thank you."

"Any time, man. I wish I could've done more."

Those words would've knocked me off my feet if I hadn't been securely strapped into Sol's passenger seat.

How many times had he murmured them to me the morning after? Stroking my hair. Rubbing my neck. Gazing at me with worry and sympathy all over his face.

"I wish I could've done more," he'd said so, so many times.

"I wish I could've done more," he'd said just now, the morning after he'd had to jump into the net to fill in for me, but had stopped on his way to the ice to tell someone as much as he could remember about what I needed.

A lump rose in my raw throat. Did he have any idea how long it had been since someone gave that much of a shit about me?

The training center came into view up ahead, and I stared intently at it. "The migraines—I haven't had many people who did as much as you do when I have one."

Sol didn't speak, but I could feel him tense beside me.

I moistened my lips. "Like I said, they got worse after that one concussion. I was having them a lot, especially the first few months." I swallowed hard. "Drove my ex-husband insane."

"What? Please tell me you mean he just hated seeing his husband in pain."

"If by that you mean he hated having to walk on eggshells, cancel plans at the last second, and—"

"For fuck's sake," Sol growled with sudden vehemence. "Are you serious?"

"Completely. It was..." I chewed the inside of my cheek, not sure if I wanted to show this card. I was ashamed of it, even if I couldn't articulate why, but I also just hated talking about it. The divorce, the last year or so of my marriage, my ex-husband—all of it. But I'd already nicked the vein. Might as well open it up completely.

I took a deep breath. "He didn't think a headache could

really be that bad. I mean, he was accommodating the first week or two after the concussion. When I was still having symptoms months later, though, like the cognitive issues— memory, speech, that kind of shit— or when the migraines kicked in worse than before...when I was getting them all the damn time..." I sighed. "That drove him nuts."

"What was his problem?" Sol shifted in the driver seat. "Did he think you were faking it?"

"Don't know if he thought I was faking it. Just that I was exaggerating. He didn't believe it was possible for a headache to be that bad because no one could possibly handle it." I laughed bitterly. "Isn't like I had much choice, you know?"

Sol didn't laugh. "There's no way anyone can see you like that and think you're in anything but awful pain." He adjusted his grasp on the wheel, which was when I noticed his knuckles had been turning white, as if he'd been taking out his frustration through a death grip. "That's...God, that's even more infuriating than those stupid reporters thinking you embellished when you got hurt. Like, it's..." He huffed sharply and shook his head. "It's fucking bullshit. And your own husband? What the hell? After a hit to the head like that, of course you were going to be fucked up for a few months. Migraines, cognitive shit—I mean, what the fuck did he expect?"

I stared at him, startled by the anger.

"Jesus Christ." Sol pulled into the parking garage, and he continued ranting as he looked for a space. "Did he not understand what he was signing up for when he married a pro athlete? Injuries are a thing. And like, you've had migraines since forever."

"Yeah," I said with a humorless laugh. "And they drove him nuts from day one."

"Ugh." Sol rolled his eyes and swore as he eased into a parking space. He killed the engine and set the brake, but he didn't open the door. Instead, he turned to me, and we locked eyes over the center console. "I don't know if anyone's told you this, but your ex is a dick, and you deserve better than that."

I blinked.

"I'm serious. Being compassionate and helping out when you're hurt or when you're dealing with a fucking migraine—that's like the bare goddamned minimum. That's right up there with not cheating or not setting your stuff on fire—anything less makes him a terrible partner and an awful human being, and even though I've never even met the guy, I can tell he's not worthy of someone like you." He made a disgusted sound. "I know the divorce was tough on you, but just from what little you've said? Good riddance to that jerk."

I chuckled with some actual feeling. "Jesus, Sol. Tell me how you really feel."

His lips quirked. "Well, I'd say he deserves to catch rabid crabs, but I feel like the crabs don't deserve to live in such inhumane conditions."

The laugh that burst out of me was genuine, and despite the lingering throbbing in my skull, it felt amazing. Almost dizzying. "You know, I think you missed your calling." I unbuckled my seat belt. "You'd have been amazing at writing greeting cards."

Sol laughed as genuinely as I had, and I tried to ignore the rush of warmth that sent through me.

Tried.

But failed.

And as we gathered our luggage and headed in to meet up with our teammates, I was off-balance. Because while I'd tipped my hand a fair bit during our conversation, I hadn't told him everything.

The part I couldn't say out loud was that my ex had been convinced I was still in love with Sol. That if I'd had the faintest whiff of another chance with Sol, I'd have dumped Damon for him in a heartbeat.

The accusations had been absurd. I'd never have cheated on my husband or anyone else. I'd always been faithful to any man I was with.

But right now, I couldn't look anyone in the eye—not Damon, not Sol—and say that *all* of his concerns had been wrong.

Because I *was* still in love with Sol.

CHAPTER 33

SOL

Seattle Sasquatches Continue Comeback Season: Shut Out Reigning Cup Champions

Rookie Forward Suspended for Two Games Following Cross Check to Bouchard's Face

SEATTLE – Thursday night's crowd-pleasing Montreal-Seattle game stunned hockey fans, with the Sasquatches shutting out the Royales—and Seattle's own former star netminder, David Barnaby—in a 5-0 blowout.

Seattle was backstopped by one of Barnaby's replacements, Josh O'Brien, who was recently reactivated after suffering a concussion. O'Brien recorded his twenty-second career shutout with an impressive forty-three saves against Montreal. Sasquatch center and captain Patrice Leclerc got a piece of each of Seattle's goals—two goals and three assists.

The third period brought out the spicier—and arguably more entertaining—side of hockey, with Montreal's frustration boiling over into three separate fights. Seattle's

Konstantin Volkov and Montreal's Nils Olsson dropped gloves two minutes after the puck dropped.

Both were still in the box when Seattle rookie forward Axel Egillsson fought Montreal defenseman Mike West after West's uncalled slash on Antero Järvinen. Shortly after leaving the box for his penalty, Egillsson exchanged slashes with Jean-Marc Bouchard behind Montreal's goal before delivering a cross check to Bouchard's face. Bouchard left the ice for stitches. Egillsson was ejected and, following a hearing this morning, suspended for two games.

The young forward had a reputation in major juniors for being extremely well-disciplined and rarely taking part in fights or scrums. Since his league debut, though, and especially in the weeks since the holiday break, he's proven to be increasingly aggressive, racking up more penalty minutes in the past ten games than in his entire last season of juniors.

During this morning's media availability, Coach Maines said of the suspended rookie: "It's tougher at this level, and some of the young guys learn the hard way they have to be more aggressive. Sometimes that pendulum swings a little too far. The kid's got a good head on his shoulders—he'll level out."

Teammate Troy Colfax said about Egillsson: "He got pushed around a few times, and he learned to push back." With a chuckle, he added, "Somebody woke up the sleeping dragon."

Egillsson is due to return to play Tuesday night when Seattle plays in Portland. Bouchard received three stitches after the cross check but is listed as available to play. He had no comment regarding last night's incident.

Seattle plays Houston tomorrow at home. Montreal plays tonight in Vancouver.

. . .

Seattle Racking Up Wins, Penalty Minutes

SEATTLE – In a season that has proven to be anything but boring, the Seattle Sasquatches have been putting up unusually high numbers in two categories: wins and penalty minutes.

Seattle has held the first-place spot in the Pacific Division for five straight weeks, the longest in team history. The team has performed exceptionally well both offensively and defensively, boasting three players on track for 80-point seasons and some of the finest and most consistent goaltending in the league.

The latter is especially surprising given what many had called a foolish desperation play by Seattle—signing goaltenders Josh O'Brien and Cary Solomon. Both O'Brien and Solomon had abysmal stats in their last two seasons, but have flourished in Sasquatch sweaters.

But perhaps even more surprising than Seattle's record is the number of penalty minutes the team has incurred. The Sasquatches typically average 6-8 penalty minutes per game. This season, the average is 9.6, and 11.2 in the last ten games.

While fighting in hockey is hardly uncommon, Seattle has been an historically well-disciplined team under Head Coach Heath Maines. This season, however, the Sasquatches have already incurred nearly as many fighting penalties as they did in their previous three. Defensemen Troy Colfax and Connor Darby account for the majority of those, but forwards Antero Järvinen and Axel Egillsson have also spent time in the box for dropping gloves. Colfax,

Darby, and Egillsson have also served brief suspensions for on-ice aggression—Colfax and Darby for hits with intent to injure; Egillsson for an egregious cross check.

Asked about his team's surge in aggression, Coach Maines said that it's "something we're working on in practices." He went on to add that, "A fight or a scrum now and then is fine. But this isn't how we play. Not in this town. They know that, and it'll change going forward if they want to stay on this team."

None of the players in question are expected to be benched for the next game in Philadelphia, but Coach Maines wouldn't rule it out if the problems continue.

"Now in goal for Seattle," the announcer's voice echoed through the arena behind me as I retreated to the dressing room, "Number thirty-two—Joshua O'Brien."

I winced. Fuck. What a shitshow. Hopefully Josh would play better than I had tonight.

Every goalie had terrible games. And they happened every season. It was just one of those things that everyone in hockey knew and accepted, even if they acted like it was a shock every damn time. Cam Xavier himself, the legendary Hall of Famer and namesake of the most coveted award a netminder could earn, had some spectacularly awful performances in his storied career. Sometimes it was an off night. Sometimes we were just outplayed by the other team. Sometimes...hell, sometimes it was unlucky bounces and the hockey gods laughing at that goalie's expense. It happened.

And tonight, as Seattle played in Atlanta, it happened to me.

I had no explanation. No excuse. There'd been a time when I probably would've blamed my team for allowing so many breakaways and not keeping the puck out of our defensive zone, but my job wasn't to sit there and look pretty while they hammered away at the other team. My job was to keep whatever pucks came at me from getting past me, and I wasn't doing that.

No excuses—I fucking sucked tonight, and my team was paying for it.

Being pulled early was always humiliating, but it was a relief, too, especially when I knew deep down that there was no salvaging this performance. As I'd skated toward the bench before the first period had even ended, I'd felt like absolute shit. But when I'd exchanged glances with Josh while he'd put on his mask and I'd taken mine off...

We were in good hands.

With Josh out there to stop the bleeding, our teammates could focus on making up for the deficit I'd allowed. Even if we couldn't win this one—and with a four-nothing score at the end of the first period, there wasn't a lot of hope—we could at least salvage some of our collective dignity.

I dropped onto a bench in the locker room and sighed as I put my mask down beside me. Well. That fucking sucked. I couldn't wait to hear what fans and reporters had to say about me after this. Probably a good night to stay off my phone.

The period ended shortly after that, and my team filed in. I got a few encouraging comments from my teammates, but they were obviously demoralized, and I felt awful about that. The goalie's performance could make or break a game, and I never felt that weight more profoundly than I did on nights when I shit the metaphorical bed.

As I lethargically stripped off my gear, I told myself over

and over that this wasn't the end of the world. No team won every game in a season. We were holding steady at first place in our division, with only one point currently separating us from Los Angeles, while there was a solid seven-point gap between L.A. and Portland, who'd been sitting firmly in third place. Plus we still had three games in hand on both teams, giving us a comfortable cushion. No matter how disastrously we lost tonight, the worst-case scenario was narrowing that gap to five points, assuming Portland won their game tonight.

But as I did every time I had a bad game, I worried this was the beginning of a downturn. A losing streak for my team. A string of bad games for me.

Shuffling off to take a shower, I tried to ignore the sick feeling in my stomach, but I couldn't shake it. What if this *was* the start of another slump? Because I couldn't fucking afford a slump. Not even a brief one. With the way last season had ended, that didn't just make me nervous. It scared me. It reminded me of how much was on the line, that my career was hanging by a thread, and just how thin that thread really was.

What if this is the beginning of the end?

Of course, that line of thought sent me right down the predictable spiral.

I just need to focus.

I need something to help me focus.

I know exactly what'll help me focus.

I closed my eyes and put my face right into the hot spray. My therapists had told me over and over that the little voice in my head would probably be with me forever, and a lot of the fight with addiction was just learning to ignore it or redirect myself to something less destructive. Usually, I could deal with that. Over time, it really did get easier, even if I did still struggle sometimes.

Nights like this, though? Fuck my life. This wasn't just a random craving out of the blue. There was so much pressure. So much riding on me. I told myself over and over and over again that everyone was depending on me staying sober so I didn't fall apart. But that little voice reminded me over and over and over again what a difference one sharp sniff of white powder could do to my performance. Which was worse? Being a terrible goalie while I was sober? Or giving in to the craving and being what my team was paying me to be? I'd come within spitting distance of the Xavier trophy—second place by a *razor*-thin margin—exactly one time in my career, and my brain never let me forget that that was the season before I went to rehab.

Cocaine got me the best stats of my career.

A night like tonight barely registered when my numbers were that good.

What am I waiting for?

I turned around to let the spray beat on my neck. Staying sober was better and I fucking knew it. Cocaine would help in the short term, but it wasn't worth the long-term problems.

And what if tonight is the beginning of a long-term disaster?

What if this is the beginning of backsliding right into last season?

Is a nose full of cocaine really worse than that?

Yes, I told myself emphatically. *Yes, it fucking is.*

Frustration and humiliation alike had me on the brink of tears. I hated everything about this. Did other goalies fall apart like I did after a piss-poor performance? Or did they pull themselves together and tell themselves they'd do better next time? Did they have this stupid, persistent, incredibly persuasive voice in the backs of their minds?

Was that why everyone thought goalies were insane? Because on some level, we kind of were?

No, that wasn't it. Yeah, you had to have a reckless streak to sign up for this job. Nobody with a healthy sense of self-preservation volunteered to be a human shield for frozen discs of vulcanized rubber flying at a hundred miles an hour.

But given that most goalies didn't land in rehab after destroying their lives and careers one line at a time, I was pretty sure they didn't have this asshole voice in their heads. That, or they had a better ability to ignore it than I did.

Well, whatever. I was stuck with it. And I needed to ignore it so I could put tonight behind me and be the goalie I'd been all season.

I shut off the shower and reached for my towel. What the hell had changed, anyway? Was this really just an off night? Or was I falling apart again?

Then it occurred to me that when I'd been performing at my very best since the start of this season, there'd been a strong motivator that I hadn't had before—spite. Competitiveness. The absolute refusal to play backup to my ex-boyfriend.

Had I lost my edge tonight because I wasn't trying to outperform Josh anymore?

Great. We'd come to an understanding and were civil to each other—hell, we were actually friendly to each other—and we weren't competing for the starter position anymore. No spite, no competition, and now I couldn't do my damn job. Awesome.

Maybe I needed a distraction.

There's a ton of gay bars in this town. Wouldn't take much to find someone there who wants to—

To get laid. Not party. Get laid. Sex, not cocaine.

Except sex wasn't what I wanted tonight. Falling into bed with a stranger could be fun, but I felt too low and defeated for that right now. What I wanted was something to quiet all the self-loathing and fear about my career being over, and yeah, a gay bar wasn't a bad place to go look. Anywhere there were people drinking and looking for a good time—gay bar, sports bar, wherever—there was inevitably someone who either had some blow or knew where to find it.

"Stop," I told myself out loud. "Just...no."

I was a mess, and I probably would be until I won my next game, and no matter how good it would feel in the moment, cocaine would *not* solve the problem.

Not today, Satan. Not today.

With my head still swimming with a million thoughts, and with that stupid voice still nagging at me to put some relief up my nose, I left the showers and returned to the dressing room. There, I put on a pair of sweats and a T-shirt. I'd change into my suit before we left for the hotel, but I wanted to be comfortable right now.

Don't want to look like I'm ready to hit the club, I told myself.

Except I would look the part when I left, and given the choice between going back to my hotel room and going to the bar with my teammates... Damn. That was a tough one. Especially when I knew there were guys on the team who were using.

So which was more dangerous in this state of mind? Alone with my craving? Or in a group with people where the liquor flowed and the cocaine was readily available?

Goddamn, I missed the days when I could just have a bad night and be miserable for a little while without this constant drumbeat of *"you know how to feel better."*

As I was zipping up my bag, footsteps raised the hair on my neck. No skates, so it wasn't a teammate. Definitely wasn't Josh. Why would it be? He was busy minding the net after I'd been a goddamned sieve out there. Probably just one of the trainers or another staff member.

But when I turned around, it was Kayla. And she was watching me.

"Hey." I forced a smile as I sat down to put on my sneakers. "Is the second period going better than the first?"

"So far, so good. We're on the power play right now." She gestured over her shoulder. "And Benning scored, so their goalie won't be getting a shutout tonight."

Well, that was something. When it came to adding insult to injury, few things stung more than having a terrible night in goal while the guy at the other end of the ice got a shutout.

"Let's hope the power play does something," I muttered as I leaned down to tie my shoe.

Kayla was silent for a moment. Then she crossed the room and sat down on the bench with my mask between us. "You know, you're having an incredible season."

I glanced at her before returning my focus to my shoelaces. "Sure doesn't feel like it tonight."

"It's one game. You're allowed to have a bad game."

I knew that. I really did. I'd been telling myself that for my whole career, and ever since that second puck had gone in tonight. What I couldn't explain to her was the path my brain went down whenever I caught a faint scent of failure, because I'd crashed and burned so many times, I was scared to death that if I wasn't at the absolute top of my game, I was on my way back down to rock bottom.

"Sol. Look at me."

I swallowed hard and made myself look at her again. She could be a total hardass, and she had very little patience for things like the conflict between me and Josh. Right now, though, her expression was soft. So was her voice.

"Listen, I know as well as anyone how much a bad night can screw with a goalie's head. Been there."

I dropped my gaze to avoid hers. I wanted to laugh bitterly and say she had no idea, but even if she didn't know what it was like with the added layer of addiction, she *was* a goalie. As much as anyone could, she did get it.

"I also know what it's like to be a goalie with ADHD."

At that, my head snapped up. "What?"

She smiled sympathetically but genuinely. "You didn't think I knew?"

"I, uh..." I racked my brain, trying to recall if that was something that had ever made it into the media. I'd never mentioned it after the first time someone told me I was just making excuses to be a cokehead, and I didn't think the medical staff had said anything to—

"I can tell, hon. It's not hard to miss if you know what you're looking for."

Heat rushed into my face. "Oh. Damn. I didn't think..." That was a lie. It was obvious as fuck, especially if someone knew what ADHD could look like.

"That's the whole reason I got into hockey." She sat back, watching herself thumbing the hem of her suit jacket. "It doesn't always look the same in girls as it does in boys. The hyperactivity..." She shook her head. "It's usually not the hyperactive and inattentive version like it is in boys. Not...it's not usually the same as... Anyway, the point is, my parents thought I just needed an outlet for my energy, so they stuck me in hockey."

I swept my tongue across my lips. "Yeah, that's... Me too. I was a hyper kid, so they put me on skates and figured I'd burn it off."

Her laugh was gentle and kind—the sound of someone who empathized, not someone who was laughing at me. "Ever wonder if our parents knew what they were signing themselves up for in exchange for maybe getting us to sit still in class?"

I managed to chuckle. "My mom actually complained about that."

"Did she?"

"Uh-huh. Every time she had to cut a check for another piece of equipment or another tournament, she was like, 'What the hell? I thought we were just burning off his energy, not bankrupting ourselves.'"

Kayla giggled. "Yep. Same boat." Sobering, she said, "It did help a little. I still couldn't focus for shit in school, and my grades were..." She groaned and rolled her eyes.

"Ugh, me too. They had me tested for all kinds of things like dyslexia and whatnot, and they kept threatening to make me quit hockey if my grades didn't improve." I rubbed the back of my neck and exhaled. "They actually did for a little while. Made me quit in eighth grade. My grades got even worse and my focus went all to shit. My guidance counselor told them it wasn't an effective punishment—it was just making me miserable by taking away the one thing I was good at because I struggled at everything else."

"That happened to me too," she said quietly. "Lasted about a month before my dad called and begged my old team to let me register. My grades were never great, but I was good at hockey, so..." She shrugged as she trailed off.

I faced her. "How do you deal with it now?"

"Meds, mostly." She wrinkled her nose. "I don't like some of the side effects, but they help."

Sighing, I let my shoulders sag. "God, I wish I could take something."

The question was written all over her face, but she seemed to work out the answer before she spoke it out loud. "You can't take stimulants."

Renewed heat rose in my face as I shook my head, and acidic shame rose in my throat as I croaked, "Nope."

"Jesus. So you just have to live with it? Work around it?"

I looked down and thumbed the edge of the Sasquatches logo silkscreened onto the thigh of my sweats. "It's all I can do."

She was quiet for a long moment. Then, "You know, you've had a phenomenal career by any standards."

I met her gaze but didn't speak.

She continued, "Making it to this level isn't easy for people who *don't* have ADHD or struggle with addiction. And your stats—yeah, you had some bad seasons, but for someone to have come back from the things you have and still maintain your record?" She whistled. "Sol, that's impressive as hell."

I couldn't look at her anymore, so I lowered my gaze to the logo again, watching my thumbnail trace the white outline. "Gotta wonder how much better I'd be if I hadn't fucked myself with the drugs."

"And we can always wonder how much better Chip Harrison would've been if he hadn't missed three seasons to injuries, or how many more goals Bobby Wilson would've scored if he hadn't had to retire so young. What they accomplished is still incredible, especially since they had less time and had to work through a lot more pain and problems than their peers to get there."

"Yeah, but what I had to work through—I did that to myself."

"You also *un*did it yourself."

"With help."

"Yes, with help. But you still did the work." Kayla sighed. "Listen, I've read the articles and watched the interviews. And I've been watching your career since long before either of us came to Seattle. I don't care how you got started with cocaine, because I'm too impressed by how well you bounced back after, and how far you've come since."

I swallowed hard against the sudden lump in my throat, and I made myself meet her gaze.

"I'm serious," she said. "And I know you're being hard on yourself because you had a bad game tonight. But you've had so many good games in your career, I think you can cut yourself some slack for this one."

It was still tough to swallow, but I managed. "What if it's not just one night?" God, I sounded pathetic. "What if this is the start of a slump, or—"

"That won't happen." She sounded absolutely certain. "I'll work with you. Coach Maines will work with you. And it isn't like you have to carry the team yourself." She motioned toward the ice. "Obie's holding his own, too. Sooner or later, he's going to have a bad night, and I have complete faith you'll step in and take over for him like he's doing this time. Same as you did the night he went down with a migraine." She paused. "And do I have to remind you that while Obie was injured, *you* carried this team? There was a ton of pressure on you, and your only backup was a third-string goalie who really isn't ready for this level, and you pulled it off." She reached over the mask sitting on the bench between us and put her hand on my forearm. "Tonight is one bad night after you've spent the whole season blowing everyone's expectations out of the water. Cut yourself some slack."

I held her gaze, still trying to digest what she was saying. As it slowly settled in, so did a sense of calm that I'd desperately needed. That obnoxious voice still yapped at me, encouraging me to find some powdered relief, but Kayla's voice was louder.

Louder, and a hell of a lot more convincing, especially since she understood me in a way very few people did.

From up the tunnel, the buzzer sounded, signaling the end of the second period, which meant the team would be filing in shortly.

I rolled my shoulders. "Thanks. I needed to hear all that."

"I figured." She rose, straightening her suit jacket. As the sounds of voices and clomping skates approached, she added, "If you feel like you need some extra practice just to get in the groove, let me know. I'm here to help."

"I will." I smiled with some actual feeling. "Thanks."

The team and I tried our damnedest to make up for Sol's disastrous first period, but it didn't happen. I didn't let anything through, and Seattle managed shrink our deficit to one, and we hung on with a score of four-three. During the last two minutes of the third, Coach pulled me so we'd have an extra attacker, hoping to tie up the score and go into overtime. At least we could salvage a point, right?

As often happened during the empty net Hail Mary, though, the other team managed to get control of the puck, and despite a valiant effort by our defense, put up another goal to secure a five-three win.

Not good for morale, but everyone tried to stay optimistic. We were, after all, securely in the top three in our division. Our next game was against New Jersey, and they were having an awful season, so we had a reasonably good chance at beating them.

We'd be fine.

But what about Sol?

With my heart in my throat, I went through my post-game routine as quickly as possible. I spoke to reporters with all the professionalism that had been trained into me over the years, hoping none of them caught on to how much I wanted them to get the hell out of my face so I could shower, dress, and check on Sol. I was starving, too, but that could wait.

Once the reporters were done with us, the locker room cleared out pretty quickly, with almost everyone going off in search of food. I would be right behind them...in a minute.

Much like I had after that awful game in Phoenix, I found him lingering in the mostly empty locker room. He was sitting on the bench by his stall, dressed casually, and he had his phone in his hand, which he was staring at as if he couldn't remember what to do with it. Or as if he'd gotten sidetracked and forgot it was there at all. Either was a possibility if his head was scattered enough.

"Hey." I studied him as I came closer, and when he looked up at me with tired, defeated eyes, I asked, "You doing okay?"

"Yeah, yeah. I'm good." He waved a hand. "Felt pretty shitty after that first period, but I cooled off, and Kayla talked me down."

"Did she?"

He nodded but didn't elaborate. That was fine—whatever they'd talked about was their business, and I was relieved to know that someone had been able to break through Sol's mood. When he'd left the ice after that fourth goal, he'd looked absolutely destroyed, and that was never a good state of mind for him. I'd been relieved to see him still in the locker room during the second intermission and after the game; though he was obviously trying hard to stay sober, a bad night on the ice had always been something that could send him looking for a chemical distraction.

That he was still here, still sober, and actually smiling a

little instead of being folded in on himself—talk about a relief. I didn't need to pry into what he and Kayla had discussed. I was just glad for whatever she'd said to him.

Okay, so I'd worked myself up over nothing. I could live with that.

"Do you, um..." I gestured toward the door. "We should probably both get something to eat."

He looked at me through his lashes, then pocketed his phone. "Yeah. Probably. I'll be there in a minute." He nodded at the door. "I don't want to keep you from eating. Especially after you stood on your head to make up for my shit."

Maybe it wasn't nothing after all.

I sat down on the bench beside him, leaving some breathing room between us. "I can wait a minute. It's fine."

He glanced warily at me. "You don't have to wait for me, though."

"I don't mind."

I braced for a venomous look and an irritated, *"What I mean is, don't wait for me—get the hell out of here."*

Those didn't come, though. He met my gaze again for a second, but quickly looked away, fiddling with the drawstring on his hoodie. "You won't have to step in for me next game. I promise."

"I know." I paused. "Though maybe don't tempt the hockey gods."

His fingers stopped on the string, his brow furrowing as he eyed me. Then he chuckled. "Okay—you won't have to step in for me because my dumb ass forgot how to tend the goal. Hopefully you won't have to step in because I'm hurt, either."

"Yeah, hopefully. You don't want to get hurt—watching

games from the press box?" I wrinkled my nose. "It fucking sucks."

Sol laughed with some actual feeling. "Oh, I know. I've done my time in there." He pushed himself to his feet, and as I stood too, he said, "I spent *ages* up there that year I broke my collarbone." He groaned and rolled his eyes. "And wouldn't you know it, that was the same time one of our defensemen was out for hernia surgery. That guy..." Sol pushed out a harsh breath through his teeth. "Would. Not. Shut. *Up.*"

I grimaced. "And you were stuck sitting with him at every game?"

"Pretty much."

"Eww."

Sol nodded grimly. "I seriously considered smacking him a few times, but that would've just extended his recovery time and kept him up there with me longer."

"And probably would've hurt *you.*" I tapped my collarbone. "I've broken mine before, too, and I've heard decking someone doesn't bode well for healing."

Sol's lips quirked. "Huh. I hadn't actually thought about that, but yeah, you're probably right." He motioned toward the door. "Anyway, let's go eat. I'm starving."

I chuckled and followed him, and a few minutes later, we were eating with our teammates. No one was giving him grief for his performance tonight. It was business as usual in here, which was a relief to me. Probably for him, too.

While Volkov and Leclerc exchanged snarky chirps over the table, making everyone howl with laughter, I surreptitiously watched Sol. Sometimes I thought I was going to get whiplash from the way we blew hot and cold with each other.

One night, he was on my last nerve. The next, he was

going to bat for me when the media tried to accuse me of embellishing.

One night, I was so frustrated with him, I wanted to scream. The next, I was worried sick about him.

One night, we could drop the temperature in the locker room by exchanging a look. The next...

Well, the next, we could be friendly and supportive like teammates should be. Even bantering a little as if everything was fine. Or we could be a breath away from being everything we'd been years ago.

I had no idea what any of it meant. Where we'd be the next time we crossed paths. After the way we'd been interacting recently, I could almost believe we were settling into this reality where we coexisted and functioned as if we'd never been the catalysts for each other's heartaches.

Some part of me wondered, though, if it was the opposite. If I'd let my guard down, and then things would blow up in a way that I couldn't quite picture yet but would feel like it had been inevitable from the moment I'd committed to playing for Seattle.

Everything seemed fine between us right now, and that made me suspicious as hell.

Are we heading for disaster?

And will either of our careers survive the fallout?

The next time we played Phoenix was at home. Coach Maines asked before the morning skate if Sol wanted to sit this one out, given our previous meet-up with his old team, but Sol insisted he was fine. His head was in a better place, and he wanted some redemption.

It hadn't been very long since Sol and I had both been

on thin enough ice that Coach would've told him, "All right, you can have your shot. But if I think for a second you're not going to hold it together, I'm pulling you, even if it's five minutes into the first period. You hear me?"

Today, he just nodded sharply and left us to get dressed. Even Sol had seemed a little shocked by that, staring at Coach's back like he was sure the man was going to remember what a mess he'd been.

Coach just kept walking, though, and his voice echoed down the hall as he called out to one of the trainers for something.

Still wide-eyed, Sol turned to me, his expression screaming, *"Did that just happen?"*

I just shrugged. So did he.

And when he stepped into the net tonight, he had his game face on. If his former teammates were giving him any grief like they did last time, the roar of the crowd undoubtedly drowned it out. At one point, he'd come to the bench during a commercial break, mask pushed up onto his head. As he was taking a drink near where I was sitting, one of the guys from Phoenix skated by. The jackass called out something I didn't quite catch, apart from the word "snowman." Sol rolled his eyes and swore—hopefully not within range of any cameras or hot mics—and took another swallow of water.

"Don't let 'em get to you," I told him. "They just want to get in your head so they can get in your net."

He nodded slowly as he put his water bottle down. "I know. Just wish they wouldn't pick that nerve to step on."

I could do the math. "All the more reason to beat two points out of them and send them home empty-handed."

He met my gaze as he was reaching up to pull down his mask. He didn't say a word—just shot me a sly grin, lowered his mask, and skated back toward the net as the ice crew left the sheet.

Whether it was my advice, Sol's determination, his skill as a goalie, our team's defense, sheer spite, or some combination thereof, Phoenix didn't get another puck past Sol. Their goalie put up a solid fight, too, but he wasn't the brick wall that Sol was out there. In the end, we beat them three-one, and Phoenix would, indeed, go home empty-handed while we racked up two more points.

Sol was all smiles all the way back to the locker room. He got first star, too, and when the wrestling belt was given out, we all would've been shocked if it had gone to anyone but him. I didn't think I'd seen him this happy in a long time, beaming with pride and laughing with the guys as he put on the belt and posed playfully. He happily chatted with reporters, and he looked like the weight of the world had been pushed off his shoulders.

Good. He deserved a night like this. This was the kind of redemption every hockey player lived for, and I was glad to see him get it.

Eventually, the noise and excitement in the locker room ebbed, and the guys started heading out for the night. After away games, a lot of the team would hang out in a hotel bar or some other place nearby. At home, it was a smaller crowd, especially since the guys who had families wanted to spend as much time with their partners and kids as the regular season allowed.

The single guys had a few bars near the arena that they liked to close down if we didn't have an early practice or flight the next day. I probably went about half the time. Sometimes I just wanted to go home and enjoy some quiet downtime while my ears continued ringing from the game.

Other times, I was still too energized, and like many of my teammates, wanted to ride that while it lasted.

Tonight, I joined them at a place two blocks over from the arena. I looked around when I walked in, taking stock of who was here. Colfax was almost always out with the team, whether the game was home or away, and tonight was no exception. He'd already grabbed a table with Darby, Axel, and Järvinen, who'd been hanging out with us ever since he'd come back off the injured list.

I had to smile as I watched the two rookies bantering with the older guys. Sometimes it was hard to find a place on the team, especially for the really young rookies. The guys who came up through college had a little more time to mature, but the kids who were barely out of high school and suddenly found themselves skating with veterans—hell, with living legends—could get in over their heads really fast. Especially the ones who had the talent to land them on a major league roster right out of the gate instead of spending some time cutting their teeth and developing their skills in the minors. Didn't I know it.

So I was glad that Axel hadn't struggled quite like I had, especially while his friend was gone. He was still a bit starstruck sometimes, and the brutal travel and game schedule obviously took their toll, but he was finding his footing. Playing well, too—he'd already racked up several assists and his first pro goal. We'd even won the night he scored his first goal, which always made that milestone sweeter.

I was glad to see him finding his footing on the ice, and also his place within the team after hours. He and some of the guys had clearly hit it off—especially Colfax and Darby—and he'd found his groove chirping and pranking like everyone else.

And admittedly, I was kind of glad to realize that Sol wasn't here. Surprised, too, but relieved he wasn't at that table with Colfax. Though Sol had been in a great mood when we'd left the arena, partying was still dangerous, especially with another cocaine user. Back in our younger days, those had been some of the worst nights, especially when he was perfectly fine until everyone started winding down, and then he'd go looking for a way to keep the high rolling for as long as he could. Usually on his own, especially since everyone else—including me—would be too tired to stay up any longer. *Those* nights had ended badly, and though I was still mostly confident he was sober at the moment, I couldn't convince myself a night of partying wouldn't end badly for him now.

That wouldn't be an issue tonight, though, because Sol wasn't here.

And honestly, I felt like a dick for even thinking it. Sol hadn't given any indication that he was using again. In fact, he'd come to me begging for help when temptation had nearly gotten the best of him. No one could deny that he was trying like hell to stay sober.

But he *had* those temptations. And he'd had one of those great nights that could be as dangerous as a bad one— instead of trying to quiet his brain and numb himself, he'd be looking for every way possible to hold on to that feeling. And I'd had a front-row seat to too much of Sol's past to be comfortable watching him hang out with a young player, least of all one so eager to find his place among his teammates, when Sol was in any state that might lead him to use again.

"No Sol tonight?" I asked casually as I joined everyone with a soda in my hand.

"Nah." Colfax waved a hand. "Said he was going out with some of the boys from Phoenix."

That prompted a chorus of "boo" and "traitor" and "consorting with the enemy," but everyone was chuckling. We all got it. Very, very few hockey players stayed with the same team their entire career, and with as close as we got to our teammates, it stood to reason we'd stay friendly even after we moved on.

It did catch me a little off-guard that Sol was going out with those teammates, though, considering how they'd treated him. Maybe there had just been a few who were dicks to him. Hopefully none of those assholes would be there this evening; he deserved a night to wind down with friends.

What about the guys he used to do blow with?

That thought gave me pause. I actually took out my phone, pulled up the current Phoenix roster, and scrolled through it. There were only three guys left from when I was on the team, and none of them had, to my knowledge, ever been involved in illegal substances. Sinclair, the player who'd gotten Sol into it was long gone, having flown under the radar long enough to retire about a year after Sol went into rehab. Last I heard, he'd wound up in rehab himself, but it "hadn't worked out." I didn't know what that meant—if he'd bailed, if he'd been booted out, or what—only that he'd dropped off the map and I had no idea where he was or what he was doing now. Or if he was even alive.

A ball of lead formed in the pit of my stomach. I'd known a handful of people in the league who'd been addicted to something or another—cocaine, painkillers, alcohol—and so many of their stories ended the same way. Rehab. Relapse. Vanished from the face of the earth.

The ball of lead grew bigger and colder as my mind

went back to Sol. He'd relapsed twice in the last seven years. Both times, he'd managed to keep his career and his reputation, even hiding those relapses from both his club and the media. What if that lightning didn't strike a third time? What if the next one was more public? More catastrophic?

I rubbed my suddenly tired eyes with my thumb and forefinger.

Sol was doing well these days, I reminded myself over and over. He was sober. He was committed to staying that way.

Disaster wasn't right around the corner. That was just my too-many-times-bitten brain jumping a gun that wasn't even there.

Things were *good*.

All I could do now was hope like hell that continued.

And that this ominous feeling really was all in my head.

CHAPTER 35

SOL

When Seattle had played in Phoenix, I'd wanted to meet up with some of the teammates who I still talked to. Tracer, especially.

Unfortunately, that hadn't worked out. Schedules just hadn't lined up, and in hindsight, I was ckay with that. As miserable as I'd been after that awful game, I hadn't felt like socializing with anyone.

Tonight, though, my old teammates had some time, and I still had plenty of gas left in the mental tank, so I joined them in the bar at their hotel.

Admittedly, I was a little worried about who would show up. The only real in-person interaction I'd had with anyone this season had been on the ice, and that had mostly consisted of dickholes like Carver making cracks about me snorting lines of snow, or him and Bailey calling me Snowman, since they knew that got under my skin. Given how viciously guys could chirp on the ice in order to gain an advantage, I wouldn't have been surprised if they showed up at our table and acted like it was just friendly shit-talking.

That would get awkward. I had as thick a skin as anyone needed to stay sane in this sport, but my addiction wasn't funny. If they thought they could use it as a punchline and then have a beer with me like everything was normal, they could go fuck themselves.

To my great relief, Carver and Bailey were nowhere in sight. Instead, it was Tracer and five of the guys who'd been fiercely protective of me while I'd been on the team, including Petrovich and Nilsson. Instead of putting up defenses at the sight of assholes who thought "Snowman" was hilarious, I had to force back a lump in my throat as I joined half a dozen men who'd tirelessly kept me on the rails while we'd been teammates.

"Hey, there he is!" Tracer gathered me into a bear hug. He was easily six inches shorter than me, but he was built like a brick shithouse. His hugs actually made me feel small —in an endearing way, not a vulnerable one. He'd been like my big brother all this time, and he'd pulled me out of more than one fire of my own making. I almost cried as I hugged him back, realizing right then how grateful I was to still have him as a friend and a support person. The world I lived in would've been way darker without this guy and his bear hugs.

The rest of the boys greeted me the same way—hugs, back slaps, and of course, trash talking.

"Oh, man." Nilsson made a big show of shielding his face as if something were blinding him. "You were already pale as fuck, but Seattle is making you—"

"Oh fuck off," I said with a laugh as I took my seat. "Your mom doesn't think I'm too pale."

"Ooh," the other guys said as Nilsson rolled his eyes.

"Eat a dick," he muttered into his beer, but he was chuckling.

I laughed, too, and ordered a soda. While I waited for it to arrive, I turned to Tracer and gestured at my chin. "Looks like you finally made it past puberty!"

That earned me a punch to the shoulder that smarted a little. "Says the guy whose playoff beard is whiter than he is."

"Mmhmm, whatever you say, Chin Pubes."

Another punch. More laughter. Yeah, it was good to be back with the boys.

About the time my drink arrived, a couple of guys came strolling into the bar. As soon as I made eye contact with one, my spine straightened. He halted in his tracks and glared right back at me.

Then he turned on his heel and walked back out.

"Aww," I said, letting the sarcasm drip, "here I thought Carver was about to join us."

My old teammates all glanced in his direction, then shook their heads and rolled their eyes in unison.

"Man, don't let him get to you." Tracer picked up his beer bottle. "He's a dick."

"Coach had some words with him, too," Nilsson said.

I blinked. "He did?"

"Oh, fuck yeah." Nilsson gestured with his glass. "One of the refs told him last game about the 'Snowman' shit. Said if he heard it one more time, Carver was getting a penalty for unsportsmanlike."

My lips parted. "Seriously? I didn't think the refs heard it." Nah, that was a lie. I was pretty sure everyone in the circle for that faceoff had heard it. I just hadn't thought anyone cared.

"Didn't even matter what the ref said," Nilsson grumbled. "By the time Coach got to him, Carver'd already got an earful from the captain."

I could barely process that. "Oh. Wow. I, um...I didn't think anyone..."

"Fuck that," Tracer said. "There's chirping, and there's that trash." He shook his head sharply before taking a pull from his beer. "Not cool."

"I don't think it was you he was avoiding." Nilsson nodded toward the bar's entrance, where Carver had come and gone. "I think it was us."

I cocked my head. "How do you figure?"

Tracer grunted. "Because he knows damn well he crossed a line, and if he came over here to give you shit, all six of us"—he gestured at himself and his five teammates —"would take suspensions in a heartbeat for kicking his ass."

The comment made my heart flutter. So did the solemn nods all around the table from guys, a couple of whom I'd seen throw down on the ice for far less.

"Damn right," Nilsson said. "Maybe we'll get lucky and he'll get traded."

"Right?" Petrovich rolled his eyes. "How did we end up keeping Carver and losing Sol?"

I laughed uncomfortably. "To be fair, his stats are a lot better than mine were." And more consistent. And he didn't have a questionable history. And he wasn't the one who'd gotten us knocked out of the playoffs. And he—

"His stats aren't *that* good," Nilsson said coldly. "I don't fucking care if they are, though—I don't even want a league MVP on the team if he's a cancer in the locker room."

Again, nods all around.

I swallowed. "He isn't that bad, is he?"

"Didn't used to be," Nilsson said.

"Oh, he was," Tracer grumbled. "He was just more

subtle about it." He pursed his lips. "I think Bows was keeping him in check."

That made sense. Bows—Mark Bowman—had been the team captain for my entire tenure, and he had some history with Carver that predated either of them coming to Phoenix. Looking back now, I could believe Bows had tempered Carver's bullshit. He hadn't tolerated toxic behavior from anyone in the locker room, and he'd had enough clout that if he decided someone was dragging down the entire team, the club would listen. He and another forward had nearly gone to blows one time after some crap had been building for half the season, and the other guy was traded almost immediately after that.

That wasn't to say he'd abused his power. He was fair and reasonable, not a diva who demanded things be run his way. He just knew when to put his foot down for the sake of the team.

At the end of last season, he'd been an unrestricted free agent, and Toronto had made him an offer no one could blame him for accepting. Now Carver wasn't on a short leash anymore.

At least the team didn't seem to be putting up with it. Somehow, despite me convincing myself that everyone would wash their hands of me given half a chance, my former teammates—men who had no obligation to stand up for me or even get involved in conversations about me—had made their support of me clear. A ref had told Carver to can it. So had his coach and the Firebirds' new captain.

The end of last season had felt like one of the lowest points of my life, and that was saying something.

But tonight, sitting at a table with former teammates I could still call friends, I was in a good place. My stats were better than they'd ever been. I was part of a winning team.

These guys still had my back. The people who sneered at me and hated me were getting shut down.

More and more, I believed things were getting better for me.

Please, please, let them stay that way.

My old team had to fly out early in the morning, so they called it a night around eleven. I didn't blame them, even if I was disappointed to see the evening end.

"Next time you're in Phoenix," Petrovich said, "beers are on us."

"Damn right they are," I said, even though we all knew that "beers" meant beer for them and soda for me. "I'm holding you boys to that."

"Deal," they all said.

"Take care of yourself, man." Tracer clapped my arm. "We're all proud of you. You're killing it up here."

I smirked even as heat rose in my cheeks. "It helps when the other team can't get the puck to the net."

"Oh, fuck you." Tracer rolled his eyes and punched me playfully. The other guys chimed in with some chirps, and we all exchanged quick hugs.

"I'm serious," Tracer said. "Take care of yourself."

I smiled. "I am. I promise."

It felt good to mean that.

They headed back upstairs, and I went outside to get an Uber. Before I'd finished entering the request for a ride, though, I paused. It wasn't what I'd call early, but I still had too much energy to just go home. All I'd do there was toss and turn for half the night.

I texted Darby to see if they were all still hanging out at the bar by the arena. He confirmed they were.

Some of the guys have left, he said. *But there's a few of us hanging out till last call.*

Perfect. That bar was walking distance from here, so I closed the Uber app and headed up the sidewalk, letting the brisk wind rush over my face. I didn't know which had left me flying higher—the game or the evening with my old friends. I still couldn't get over the realization that when I'd hit what felt like rock bottom this time, I hadn't lost everything. I still had my career. My sobriety. My health. And yes, my friends.

I was still going to have bad nights on and off the ice, and I was still going to have moments when cocaine sounded as necessary as air. But I was also going to have nights like this, and if I could hold on to everything about it —this feeling, this reality—then maybe that would be enough to carry me through those cravings.

Or maybe it wouldn't, but that would be okay, because I had people. The boys in Phoenix. Eventually, I'd get there with the boys here in Seattle.

I have Josh.

The thought almost made me trip over nothing. Yes, I did still have him. And he'd already proven that, even when we were still hostile toward each other, he'd see me through a weak moment so I could stay sober.

As I waited for a crosswalk light to change, I closed my eyes for a second and took in a deep breath through my nose. I felt fucking amazing, and there wasn't a grain of cocaine in sight.

Remember this, I reminded myself. *Remember it for the bad nights.*

A few minutes later, I walked into the bar where some

of my teammates were hanging out. Only a handful remained, which made sense, given how late it was.

Was it weird that I was disappointed that Josh wasn't here? I thought I'd heard him telling Johnson in the locker room that he'd be joining them. Maybe he'd been here and gone already. Damn.

And why did I care? If he was here, he'd probably be giving me the stink eye for hanging out in a bar. He'd be a downer. I didn't want him here.

Why didn't I believe any of that?

"Hey, Sol!" Colfax grinned as I came in, and he pulled my focus away from my scattered and contradictory thoughts as he called out, "There's the star of the night!"

I laughed, getting a little rush at the reminder that I'd been first star of the game. I'd told Coach Maines I wanted redemption tonight, and I'd gotten it in spades. Fuck yeah.

"How about a drink?" Colfax gestured for a server. "What are you drinking, man?"

"Just a soda." I smiled and craned my neck so I could see the labels on the soda fountain. "Do they have Dr. Pepper? Oh, they do. Fuck yeah."

"Just Dr. Pepper?" Johnson clapped my shoulder. "Come on, we're celebrating! Get yourself a—"

"Hey." Darby tapped a knuckle on the table and looked pointedly at Johnson. "He said he's not drinking. Leave it be."

Johnson froze, then nodded and squeezed my shoulder. "Right. Right. Sorry, man." The server appeared right then, and Johnson said, "Hey, can you get my buddy here a Dr. Pepper?"

"Of course." She looked at me. "Can I get you anything else?"

I was still gobsmacked that a teammate had stepped in

and told someone to back off, but I recovered, offered a smile, and shook my head. "No, just a Dr. Pepper. Thank you."

She smiled back, then disappeared to get my drink.

"Sorry about that, man." Johnson nudged my shoulder. "I forgot you don't drink."

I shrugged. "Don't worry about it." It was funny how no one had ever pressured me to try some blow, but ever since I'd stopped drinking, I'd had to fight off well-meaning people who just wanted me to "loosen up" and "have fun."

Yeah, bro. That's the problem. If I drink, I will loosen up and have fun...in ways that will ruin my life again.

I caught Darby's eye across the table and mouthed, *"Thank you."*

He tipped his beer bottle in a subtle toast and gave me a nod.

After that, my Dr. Pepper came, and the moment of awkwardness was forgotten. I fell into bantering and laughing with my teammates, who had apparently been trying to bribe Axel to bring them some more of those Icelandic chocolates his family had sent him before the holidays.

"I can get them," he said with a shrug. "My aunt always sends me a few boxes, but if I tell her the team wants them..." Another shrug.

He was right across from me, so I tapped him under the table with my foot. "Why the hell is this the first I'm hearing about your fancy imported chocolates?"

He brought his drink up to his lips. "I didn't have any goalie chocolates."

I snorted and rolled my eyes as our teammates laughed around us. "Fuck you."

Axel flashed me a grin, then took a swig of his beer.

"Nah, seriously, I can get more. I can also—" His teeth snapped together, and he sobered. "You, uh, probably don't want the other stuff she sends me."

I cocked a brow.

"Brennivín," he said sheepishly. "It's a liqueur. And also whiskey and some other stuff."

"Got it." I nodded sharply. "Nah, I'll stick with the chocolate."

"Cool. I'll let her know. Do you cook at all?"

"A little. Why?"

"Oh, dude." Colfax leaned in, wrapping his arm around Axel's shoulders as he said, "His grandma sent over this—what is it, lava salt or some shit?" He shook his head. "Shit's amazing for cooking."

Axel blushed, gazing at Colfax like a starstruck kid who was giddy over his idol's approval.

"Oh yeah?" I asked. "What's so special about it?"

Axel shyly started explaining it, but before long, he had me and the other guys leaning in and listening intently to all the different kinds of salt Iceland was apparently famous for. I was dubious, especially after so many people had insisted the pink Himalayan salt was supposed to be spectacular—maybe it was, but I'd sure never tasted a difference—but I was willing to give it a try.

Before long, the kid was making a list in his phone of what everyone wanted, from salt and booze to chocolate and a bunch of other candies. That led to him and a couple of the guys comparing notes on different baked goods, and I had a feeling there would be tons of bread and cookies in the lounge after our next practice. Oh my God. As if I hadn't stuffed myself after half the team had brought in food before Christmas, not to mention at both the Thanksgiving and Christmas parties at Leclerc and Volkov's houses, respectively.

"Go easy, boys," Coach Maines had warned. "We do have practice tomorrow."

"Uh-huh." Leclerc had shot him a look. "Says the guy with chocolate on his face."

We'd all cracked up as Coach blushed and wiped away the incriminating smudge.

I fucking loved this team.

Around one in the morning, I was starting to finally run down a bit. All the caffeine had mellowed me out enough that it was a good thing I wasn't driving; I wasn't drunk like Axel, Johnson, or Darby, but falling asleep at the wheel was a real possibility.

I'd also had several sodas tonight, so I stepped out to use the men's room. When I came back and rejoined the group, I noticed the chair across from me was empty. That wasn't unusual—we all kind of came and went at these things, and people went up to the bar, went to the restroom, or peeled off to call it a night. Still, I noticed this time because the person who'd been sitting across from me was Axel.

Trying to look casual and not at all bothered, I glanced around, searching for that distinctive red hair and the gray shirt he'd been wearing.

He was nowhere in sight.

Okay. He was an adult. I wasn't his babysitter. He didn't answer to me and I didn't need to know everywhere he went.

But I was still concerned...especially when I noticed another empty seat at our table.

Colfax's empty seat.

Oh.

Fuck.

Panic surged through me. Had they left together? Did it mean anything at all that, in the time I'd been away from the table, they'd both disappeared? Or was I reading way into something that meant absolutely nothing?

Trying to stay cool and collected, I leaned over to Darby. "Hey, did Eggs leave?" I gestured at Axel's empty seat.

"Oh, yeah." Darby motioned toward the door. "Colfax was giving him and Järvinen rides home."

My blood turned cold. "Oh. Uh."

Darby must've seen my sudden concern, because he shrugged. "Dude, it's all good. Colfax stopped drinking like two hours ago."

"Right. Right. Yeah. It's not... It wasn't that." I shook my head, then said with a forced smile, "Just, uh...I was going to have Eggs add another box of those chocolates to my order."

Darby laughed. "Oh, yeah. I don't blame you. Those things are so good. I should have him get me another one too." He took out his phone. "You want me to text him?"

"Nah, it's okay. I'll catch him at practice."

I bowed out a minute or two later, and as I waited for my Uber, I rocked on my feet on the sidewalk. The calming effect of the caffeine I'd been drinking was a distant memory now. I was wired, and I doubted my ADHD was the culprit this time.

What was I supposed to do? I couldn't randomly text Axel. Couldn't grill him about where he'd gone with Colfax and what they were doing. Couldn't tip my hand and tell him I had my suspicions, especially because I was starting to wonder if I'd imagined it all anyway.

I mean, so what if Colfax could ping-pong between moods? So what if he sniffled sometimes? Being out on the ice did that to some people. So did exertion. And who cared if he was sweaty a lot when we went out? Every time he was eating anything, it was five-alarm spicy. Which probably accounted for some of the sniffling, too.

Was this all in my head? Or was I gaslighting myself into doubting I'd seen what I knew I'd seen?

I closed my eyes and pushed out a breath into the crisp night. What if I was wrong? Or worse, what if I was right? What was I supposed to do? I couldn't just accuse Colfax or Axel of using. I couldn't just elbow my way in between them and tell Axel he needed to stay away from Colfax. If I started doing shit like that, I'd get a reputation as a locker room cancer and a troublemaker, and what little credibility I had would be trashed. No one would listen if I did have proof that someone on the team was using. Would they listen even then? Because if I said someone was using cocaine and I could prove it, then all eyes would be on me and my sobriety.

"If you know he's using cocaine, you must be doing it, too."

Didn't really work that way, especially since the signs were painfully obvious to anyone who knew what they were looking for, but since when did anyone take anything a former cokehead said without a giant grain of—

A car pulled up right in front of me. I opened my eyes. The driver peered at me.

Then I saw the Uber sticker.

Oh. Right.

I confirmed she was my ride, then climbed into the backseat. She tried to chat with me, but my mind was going way too fast to hold on to any conversation. I felt bad, but I just couldn't focus. My head was too full of red flags and blaring alarms.

It didn't necessarily mean anything that Axel had left with Colfax. Even if Colfax was a cocaine user, he could still do things like give someone a lift home, just like he could still play hockey, buy groceries, put gas in his car. He was a high-functioning user—so high-functioning I couldn't be as sure as I wanted to be that he was using at all—so he lived his life and did normal things in between lines. He might not have any interest at all in getting a teammate, least of all a young one, to start using. Hell, for all I knew, he was giving Axel a serious lecture about staying away from all that.

"Do as I say, not as I do, because you don't want to go down this road, kid."

Closing my eyes again, I pressed back against the seat. I took a few slow, deep breaths, and I tried to pull my thoughts into order. Simplify the situation.

The possibilities were endless, but there was one fact I could be absolutely sure of, and one I'd be willing to bet serious money on.

The certainty—that Axel was a young player trying to find his place in this sport and on this team.

The *almost* certainty—that Colfax was a habitual cocaine user.

I stared up at the car's ceiling. I had to take those two things seriously, even the one I wasn't a hundred percent sure of.

Question was, what the hell did I *do* about it?

CHAPTER 36

JOSH

The banging on my apartment door pulled me out of a sound sleep. What the hell?

Sol's face on the Ring camera definitely startled me wide awake and had me hurrying across my apartment with panic in my throat. Another craving? Had he gone out partying like I'd worried he would? Or was he trying to stop himself from giving in to that temptation?

Mind reeling with all the possibilities that could have driven him to my door, I turned the deadbolt and opened it. "Hey. What's up?"

He shifted his weight, his body almost vibrating with anxiety. "I need to talk to you about something."

"At two in the morning?"

He bit his lip and avoided my eyes. "It's... Shit. Maybe it can wait. I'm sorry. I..." He raked a hand through his hair and exhaled. "I don't know."

I studied him, not sure what to make of him. Being wound up and agitated wasn't out of the ordinary for him, but the fear and worry in his eyes—that wasn't normal. Not unless...

"Is this another craving?"

Sol jumped like I'd backhanded him. "No! No. It's... No." He shook his head. "It's nothing like that."

Okay, this was weird. Really, really weird. And alarming as all hell. Two in the morning or not, I was wide awake now, and I wouldn't be able to sleep until I knew what this was all about.

Am I going to be able to sleep after *that?*

Sol raised his eyebrows, and I realized we'd been standing there in silence for a long time. Chewing my lip, I stepped aside to let him in. Then I closed the door and faced him, both concerned and guarded. "So, what's going on?"

Sol couldn't stand still, which wasn't a surprise. I didn't try to calm him down or get him to stop moving. I knew better. Between his ADHD and the fact that something was clearly bothering him, it was a miracle he wasn't pacing or, hell, levitating or something. So I just leaned against the wall and waited for him to collect his thoughts and say whatever was on his mind.

"It's the rookie. Eggs." Sol ran a hand through his hair. "I'm, uh...I'm concerned about him."

That caught me off guard even more than him showing up at my door in the middle of the night. Folding my arms, I cocked my head. "Why? What's going on?"

Sol moistened his lips, and when he met my gaze, he wasn't just worried. He was legit scared. Alarm raced through me as my brain tried to anticipate what he was going to say next. What the hell was happening? Was the rookie in some kind of trouble?

Talk to me, damn it.

Sol took a deep breath. "I'm worried he might be using."

I blinked. "Using? As in..."

"Cocaine," he said bluntly. "I think he's using cocaine. With Colfax."

My jaw fell open. So I hadn't imagined it with Colfax, but *Axel*? And then I remembered they'd both been at the bar tonight, and ice slithered through my veins. "Oh shit. They were hanging out tonight. Not, like, together, but with the team. At—"

"At the bar by the arena."

I blinked. "How did you know?"

"I was there." Sol started pacing again. "After you left, I guess. And they were definitely being friendly."

My stomach dropped into my feet. "They're...they're always friendly."

He stopped and looked right at me. "I know. That's what I'm worried about."

The words, *"So, what? You think because they're friends, they're doing blow together?"* died on the tip of my tongue. Because...

Because I'd known for a while now that Colfax was probably using. And I'd known he was friends with Axel. But those two things hadn't connected because I'd been happy to see Axel making friends on the team...and because I'd been *way* more concerned about who *else* Colfax was friends with.

"Oh, God." I sank onto my couch. "I'm so sorry."

He eyed me. "For what?"

"I thought..." I scrubbed a hand over my face, then dropped it into my lap. "When I saw you hanging around with Colfax and the rookie, I thought.." God, I couldn't even say it, I was so ashamed. Had I always had this kind of tunnel vision when it came to Sol? Holy shit.

Sol wasn't quite as hard up for words as I was: "You thought I was going to get coke from Colfax. Or get Axel into something he shouldn't." He didn't even sound angry. Disappointed, maybe? As if he wasn't at all surprised I'd gone there, but had held out hope that I wouldn't.

I had, though, so, avoiding his eyes, I nodded. "Yeah. I didn't realize... I don't..." What was the point of even trying to make excuses? Pulling in a deep breath, I met his gaze. "I'm sorry. I was wrong."

He studied me for a moment, but to my surprise, he didn't get mad. Instead, he leaned back against the couch and rubbed the back of his neck. "I can't really blame you, to be honest."

"Still, I..." I pushed a hand through my hair and swallowed the acid rising in my throat. "God, I feel like such an asshole now. And so damn stupid. Because I picked up on Colfax early on. I mean, he pretty much screams 'cocaine user.' But I was so worried about him being around you, and about you being a bad influence on the kid, I never even thought about... Jesus fuck." I stared up at Sol. "I didn't realize Colfax might be the one leading Axel astray."

Sol's expression was a mix of hurt and fatigue. No anger, though. Not even any surprise. Which made me feel even worse. He expected people to do what I did— expecting him to be a breath away from falling off the wagon.

"I'm sorry, Sol," I said again. "I really am."

"No, you shouldn't be." He sounded resigned but genuine. "I get it."

I looked in eyes again. "But I was so focused on you with Colfax, I completely missed that he was getting in so tight with Axel. Or, well, what it might *mean* that they were so..." I leaned back against the couch and swore. "Jesus Christ. For all I know, he was getting Axel into cocaine right under my goddamned nose, and I didn't see because—"

"Because if anyone had to guess," Sol said quietly, "they'd put money on me being the one who started using with Colfax. Not Axel."

"Still," I whispered. "I'm sorry."

"I know. For what it's worth, I was sticking close because I was trying to keep Colfax from getting him started. Thought maybe if I was around, I could keep Axel from leaving with him, or pull his focus, or..." He flailed a hand. "I don't know. And...I mean, there was at least one night where I'm almost sure he was high. More than one, but... He's been more aggressive on the ice. He's got some of those tics that users get."

"Like sniffling all the time??"

He nodded. "Yeah. But people do that without using cocaine, so it's possible... It's possible for him to start sniffling *and* start getting noticeably more aggressive on the ice without..." He threw up his hand. "The point is, I'd bet money he's using, but I haven't actually *seen* him touch the stuff. For all I know..." He rubbed the back of his neck and sighed as if the game and the long night were catching up with him on top of everything else. "Maybe this is all in my head. I don't know."

"I think this is one of those times where it's better to err on the side of *extreme* caution. I don't want to assume Axel isn't using, and then find out later that he is."

Sol looked at me, and the desperation and fear—hell, the *brokenness*—in his eyes brought me up short. So did the unsteadiness of his voice. "So what do we do? Because I can't let him end up like I did."

If ever there was a moment when I believed without a shred of doubt that Sol was committed to staying sober—that he was absolutely going to fight those demons with everything he had, even if he didn't always win—it was right now. He understood to his core how horrible this addiction was to live with, and the thought of someone else getting swept into it was tearing him apart.

I swallowed hard and reached for his hand. "I think we should go to Coach. He needs—"

"*No.*" Sol shook his head decisively. "We can't turn them in."

"What?" I blinked. "We can't just let them—"

"They're *addicts*."

I stared at him, hoping he'd clarify where his train of thought was going.

Sol exhaled. "Look, it's hard to explain. It's a messed-up mindset, but that's...I mean, that's what addiction *does*. If the league or the team decide to go scorched earth on them, then they'll lose hockey. They could wind up in prison, or both! It'll wreck their lives and make them even more desperate to use, and—"

"Okay, I get that. I honestly do. But what else can we do?"

"Get them help." His expression was filled with a million emotions as he whispered, "We do what my team-mates did for me when I relapsed, and... And what you tried to do for me in the beginning."

The honesty caught me off guard. "And if...if it doesn't work?"

He sighed, shoulders sinking. "Then we do what you ended up doing for me. Tell the staff and let them take it from there." He chewed his lip. "I know it seems counterin-tuitive, but that should be our last resort." His eyes pleaded with me to understand. "Because the league is punitive about it. Yeah, they stick you in rehab, but there's all kinds of threats hanging over your head, and..." He swallowed like he was struggling to keep it together, and his eyes welled up.

"Once the league gets involved, it'll be an uphill battle. For the rest of their careers. I want to help them, but if we can avoid that..."

Still stunned by everything he was saying, I asked, "It was that bad?"

Staring down at his wringing hands, he nodded. "The rehab wasn't so bad once I finished detoxing. But the league has treated me like a pariah ever since. I always have some teammates who are suspicious of me, and players on other teams like to use it as a fucking punchline. And the fans... the press..." His shoulders dropped a little more. "It's miserable."

"Jesus." I pushed out a ragged breath. "I'm sorry I put you through that."

Sol was already shaking his head, and he met my gaze. "It wasn't your fault. In fact, I get it. Completely."

"You do?"

"Yeah." He held my gaze. "It was either that or let me kill myself."

My heart flipped, both at the memory of that hellish period and the realization that, after all this time, Sol understood. Somehow I found my voice and whispered, "That was the only reason. I couldn't..." It took some work to push back the sudden rush of emotion, and I had to clear my throat a couple of times. "I didn't want to lose you, but I was scared shitless I was going to no matter what."

"I know. And I know you tried a million other ways to get through to me." He reached across the space between us and touched my face. Voice so soft it barely carried to me, he said, "You went to the team because I didn't leave you a choice."

The wave of emotions that crashed over me right almost sent me tumbling to the floor. There would probably always be some guilt there, but the relief of hearing him acknowledge everything seemed to wash away years' worth of resentment.

No, he hadn't left me a choice. I'd hated him for that, and I'd hated him for not seeing it.

But now he *did* see it. He got it. And with as earnest as he was about protecting Axel and Colfax while also helping them, with as torn up as he was over the prospect of pulling that trigger, I believed wholeheartedly that he understood what I'd been up against. That I hadn't had a choice.

The next thing I knew, I was wrapped up in Sol's arms, and he whispered, "I'm sorry," into my hair.

Burying my face in his shoulder, I closed my eyes, squeezing a few hot tears free. The last couple of years had been hell for a lot of different reasons, and that had been on top of all the hurt and resentment I'd been carrying from my time with Sol. Things had been getting better across the board lately, but tonight, even as we both worried ourselves senseless over our teammates...

Oh my God, it was liberating. Sol got it. Maybe he'd known all along. Maybe he'd just figured it out tonight. But he realized that I hadn't done what I did back then to hurt him or to ruin his life or so I could abandon him.

He hadn't left me a choice.

And he understood that.

So many things I'd been carrying all this time just...fell away. Not all of it—there was no such thing as a quick fix for something that heavy—but it helped. It was suddenly lighter. The resentment wasn't quite so cold. The hurt wasn't quite so hot.

I drew back to meet his eyes, pausing to wipe at my own. To my surprise, he was doing the same. Neither of us had been particularly emotional in the past, but I guess it was to be expected for us to both be a bit raw when we started pulling at years-old wounds.

Sol sniffed sharply, and it was surreal to not be instantly suspicious that he'd been using. I knew without a doubt that he was completely sober right now. That he had been for a long time, even if it might not have been as long as he would've liked.

Cautiously searching my eyes, he asked, "What do we do now?"

I chewed the inside of my cheek. "About Axel and Colfax? Or..."

I held his gaze. He held mine.

Neither of us had to be clairvoyant to know what I was getting at. We knew each other and our history way too well, and there was no denying that we'd been closer lately. Tonight, we'd broken through some of the barriers we'd put up between us. But what did that mean going forward?

"I don't want to complicate things." Sol swallowed. "I'm worried if we... I mean, we still have to be on the same team, and—"

"I know." I covered his hand with mine on his knee. "Let's put a pin in..." I hesitated, trying to find the right words. "We can be teammates. We can be friends, maybe." I raised my eyebrows.

Sol nodded. "Yes. Please."

Fuck, I was going to lose it again. I didn't think relief had ever been this profound.

Somehow, I managed to force back those emotions. "Okay. So friends and teammates. And we focus on figuring out what's going on with Axel and Colfax. Maybe after the season is over and everything quiets down..." I trailed off into a hopeful shrug.

The soft smile on his lips made me reconsider putting a

pin in anything. He was so damn beautiful, and tonight he was everything I'd *ached* for him to be back then.

But we had to stay this course. Assuming one of us didn't get traded or something (and that was highly unlikely if some recent comments from Coach Maines were anything to go on), neither of us was going anywhere. We could put our teammates and our team first. When the season was over...

Well, we'd see what happened.

"In the meantime," I said, "I guess we keep an eye on Colfax and the rookie until there's an opening to make our move. Maybe try to get the kid one-on-one and feel him out?"

"Probably the best thing. Getting him alone will be tough, though."

"Yeah, I know. But that's probably better than bringing it up around anyone else."

Sol shuddered. "True. Okay. We'll..." He exhaled. "Look for an opportunity and grab it when it comes, I guess."

"About the only thing we can do at this point." I squeezed Sol's hand. "We've got this. One way or another, if they really are using, we'll get them some help."

His gaze turned distant as he nodded. Ideally, we could do this the easy way—talk to Axel and Colfax, convince them to quietly get some help if they needed it—instead of potentially setting fire to their careers and lives.

But neither of us was naïve enough to believe it was going to play out that way.

CHAPTER 37

SOL

Figuring out how to intervene with Axel and Colfax was easier said than done. It was difficult to get someone alone in between practices, travel, games, meals, and team meetings, and that got even harder when the team embarked on one of our long road trips.

Road trips were brutal, especially the ones that took us through multiple time zones. Right now, we were on a beast of a trip through Canada: Vancouver, Calgary, Edmonton, Toronto, and Montreal. The Calgary and Edmonton games were back to back, though we were blessedly off for two days between Toronto and Montreal. The night after Montreal, we'd fly home, and we'd have a home game two nights after we got back to Seattle, but I'd process that nonsense later. Right now, I was just trying to survive this stupid trip.

We beat Vancouver by the skin of our teeth (mostly thanks to Josh standing on his head), and I managed a shutout in Calgary. Edmonton was a grind that ended in a three-two regulation win with Josh in the net. He'd also played last night in Toronto, which we'd lost in a shootout; Josh had felt awful afterward, but there wasn't a goalie on the planet—not even Cam Xavier himself—who could've blocked that shot from Toronto's sniper. Sometimes there was just nothing a goalie could do.

This evening, we were in Montreal, and we'd play tomorrow night. We'd had a light practice this morning, then the rest of the day to relax a little. Some of the guys had a media thing tonight—I didn't know the details, because I was mercifully not part of it, but they were chilling in the bar while they waited for their ride.

"Ugh." Axel groaned and rubbed his eyes, then dropped his hand to the table with a heavy smack. "These road trips fucking suck. How do you guys not just, like, faceplant?"

"Coffee," Leclerc said solemnly.

"Lots of coffee," Johnson agreed.

"Coffee is not enough," Järvinen muttered.

Axel grunted in agreement.

"Don't worry." Colfax gave Axel a knowing look. "You'll get used to it."

"Yeah, I know." Axel chuckled. "It's been getting easier."

Colfax grinned. "I figured it would."

Something unspoken passed between them through barely perceptible nods and glances. The other guys at the table didn't even seem to notice, but I had alarm bells clanging in the back of my mind.

My heart sank just like it always did when I got some confirmation that the kid was probably using. More and more, I was convinced there was no way he *wasn't*. And right now, it was even more complicated than usual. If he did a line or a bump tonight—I mean, we were in another country, for fuck's sake. If he did something stupid on this trip and got busted... Jesus.

And how many times did I flirt with going to prison in Canada before I sobered up?

I shuddered. Canadian prisons didn't have some horrific reputation or anything, but getting locked up in a country other than my own sounded terrifying. Not that American prisons were exactly something I wanted to sign up for. My mind suddenly wanted to tumble over all the awful detours my life could've taken back then, same as it always did when I caught the scent of a possible cocaine habit on someone, but I made myself focus on the here and now.

On Axel.

On what I could possibly do to get him off the horrible road I'd already been down.

I needed to talk to him, and I needed to do it as soon as possible. But not with our teammates around. Especially not with Colfax in the room.

I glanced around to see if Josh had come in. He'd gone up to his room, and I hadn't seen him since I'd sat down here in the bar.

Where the hell are you?

As everyone laughed and talked and chirped about a recent card game, my heart raced as if I'd just done a line myself and the drug had hit me the way it hit everyone else. This was straight-up nerves, though. I was stone-cold sober and nervous as hell—scared out of my mind, if I was honest. What if I did or said the wrong thing? What if I made things worse for Axel? No, I hadn't been the one to get him started putting powder in his nose, but I was absolutely certain that if I didn't handle this with a perfectly delicate hand, I'd make things exponentially worse. How much of that was irrational and how much of it was based on my own experience, I couldn't even say.

But it was a risk I had to take. I couldn't just do nothing

while my rookie teammate got hooked on that fucked-up drug, and I couldn't wait until Josh was here to have my back. Especially now that Axel was quite possibly using it in another country.

My opportunity came when Axel stepped away to use the men's room. Under the pretense of needing something from the hotel's shop, I also slipped out of the bar. I didn't chase him into the restroom, but waited outside instead.

When he came out, he was—unsurprisingly—more awake than he'd been a moment ago, and I didn't imagine it was because he'd just splashed some cold water on his face.

As soon as he saw me, he jumped. Speaking fast, he said, "Oh. Hey. Did you need...?" He gestured over his shoulder at the restroom. "It's not just one stall, so—"

"No, I came looking for you."

"What?" He peered at me with bloodshot, dilated eyes, and I could practically feel his walls going up. "What do you want?"

I wanted to be gentle about this, but he was already on the defensive. And I needed him to listen to me, which meant I might need to bite the bullet and use the direct approach to—

Axel swiped at his nose and glanced toward the lobby, and my heart dropped as the warm overhead light illuminated a faint but telltale dusting of white powder above his lip.

"Jesus fuck, dude," I hissed, and I took him by the arm and marched him back into the restroom.

"Hey!" He wrenched his arm free. "What the fuck is your problem?"

"You're using, aren't you? Cocaine?"

His eyes widened, then immediately narrowed, and he gave a caustic laugh. "What? No! Why the hell would—"

"Don't bullshit me. I can see all the signs because I've been you before, and I—"

"No, the fuck you haven't," he snapped. "*You* were a damn cokehead. That doesn't mean—"

"It means I can spot another cokehead from a mile away," I threw back.

He blinked, but the surprise vanished in favor of renewed anger. "What the fuck? Who the hell do you think you are? I'm not—"

"Dude, you don't think it's obvious when you leave for a few minutes, and you come back sniffling and clearing your throat every two seconds?" I gestured at my own face. "Or that you don't have goddamned cocaine eyes?"

"Cocaine eyes? What the—" Axel scoffed and rolled his conspicuously dilated eyes. "Dude, fuck off. The bar is dim as hell. Everyone's pupils were dilated in there."

"Uh-huh." I inclined my head. "And in here?" I motioned toward the bright lights above us.

"That's—"

"Bullshit." I stepped closer. "How do you explain this?" I gestured below my nose.

"Explain what? What are you even talking about? I don't see a—" But then he looked in the mirror, and he swore under his breath and quickly wiped his nose. "Shit."

"Yeah. Shit." I ran some water on a paper towel and handed it to him. "Now can we cut the crap and talk about this? Because we both know what's going on." I softened my voice. "I want to help, okay?"

"Fuck off," he growled, dabbing away the powder.

"Look, I'm not trying to get into your business," I said quickly. "I'm trying to keep you from getting fucked over like I was. Especially right now, when we're—I mean, did you forget you're using a highly illegal substance *in Canada?*"

His hands stopped mid-dab, and the fear that flashed over his face left no room for doubt that I was correct in my suspicions.

"A possession charge in another country is a serious, serious charge," I went on. "Especially if they find out you transported it over the border or on a plane."

"I...I didn't bring anything over—"

"Good. Great. But don't you think it'll be an uphill battle to convince the RCMP or whoever if you get busted for being high as a fucking kite?"

"I'm...I'm not..." he stammered, but then he pulled himself together, and anger took over again. He balled up the wet paper towel and tossed it into a trash can before whirling on me. "I am *not* high as a kite. Maybe *you* couldn't handle your shit, but I'm fucking fine."

"You're using," I said. "And you're fucked up enough you didn't even check your damn face to make sure there wasn't—"

"I'm *fine*," he snarled.

"You're going to destroy your life and your career." My voice had turned plaintive. "Axel, please. Listen to me. I've been there, and you're going to ruin—"

"Fuck you." He gave another hollow, humorless laugh. "People ruin their lives and careers with alcohol, too, but I don't see—"

"This isn't the same," I hissed. "Look, I know it feels great, and it's giving you the energy you need to play and while we travel. But it's *going* to blow up in your face. Let me help you before—"

"I don't need your fucking help!"

"You don't need the fucking blow, either!"

As soon as the words had left my tongue, Axel's fist came out of nowhere and connected with my face.

I staggered back, catching myself on one of the sinks before I stumbled, my dress shoe sliding on the tile floor. With a couple of curses, I landed on my ass, snapping my teeth together painfully in the process.

Axel loomed over me. "Back. The fuck. *Off.*" Then he stalked out of the men's room, leaving me stunned with my cheek throbbing and my ears ringing.

The door thudded shut behind him, and I let my head fall back against the wall. Goddammit. I wasn't going to get through to him while he was high. But then when would I? When he was coming down? When he was going through withdrawal? When he was looking for his next line?

I rubbed my eyes, suddenly exhausted and on the verge of tears, and it had nothing to do with the way my cheek hurt. I had no idea what to do. I couldn't just leave him to the wolves, but I had to—

The air pressure changed, signaling that the door had opened.

Shit. I started to get up, but then a voice called out and had me swearing all over again:

"Sol?"

Just what I needed—for Josh to find me like this. I scrambled up so I could unfuck myself, but I wasn't fast enough. My ex walked in and looked right at me as I was using the sink to pull myself up.

"Holy shit." He crossed the restroom. "Are you okay? What happened?"

"I'm fine." I winced as my own answer echoed the one Axel had given me when he clearly wasn't. Did that mean I wasn't? Did anything mean anything right now? Sighing, I gingerly touched my tender cheek. "Guess Axel didn't like what I had to say."

Josh's eyebrows rose. "What...what *did* you have to say?"

"That he's going to find himself in a world of hurt if someone busts him with anything while we're north of the border."

Josh blanched. "Oh. *Shit*. He's... Up here? Seriously?"

I nodded grimly. "The eyes, the way he's sniffling—no way he isn't high right now. And that temper?" I grimaced. "He was mellow as hell when the season started. I don't think he was only blowing his stack because he didn't like what I was saying."

"He's had a hell of a temper lately," Josh said quietly. "On the ice..."

I closed my eyes as the last few weeks snapped into focus. I'd wanted to blame it on stress. On his best friend being on LTIR up until fairly recently. On anything except the obvious cause that I'd known was there because all the signs were right in front of my goddamned face.

Meeting Josh's eyes again, I exhaled. "Maybe I came at him too hard, though. Should've—"

"I doubt it." Josh shook his head. "You've tried to the nice approach, and it didn't work."

"Neither did this."

A million emotions played across his face as he looked me in the eyes. Voice soft, he said, "The first approach usually doesn't."

I flinched.

We held each other's gazes for a second. Then he cleared his throat and gestured at his nose. "You might want to... uh..."

I had a flash of memory of him catching me with the

same incriminating dusting of white I'd seen on Axel, and anger tried to bubble up as if it were muscle memory, reacting to an accusation. But then I touched my nose, and my fingers came away, not with a dusting of white, but with a smear of red.

"Oh. Damn." I peered at the mirror, and sure enough, my nose was bleeding. Not badly—my cheekbone had taken the brunt of the hit, so Axel must've grazed the cartilage when he followed through on his punch.

Josh pulled a paper towel from the dispenser, ran it under some water, and handed it to me, unaware of how eerily similar this moment was to my exchange with the rookie a few minutes earlier.

"Thanks," I murmured, and I dabbed at the blood with the cool, damp paper towel.

Neither of us spoke as I cleaned myself up. I couldn't imagine what was going through his mind. Then again, maybe I could. After all, the more my encounter with Axel sank in, the more I hurt, and not because of where he'd hit me or where I'd smacked into the edge of the sink on the way down.

No, it was because I'd been in Josh's shoes before. I knew more than most just how difficult it was to crack through that shell of denial and dependence.

I knew how fucking hopeless this was unless we did something drastic.

My gaze slid toward my ex-boyfriend, and cold guilt coiled in the pit of my stomach. In my mind, I saw him in those last few months of our relationship. I'd been so far into my habit, I'd been mostly oblivious to what he was going through, but as images from that period played out side by side, it was impossible to ignore. The anger. The hurt. The frustration. How many times I'd thought he was cold-shouldering me, but now I could remember the tears in his eyes just before he'd look away, or how he wouldn't just recoil from my touch, he jerked out of my reach as if even my gentlest caress was painful.

I was killing you, and I didn't even know it.

That was something I needed to atone for. Sooner than later, that was for sure. But tonight, there was a more immediate problem, and I hoped Josh understood.

He probably does. More than most people ever will.

I indulged in a second to wince at my own thought. Then, staring at him in the mirror because it was easier than looking at him directly, I said, "I think we need to get the staff involved."

Josh's head snapped toward me, meeting my reflected eyes. "You do?"

My stomach churned with nerves and nausea. "Yeah. Axel isn't going to listen. I...I think we can both be pretty sure about that."

Avoiding my gaze, Josh nodded slowly, some of that fatigue and defeat from years ago radiating off him. "Yeah. You're right."

I swallowed my emotions. "How, um...how do we do this?"

He met my eyes again, looking at me in the mirror through his long lashes.

"I have to follow your lead," I confessed. "I don't want to put this on you. But all I've ever been is..."

He pressed his lips together. Then he nodded. "Okay. Well. I think you're right about involving the staff. First things first, we should have a meeting with Coach Maines."

"Do you think he'll listen?"

Barely whispering, Josh said, "I don't know. Only one way to find out."

I tossed the paper towel in the trash, rested my hands on the sink's cool edges, and turned to look at Josh directly. "What about tonight?"

"What do you mean?"

"He's high. Guaranteed." I exhaled. "We won't be getting through to him, but God knows what he'll do while he's—"

"Slow down, slow down." Josh put up his hands. "He's not going out partying tonight, remember?"

I blinked. "He's... Oh. Right. The media thing." Grimacing, I said, "If he gets busted there..."

"Well." Josh half-shrugged, looking more apologetic and resigned than dismissive. "There isn't much we can do about that. But one way or the other, he's safe right now. He's out with the media team, and..." Josh waved his hand. "He'll be fine for tonight."

That much, I could agree with. Axel would be in good hands for the next few hours. He was with safe, responsible people at a professional event. For that matter, he wasn't a *heavy* user (yet), and he wasn't so deep into his habit that he'd risk using around anyone who wasn't *also* using. Plus, one of the guys in that group was Järvinen, Axel's friend and roommate—that meant the rookie wouldn't be alone even after they made it back to the hotel. When the coke wore off, he'd be tired and sluggish, but he'd mentioned more than once he was struggling to get used to the heavy travel, so I doubted anyone would suspect he was coming down from an illicit substance.

So...as much as he could be under the circumstances, he was reasonably safe and in good hands. Josh and I needed to do something sooner than later, but if ever there was a moment when we could catch our breath and strategize, this was it.

"Come on." Josh gently guided me out of the restroom. "Let's sit and regroup. We can figure this out."

I followed numbly. Axel was going to hate me after this. I hoped someday he understood.

Glancing at Josh, I cringed inwardly.

I hoped it didn't take Axel as long as it had taken me.

CHAPTER 38

JOSH

There was a time in the not-too-distant past when, had I seen Sol this distraught over not being able to get through to someone about their drug use, I'd have been... I don't know if "smug" was the word, but there would've been a certain amount of, *"Sucks to be on this end of it, doesn't it?"* Because goddamn, I knew exactly how much it hurt. I knew exactly how heartbreaking and frustrating it was to try to stop someone from self-destructing as badly as they were determined to. Or, maybe more accurately, to show them that they *were* self-destructing when they were completely convinced everything was fine.

Tonight, I didn't feel any of that. This wasn't karma. It wasn't Sol getting a taste of his own medicine. It wasn't satisfying in the least to see him walking in my shoes any more than it was to see that bruise slowly darkening on his cheek.

Sitting on the couch in my hotel room, I wrapped a comforting arm around Sol's shoulders. "This isn't over. We'll get through to him." I didn't even know if I was lying; just because I'd finally succeeded with Sol didn't mean we would with Axel. That was one of the painful realities of addiction—just because one person managed to get help and sober up didn't mean the next one would.

Maybe there was hope this time because we were cutting right to the professional intervention instead of getting in over our heads like I had with Sol. I'd been so far in denial myself, and then so helpless and conflicted, and I'd let things get seriously out of hand before finally sounding the alarm. Sometimes I wondered if it was my fault Sol's addiction had gotten so bad. If I'd reached out for help sooner... If I'd ignored his gaslighting about how he was fine... If I'd done something—*anything*—other than try to save him myself...

We weren't going to make that mistake with Axel. Hopefully that was enough.

"We're doing the right thing," I told Sol.

He gazed up at me with worried, hurt-filled eyes. "Are you sure?"

"What else can we do?"

He chewed his lip, then shook his head. "I don't know. I'm just so worried we're... *Are* we doing the right thing? Getting the staff involved?" He exhaled and wiped his hand over his face. "God, how do we do this?"

In some parallel universe, a far more vindictive version of myself snarked back, *"Oh, gee, I don't know. What would've gotten through to you?"*

But in this universe, Sol's earnestness to help Axel despite risking his own sobriety in the process had softened me to him. Yes, I still had a lot of anger and resentment about the past, and a lot of that simmered close to the surface right now as things played out in an all too familiar way, but mostly I was worried sick over Axel and... Yeah, I empathized with Sol. This was killing him right now, and I didn't feel the least bit vindicated by watching him get torn up the same way I was back then.

I took a deep breath. "We do exactly what we're doing. We bring in the team staff, and we let people who know how to do this step in."

"But what if it doesn't work?" Sol's eyes were wet as he met my gaze again. "Addiction is a fucking beast, and getting through... It's..." He exhaled, shaking his head.

"I know it is," I said softly. "And if this doesn't work, then..." I chewed my lip.

Sol studied me, brow furrowed as he silently asked me to spell it out.

If the team couldn't get him into rehab...

If the rehab didn't help...

That was out of our hands, though. This whole thing was really out of our hands—all we could do was get trained professionals involved and hope for the best. Whether they could help Axel sober up depended on him more than anything.

I swallowed. "It was a last resort, you know. When I did that for you. Sometimes I wonder if I should've done it sooner."

For a heartbeat, I expected him to get angry and defensive. Maybe that wouldn't have hit me in the chest quite as hard as the defeat and resignation in his expression as his shoulders sank under my arm.

"I know," he breathed. "I, um...I didn't really leave you any choice."

Even after our recent conversation, the admission caught me off guard, and I had no idea what to say.

He searched my eyes, then sighed. "I meant what I said —I get it. Honestly. It was either do what you did, or let me..." He flinched and lowered his gaze. Had I not been touching him, I might not have noticed the subtle shudder that went through him.

He didn't have to finish the sentence. I knew all the things that could've happened to him had he not gone to rehab when he did, and every one of them had been bleak. Anything from a prison cell to a morgue slab. The fact that *he* understood that—that he *admitted* it—still took my breath away, though. All this time, he'd hated me and resented me, but on some level...

"So you know why I did it," I ventured cautiously.

He looked up at me again, raw and unsteady. "Of course I do."

I hesitated, then barely whispered: "But you hated me for it."

The wince was so pained, I swore I felt the way my own words had punched him in the gut.

"No. I didn't." His voice was soft and full of hurt and regret. "I guess I did for a while. It was... Rehab is hard. Admitting you're an addict is hard. I thought I was going to lose everything." With a brittle laugh, he added, "Including the cocaine, because I didn't want to lose it back then." The humor, such as it was, faded, and he turned to me again. "In the beginning, yeah, I hated you for what you did. But after I'd detoxed and the people at the rehab place got through..." He shook his head as he dropped his gaze to his feet. "I knew you did the right thing."

My heart pounded because this conversation was a minefield. We'd veered way off course from talking about Axel, but maybe we needed to stomp on some of these land-mines so we could work together to help our teammate. Maybe we needed to do this so we could really, truly be teammates.

Nervous as hell and with no idea what the answer

would be, I said, "But you did still hate me. When we were assigned to Seattle, I saw it." I swallowed hard and barely managed to whisper, "Why?"

Sol kept his gaze fixed on the carpet as he wrung his hands and gnawed his lip. From the furrow in his brow, I had to guess he was trying to pull his thoughts into order so he could answer me. That was hard for him under the best of circumstances. Under pressure? When we were talking about something this volatile? I could give him a moment.

After a long silence, he pulled in a deep breath. Without looking at me, he said, "I hated you because you left."

Somehow, his answer simultaneously startled me and... didn't. It was like when I knew a slapshot was going to hit me—I saw it coming from a mile away, knew I couldn't avoid it, and *still* jumped when it slammed against me.

My mouth had gone dry. What was I supposed to say?

Before I could think of something, though, Sol asked, "Will you answer something honestly?"

I blinked, definitely not sure where this was going. Tonight was apparently a night for brutal truth, though, so I nodded despite my uneasiness.

Sol held my gaze. "This thing we're doing—trying to help Axel—it's..." His eyes welled up and he paused to clear his throat. "Was it this hard for you back then? With me?"

Oh. Hell. As if this conversation wasn't already a minefield. He wanted honesty, but did he really? Because I could tell by the bone-deep pain in his eyes that he already knew the answer. Was he trying to self-flagellate? Trying to punish himself? Or did he need to hear me say it out loud so we could somehow move past it after all this time?

There was no way for me to know what it was he wanted out of my answer, but he had asked for honesty.

And maybe, after all these years, what I needed was to look him in the eye and *give* him this truth.

"No. It wasn't this hard back then." I tried to keep my voice even, but it wavered anyway. "It was a million times harder."

Surprise flickered across his face. "It was?"

I nodded slowly, struggling to hold his startled gaze. "I care about Axel. I want him to get help before this gets out of control. But you?" I had to swallow hard, and even that didn't help much. "That was hell. I can't describe it any other way." My throat was raw and my voice was barely a croak as I said, "It was hell because I loved you."

Sol always wore his emotions on his sleeve, and this time was no exception. There was no denying that I'd cut him deep. Hurting him made my chest ache, but finally saying those words to him was so cathartic, it almost made me cry with relief. Guilt, too—I didn't feel good about hurting him—but also an almost euphoric feeling like I'd cut away a heavy weight I'd been dragging around all this time. No, I didn't want to kick him while he was down, and no, contrary to what I'd told myself for so many years, I really didn't want to hurt him, but some part of me had spent almost a decade *needing* to say those words to him. And now I had. And it was liberating, and excruciating, and too many other things I couldn't even define.

Sol wiped his eyes with a shaky hand, but they were still full of tears when he turned to me. "I'm sorry, Josh. For everything. You saved me. My career. My *life*. All of it. If you hadn't done what you did, I have no idea what would've happened to me, only that it would've been really, really bad. I just..." He shook his head and looked away as another tear slid down his cheek. "I'm sorry."

That, too, was a mixed bag of emotions. The pain in his

voice broke my heart, but hearing him actually apologize, believing right to my core that he *meant* it... Fuck, that was an even bigger and more euphoric relief than telling him how much it had hurt me to do what I did.

I didn't know what to say, so I just wrapped my arms around him, and as he returned my embrace, the way he sagged against me spoke of relief, too. As if he'd also needed to get that weight off for a long time. He trembled against me, and we just held each other for the longest time. Sol had already broken down. I probably wasn't far behind him, but for whatever reason, I needed to hold myself together. Wasn't like he'd never seen me cry before, but it seemed like one of us should stay strong right now. I couldn't explain it —I just ran with it.

After a while, Sol murmured into my neck, "I'm so sorry."

"I know." I closed my eyes and stroked his hair. "I am, too. For leaving. I could've—"

"No." He pulled back, and as we separated, he wiped his eyes again. "You had to go. I get it."

"But I could've..." I stopped, because anything that might've come after that felt like a lie. Yes, I felt guilty for disappearing on him, but in the moment, I'd had no other choice. I'd had nothing left. I'd had to walk away. But I still hated myself for it. "I'm sorry. You deserved more support." That much was true.

Sol shook his head slowly. "I had it. And yeah, it sucked, realizing you were gone. But I mean, just trying to get Axel's attention and show him he's going down a really bad path—that's exhausting. It's killing me." He looked right in my eyes, his still brimming with tears. "I'm nowhere near as invested in him as you were in me. I was so far gone back then, I didn't even realize what I was losing. Yeah, it sucked, and I was angry about it for a long, long time, but now that I've had even a taste of what it's like to get someone off that train..." He shook his head again, fatigue and regret both radiating off him. "I don't even want to imagine what it would've done to you if you'd stayed."

Well, so much for being the stoic one.

Sol was the one to wrap me up in his arms this time, and almost a decade's worth of pain shook itself out of me. All the regret. All the love I still had for him and tried to ignore. How I'd worried myself sick about him over the years, but never had the courage to pick up the phone or send him an email. I'd wondered for so long if he was okay, and it turned out that I was the one who wasn't okay.

As I slowly started to pull myself together, another confession rolled off my lips: "I missed you."

Sol's breath hitched, and he held me tighter. "I missed you, too." He sniffed, and as he stroked my hair, he whispered, "I'm glad you protected yourself. I'm just sorry I put you through all of that."

I squeezed my eyes shut, letting a couple more hot tears slip free. "I'm sorry I didn't do more for you sooner."

"I didn't want you to. I'm grateful you stuck around as long as you did, and that you didn't give up until I was in rehab." He pressed a soft kiss to my temple, which damn near broke me. Then he whispered, "You were the best thing that ever happened to me. Not just for what you did in the end, but the whole time we were friends and..." He pushed out a ragged sigh. "I don't have anyone but myself to blame for you hating me now."

"I don't hate you." I lifted my head and met his gaze. "I did. I *tried* to. But...I don't think I ever stopped loving you enough to hate you like I wanted to."

I'd told him as much before, but saying those words

now was like carving out my own soul and showing it to him. It hurt. God, it hurt. The shame. The regret. The painful cascade of what might have been if I hadn't wasted all those years convincing myself I *could* stop loving him.

Sol stared back at me. After a couple of seconds, I realized he was looking at me the same way he had that night in our apartment's parking garage the first time I'd let too much truth come tumbling out.

And just like he had that night, he closed the distance between us, wrapped his strong arms around me, and pressed his soft, gentle lips to mine.

Unlike that night, though, this felt right. Completely right. And long, long overdue.

I slid a hand up into his hair and opened to his kiss, and that soft little moan took me back to some of the best days of my life. Before Seattle. Before my divorce. Before his cocaine.

The kiss deepened. Heated. Sol's fingers drifted down the side of my face, raising goose bumps all along my spine. He wasn't wearing his usual cologne tonight, but he made me dizzy all the same. I knew his scent. This was him when we weren't going out clubbing. When he wasn't dressed to impress. When it was just the two of us, alone behind closed doors. It was just...*him*.

And my God, I wanted him.

Not on this stupid couch, though. No way in hell it was big enough for two guys our size.

"Come on." I gently freed myself from his arms and got up. "Let's take this over here."

He looked puzzled for a moment, but when his gaze landed on the bed, I could practically hear the pieces click in his head. Instantly, he was on his feet, and before I could take a step, he had his arms around me and his mouth against mine.

Neither of us held back.

Kissing. Groping. Unbuttoning. Unzipping. Our shoes came off somewhere in the mix. One of our phones hit the floor with a dull *thud*. He didn't make any move to find it or pick it up, and I forgot all about it when his hands slid down over my ass.

By the time I was straddling his gorgeous body on the mattress, we were…not undressed, but we'd made headway. Shirts were gone, so that was a start. Pants were undone and rucked down enough that I could stroke him while I made out with him. His kisses were breathless and hungry, and I loved how his breath stuttered and his back arched as I teased his fully hard dick. Then he was doing the same, strong fingers wrapped around my shaft, and I could barely breathe at all, never mind kiss.

Sol gently rolled me onto my side, and we kept on kissing and touching and winding each other up. When he touched his forehead to mine, he was panting hard and trembling.

"I want to fuck again so bad," he murmured. "But I don't want it to be a mistake like before."

"It won't be." I touched his cheek. "I think the only mistake we made before was not saying everything we did tonight."

He met my gaze with uncertainty written all over his face.

"This isn't a mistake," I whispered, my voice as unsteady as the hand I stroked along his sharp jaw. "Not this time."

Those blue eyes were still so full of questions.

I curved my hand behind his head, drew him in, and

kissed him, and he sighed as he relaxed against me. There was probably still so much left to say, but I was out of words. And we'd said enough for the moment. We'd said what had needed to be said for way too long, and all I wanted right now was this.

When Sol broke the kiss and looked at me this time, there was nothing but pure fire and need in his eyes. He swept his tongue across his lips and rasped, "Any chance you feel like bottoming again?"

Just thinking about taking him had my dick even harder and my body absolutely covered in goose bumps. I wondered for a moment if I might've been too tense, though —that conversation *had* been pretty fraught, after all. But in Sol's arms right now...no, I wasn't tense at all. I was probably more relaxed than I'd been in a long, long time.

"Yes," I breathed. "Fuck me."

His face lit up with a hunger I recognized from a lifetime ago. Back when things had still been new between us and cocaine hadn't crossed either of our minds.

Oh, God, I wanted him.

"I have condoms," I said quickly. "And lube. In my bag."

"Good," he growled. "Because my room is way too far away."

I laughed, which was as amazing and liberating as everything we'd done so far. "Now I kind of want to make you go get them just so you—"

"Shut up," he said, chuckling. He kissed me again, and then he let me get up so I could get everything we needed.

When I joined him in bed again, he didn't waste any time getting on the condom, opening the lube, and telling me to lie on my back with my legs apart, but he wasn't in a huge hurry, either. Lying beside me, he gently teased my hole, then eased in one finger. After a minute or two of that, he added a second, and as he slid both deeper, he purred, "Fuck, baby..."

I needed his mouth, so I kissed him again, and we made out as he fingered me. Even after I was long past ready for him, we just kept going, exploring each other's mouths as he drove me wild with his talented hand.

Abruptly, though, he broke the kiss and panted, "Fuck it. I can't wait. Turn on your stomach."

Oh, hell. I'd always loved it when he topped me like that. Something about his warmth and weight on top of me, the friction of my cock against the bed, and the way he'd kiss my neck and rumble praise and curses into my ear as his thrusts picked up speed. And feeling his orgasm from his lips against my neck all the way down to our feet was just sublime.

So as soon as he'd slipped his fingers free, I did as I was told, and my head spun with anticipation as he positioned himself over me. I slid my arms under the pillow and held on to the edge of the mattress as Sol guided himself in, and he groaned into my shoulder as he started to push in.

"Fuck," he murmured. "Oh, baby. That's... Is that good?"

"Yeah." I bit my lip and shivered. "Holy..."

A warm breath of self-satisfied laughter gusted my shoulder, but before he could say something smug, he gasped, and then he cursed softly as he pressed in deeper. He kissed my shoulder. "Oh my God..."

I moaned in response. Words weren't happening. Overwhelmed as I was, it was just as well I was already on my stomach, because otherwise I'd have collapsed.

This was so different from the last time. The motions were the same, yes—Sol on top, riding me perfectly as he kissed my neck and shoulders—but *we* were different. It was like everything we'd talked about earlier was becoming more real now. I'd never imagined how much repentance and forgiveness could be conveyed without anyone breathing a single word. Every touch, every kiss, every shiver from Sol promised he knew what he'd put me through and begged me to forgive him. In the same way, I tried to tell him that I knew he wasn't the man he was back then. That I'd forgiven him long before I'd ever even realized it.

That I meant it when I said I'd still loved him all this time.

"Sol..." I couldn't manage anything more than that. Wasn't even sure what I would've said.

He groaned softly and kissed beneath my hair, lighting up every nerve ending along my spine. I closed my eyes and stopped trying to make words or make sense of anything, and as Sol picked up some speed, I just surrendered. Fuck. This was so good. So incredible. Could we do this all night?

Forever?

"Fuck, Sol..." The words tumbled out in something close to a sob.

"Come for me, baby," he mumbled as he thrust in just right. "God, I want to feel you come. You getting there? Ungh, baby, I want..." He trailed off as a shudder interrupted his rhythm, but then he recovered, and I was a moaning, gasping mess as he kept driving me higher.

"Like that," I pleaded. "Ooh, yeah. Just... oh yeah."

"Yeah?" He brushed his lips across my shoulder and picked up some more speed, fucking me perfectly and creating the most amazing friction between my dick and the sheet. I clawed at the edge of the mattress, desperate for some kind of purchase, and Sol slammed into me hard enough to drive the breath right out of me.

"Come for me," he said again, purring the words into

the side of my neck. "Please, baby. You're so damn hot like this. So fucking hot. God, you feel so good. I want to—"

The rest of the words were just sound. Sound I could barely hear over my own voice crying out with the force of my release. The grip I had on the mattress didn't seem like enough to keep me grounded, but I held on for all I was worth anyway, and I murmured and mumbled absolute nonsense as Sol fucked me through both of our orgasms. I'd lost track of almost everything, but I homed right in when Sol gasped, forced himself deep, and swore through clenched teeth as he shuddered against me.

Then...we were still.

He was over me, holding himself up on his forearms. His breath rushed across my neck. I couldn't tell who was trembling more. Was his head spinning as much as mine was? I hoped so, because this was amazing.

Slowly, the smoke began to clear. I caught my breath. He seemed to catch his. He pulled out, making both of us gasp, but he didn't get up right away.

Instead, he kissed my shoulder. "I love you, Josh."

I closed my eyes as too many emotions tumbled through me. I did finally find my voice, though: "I love you, too."

CHAPTER 39

SOL

Lying beside Josh in his hotel bed, I couldn't quite relax. That was, no exaggeration, the best sex I'd ever had, but I was sure the other shoe was about to drop.

It had been easy to say in the moment that this wouldn't be a mistake, but last time hadn't seemed like a mistake until after the fact. What if that happened this time, too? Because right now, I felt closer to him than I ever had, and if there was one thing I could never get used to, it was losing Josh.

The vague throb in the side of my face reminded me that a world—and a crisis—still existed outside this room. Regardless of how things went down in here, Josh and I needed to be a united front more than ever. It was one thing when we acted like idiots and ruined things between us. It was another when we needed to work together to help someone else. Our team was relying on us, but especially right now, Axel needed us in ways he probably wouldn't fully grasp any time soon.

He's going to hate us when this is over.

I pulled Josh a little closer and kissed his temple.

I can't handle you hating me, too. Not again.

But I also couldn't handle not knowing. The suspense, as they say, was killing me.

I shifted onto my side and faced him. He did the same, and oh, man, he was so beautiful like this. The sleepy satisfaction in his eyes. The way his dark, wet hair was mussed. The little grin on his lips.

Do you have any idea how much I've missed you?

I touched his cheek, trailing my fingertips along the light stubble. "So what do we do now?"

Some of the sleepiness faded, and his expression sharpened into one of concern. "About us? Or our teammates?"

"Us," I whispered.

He swept his tongue across his lips. "What do you think we should do?"

He had to throw it back to me, didn't he?

I considered my answer. I could punt. Come up with some noncommittal answer that wouldn't make things weird.

Or I could do what would've saved us a ton of heartache years ago—tell him the truth.

I took a deep breath. "I know what I *want* to do, but I'm not sure if it's what we *should* do." I ran my fingers along the edge of his jaw, quietly memorizing his face again just in case I didn't get another chance.

"Start with what you think we should do," he said softly.

I gulped. "Probably the same thing we did last time this happened. Be teammates and..." I half-shrugged.

"And what you want us to do?"

It was a struggle, but I made myself look in his eyes. "Be together. Not...not like pick up where we left off before, because that was a mess. But like, start over. With both of us being more mature now, and me being sober." I exhaled and broke eye contact. "I know, I know, we can't, but—"

"Yes, we can." His voice was soft but froze me as if he'd shouted.

I met his gaze again. "We can?"

"Yes." He paused as if he needed to collect his thoughts. "I'm not saying it'll be simple, but...I think we can."

I watched him uncertainly. "Do...do you *want* to?"

"I meant what I said." He ran his thumb along my unbruised cheekbone. "I love you. I never stopped."

Emotions threatened to choke me, but I managed the clear my throat enough to whisper, "But why? I made such a mess of things back then."

"Your *addiction* made a mess of things," he corrected softly.

"It was my choice to start."

"I know." He lifted his chin for a light kiss. "But once you were in over your head..." He sighed. "Yeah, it hurt. It was hard. It was hell." He smoothed my hair, and his voice was so, so gentle as he whispered, "But it wouldn't have been that awful if I didn't love you like this. All I ever wanted was for you to be okay." He smiled faintly. "And you are now."

"I'm still an addict."

"You're still you."

I chewed my lip. I wanted so, so badly to believe him that we could do this, and that he wanted to do this. But I was quickly talking myself out of it because all I could see now was what a disaster we'd been in the end. I couldn't go through that again. I definitely couldn't put him through it. And could I promise it would never happen? No, because my two relapses were proof that there was no such thing as permanently sober.

Josh broke the silence. "You want to know something I haven't told anyone?"

I stilled, watching him with no idea what this could possibly be about. "Um. Sure?"

He moistened his lips as he watched his fingers playing with the edge of the pillowcase. "The way I feel about you— that was part of why my marriage fell apart."

My heart stopped. "It... Are you serious?"

He nodded slowly, still watching his fingers on the sheet. "Damon. He knew. We had to stop watching games together because whenever the commentators mentioned you for some reason—even just saying something about a highlight from another game or whatever—he'd pick a fight. And one day he was using my iPad and he saw that I'd opened an article about you." Josh sighed like the whole topic exhausted him. "God, he was pissed. Just absolutely lost his shit."

"Because you read an article about me?"

He nodded. "He was convinced I was pining after you. Really, I just saw your name in the headline, and I read it because I was curious if you were doing okay."

"He just...he thought you wanted me more than him?"

"He was convinced I was still in love with you." Josh locked eyes with me. "And I think he was right."

My teeth snapped together.

"I meant it when I made a commitment to him," Josh went on. "I married him in good faith because I loved him, not because he was a placeholder or because I had to settle since I didn't have you anymore." He took a deep breath. "But looking back, I guess I get why he thought that. Because no matter how much I wanted to, and no matter how much I tried to, I've never loved anyone the way I still love you."

I could barely breathe. "But...everything I put you through..."

"Sol." He brought up my hand and kissed my knuckles. "Ever since we both came to Seattle, you've made it painfully clear that you're busting your ass to stay sober. You were in denial back then, but you're not now."

"That doesn't mean I won't relapse again."

"No, but you're working hard not to. And if you do, you're more receptive to help than you were back then." He squeezed my hand. "On top of that, you were willing to risk your sobriety—not to mention put yourself in a position for your sobriety to be scrutinized—in the name of helping your teammates. Yes, you're still an addict, and you'll probably always struggle with that, but you aren't your addiction. You're a sweet, caring man, and you're still the man I've been in love with since we were kids." He kissed my fingers again. "You're an even better version of that man now. And you're damn right I want to give this a chance to work."

By the time he was done, I was in tears, and I wasn't even a little bit ashamed of it. I did the only thing I could do —I pulled him to me and held him tight as the tears fell. From the his occasional sniffle, I wasn't the only one.

If there was anyone in this world who had every right to walk away from me with both middle fingers held high, it was Josh. But somehow, even through the years when we'd been estranged, he'd still loved me. Enough that it had caused problems in his marriage. Where I saw myself as weak and broken, he saw me as stronger than ever.

By some miracle, in the eyes of Josh of all people, I was worthy.

Of forgiveness.

Of love.

Of *him*.

"I love you," I whispered shakily.

"I love you, too." He stroked my hair. "We can do this. I know we can."

I closed my eyes. It wasn't that simple. I knew it wasn't. And we'd have to talk this through once we were both less raw.

But for tonight, I held on to it with all I had.

I loosened my embrace, and when our eyes met, his sweet smile almost broke me all over again. I kept it together, though, and I touched his chin as I leaned in for a kiss.

I'd only meant for something soft and affectionate, but it went on. Deepened. Intensified. As his fingers carded through my hair and he pressed closer to me, my thoughts scattered, and I made no attempt to collect them.

Thinking could wait. Worrying could wait.

The naked man whose cock was hardening beside mine?

I wasn't about to keep him waiting.

CHAPTER 40

JOSH

Sitting down with Coach, I was hit with a nauseating sense of déjà vu.

This was a hotel room in Montreal, not an office in Phoenix. It was Coach Maines, not the head coach and general manager of our old team. And instead of having Sol's name on my lips, I had him here by my side.

"All right." Coach sat back in one of the chairs. "So what's on your mind, boys?" He was clearly guarded and uneasy; I could only imagine what his guesses were about why we'd needed to talk to him this late at night.

On the couch, Sol and I exchanged glances. He was the one to break the silence. "We're concerned about Egillsson."

Coach's eyebrows shot up. Not the answer he'd expected. "What about him?"

Sol chewed his lip. "He's, um... We think he's..."

"He has a substance abuse problem," I said bluntly. I sensed Sol flinching, but he didn't try to gainsay me.

"Substance abuse?" Coach's eyes were huge. "How do you figure?"

Sol shifted on the cushion, and his voice was heavy with

resignation when he spoke. "Because I know the signs. I suspected he was using, and I tried to get him to stop, but..." He shook his head.

Coach watched him for a moment. "Does this have anything to do with...?" He gestured at his own cheekbone. "Because you didn't have that this afternoon."

Wincing, Sol dropped his gaze as color bloomed in his face, almost hiding the deepening bruise on his cheek. "I caught him. I tried to convince him he needs to get help, but he, um... He didn't like that."

Our coach seemed to digest that for a moment before quietly asking, "Do you know what substance he's abusing?"

Just as quietly, speaking it almost like a confession of his own, Sol said, "Cocaine."

Coach stared at him. Then at me. I nodded. The chair creaked as Coach leaned his elbow on the table. "Jesus Christ."

"We wouldn't bring this up if we weren't sure," I told him, my heart pounding with the same desperation it had the day I'd had this conversation with another coach in another lifetime. "He needs help."

"So does the player he's using with," Sol said softly.

Coach eyed him. "Which player?"

Sol glanced at me, chewing his lip. I nodded subtly— there was nothing to be gained by keeping any cards close. Facing Coach again, he sat up a little. "I'm almost certain Colfax is using, too."

Coach's lips parted. "Colfax? Are you fucking *kidding* me?"

"No." Sol shook his head slowly. "I've never seen him actually use, but all the signs are there."

"Which signs?" Coach didn't sound skeptical or like he

was looking for a reason to dismiss the accusation. More like he wanted all the information.

"Have you seen the way he sniffles all the time? And his jaw?" Sol motioned toward his own. "Watch him on the bench—the way he grinds his teeth? That's a sure sign. Plus his temper on the ice. He can be so chill, and then he's just..." Sol grimaced.

"Eggs, too," I said quietly. "He didn't used to get into fights or just...get that fucking mad out there, but lately..."

"Shit," Coach breathed. "I've noticed that, too. Thought he was just feeling the pressure."

"I don't think so," Sol whispered. "It's a new pattern, though. Means he probably hasn't been using as long. The sooner someone can intervene and get him help, the better." He drummed his fingers on the armrest in a rapid, nervous rhythm. "Colfax... He's probably been at it longer. And I mean it—he needs help, too."

"I'm not going to help someone who's getting my young players hooked on illicit substances," Coach growled.

"He's an *addict*," Sol protested. "Yeah, it's shitty to pull someone else into it, but that stuff messes with you. It changes you." He fidgeted, fingers still tapping. "If they get thrown out of the league or wind up in jail or something, they're only going to get worse. The cocaine is going to be the only thing they have left."

Coach's expression was hard. He looked for all the world like he was about to tell us both that everyone—with the possible exception of Axel—was getting disciplined within an inch of their lives, and they could otherwise go fuck themselves.

After a moment, though, he sighed. "Rehab doesn't work for everyone, kid. You of all people should know that."

"I do," Sol admitted. "But at least give them a shot at

pulling themselves together. It's hard as hell to get off something like that, but punishment—treating them like criminals—it *doesn't* help. At all."

Coach chewed his lip for a long, nerve-racking moment before he sighed and looked right at Sol. "All right. But there's only so much I can do. I can have them tested, and if they come up positive, then they can either go into rehab or..." He gestured over his shoulder with his thumb.

Sol winced, but he nodded. "Just give them a chance. Please."

"I will," Coach said quietly.

"Thank you," Sol whispered.

"When is a good time to test people?" I asked Sol. "You know Axel's using tonight, but—"

"Oh, shit!" Coach straightened. "We're in Canada. He's using in *Canada?*"

Sol and I both nodded grimly.

"That's one of the reasons I tried to stop him tonight," Sol said. "And I told him he can't fuck around when we're in another country, but..." He trailed off, shaking his head.

"Jesus Christ," Coach ground out. "I... Okay. Okay. So we need to do something about this before we go back into the States. I'm not risking any of them transporting it in their luggage."

I didn't think they'd be stupid enough to do that. On the other hand, Sol had done some stupid shit back when he'd been balls deep in his addiction, so maybe we shouldn't overestimate anyone.

"Test them close to the game," Sol said. "Or after the game. Because I can almost guarantee they're all using before and during games."

"During?" Coach asked. "Are you kidding me?"

"No." Sol dropped his gaze and watched himself

wringing his hands. "I used to do a line before warm-ups and a bump during every intermission."

"Holy shit." Coach turned an odd look on me. One I couldn't quite read. If it was *Can you believe this shit?* Or maybe *Did you know about this when he was doing it?* The answer to both was, unfortunately, yes, but I didn't say anything.

Sol sounded absolutely defeated as he said, "And I won't be offended if you want to test me too."

I was genuinely surprised a question mark didn't appear above Coach's head as he eyed Sol. "Why would we test you?"

Sol sat back, his expression echoing the resignation in his tone. "Because any time anyone gets tested, I always get"—he made air quotes—"randomly selected too. I get it." He shrugged tightly, as if he didn't like it but he'd more or less made peace with it. "I'll piss in a cup or do a blood test if it means someone's doing something to help them."

My throat tightened around my breath, and I wanted so, so bad to put a hand on his arm right then. This wasn't the selfish, cocaine-consumed addict who'd shoved me away all those years ago. This was the kind, sweet man who I'd fallen in love with back then and loved even more today. It was a small thing, letting himself be tested, but it also *wasn't* a small thing. Not for someone who still ached for people to believe him that he really had put all that behind him. Letting himself be treated with suspicion or like a relapse waiting to happen was a price he was willing to pay in order to help his teammates.

Oh God, I love you so much, Sol.

Coach Maines watched Sol for a long time. Then he sighed. "All right. All right, we'll..." He chewed his thumbnail. "I need to talk to Dr. Green and a few other people.

Figure out the right strategy." He studied us. "I trust we can all keep this on the downlow until we're back across the border?"

Sol and I both nodded.

So did Coach. "Thank you for letting me know about this. I'll see what I can do."

He dismissed us after that, but we didn't get far.

"Actually, before you go..." Coach Maines sat back and tilted his head. "Is there anything else you boys want to tell me?"

My spine straightened. I glanced at Sol, who seemed as clueless and caught off-guard as I was. Facing Coach again, I cautiously asked, "Tell you...about what?"

His eyes flicked back and forth between us. "Really?"

I blinked. Beside me, Sol didn't move or make a sound.

After a long, silent moment, Coach rolled his eyes and wiped a hand over his face. "So it's all in my imagination. The two of you... You're not, uh, together."

My stomach flipped. "Uh..."

Sol coughed a laugh, and when I glanced at him, his blush went to the tips of his ears. He met my gaze and shrugged, a lopsided *what can you do?* smirk on his face.

"Yeah," Coach said. "That's what I thought. Well, it's better than you boys wanting to kill each other." He motioned toward the door. "Get out of here."

We both chuckled as we ducked out of the room. As soon as we were back in my room, Sol exhaled with obvious relief. "I'd say I'm glad that's over, but...it's not."

"No, it isn't." I slid my hands over his waist. "This part is, though."

Avoiding my gaze, he nodded. "Yeah. But the next part is going to suck."

"Sometimes things have to get worse before they get better."

Another nod, though he didn't speak this time.

"Hey." I gently lifted his chin and made him look me in the eyes. "It's going to get better. You did the right thing. We both did. I know it sucks right now—believe me, I do—and it's going to suck for a while. But in the end, it's the best thing."

"I know," he whispered, wrapping his arms around me. Then a cautious smile formed on his lips. "Guess we don't have to hide from Coach."

I snorted. "I guess you're right. I mean, maybe we could keep it quiet for a little while, until we find our footing, but I like not having to keep it a secret."

His smile came fully to life, and he pulled me in closer. "Me too."

I kissed him, and we both let it linger for a while. Neither of us tried to get anything started—he was probably way too wrung out both physically and emotionally, and I definitely was. Instead, we indulged in this long, lazy moment of gentle intimacy. I savored all this closeness I'd been missing for so damn long.

No, this wasn't going to be easy going forward. Not just the issues with our teammates, but our relationship. We had a lot of history and a lot of minefields, and no amount of romance or bliss made those magically disappear. Maybe a counselor or two, both for us and for me, so we could navigate the hard parts without imploding again.

I didn't think we would implode again. We were both well aware of where we'd been and what we had to lose. But some professional, objective guidance might be a good idea.

So, as soon as I had some time and I'd run the idea by

Sol, I'd start sniffing around for a couples counselor and a therapist for myself.

In the meantime, though, I was going to do what I hadn't done in far, far too long:

Enjoy being in love with the most amazing man I'd ever known.

CHAPTER 41

SOL

It all happened so fast. I wondered if it felt like it for Axel.
Or if this was how it had been for my teammates—for Josh,
especially—when I'd gone into rehab the first time. It
seemed like one minute we were talking to Coach, and the
next, Axel was gone.

Truthfully, a lot of time stretched between those two
minutes, and a *lot* happened. No one wanted to make any
waves about illegal substances while we were in Canada, so
nothing went down until we were back in Seattle. We'd
played in Montreal the day after the conversation with
Coach, then flown home late that night. At our next
morning skate, several of our teammates— myself included
—were "randomly selected" for drug tests.

That night, we played at home. The next morning,
when we showed up for practice, the news almost knocked
me on my ass:

Four of our teammates had tested positive for cocaine.

A couple of forwards and a defenseman from the farm
team were immediately on their way to the airport to meet

us in Portland in time for the next night's away game. Axel, Colfax, Darby, and Järvinen were suspended effective immediately—twenty games apiece—and they were all headed into league-mandated rehab programs.

The emotions that rocked me after I heard the news—I couldn't even define them all. There was profound relief that Axel and our other teammates were getting help sooner than later, but also deep, icy guilt that I was responsible for this. Especially when it came to Axel. Not for getting him hooked, but for his career being on the line. For his addiction becoming public. I knew to my core that there hadn't been any other choice, but that didn't stop me from feeling like shit for pulling the trigger.

I felt like shit for being completely oblivious that Darby and Järvinen were using too—I'd been so focused on Axel and Colfax, I hadn't even paid attention to them, much like Josh hadn't noticed Axel using because he'd been too focused on me. Tunnel vision, I guess. I definitely felt like shit for it.

I also felt like shit for doing this to them at all. Even though it was necessary, their lives and careers were being upended, and they'd be going through hell for a while. If they came back to the league, their names would always be synonymous with addiction and cocaine, same as mine was, even if they never touched another grain of blow for the rest of their lives. I hated that this couldn't happen privately. That there would be pressure and stigma on them forever, especially since those things could drive someone back to using again. Ask me how I know.

But the alternative was letting them continue to use until they destroyed their lives and careers more than this shitshow ever would. It hadn't been an easy thing for Josh and me to do, but it had been the only thing we could do apart from sitting back and letting our teammates crash and burn. That wasn't an option.

I was itching to go see Axel. I needed to look him in the eye. Apologize. Tell him I was happy to support him and help him any way I could.

It was Josh who suggested waiting a few days. Neither of us knew if Axel would have to detox like I had—if he'd been using anywhere near as much as me—but Josh assured me that we'd be better off giving him a little time.

Given my memories of detoxing, he was probably right.

When we did finally get in to see him, that visit lasted all of two minutes.

"Fuck you both," he snarled. "Get the hell out of here."

"Axel, we're—"

"I said get out!"

We got out.

On autopilot, I numbly followed Josh out of the facility and into the parking garage. I dropped into the passenger seat, and I stared out the windshield, my mind whirring as I tried to figure out what to feel.

Josh took my hand. The contact startled me. How long had I been sitting like this? And when had he started the engine?

I turned to him, and his expression was full of sympathy. "It's hard," he said softly. "You still did the right thing."

I nodded. I wanted to ask if this was what it was like for him after he'd come to see me in rehab and I'd told him to leave.

But I didn't ask because I already knew the answer.

"*No,*" he'd have told me sadly. "*That time was way worse.*"

Because he'd been alone. Because he'd been hurt in ways Axel couldn't hurt me. Because he'd loved me, and I'd...

I turned my hand over under his and clasped our fingers together. "You know I still loved you back then, right?"

Josh blinked as if he didn't quite follow. Right—because this conversation had been playing out in my head, not in his car. He seemed to catch up, though, and he brushed a tear off my cheek with his thumb. "I know you did. Maybe I didn't know it back then, but...yeah. I know."

"I don't blame you for leaving, though." I motioned toward the building. "Why come back for more of that?"

He grimaced and nodded. "Yeah. It's tough. But give him some time. Also, you and he don't have the history that we did back then. It's not as...complicated, I guess?"

I nodded. "True." I glanced at the building. "Do you think he'll reach out?"

"Don't know." Josh squeezed my hand. "But if he does, and you need someone to come with you, I'm here."

I turned to him again. "Thank you. I wish you'd had this much support when I was..." I nodded in that direction.

"I wish you did, too," he whispered. "But he's got it now, and so do you."

"Thank you." I tipped up his chin and kissed him softly. "I guess there's nothing to do now except wait for him to reach out."

"Hopefully he does."

As Josh drove us away from the facility, I gave it one last glance.

You don't have to do this alone, Axel. I promise.

If you have time, will you come see me?

The text came almost three weeks after Axel went into rehab, and for a good ten minutes, I genuinely thought my phone must've been hacked.

But then I came to my senses, got over the shock, and wrote back.

Are you sure? I'll be back in town on Wednesday. Can come that afternoon?

Please. Then he was typing again, and another message came through: *They switched me to outpatient. I'm at home.*

Well, that was a good sign. I'd switched to outpatient partway through my rehab, too; the counselors had said outpatient was fine for a lot of addicts, but the league insisted on inpatient, at least in the beginning. It had probably been just as well for me, since I'd been an absolute wreck. Axel, though—he'd been pretty functional. At most he'd been using for a handful of months, and I didn't think he was a heavy user. Not like I'd been. If he was outpatient already, then he was probably making a lot of progress.

Do you want me to come alone? I wrote back. *Or should I bring Obie?*

No hesitation at all: *Please bring him too.*

So, as soon as we were back in Seattle, Josh and I grabbed the first chance we could to go to see Axel. He lived in an apartment in Queen Anne, not super far from our building in Green Lake. It was a nice place, too—lots of light, especially in the afternoon, and a stunning view of the Space Needle and downtown.

Axel didn't look great. He'd been exhausted by the constant travel, practice, and play of the regular season, but he'd never looked as wrung out and rundown as he did today. Except maybe the day we'd seen him in the rehab facility, though the fury had masked a lot of the fatigue and misery. In a more subdued state of mind now, he looked like shit.

At the same time, though, his eyes were clear. Tired. Downcast. But clear.

He handed us each a glass of iced tea, and we all sat down in the living room. "Thanks for coming. I'm, uh...I'm sorry. About last time."

"Don't mention it." I rested my glass on my knee as I sat back on the couch. "I wasn't any better when I started rehab. It sucks. Trust me—I get it."

He nodded. "Yeah, it does."

"How is it going, though?" Josh asked. "The program?"

"It's been good. It's hard, and I won't call it fun, but it's...it's been good." Axel ran a hand through his short red hair. "I think I've been getting more from the other people in the program than the people running it."

"Yeah?" Josh asked.

Avoiding both our gazes, Axel nodded. "Yeah. Hearing them talk about how much their lives revolved around using..." He closed his eyes and pushed out a long, heavy breath before he finally looked at us again. "Scared the shit out of me. Like...I figured I could just use it occasionally when I needed to be on for a game, or..." He rolled his eyes and shook his head. "Same thing everyone in the group says. The only difference is they had time to get out of control—way, *way* out of control—before they got help."

"Been there," I said dryly.

Axel's eyebrows rose. "Yeah? I mean, I've heard the stories about... Was it really that bad for you?"

I glanced at Josh, then looked down at my wringing hands. "It was pretty bad. I completely lost touch with who

I was. Ruined a lot of friendships." I paused. "Ruined a really important relationship."

Josh put his hand on my forearm. "Not beyond repair, though."

I glanced at him again, and when he smiled, I managed to return it. Sliding my hand over the top of Josh's, I faced Axel. "I got incredibly lucky. We lost a lot of time together."

Axel's eyebrows rose. "So you two really are a thing now?" He didn't seem *too* shocked. More like he'd had something unexpectedly confirmed.

Josh chuckled. "Rumor mill's been busy, I guess."

The rookie shrugged, laughing almost soundlessly. "I've kept in touch with some of the guys, and Volkov said something about it. So did Leclerc. And Järvinen and I text and FaceTime a lot."

I winced. I still couldn't believe I hadn't noticed Järvinen getting drawn in as well. It was amazing how easy it was to hyperfocus so hard on one problem that you overlooked another that was right in front of your own face. "How is he doing?"

"Good," Axel whispered. "He's doing his treatment back in Finland. The league said it was okay, and being close to his family helps. I think being so far away—that was tough. But being back there, close to people he knows... It's been good for him." He chuckled and added, "By the way, he thinks you guys are cute together."

Josh laughed softly. My heart fluttered. Not at the realization that our teammates had been talking openly about us—wasn't like we were a big secret *or* a sensational story—but that they'd been talking with Axel. I'd have sold my soul for that kind of connection to my team during my first stint in rehab.

"I'm glad everyone's stayed in touch," I said. "Going through this—it's hard, but it's even worse to do it alone."

"Seriously." Axel blew out a breath. He gazed out the window for a moment, and when he faced us again, I was startled to see an extra shine in his eyes. "I wanted to thank you."

"Don't mention it," I said gently. "I've been there. I get it."

He seemed to sag against his chair, and his voice was unsteady as he asked, "How do you do it? Staying sober?"

I pressed my lips together as I considered my answer. People at his stage of recovery needed all the encouragement and optimism they could get, but I remembered from my own uphill climb to sobriety that truth was also necessary. Honesty. Reality.

"It's really hard," I admitted. "I won't tell you it isn't. Even today." I flicked my eyes toward Josh, then swallowed hard and met Axel's. Shame weighed heavily on my shoulders as I said, "I've backslid a couple of times."

Axel's eyebrows shot up. "You have?"

I nodded slowly. "I was lucky the league never found out. And that I had friends who saw the signs and got me help before it got out of hand."

"Like you guys getting me help."

"Yeah. Exactly." I hesitated, then decided to hell with it. "Listen, you *can* recover from this. I'm not going to blow smoke up your ass and tell you that it won't be a struggle going forward. I mean, maybe it won't be—you got help early—but it probably will be, and that doesn't mean you're a failure. Even backsliding isn't a failure. It's just a setback."

Something unwound in Axel's posture, and I wondered if he'd been needing to hear that all this time. That was the thing about rehab—there was no such thing as one size fits all when it came to addiction, and sometimes there was that one piece of the puzzle that was just out of a person's reach. For me, it had been realizing I wasn't a failure or a hopeless junkie just because I was aware of the good things cocaine had done for me. The moment a therapist had told me that it was no different than a person with chronic pain being hooked on painkillers—fully cognizant of both the cons *and* pros of their substance of choice—had been a gamechanger for me.

Maybe for Axel, that gamechanger was knowing that a relapse didn't mean he couldn't get sober again, or that he was doomed to use for the rest of his life. That had never been a huge thing for me—maybe because, as a goalie, I was well-accustomed to the idea that I could absolutely go down in flames one night, then pull it together and have a shutout the next. The idea of being able to course correct after a seemingly catastrophic failure wasn't alien to me, even if it sometimes felt like it in the moment.

We stayed for a while, talking about Axel's rehab, but also hockey, because you couldn't put a bunch of hockey players in a room without the conversation turning to sticks and stats.

"Hopefully I'll be back in time for the playoffs," he said with a smile. "I'll be cutting it *really* close, but Coach says as long as I keep my conditioning up, I should still be able to play."

"That's great," Josh said. "Hey, if you want to get in some ice time, let us know." He nudged me with his elbow. "We can work on some practice by the crease with you."

Axel's face lit up. "That would be awesome. Thanks!"

We stayed long enough that we ended up ordering

pizza and watching the New York-Pittsburgh game. By the time Josh and I headed for the door, it was almost eleven.

"Thank you guys so much for coming." Axel hugged me tight. "And thank you again. For everything."

"Don't mention it." I returned his embrace fiercely. "And I'm serious—you can always come to me if you need help. Even if things change down the line and we're not on the same hockey team. Got it?"

Drawing back, he nodded, a tired but genuine smile on his lips. "I got it. Thank you."

We headed downstairs after that. I felt great, flying high from seeing that our teammate was well on his way to staying sober. Josh, though, was unusually quiet on the way out of the building. He didn't look at me. Just sort of folded in on himself and shut out everyone and everything.

In the parking garage, I stopped at my car and turned to him.

"Hey." I touched his back. "You all right?"

He swallowed and nodded, but he still didn't look at me.

"Josh? What's going on?"

He chewed his lip and didn't answer immediately. After a moment, though, he finally met my eyes, and there was a faint shine in his, which almost sent me back a step. I definitely wasn't prepared when he whispered, "I'm sorry."

My heart dropped into my feet. Was he dumping me or something? Right here? Now? What was going on?

Despite my suddenly dry mouth, I managed to ask, "For what?"

He winced and broke eye contact again as he leaned against the car. For long seconds, his jaw worked as his eyes welled up and he seemed to think about what to say next.

Panic and confusion twisted beneath my ribs. What the hell was happening?

It seemed like ages before he broke the odd silence: "I left you there. In rehab. You..." He wiped a hand over his face, then let it fall to his side as he looked at me again. "You should've had support. Everything you're doing for Axel—you should've had that."

I stepped closer and reached for his waist. "Josh. It wasn't your fault."

"But I should've been there." A tear slid down his cheek. "I left you to the wolves when you needed me the most."

I brushed away the tear with my thumb. "I *pushed* you away."

"So did Axel." He flailed a hand toward the elevators. "But we're here now."

"Because Axel reached out to us. He *asked* us to come back." I sighed. "I was too fucked up and way too proud to reach out to you or anyone else. It was my own damn fault that I was alone."

Josh swiped at his eyes. "Still. I should've done more than I did. I shouldn't have just...*left* you there."

"Baby." I pulled him into a tight embrace and stroked his hair. "No one expected you to know how to handle everything back then. You were a kid. So was I."

"But I loved you," he whispered into my shoulder. "I wanted you to be okay. I just..."

"You didn't know how. Neither of us did." I pressed a kiss to his temple. "You saved me, though. That's what matters."

"I also lost you." He drew back and looked in my eyes. "I have you back now, but God, we lost so much time because I—"

"Because *I* was too deep into my addiction to know which way was up." I caressed his damp cheek. "We lost a lot of time, but maybe we needed that so we could get here."

His shoulders sagged. "Maybe. I don't know."

Fuck. It always hit me in the chest to see him hurt, and it was even worse when he was hurting because of me. I had done this to him. Because of shit I did years ago, sure, but still—because of me.

And who was to say I wouldn't do it again?

Josh cocked his head and peered at me like he was reading something in my expression. "What's wrong?"

"I, um..." I couldn't get my thoughts into enough order to articulate them eloquently or gently or whatever. Finally, I just blurted out: "I don't want to be an addiction for *you*."

Josh blinked, his spine straightening. "What?"

"You're..." I couldn't hold his gaze, and I dropped mine to the concrete between us as I rubbed the back of my neck. "I love you. I've always loved you. But I've hurt you so fucking much, and I..." I took in a deep breath, and from some deep reserve I didn't know existed, found just enough courage to look in his eyes again. "What if I'm your drug? Like cocaine was for me? Yeah, being with me feels good in the moment, but..." I trailed off.

Josh studied me. Then he shook his head. "Sol." He tipped up my chin. "Listen to me: you are *not* a drug, and you're not an addiction. I love you."

"But all I've done is hurt you," I whispered. "Yeah, the high is fun and everything, but then it all comes crashing down and—"

Josh stopped my rambling with a soft kiss.

When he broke that kiss, he had my face cupped in both hands, and he looked right in my eyes. "If you were abusive, or you kept cheating on me, or..." He waved his hand. "Then, sure, you'd have a point. Coming back to that over and over—like if I'd gone back to Damon after the way he treated me—then I guess you could say that's kind of like an addiction." With that same hand, he caressed my cheek. "But that's not what's happening here. Not even close."

I searched his eyes, silently begging him to explain it and make me believe him, because my God, I wanted to.

"You're so much more than your addiction, Sol," he said softly. "You're an amazing friend and boyfriend. Yes, watching you self-destruct—that hurt. But it's painfully clear that you're trying your damnedest not to go down that road again. You're a different person than you were back then—we both are—and I have complete faith that you can stay sober now. That you want to."

I nodded slowly, trying like hell not to cry. "I do want to."

"I know you do. You were in denial back then, and you were so far into your addiction that none of us could reach you. But now, when you feel yourself sliding even a little bit in that direction, you *ask* for help." He ran his thumb along my cheekbone. "That person? The one who's worked so hard and is trying like hell to stay sober? That's who you are now, and I'm not addicted to that person. I'm in love with him."

I squeezed my eyes shut. "But there's still no guarantee I won't relapse."

"I know. And if you do, I'll be here. So will your friends."

"I can't keep asking you guys to—"

"Are you going to bail if my migraines get out of control?"

My eyes flew open and I gazed at him in horror. "What? No! Of course not!"

He inclined his head.

I exhaled. "Come on. That's not the same. I did this to myself. Migraines are a medical issue."

"One I made a hell of a lot worse by playing hockey, so..." He shrugged. "You could kinda argue I did it to myself."

Pursing my lips, I held his gaze, not sure how to respond.

"The point is," he went on, "living with someone who has chronic migraines, or old injuries, or depression, or..." He waved his hand again. "It's not easy. Not for the person who has it, and not for their partner. But it's what people mean when they talk about 'in sickness and in health.' You don't just come for the good stuff and bail for the rest, you know?"

I swallowed hard. As much as my therapists and everyone in rehab talked about addiction being a disease, most people brushed that off. It certainly wasn't a disease on par with a *real* problem like migraines, depression, or chronic pain (not that any of those were taken as seriously as they should've been). But to Josh, addiction *was* a disease. In his eyes, somehow, my struggle with cocaine wasn't a character flaw—it was something we both had to live with and work around, same as his migraines or the various aches and pains we both had from years of hockey.

"You're amazing," I whispered, and hugged him again, just marveling in how incredible it was that this man had taken me back, addiction and all.

Holding me close to him, Josh stroked my hair just like I had his a few minutes ago. "We can get help, you know. As a couple, and also on our own."

"I already have a therapist," I murmured.

"Okay. Well. Maybe *we* should get one. Someone who

knows how to navigate a relationship with a recovering addict."

I thought about it, and nodded. "You're probably right. In fact, it, um... It wouldn't hurt for you to get one, too. For yourself."

His eyebrows rose. "I've been thinking about that, too, honestly. But what makes *you* think I should?" He sounded curious, not defensive; interested in my line of thought rather than preparing to shoot it down.

"Your ex treated you like shit and so did I," I whispered. "And I'll always be an addict. I could relapse again."

"You won't." He squeezed my hand. "Jesus, Sol. If you were going to relapse, you would've—"

"It's always a possibility," I said softly. "It always will be. I'm working as hard as I can to keep it from happening, but...I mean, you should have some backup, you know? And someone to help you with setting boundaries. Not *just* with me, but...with me."

Josh stared at me, as if he didn't quite understand what I was saying.

"I don't want to be what your ex-husband was for you," I went on. "I definitely don't want to be what I was for you in the past. You can bet I'm going to bust my ass to be anything but those two jackasses." I ran my fingers through his hair. "But having an uninvested third party in your corner, or just to help you deal when I'm struggling..." I half-shrugged. "Might not be a bad idea."

He watched me for a moment like I'd lost my mind, but then he slowly deflated. "Yeah. You're right. Something to look into, I guess."

"Definitely." I wrapped my arms around him again. "And thank you," I whispered against his neck. "For never giving up on me."

He lifted his head, but instead of saying anything, he kissed me, and my God, the whole world listed under my feet.

I would never stop marveling at the miracle that was having this man back in my life and in my arms again.

And I would never stop doing everything in my power to make up for our past.

CHAPTER 42

JOSH

Sasquatch Fans Welcome Players in Emotional Return After Rehab For Substance Abuse

SEATTLE – Veteran defenseman Troy Colfax and rookie forward Axel Egillsson both returned to the ice with the Seattle Sasquatches Thursday night in a home game against Cleveland.

Both players were among four suspended from the team after testing positive for cocaine, and they made their joint comeback in a wild 5-3 win. Colfax came away with two assists, and Egillsson, in addition to an assist, scored his fourth professional goal—the game-winning goal on an assist from Leclerc and Johnson.

Asked about their struggles, both men expressed gratitude to their teammates who intervened and got them help.

"Sol knew," Egillsson said, referring to goaltender Cary Solomon. "He tried to help me, but when I wouldn't let him, he got the coaching staff involved. I'm pretty sure he saved my life and my career."

Colfax also credited Sol for the intervention: "If you asked me the day it happened, I'd have had a very different opinion. But now? I don't know where I'd be if they hadn't stepped in. My career would be over, that's for sure."

Solomon famously struggled with his own cocaine addiction in the past, and he too credits his sobriety to those who refused to stand by and watch him self-destruct. In particular, teammate and fellow goalie Josh O'Brien.

"He put a lot on the line for me," Solomon told reporters. "I owe him my life and my career. Hopefully helping Colfax and Axel pays that forward."

Egillsson and Colfax were among four Sasquatches to test positive for cocaine earlier this season. Antero Järvinen remains in rehab near Helsinki, where he transferred to be closer to his family during his recovery. A timeline for his return is unclear.

Connor Darby checked out after just seventeen days and has been released from his contract with the Sasquatches for failing to complete the program. Requests for comment were unanswered.

What a Redemption: Sasquatch Goalies Both Vying for Xavier Trophy After Western Conference Championship Win

SEATTLE – Hockey has been abuzz all season about the startling comeback of both the Seattle Sasquatches and their Hail Mary netminders—Cary Solomon and Josh O'Brien—and despite losing in the Cup finals this weekend, the story isn't over yet.

The Sasquatches have missed a playoff berth six seasons in a row, and stunned hockey fans by not only making the playoffs but securing the Western Conference Championship for the first time in franchise history. While head coach Heath Maines was understandably disappointed to see Seattle defeated in the finals, he was effusive about his team's efforts this season.

"They proved everyone wrong," he said after the loss. "They made it farther than anyone thought they could, and they went down swinging in the end. I couldn't be prouder."

His pride no doubt extends to five players whose performances were as surprising as the team's. Axel Egillsson and Troy Colfax both missed twenty games while in rehab for cocaine use. Antero Järvinen missed twenty-seven while in Finland, also undergoing treatment for cocaine use, before returning three games into the postseason.

Egillsson and Colfax performed stronger than ever after their respective returns, each putting up impressive numbers during their shortened seasons and scoring multiple times apiece during the playoffs.

Järvinen hit the ground running as well, impressing fans and critics alike with his confidence on the ice.

"It was terrifying, the first time I saw my team after rehab," he told reporters. "But when you realize your team has your back like that, it's huge. You don't feel like the rookie trying to find his place anymore. You know these guys will do anything for you off the ice, and that carries over into the game."

Among those teammates? The two men who sounded the alarm about the substance abuse in the first place, and who are also among the major contributors to Seattle's shocking success.

Netminders Solomon and O'Brien were signed before the season started when Seattle was suddenly desperately short on goaltenders. With dismal stats in recent seasons, neither goalie was expected to perform well in Seattle.

Instead, Solomon and O'Brien will attend the league's year-end awards ceremony tonight, where they are both finalists for the coveted Cam Xavier Trophy, awarded each season to the best-performing goalie. Boasting an impressive 0.932% save percentage and 2.07 goals against, Solomon will eke out his teammate by a slim margin, with O'Brien coming in for a very respectable second place with 0.929% and 2.17. The next goalie behind O'Brien—Tanner Croy from Houston—recorded a save percentage of 0.912% and 2.54 goals against.

When asked about losing to his rival-turned-teammate, O'Brien smiled and replied, "He earned it. I'm proud of him. And hey, I'll still get to look at the trophy every day, so I can't complain too much."

Presumably this remark is in reference to the West Seattle home he and Solomon will be moving into this summer. Both have signed four-year extensions with the Sasquatches, and several of their teammates have alluded to a wedding in the coming months.

"We'll see," O'Brien said with a laugh when asked. "This summer is all about moving. Maybe next year?"

Asked how he feels about two of his players dating and potentially marrying, Maines just shrugged and smiled. "You always want your players to get along."

With two former rivals now engaged and three players successfully recovering from addiction, the Seattle front office is optimistic about an even better collective performance next season.

· · ·

I chuckled as I handed Sol back his phone in our hotel room. "They really want us to get married. don't they?"

"No kidding." He slid it into the inside pocket of his tuxedo. "Did you really tell them 'maybe next year'?"

My cheeks warmed, and I offered a sheepish grin. "I...I mean, I figured it would get them off our backs for a while. Buy us some time, you know?"

"Fair enough."

I checked the time on the microwave. "We should get going. The car is going to be here soon."

We gathered our wallets, phones, and room keys, then headed downstairs to meet the car that would take us to the awards banquet. It was a fancy-ass stretch limo, too—if being up for a big award meant getting driven around in cushy shit like that, I'd definitely bust my ass next season.

As we left the hotel, I caught Sol skimming over the article again on his phone, his eyes sad.

"What's wrong?" I asked.

"Nothing." He shook his head and exhaled as he put his phone away. "I just wish we could reach Darby."

My heart sank at the reminder. "Yeah, I know." I squeezed his hand. "But you know how it is—you can't help someone who doesn't want to be helped."

Sol nodded slowly. "It just sucks. He has so much support."

"Hopefully that'll be enough to get him back on the rails. Some people really do have to crash and burn before they can get up again."

"Don't I know it," he murmured.

We exchanged glances. I brought his hand up and pressed a kiss to his palm. "You made it. There's hope for him, too."

"I know." He leaned across the seat and brushed his lips across mine. "Wouldn't have made it this far without you."

I smiled, caressing his cheek. "And now you're stuck with me."

"Oh no." He laughed and rolled his eyes, then kissed me again before returning to his seat. "How will I ever manage?"

I was pretty sure we'd both figure that out.

CHAPTER 43

SOL

This car really was amazing. I'd been living the pro hockey life for a long time, and I still loved stuff like this. Kind of made me feel like a movie star sometimes. What could I say? I was still a kid at heart.

But even more amazing than the limo, the tuxes, and the awards was the man sitting beside me.

It blew my damn mind that he was here. With me. Dating me. Practically living with me now, and we were moving in together as soon as we'd closed on the new place. The team's travel coordinator even had us rooming together. Of all the ways I'd imagined my future, I hadn't even let myself dream of being with Josh again, but....here we were.

As the car continued through downtown toward the awards ceremony venue, I thought about the article he'd shown me before we'd left the hotel. It felt like years since we'd dropped that bomb on Coach, not something that had happened in the hockey season that had just recently ended. Maybe because the playoffs made time go wonky. Maybe because being with Josh had done the same thing. Our relationship felt like a weird combination of something brand new, something we'd been settled into for years, and something that had been gone for so long, I'd been sure I'd never have it again.

We weren't back to the young, carefree life we'd had before my addiction. We were in our early thirties now instead of barely out of our teens. We'd been through enough hell—together and on our own—to be cynical beyond our years, but also to deeply appreciate the good things. Kind of how we were as hockey players, too, if I thought about it.

We were also out and proud this time, instead of keeping things a secret like before. In fact, it was kind of funny when people realized we weren't a new couple at all, and that we'd dated for a while in the past.

It was also funny how quickly reporters had gone from being surprised that we were together to asking if and when we were getting married...especially once they figured out this was our second time around. I swore it was like the media had collectively turned into that mom who started tapping her watch and saying, *"You've been together forever—when are you getting married?"*

And...in fact...

It occurred to me now that while we'd both fielded a *lot* of marriage questions from reporters, Josh and I hadn't really talked about it. We were out, and we were closing on a house together next week, and though we hadn't been together all that long, every sign pointed to us being in it for the long haul. We'd just never actually discussed that level of commitment with anyone other than the press.

I reached across the seat and slid my hand into his. "That thing you said to the reporters...about us getting married..."

He turned to me, brow furrowing. "Was that the wrong thing to say?"

"No, no." I shook my head. "I was just thinking, though..." I chewed the inside of my cheek. "Do you *want* to get married next year?"

"I..." He studied me. "Are you asking if I want to get married? Or if I want to do it next year?"

"Um." I had to be as red as our old Phoenix sweaters by now, and I gripped his hand a little tighter. "Both, I guess? We haven't really talked about it."

His expression was guarded. "No, we haven't. Do, um..." His forehead creased. "Is that something you'd want to do?"

"I...I mean..." Why was my heart going so fast? "I'm not...*opposed* to it?"

Josh's eyebrow flicked up. "So, if I did the whole get down on one knee thing, you'd be...not opposed to it?"

I inclined my head. "Were you planning to do the whole get down on—"

"I asked you first." There was a playful challenge in his eyes, but also—I thought—genuine interest. Maybe even some worry.

So, I thought about it. Then I smiled. "Might depend on how impressive the ring was, but..."

Josh barked a laugh and rolled his eyes. "Oh my God."

I snickered. "I'm kidding." Sobering, I slid my hand over his, and my voice actually got a little thick as I said, "Yeah. I would."

"Be opposed to it?"

"Oh, for fuck's sake." I pulled my hand back. "You are such a brat."

"Yeah, and you love it." He unbuckled his seat belt and

slid a little closer. "So if I hypothetically got down on one knee, with an impressive enough ring..."

I cupped his face. "You know damn well I'd say yes."

He grinned and kissed me.

Drawing back, I said, "But what if *I* got down on *my* knee and asked *you*?"

"Eh, we don't need to entertain that hypothetical."

"What?" I scoffed. "Why the hell not? You don't think I'm romantic enough to—"

"No, no, it's not that." His grin was wicked. "It's just that there's no way you're going to beat me to it."

Before I could say another word, he proved how right he was:

Right there in the limo, he slid down to the floor in front of me on one knee. And apparently while I'd been distracted during our interplay, he'd managed to get something out of one pocket or another.

He held up the band, which had several good size diamonds embedded in a channel of white gold or platinum or something. "Is this an impressive enough ring?"

I stared at the ring, then at him, completely stunned at the direction this had gone. "Are you..."

"I was going to do this on the red carpet." He swallowed, expression turning completely serious. "But I kind of want this to be just you and me. I want the *future* to be you and me. So..." He raised his eyebrows. "Marry me, Sol?"

My throat was too tight around my breath to speak, so I did the next best thing—I unbuckled my seat belt, threw my arms around him, and kissed him. We held each other tight, both shaking a little. We were... He wanted...

Holy shit.

After a moment, Josh grinned against my lips. "So the ring is up to your—"

"Shut up." I kissed him again, and he pulled me in even tighter. His whole body seemed to relax, as if he'd been carrying all kinds of unseen tension, and now it was gone. Drawing back, I met his gaze. "Were you afraid I'd say no?"

He moistened his lips as a blush rose in his cheeks. "I wasn't sure. I'm not exactly batting a thousand when it comes to making marriages work, you know?"

"To be fair, you were married to a sentient bag of dicks."

He barked a laugh. "Okay, you're not wrong."

"To be serious," I said, "I've known for a while I wanted to get married, but I was afraid to ask myself. I had no idea if you... I mean, hitching your wagon to me in the long run is—"

He cut me off with a gentle kiss. "I know exactly what I'm getting into."

I watched him uncertainly.

"I love you, Sol," he whispered. "And I know you. I know everything that goes along with being with you." He brushed another kiss across my lips. "We've got counselors to help us through the rough parts."

"There *will* be rough parts, though," I said. "I'm an addict, so—"

"There would be rough parts even if you'd never touched cocaine and I'd never been through a messy divorce." Josh shrugged. "What we've got is worth the work it'll take to get through anything."

I held his gaze a moment longer, and all I saw in his was sincerity. And love. So much love. Smiling, I drew him in again. "You're amazing."

He stole a gentle kiss. "And you're stuck with me."

I chuckled and kissed him again.

Josh let me go and held up the ring. "So, do you want to actually wear this?"

"Are you kidding?" I made a grabby hands gesture. "Let's give the reporters something to go nuts over."

He laughed for real, and I swear I almost melted as he slid the ring onto my finger. Wow. A wedding ring. Engagement ring. Whatever. A big sparkly thing that said Josh really did want to spend the rest of his life with me. Despite everything, we'd made it back to each other. We'd made it to this.

"Do you like it?" he asked softly.

"I'd have been happy with anything you gave me." I grinned up at him. "But this thing is sick as hell. I love it!"

He snorted. He started to say something, but then the car stopped and one of the front doors opened. Josh looked around. "Oh, shit, are we here already?"

I craned my neck to look outside, and sure enough, there was a flock of reporters and camera lenses behind the velvet rope. "Yep. Looks like we're here."

He grinned at me as he tugged at his jacket sleeves. "Ready to get asked a million questions about when we're getting married?"

"Are you?"

His smile was the most beautiful thing I'd ever seen.

Hell yeah, I was ready for anything.

And just before the driver opened the door to let us out, I said, "Let's do this."

The End.

AFTERWORD

If you or someone you know is struggling with addiction, please contact the Substance Abuse and Mental Health Services Administration at 1-800-662-HELP or by visiting their website, https://www.samhsa.gov/find-help/national-helpline, or reach out to available rehab and information services in your country.

ABOUT THE AUTHOR

L.A. Witt is a romance and suspense author who has at last given up the exciting nomadic lifestyle of the military spouse (read: her husband finally retired). She now resides in Pittsburgh, where the potholes are determined to eat her car and her cats are endlessly taunted by a disrespectful squirrel named Moose. In her spare time, she can be found painting in her art room or destroying her voice at a Pittsburgh Penguins game.

Website: www.gallagherwitt.com
    Email: gallagherwitt@gmail.com
    Twitter: @GallagherWitt

For more books by L.A. Witt, please visit

http://www.gallagherwitt.com

Romance * Suspense

Contemporary * Historical * Sports * Military

Titles Include

Rookie Mistake (written with Anna Zabo)

Scoreless Game (written with Anna Zabo)

The Hitman vs. Hitman Series (written with Cari Z)

The Bad Behavior Series (written with Cari Z)

The Gentlemen of the Emerald City Series

The Anchor Point Series

The Husband Gambit

Name From a Hat Trick

After December

Brick Walls

The Venetian and the Rum Runner

If The Seas Catch Fire

...and many, many more!